You married the man. I told ~~myself~~
What did you e~~xpect~~

I was tempte~~d~~ ~~ry~~,
to whimper that I ~~was as much a~~ victim of my
uncle's scheme as he was, but I could not get the
words to come. They were untrue, anyway. We both
knew that I stood to lose nothing by this marriage,
while he had lost everything.

He looked down at me, his face hard, his
eyes narrowed. My stomach tightened. I said, "I
have told you I was sorry, my lord. I will do whatever you want me to."

His eyes flicked to the bed behind me, then
back to my face. "Will you?" he asked.

My heart began to thud. The thought of
going to bed with such an angry male scared me to
death. I do not welsh on my bargains, however. I
made myself as tall as I could and said baldly,
"Yes."

And before I realized what was happening,
he had reached out, grabbed my arms, and pulled
me against him. I opened my lips to protest, but
before I could speak his mouth had come down on
mine.

❧

PRAISE FOR JOAN WOLF

ॐ

"A master storyteller."
—*Publishers Weekly*

"Joan Wolf writes with an absolute emotional mastery that goes straight to the heart."
—Mary Jo Putney

"No matter in what time period Joan Wolf writes, the results are the same: a superb story with wonderful characters and romance that touches the heart."
—Fayrene Preston

"The only thing that could be better than one of Joan Wolf's wonderful romances would be two of them! She writes with such grace and ease that you're halfway through her book before you know it—and sorry it will have to end soon."
—Edith Layton

ॐ

The
Deception

Joan Wolf is a native of New York City who has resided in Milford, Connecticut for the last twenty-one years. She lives with one husband, Joseph; two children, Jay 21, and Pam, 17; one dog and three cats. Her hobby is attempting to ride dressage.

JOAN WOLF

THE
DECEPTION

WARNER BOOKS

A Time Warner Company

WARNER BOOKS EDITION

Cover design by Diane Luger
Cover illustration by Vittorio Danglico
Hand lettering by Carl Dellacroce

Warner Books, Inc.
1271 Avenue of the Americas
New York, NY 10020

Visit our web site at
http://pathfinder.com/twep

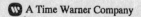 A Time Warner Company

Printed in the United States of America

First Printing: November, 1996

10 9 8 7 6 5 4 3 2 1

For Pam, a book of her very own

CHAPTER
one

IT BEGAN WITH THE DEATH OF MY FATHER. IF I LIVE TO
be a hundred, I shall never forget that day. The sky was gray
as gunmetal and the bare tree branches were black with damp.
The men carried him into our lodging on a hurdle and his face
was as gray as the sky.

"Some damn fool was after shooting in the woods, Miss
Cathleen," Paddy said. His weather-beaten face was red with
emotion and cold. "He must not have seen Mr. Daniel riding
by. Freddie's gone ta fetch the doctor."

"Papa." I knelt beside the bed. A cloth that had once been
Paddy's shirt was balled up and stuffed against the wound in
his chest. It was drenched with blood. My father's eyes flickered at the sound of my voice. His lashes lifted, and for the
last time I gazed into their familiar brilliant blue. "Kate," he
said. "Jesus. I'm done for." His eyes flickered shut.

"Papa!" I was as close as I've ever been to hysteria. I
forced my voice to a steadiness I did not feel. "The doctor is
coming," I said. "You're going to be all right."

"Didn't . . . think he . . . suspected . . . I knew . . ." my
father mumbled.

"Didn't think *who* suspected, Papa?" My voice was
sharp. "Do you know who shot you?"

He did not answer right away.

"Papa?"

"Don't know . . . who . . ." His eyes opened again and

fixed on Paddy. "Send for . . . Charlwood," he said. His voice sounded bubbly. "Lizzie's brother." Silence as he fought for breath. ". . . take care of Kate."

"No one is going to take care of me," I said. "Just be quiet and wait for the doctor. You are going to be all right, Papa."

The blue eyes remained fixed on the old groom who had been with him since boyhood. "Paddy?"

"Right here, Mr. Daniel."

"Promise . . ." More silence while he fought for breath. The agonizing struggle caused me to drive my nails into my palms. "Promise you'll send . . . for Charlwood."

"I'll do that for you all right, Mr. Daniel." Paddy's soft Irish voice was steady. "Do you not worry. I'll make certain that Miss Kate is looked after."

My father's bloodstained chest was heaving. I looked frantically toward the window of the small, shabby lodging. There was no sound of hoofbeats to signal the coming of the doctor. The only noise in the room was the ominously-bubbly sound of my father's breathing. "Don't talk, Papa," I said again. "The doctor will be here momentarily."

My father was looking at me once more. "Been a bad father to you, Kate," he said. His voice was very faint. "But. . . love you."

His eyes closed and they never opened again.

My first reaction was sheer, blinding rage. I created such a furor, in fact, that the local magistrate instituted a thorough search for my father's killer, but he came up with no suspects. Then grief set in.

I didn't cry. I cried when my mother died, but I had only been ten then; too young to realize the futility of tears. That was something I had learned over the years. Crying hadn't brought my mother back, and it wasn't going to bring my father back, either.

A cold rain began to fall as Paddy and I returned to the

lodging house after Papa's funeral. The streets of Newmarket were deserted. The racetrack was closed in November, and the bleak look of the town echoed the bleak feeling in my heart.

"Mr. Daniel would like it that he's buried in Newmarket," Paddy said, trying to cheer me up a little. "It was nice that so many of the lads came to the funeral."

There had been a large contingent of trainers, lads, and even some owners from the local racing stables at the church and the cemetery. In his own way, Papa had been a well-known man.

"Yes," I said, turning my face to the faithful friend who had been part of my life since my birth. I felt utterly forlorn. "What am I going to do now, Paddy?"

"We will wait here for your uncle, Miss Cathleen," he replied.

It was not the answer I wanted to hear. I bit my lip, bent my head, and stared at the ground. There was a stone close to my foot and I kicked it into the road. It landed in the mud with a little *plonk.* "You don't think we could carry on the business by ourselves?" I asked. "You could buy the horses and I could train them."

I felt his arm come around me. He hugged me once, hard, then let me go. His voice was regretful but firm when he answered, "Your father wanted you to go to your mother's people, girl, and I'm thinking he was right. You're eighteen years old now, Miss Cathleen. It's no life for a well-born young lady, trekking around horse farms with the likes of me."

"It's the life I've always lived," I said. "I love you, Paddy. I don't even *know* my uncle." I gave him a look calculated to melt his bones with pity.

It didn't. "He's your mother's brother and a lord," Paddy said briskly. "I would be a poor friend indeed if I stood in the way of such an opportunity."

I kicked another stone into the street. "We don't even know if he's coming."

"If he does not come, then it will be time to discuss what we will be doing next." The door of the lodging house loomed in front of us, and as we went in I offered up a silent prayer that my uncle would not show.

He came the following day. I can still remember the sound of his step on the bare floor of the hallway outside my door. I heard that firm step distinctly, and I knew.

Paddy was sitting with me, and it was he who answered the door. When Charlwood introduced himself, the old groom let him in.

"I'm thinking you look awfully young to be Miss Cathleen's uncle." Paddy's critical eyes went over the impeccable aristocrat from the top of his carefully arranged hair to the tips of his toes. The old groom had spent too many years following Papa around English estates and racetracks to be impressed by impeccable tailoring and shining Hessian boots.

"I am thirty-two," Charlwood said. "My sister was six years older than I."

"Ye have the look of Miss Elizabeth," Paddy grudgingly admitted.

It was true that he had my mother's dark auburn hair and sea-green eyes. My mother's eyes had been soft and misty, however, while his were almost startlingly clear. I had risen to greet him and we stood now, with two feet of worn carpet between us, and looked at each other.

"I have come to invite you to make your home with me, Kate," he said. "Your mother was my only sister, and I want to take care of you. For her sake."

His face looked sincere; his voice sounded sincere. I looked at Paddy. "I'm thinking you should go with him, Miss Cathleen," he said gently. "It was what your da wanted."

I nodded. My heart was breaking, but I did not cry. Instead I looked slowly around the small, faded room where Papa had died. We had come to Newmarket at this unlikely time of year because he was hoping to sell two horses to the Marquis of Stade, whose estate was nearby. Papa had not yet closed the deal with Stade, however, and we still had the two geldings stabled here in the inn. They were both big, honest hunters that I had schooled. They were worth good money.

"Take the horses," I said to Paddy.

The old man looked at the fine English lord who was my uncle.

Charlwood smiled. "Miss Cathleen will want for nothing," he promised Paddy. "You may keep the horses."

The following morning I left Newmarket in my uncle's coach. The rain had stopped overnight and the brilliant blue sky of morning gave no indication of the storms that were to follow.

Charlwood Court was huge and empty and cold. Since the death of his father some years before, my uncle had lived alone. He was not married.

He told me this when we stopped at a posting house to change horses and I felt an alarm sound in my brain. I had assumed that a man his age must be married. He saw my reaction and assured me that he had summoned a respectable female cousin to stay in the house with me. "The proprieties will be observed, Kate," he had said with a smile.

It was dark when we reached Charlwood Court, which was located five miles southwest of Reading. Cousin Louisa was waiting for us in the chilly drawing room. She was a poor timid little mouse of a thing, and if I had had any room in my heart for an emotion other than grief, I would have felt sorry for her.

She looked startled when she saw me.

"Yes," Charlwood said softly, "she is the image of her father."

There was an odd note in his voice, and I looked at him in surprise. He smiled. He smiled a lot with his mouth, but I had noticed earlier that his eyes never seemed to change.

"Louisa will show you to your room, Kate," he said. "Welcome to Charlwood Court."

To this day I have very little recollection of what Charlwood actually looked like. I know that the rooms were large, but they all seemed to be filled with stillness. It was as if no one had lived there for a very long time. The windows were all draped with heavy dark velvet curtains, which shut out the sun. Even when the fire was going and the candles were lit, the rooms looked bleak and unwelcoming. At night I would lie awake for a long time, listening to the tomblike silence of the house. It was hard to believe that anyone had ever been happy in this place; harder still to imagine my mother as a little girl here. When I finally fell asleep it was to dream of my father.

So I lived for six months, my heart as frozen as the ground outside my window. My uncle lived the nomadic life of an aristocratic bachelor, dividing his time between London and the houses of his friends, so I seldom saw him. The only person to make demands on me was Cousin Louisa, who had probably never made a serious demand on anyone in her entire life. We made polite conversation at mealtime; otherwise she respected my grief and left me to myself.

Slowly the winter passed. The dead earth softened and began to sprout forth grass and flowers. Daffodils bloomed and the scent of lilac hung in the air. The house retained its stagnant, lifeless air, but outdoors the world was alive. Unwillingly, I too began to awaken from my long hibernation.

In early May my uncle came home and told me he was taking me to London.

"London?" We were at dinner in the gloomy, darkly wainscoted dining room, and I stared at him over the candles. "Why?"

"Why not?" he replied lightly. "It cannot be good for you to remain cooped up here in the country. You are looking quite pale, my dear." He put a small piece of potato in his mouth and chewed it slowly. "You have had the winter to grieve for your father; now it is time for you to pick up the threads of your own life."

I had been thinking much the same thing myself for several weeks. Why did I so resent hearing it from him?

I pushed my food around on my plate and scowled. "What will I do in London?"

"What every normal young girl does. Go to parties. Look for a husband." My eyes jerked up at those words. He was looking at me, his eyes very direct and clear. He said, "It is not impossible, Kate. Your father was a nobody, but your mother was the daughter of a viscount."

I immediately leaped to my father's defense. "Papa was not a nobody! The Fitzgeralds are a very old Irish family."

He shrugged. "That may be so, my dear, but the Fitzgeralds long ago washed their hands of your father. Daniel was nothing more than a gambler and a horse-trader. He dragged my poor sister around from racetrack to racetrack and from one wretched lodging house to another. No wonder she died before she was thirty-five."

I was furious. On the surface what he had said might be true, but he had missed the most important thing. I balled my hands into fists and said evenly, "We were never hungry. Papa was a good man and he loved my mother very much."

"Daniel was nothing but a good-looking Irish charmer who seduced my sister so that she was forced to marry him," Charlwood said brutally.

I stood up. The footman, who had been about to pour more lemonade into my glass, froze. Cousin Louisa made distressed noises. "I will not sit here and listen to you slander my father," I said.

"Sit down." Charlwood spoke between his teeth. His face was white and his eyes were glittering in an alarming way. In fact, he looked quite frightening, but in the course of a lifetime of working with horses I have learned that if you let them know you're afraid of them, you've lost the battle. The same principle applies to men.

I said in a voice that was every bit as chilly as his, "I will sit down if you will cease slandering my father." I had enough sense not to ask him to apologize.

Silence fell as we eyed each other across the table.

"Do sit down, Kate," Cousin Louisa said nervously. I glanced at her. The poor thing looked terrified.

Slowly, I sat down. Slowly, I took up my fork. After a moment the footman carefully poured more lemonade into my glass. Another one poured wine into my uncle's.

"Will you be wishing me to accompany you to London, Charlwood?" Cousin Louisa said into the tense silence.

"Certainly."

I put a piece of mutton in my mouth and said nothing. I had my own reasons for wishing to remove to London. I looked up under my lashes at my uncle's face and let myself consciously realize what I had known deep down all along. I did not like him.

"Kate will need clothes if she is going to go into society," Cousin Louisa said. "Her wardrobe is . . . somewhat sparse."

"You can take her shopping, Louisa, and send the bills to me," my uncle said. His good humor appeared to be restored.

I bit my lip. I didn't want to take his money.

Cousin Louisa smiled at me. "You will be the most beautiful girl in London, my dear," she said.

I smiled back, appreciative of her generous attempt to raise my spirits. I was in little danger of letting her words go to my head. I might have inherited Papa's cheekbones, but I was still Irish and poor, and the chances of my making a good match were slender, to say the least. I had no intention of spending the rest of my life hanging on my uncle's purse strings, however, and in order to be independent I needed to find a way to support myself. *Perhaps,* I thought with the incurable optimism of youth, *perhaps in London something will turn up.*

*   *   *

I rose early the following morning to go for a ride. My uncle's hunters had been stabled at Charlwood since the end of hunting season in January, and I had been riding them on days when the weather was not too nasty. The sun was just coming up when I left my room and began to walk down the dark, picture-hung corridor on which all the main bedrooms at Charlwood were situated. I stopped short when I saw a girl coming out of my uncle's room.

It was Rose, the under-housemaid. She was fully dressed, but her hair was hanging in a loose tangle around her shoulders. It was very pretty hair, the color of honey. She stopped when she saw me and pressed up against the wall. I stared at her in confusion and saw that there was an ugly red welt on her left cheek. Her eyes were red as well and she obviously had been crying.

"Are you all right, Rose?" I asked.

"I'm fine, Miss Fitzgerald," she whispered.

She did not look fine. My eyes went from her marked face to my uncle's door.

"I—I was bringing Lord Charlwood his morning tea," she stammered.

As I have previously mentioned, the sun was barely up. "I see," I said in an expressionless voice.

She began to inch her way down the hall, her back still pressed against the wall. "I'd best be going now," she said.

I nodded and let her go, which was clearly what she wanted to do.

I thought about Rose the whole time I was in the saddle. Obviously she had been summoned to my uncle's bed, and obviously she had not found it to be a pleasant experience. Every time I thought of that mark on her cheek, my stomach clenched. Most frustrating of all was the knowledge that I could do nothing to help her escape my uncle's clutches.

It would be difficult enough trying to escape them myself.

*   *   *

The very air of London seemed to act like a tonic on Cousin Louisa. She dragged me around the shops on Bond Street, visibly shedding years with every purchase she made. I was appalled by the amount of money she spent, but she kept assuring me that Charlwood would not be at all surprised.

"How old are you, Louisa?" I asked as we sat having an ice at Gunther's after a particularly expensive session at Fanchon's dress shop.

"Forty-one," she replied.

I had thought she was about sixty.

"But you're younger than my father!" I blurted in surprise. My father had been forty-six when he died, and his thick black hair had not held a thread of gray. There were definite strands of gray in Louisa's soft brown locks.

She smiled reminiscently. "Daniel did not age, then?"

"Did you *know* Papa?"

"I was at Charlwood the summer he met your mother."

I knew this story well. Papa had delivered a horse to Mama's father, taken one look at Mama and stayed on to school her father's other horses. They had met secretly all summer long, and in September she had run away with him to Scotland, where they had married.

Louisa's smile became even more nostalgic. "Your father was so good-looking, Kate. Lizzie was head over heels in love with him. I helped her pack her bag the night they eloped."

I stared. I had not realized that Louisa knew my parents.

A well-dressed middle-aged woman passed our table and cast a scornful look at my old brown pelisse. I returned her look with one so haughty that she was startled. *Old harpy,* I thought.

"I have often wondered if Lizzie was happy," Louisa said.

"I think she was very happy," I said. "Papa was . . ." I

searched for the words that would describe my father. "Oh—the world just seemed so much more vivid around Papa," I finally said. "It's true that he was a gambler, and there were times when money was short. But . . ." My voice quivered, and I folded my lips.

Louisa kindly gave me a moment to collect myself. Then she said, "You are very like him, Kate."

I shook my head. It was true that I looked like Papa, but inside I was quite different. I changed the subject. "It is nice to be away from Charlwood. The place is like a tomb."

Louisa shivered. "It has always been like that. When I was young I hated having to go there on a visit."

"Was it like that then when my mother was young?" I asked curiously.

Louisa nodded, then glanced around the crowded tables as if she was afraid someone would overhear her words. "Your grandfather . . ." She stopped and looked down at her lemon ice.

"Yes?" I prompted when it seemed she was not going to speak again.

She finally said simply, "Your grandfather was a hard man."

I said nothing. On the other side of the room a little boy dropped his spoon and called out imperiously for another. A waiter hastened to his side.

Louisa looked up at me again and said, "I am sure that Lizzie found life with Daniel, however hard, infinitely preferable to life at Charlwood."

Two fashionable young men in elegant blue coats stared at me rudely as they passed our table. I ignored them and said to Cousin Louisa, "If you dislike Charlwood so much, why ever did you agree to come and stay with me?"

She sighed. "I had no choice in the matter, my dear."

"Nonsense." I was still young enough to believe that grown-ups always had a choice.

"It is not nonsense," Louisa said sadly. "I live with my

brother's family, you see, and Charlwood offered Henry a
large sum of money if he would dispense with my services
and allow me to chaperone you. My brother accepted, and so
I had to go."

"Services?" I asked, puzzled. "What services, Louisa?"

"I act as my sister-in-law's housekeeper," Louisa said.
"They don't call me that, of course, but that is what I am. And
then, because I am not an employee but a dependent of theirs,
they can ask me to do all kinds of other things."

A girl's high voice came from one of the tables around
us. "Oh, la, Mr. Wetmore! You are such a jokester!"

"What kinds of other things?" I asked Cousin Louisa.

"Oh, I go to the village on errands, sit up with the children if they are ill. That sort of thing."

"Do they pay you?"

She smiled forlornly. "They give me a home, Kate."

I put my spoon down on the table's white cloth. The ice
had all of a sudden lost its flavor. "Why do you put up with
such treatment?"

"I have no husband and I have no money of my own,"
Louisa said. "I have to live, Kate."

"You couldn't earn your own money?" I asked.

Louisa shook her head. "The only position open to a lady
with no means of her own is to become a governess, and that
is not a life I aspire to. At least now I am considered a member of my brother's family, no matter how ill-used. Believe
me, Kate, the life of a governess is much worse. You are not
family and you are not a servant. It is a wretched existence."

I thought it sounded much less wretched than the life she
had just described to me. At least one got paid for one's labor!
I drew concentric circles on the tablecloth with my fingertip
and asked thoughtfully, "Just what credentials does one need
in order to become a governess, Louisa?"

My cousin didn't answer, but I could feel her looking at
me. I glanced up, my eyes full of innocence.

"Don't even consider it, Kate," she said. "No one would ever hire you."

That made me indignant. "Why not?" I demanded. "Mama taught me herself until I was ten. And Papa was always willing to buy me books, so I learned a great deal on my own." I raised my eyebrows and gave her my loftiest look. "I assure you that I am perfectly capable of instructing young children."

Louisa said bluntly, "It wouldn't matter if you were a scholar, my dear. You wouldn't be hired because no woman in her right mind would let you near either her husband or her sons."

"Nonsense."

"It is true," Louisa said. She sounded very positive.

I decided to confide in her. "The thing is, Louisa, I do not want to go back to Charlwood, and so I need to find a way to support myself."

"Find a husband," Louisa advised.

I could feel the expression that Papa always referred to as my "mule's look" settling over my face. "I don't want a husband," I said.

Louisa smiled at me as if I were a child. "Every woman wants a husband, my dear."

I wouldn't dignify that comment with a reply. Instead I thought of our morning's shopping expedition, of the dozens of expensive dress shops and hat shops that lined Bond Street. I had a depressing feeling that Louisa was right about my chances of becoming a governess, but surely there were other ways.

"There are plenty of shops in London," I said. "Why couldn't I get a position in one of them?"

Louisa looked scandalized. "Do you really think Charlwood would allow his niece to take a position in a London shop?"

"He doesn't care about me," I said. "He'll be glad to get me off his hands."

"He will care about what society says about him if his niece is reduced to becoming a milliner's assistant!"

I had an answer for that. "Why should anyone know? I will get a position in a shop that society doesn't frequent."

Louisa looked very grave. At this point both of us had forgotten about our ices, which were slowly melting in their glass dishes. "You must not leave your uncle's protection," she said. "If you should do that, Kate, if you should try to live on your own in London, you would not be safe."

"I can take care of myself," I said.

"You would be raped within the week," Louisa said sharply. "London is not the country, Kate. It is filled with unemployed rascals who would show no respect for a solitary female."

I bit my lip. "I'll get a gun," I said. "I know how to shoot." I have never been one to give up easily.

Louisa cast her eyes upward. "I cannot believe I am having this conversation! Kate. Think. If someone jumps out at you from the shadows, you will not have time to use a gun."

I was not a stupid young girl who knew nothing of the world. I remembered the many times my father had stood between me and some man who had looked at me with hot and greedy eyes. Louisa was right. Unfortunately. I ate a little bit of my soupy ice and cudgeled my brain. Suddenly an idea exploded in my mind with all the brilliance of fireworks in the night sky.

"I could pretend to be a boy!" I said. "I used to wear breeches to school the horses. If I cut off my hair . . ." I smiled triumphantly. "What a splendid idea, Louisa! No one would rape a boy!"

"You are funning me," my cousin said.

"Not at all. I assure you, Louisa, I could get a position in any stable I applied to. I really am *very* good with horses." No point in false modesty, I thought. The more I considered this idea, the more I liked it. "Think of Rosalind in *As You Like It,*"

I said enthusiastically. "*She* fooled everyone. Why shouldn't I?"

Louisa was looking at me with a mixture of admiration and horror. "I don't care if you are a genius with horses." There was still color in her cheeks, and she looked almost pretty. "No matter what position you might manage to find, Kate, you will not be given the luxury of a room to yourself. You will have to share your living quarters, and there is no possible way you can keep your sex a secret if you have to share a room with other men."

I scowled. I did not like the way she kept pouring cold water on all my beautiful schemes. "You are so gloomy, Louisa!" I exclaimed.

"I am realistic, my dear," she said. The pretty pink faded from her cheeks. "Find a husband, Kate. It is the only solution."

CHAPTER
two

MY ENTRANCE INTO LONDON SOCIETY, OR THE *ton*, as it was called in the newspapers, was hardly an unqualified success. Because of my uncle and Louisa I was invited to a number of the larger balls, but it was clear that I would never be considered worthy enough to be admitted into that inner sanctum of the English aristocracy, Almack's Assembly Rooms.

My dance card was always full at the balls we did attend, and I was invited to a host of other parties: routs, breakfasts, musical evenings, and so on, but the young men who danced and talked with me were clearly more interested in flirting than in proposing.

Since I am being honest, I will have to admit that I was disappointed. I yearned for a home with all my heart, and, much as I might despise Cousin Louisa's advice, I knew she was right when she said that in order to find a home I had first to find a man. I suppose this strong desire for permanency stemmed from my nomadic upbringing. One always seems to want what one does not have.

My uncle had been away from Charlwood for most of the winter, so these weeks in London were the first time I had ever spent an extended period in his company, and he did not grow on one. In fact, the more I was with him, the more uneasy he made me. I kept telling myself that I was being ridiculous, that he was my mother's brother, that he had taken me in, had lavished money on me, et cetera.

But I did not like his eyes. On the surface they seemed so extraordinarily clear and direct, but when one returned his gaze, one found that one could not see in. There was something about that deceptively cloudless gaze that reminded me of someone, and it wasn't my mother. I had a feeling that this resemblance was the cause of my apprehension, but I didn't place it until the evening of the Cottrells' come-out ball for their second daughter.

I remember that I was standing in the Cottrell ballroom, in front of a very lavish arrangement of pink and white roses, waiting for my partner to bring me a glass of punch, when I happened to glance across the floor at my uncle just as his face changed. It was only a momentary lapse, and then his customary clear look returned. But in that instant I knew who he reminded me of—Sultan, the only horse my father ever had put down. The bay gelding had had the same kind of opaque brilliance in his gaze that I saw in my uncle's, but Sultan had tried to kill me.

"Only horse I ever knew who's bad through and through," my father had said. "I could sell him to some unsuspecting soul who'd buy him for his looks, but I won't have it on my conscience that I've passed on a rogue."

I looked to the door to see what had caused that momentary flicker of hatred on my uncle's face. And for the first time I laid eyes on Adrian.

He was standing at the top of the three steps that led down into the ballroom, his head bent to listen to something his hostess was saying. Mrs. Cottrell looked small next to him, but I had stood beside her earlier in the evening and I knew she was taller than I.

"Here is your punch, Miss Fitzgerald." My partner had returned.

"Who is that talking to Mrs. Cottrell?" I asked.

Mr. Putnam looked across the crowded dance floor to the man on the stairs. "That is Greystone." There was an unmistakable note of awe in his voice. "He gave up his commission a few months ago to come home to England. They say he is going to join the Government. Castlereagh wants him at the Foreign Office."

Even I knew the name. Major Adrian Edward St. John Woodrow, Earl of Greystone, Viscount Wraxall and Baron Wood of Lambourn, was one of the most notable heroes of last year's Battle of Waterloo. He had been singled out for commendations by the Duke of Wellington, and his exploits had been lauded in Parliament. He had remained in France after Waterloo to help Wellington administer the Army of Occupation the Allies had seen fit to quarter on the French nation.

The music ceased and I watched him as he crossed the crowded floor. His hair was so pale a gold that it glimmered like moonlight as he passed under one of the three crystal chandeliers that hung from the ballroom's gilded ceiling. People fell away from in front of him as he advanced, and I watched as he tossed a genial word or two in the direction of people he knew, all the while not once slowing his forward progress. He came to a halt directly in front of a tall slender girl whom I knew to be the daughter of the Duke of Wareham. They stood talking for a few moments, and when the next dance was announced they went out to the floor together.

My uncle appeared at my shoulder and claimed me from Mr. Putnam. Hiding my reluctance, I accompanied him to the floor. He inserted himself into the line next to Greystone and I took my place beside Lady Mary Weston.

She smiled at me as she made room. We had spent a few minutes together in the ladies' withdrawing room at a previous ball and she had been very pleasant to me. Many of the young ladies I met were not.

"How are you, Miss Fitzgerald?" she asked now in her soft, sweet voice. "I hope you are enjoying the ball?"

"It is very nice, Lady Mary," I replied politely.

The set finished forming up, the music started, and the dance began. It was a quadrille, one of the new dances that had been imported from France, and I had only learned it a few weeks before so I had to concentrate. When it finished, my uncle and I were left standing next to Lord Greystone and Lady Mary.

"Greystone," my uncle said with his most charming smile, "allow me to introduce my niece, Miss Cathleen Fitzgerald."

His hair was so fair that I had assumed his eyes would be light, but they were a strikingly dark gray. He had a face Michelangelo would have loved. He said in a deep, pleasant voice, "How do you do, Miss Fitzgerald. I hope you are enjoying the ball."

"It is very nice," I answered for about the twentieth time that evening. Standing this close, I could see how tall he really was.

"I believe I've come across something that will interest you, Greystone," my uncle said. "Are you still collecting Saxon weapons?"

"I am still interested in Saxon artifacts, yes." The earl's voice was coolly polite. I got the distinct impression that the antipathy I had seen earlier on my uncle's face was fully reciprocated. "What have you found, Charlwood?"

"The owner told me it was a sword that once belonged to King Alfred."

I noticed that all the people in our vicinity were trying not to look as if they were looking at us, but they were. "They all say that their swords once belonged to King Alfred," Greystone replied.

"Well, this fellow was very persuasive." My uncle smoothed an imaginary wrinkle out of the sleeve of his black coat. "Supposedly the sword's been in his family for hundreds of years." He looked up. "He has documentation."

Against his will, Greystone was interested. "It might be worth my looking at."

"I'll call on you tomorrow and we'll arrange a visit," my uncle said.

There was a pause, then Greystone replied slowly, "I will be at home in the morning." My uncle nodded and the orchestra struck up the first strains of a waltz.

"May I have this dance, Lady Mary?" my uncle promptly asked.

She glanced at Greystone, as if seeking guidance, but his face was unreadable. So she smiled agreeably at my uncle and allowed him to lead her back to the floor. This left Greystone stuck with me.

With perfect courtesy he said, "May I have this waltz, Miss Fitzgerald?"

"I suppose we shall have to," I said glumly. "It will make you look rude if you abandon me here."

His lips twitched. "It would," he agreed. "I beg of you, save my reputation and dance with me."

"We can't chat," I warned him. "I have only been waltzing for a few weeks and I still need to mind my steps."

"I will maintain absolute silence," he promised. And on that note, I accompanied him out to the floor and stepped into his arms.

When the waltz was first introduced into England after the Congress of Vienna, many people had considered it immoral, but until that waltz with Adrian, I had never understood why. We had not taken half a dozen steps, however, before I realized that the sensations the closeness of his body were provoking in mine were far too exciting to be proper. A full turn of the room convinced me they were immoral.

I had performed the waltz many times during my stay in London, and nothing like this had ever happened to me before. I didn't quite know how to account for it. He held me at the correct distance. He didn't try to squeeze my waist—as several other gentlemen had done. But I was intensely and acutely conscious of the feel of that big hand, of the closeness of that big body.

It was a thoroughly unnerving experience, and I was extremely glad that I did not have to talk to him! When the waltz was over, my uncle reclaimed me and escorted me from the floor.

"You looked lovely tonight, Kate," my uncle said as we rode through the streets of London in his coach. "Certainly the young men present thought so—you danced every dance. Even Greystone danced with you! I am impressed."

There was a silky note in his voice that was making the muscles in my stomach tighten.

"Lord Greystone was just being polite," I replied, striving for a light tone. "After all, you left him very little choice, Uncle Martin."

"He did not look like a man who has been coerced," my uncle said, his voice even silkier than before.

Cousin Louisa spoke out of the dark from the opposite seat, "It is well known that Lord Greystone is on the verge of making an offer for Lady Mary Weston."

For some reason this remark appeared to amuse my uncle. He chuckled.

My heartbeat accelerated at the sound, and for the first time I let myself acknowledge that I was afraid.

It was not an emotion I was overly familiar with, and I didn't like the feeling at all.

Don't be a fool, I scolded myself. *You may not like Charlwood, but there's nothing in him to fear!*

My heartbeat did not slow; my stomach muscles did not relax. Every part of my being shrank away from the man who was sitting so close beside me in the dark. When he reached out his hand and put it over mine, I jumped.

"Did I startle you, Kate?" he asked. He turned my hand so it lay palm-up upon my lap.

He repelled me. He was like one of the faerie folk my father used to tell me about—beautiful to look upon but fatal to trust. His finger moved across my exposed palm in a confident caress.

I pulled my hand away. In the darkness I could feel him

smile. *I have to get away from him,* I thought. *I have to get away.*

Mr. Putnam, one of the young men I had danced with at the ball, arrived at my uncle's home in Berkeley Square the next afternoon to take me driving in Hyde Park. Five o'clock was the magic hour when London society emerged into the daylight, to walk and to drive, to see and to be seen.

I assessed my escort's horses after he helped me up into the high seat of his phaeton. They were a matched pair of grays, well-proportioned and well-groomed. I regarded the young man with more interest than I had previously shown. He looked rather like a rabbit, but a man who had horses like these must have hidden depths.

"I like your horses, Mr. Putnam," I said.

He smiled. "I've only had 'em for a month," he confided. "Got 'em from Ladrington when he had to sell off his stable after playing too deep at Watiers."

We discussed the horses for the rest of the drive to the park. The late-afternoon streets of London were filled with horses and tradesmen's wagons, but Mr. Putnam handled his reins with skill. My opinion of him went up another notch. We reached the park and entered into the flow of fashionable traffic.

The wide path that bordered the Hyde Park lake was filled with a stunning array of vehicles. There were beautifully appointed traditional carriages containing stylishly dressed ladies attended by footmen in lavish livery; there were high-perch and low-perch phaetons driven by gentlemen like Mr. Putnam; there were barouches and cabriolets and curricles; there were beautiful Thoroughbred horses under saddle, ridden by ladies in elegant habits and gentlemen in top boots and leather breeches and kerseymere tailcoats.

Hyde Park at five o'clock during the Season was a horselover's dream, and Mr. Putnam and I comprehensively discussed every individual animal as it paraded by. I was thoroughly enjoying myself when a phaeton pulled up alongside of us.

"Putnam!" said an imperious voice. "Stop for a moment, if you please."

Mr. Putnam stopped his horses. The high-perch phaeton that was behind us swung wide to avoid a crash. "Lord Stade," my escort said with bewilderment, and I narrowed my eyes and stared at the man for whose sake my father had made that fatal last visit to Newmarket.

The Marquis of Stade was a broad-shouldered, bull-headed man whose unwinking brown gaze was all over me as he talked to Mr. Putnam about the upcoming races at Newmarket. My escort was obviously torn between gratitude for the attention of the marquis and discomfort with the way he was looking at me.

"And who is this young person?" Stade finally rapped out, gesturing to me.

Mr. Putnam gave me a perturbed look. "This *lady* is Miss Fitzgerald, my lord," he said. "Lord Charlwood's niece."

Stade feigned great surprise. "Are you Daniel Fitzgerald's girl, then?"

"Yes," I said, regarding him steadily. "I am."

"Now that I look at you, I can see the resemblance." He had been doing nothing but look at me for the last five minutes. Stade turned now to my escort and said disdainfully, "This chit's father was nothing but an Irish horse-trader, Putnam. Don't let yourself be fooled into thinking she's eligible goods on the marriage mart."

Mr. Putnam looked horribly embarrassed and began to blink like a frightened rabbit. Stade looked once more at me. I held his gaze and said calmly to my flustered escort, "I am ready to drive on, Mr. Putnam." He raised his reins immediately and the grays started forward with a jerk. Behind us I could hear Stade's harsh, unpleasant laugh and my fists clenched in my lap.

"I'm s-sorry about that, Miss Fitzgerald," Mr. Putnam said. "I didn't even think Stade knew who I was!"

That was interesting news. The marquis had stopped, then, because of me.

"His stable has been doing very well of late," Mr. Putnam ventured after a few moments. "He won the Guineas two years ago, and the three-year-old he has this season looks a sure bet to win it again. That stud of his is proving to be a surprising success."

"Do you mean Alcazar?" I asked.

"That's the one." The sun was glinting off the brass buttons on Mr. Putnam's blue coat, and I blinked as a flash caught me in the eyes. He said, "Horse had a mediocre career himself, but he's certainly come up trumps as a sire."

"That's not a usual thing, is it? I know my father was very surprised when he found out that Alcazar had sired the colt Stade won the Guineas with."

"Everyone was surprised," Mr. Putnam returned, "but Alcazar's no one-day marvel. The horses Stade ran last year were very good, and this year's colt is remarkable."

"Do you race your own horses, Mr. Putnam?" I inquired, and he spent the rest of the drive happily regaling me with his plans for setting up his own stable.

The following day my uncle told me that he had arranged to take Greystone to a village near Winchester in order to view the sword that was supposed to have belonged to King Alfred. I didn't pay a great deal of attention to this plan until Friday evening. That was when my uncle informed me that he had learned that someone else wanted to purchase the sword and that he was going to ride ahead to insist that the owner not sell until Lord Greystone had had an opportunity to make an offer.

"You must accompany Greystone, Kate," my uncle said. "I will write down all the directions for you and I will meet you at Squire Reston's. If I delay until tomorrow afternoon, that sword will be gone."

I did not understand my uncle's sense of urgency and protested, "Surely a few hours is not going to make that much difference, Uncle Martin."

"I have just told you that it will, Kate. The squire sent word to me that he has another buyer." He gave me a look of disarming frankness. "I have a particular reason for putting Greystone in my debt, and I badly want to be the one to find him this sword."

I had a deep distrust of that look. "Well, then, why cannot I simply give him these directions and let him go by himself?" I inquired reasonably.

"Because I wish you to come as well." How could so soft a voice be so full of menace? "I have a good friend whose estate lies near Winchester, and he has a son I would like you to meet. Bring some clothes and after we have seen the sword we will pay them a visit."

I was not overly pleased with this plan, but I did not want to argue with my uncle. I was not overly pleased with my own cowardly behavior, either, but I couldn't seem to help it. There was something about the man that made me extremely nervous.

The Earl of Greystone arrived to collect my uncle promptly at eleven o'clock the following morning. He was dressed in a four-caped driving coat, which made him look enormous, and he was not happy to discover the change in plans.

"I am driving my phaeton," he said. "There is only room for one other person. Miss Cranbourne would be unable to accompany you."

"Uncle Martin will be waiting for me at Squire Reston's," I assured him. There was skepticism in the earl's eyes as he scanned my face. "It sounded a hasty scheme to me too, my lord," I admitted, "but my uncle was quite concerned that this other buyer would beat you out of the sword."

Silence.

"I promise I will be no trouble," I said, and bit my lip as I heard the pleading note in my own voice.

He looked at me with hard gray eyes, then he shrugged. "Very well," he said. Pause. "You do realize that this is a five-hour drive, Miss Fitzgerald?"

"I am not a hothouse flower, my lord," I said with dignity. "I can withstand a five-hour drive in fine weather."

For the first time I saw the hint of a smile in his eyes. "Very well." He glanced significantly toward the street. "I would prefer not to keep my horses waiting."

"It will take me but a moment to get my pelisse and bonnet," I promised, and ran out of the room.

I am not usually shy with people, but as we drove westward out of London I definitely felt shy with Greystone. It was not his looks that overset me—after all, I had spent most of my life looking at Papa—it was his reputation as a war hero that did it. He had had three horses shot out from under him at Waterloo, and then, even though he was injured, he had led some sort of cavalry charge that everyone talked about for months.

It was hard to think of war on such a beautiful May morning, however, and by the time we were clear of the city traffic my unusual attack of reticence had disappeared. I have always found the best way to make friends with people is to ask them about the things that they like, so I asked him about his interest in King Alfred.

He replied easily, "My principal seat is near the Berkshire Downs—Alfred's own country—and I developed an interest in him when I was a boy. It was my mother who got me started actually collecting. She had a great interest in our Saxon heritage."

I knew very little about King Alfred myself and asked him a dozen more questions, all of which he answered with perfect good humor. It was just lovely to be out of London in the spring sunshine, and, defying convention, I took off my bonnet so I could feel the sun's warmth on my face. The road we were driving along was flanked by stretching fields of corn, and I admired the flush of green wheat that waved gently in the soft breeze. The grassy verge at the roadside was sprinkled with brilliant patches of lady's grove, blue speedwell, and yellow primroses. I was glad that I had made Greystone take me.

After we had finished with King Alfred as a subject, I asked him how France was recovering from the war. While he talked, I inhaled the fresh air, watching the way the sun shone on his uncovered hair, and forgot about my uncle.

Then he said, "Now it is your turn to tell me about yourself, Miss Fitzgerald. I have heard from several sources that your father was an incomparable judge of a horse. Is that indeed so?"

I was delighted to have an opportunity to talk about Papa. Greystone was such a good listener that I was still talking when we stopped at a posting inn to rest the horses, and I kept on talking while he hired a private parlor for us to partake of a luncheon. Over the cold meat and cheese I found myself telling him about the way Papa had died.

"It was such a strange thing for him to say—*I didn't think that he suspected I knew.* I keep thinking about it, my lord, but it doesn't make sense. Whom could he have been referring to?"

"Perhaps he had drifted away in his mind," Greystone suggested in a surprisingly gentle voice. "I have seen dying men do that, Miss Fitzgerald."

I did not think that Papa had drifted away, but I forbore to press the point. I didn't know what had made me talk about Papa's words with this man anyway. I certainly had never mentioned them to anyone else.

After luncheon we returned to the road, driving southward into Hampshire. We were about an hour away from our destination and progressing smoothly along a deserted country road—scarcely more than a lane, really—when the phaeton suddenly wobbled and then pitched over on its side. It was the passenger's side that went down, but fortunately I was tossed clear of the accident.

I landed abruptly in a roadside ditch, startling a fox that was curled up in its bottom, peacefully asleep. The fox streaked away, and I lay still for a moment, regaining my breath. Then I got slowly to my feet. I have fallen from enough horses to have learned how to land, so, though I collected a few bruises, I was otherwise unhurt. As I brushed the dirt off my new blue pelisse, I heard Greystone shouting my name.

"I'm all right!" I called back. My straw bonnet was hopelessly mashed, so I abandoned it, lifted my skirts, and began to scramble up the steep side of the ditch. Greystone appeared above me when I was halfway up and he bent to offer assistance. I reached my hand up and was pulled effortlessly back to the road.

"Are you certain you're all right, Miss Fitzgerald?" he demanded brusquely, taking in my torn and dirty clothes.

"I'm fine." My hair was coming down and I pushed it away from my face. "What happened?"

"The wheel came off," he answered tersely. "If you're really all right, I had better see about getting the horses out of harness. They've contrived to get it all tangled."

He had managed to keep his matched bays from running away, but they were snorting and stamping and throwing their heads around, and I went to help him. We put the leather halters he carried on them and I offered to hold them while he tried to fix the wheel.

He gave me a worried look. "Can you hold two horses?"

"Yes." Without waiting for further comment from him, I led the horses to the grass margin that lay along the side of the road. As soon as they saw the grass they put their heads down and went to work.

A field of wheat lay to the left of the road, and to the

right was pastureland upon which grazed a herd of cows. Bands of butterflies flitted here and there in the grass, and bees hummed among the clover. Nowhere was there any sign of a human person.

Ten minutes later a grim-faced Greystone appeared at my side. He had removed his coat and rolled up the sleeves of his white shirt. There was a long white scar on his bare right forearm. His shoulders were very wide. There was a sheen of perspiration on his forehead, and he was scowling. "The axle is broken."

"Oh dear." I looked at the peaceful, rural scene that stretched all around us. The white tail of a rabbit bobbed in a clump of nearby hawthorns. No one had passed us on this road yet. "You can't fix it?"

"It can't be fixed. It needs a new axle."

He was looking extremely grim. "Well," I said as cheerfully as I could, "then we must just go on to the next village and get the blacksmith to come back to replace the axle."

"According to my map, the next village is eight miles up this road."

I looked at the two horses, who were eating grass as if they hadn't seen food in a week. A bee buzzed around my ear and I brushed it away. "Can we ride these bays, my lord?"

"To my knowledge, they have never been ridden. Considering that we do not have either saddle or bridle, I do not think it would be wise to make the attempt."

I chewed on my lip. "I suppose not."

He looked around the bucolic landscape. "I cannot leave you alone here, Miss Fitzgerald."

"There is nothing wrong with my feet, my lord," I said tartly. His grim look was beginning to annoy me. "We can each lead a horse."

He ran his fingers through his disordered hair and consulted the sky. Wordlessly, I extended one of the horses' lead ropes to him. He took it, and, still in silence, the two of us began to walk down the road.

It was almost two hours before we saw the first sign that we were approaching a village. A little squat church, with neither spire nor tower, appeared on our right, fronted by a small enclosed churchyard. Next to the church, rising from behind an orchard and a forest of overgrown shrubberies, two chimneys jutted toward the sky.

"A church and a rectory," Greystone murmured. "The village must lie directly ahead."

I devoutly hoped so. The boots I was wearing had been chosen for style, not for comfort. They were definitely not the footgear I would have elected had I known I was going to be walking for eight miles.

A few minutes later we did indeed enter the tiny village of Luster. It did not take us long to discover that the sum total of Luster's amenities was one inn, The Luster Arms, which consisted of a taproom with a single bedroom above it. The landlady was out in front contemplating her one rosebush when we came limping up to her. She fetched her husband, who informed us that the village's sole blacksmith was out shoeing horses at someplace called Farmer Blackwell's.

I said to Greystone, "The first thing we must do is find a place to stable these horses."

He gave me the only approving look I had earned from him since the accident.

The landlord promptly offered to put the horses in his own stable for the evening. Next he informed us that we were in luck, his one room was not rented.

"Ye can stay there for the night. The wife will put clean sheets on the bed and we'll gif ye a grand supper, we will. In the morn Smith can fix yer axle."

It was the first time that I realized the full extent of our dilemma. My eyes flew to Greystone. He was giving the landlord an absolutely devastating smile. I blinked. "I am Mr. Grey," I heard him say, "and this is my sister. We appreciate your help, landlord, but is there no way the axle can be fixed today?"

"Smith is staying at Blackwell's for the night."

Impossibly, the smile gained in power. "I will make it well worth his while to do this job for me."

The innkeeper was not unmoved, but he could offer no help. "Smith's likely too jugged by now to do anything," he said frankly. "Farmer Blackwell makes grand ale."

"I see." The bay Greystone was leading chose this moment to nuzzle his pocket, obviously looking for a treat. The earl gently pushed him away. "Perhaps I can stay with you, and my sister can stay with your parson and his wife."

"Parson's a widower," came the reply. "Wouldn't be proper for a young woman to stay with him."

Rueful gray eyes turned to meet mine. "It seems as if we have no choice, Kate."

I said to the innkeeper, "Surely there is someone else in this village who can fix an axle!"

"Nope," the innkeeper said cheerily. "Nary a one."

"Damn," I muttered under my breath.

Greystone removed the lead rope from my hands. "Go upstairs with the landlady, Kate," he said. "You must be aching from that fall, and you need a wash. I will see to the horses."

"Oh, Jem will see to them, Mr. Grey," the landlord said cheerfully.

We all looked around for Jem. The landlord shouted his name. After a minute, a skinny young man came out the front door of the inn. At the landlord's direction, he took both of the horses' lead ropes and led them away.

"If your taproom is open, landlord, I think I will have a beer," Greystone said. He sounded as if he needed one.

The men went into the taproom and I followed the landlady up a set of battered wooden stairs to the bedroom. It was quite small, and the roof was low, and it had cracks in the plaster walls, and there was only one bed.

"Damn," I muttered again.

"I'll fetch you some water, miss," the landlady volunteered. "You'll want to clean up some."

When I looked in the small mirror that was nailed above the clean but chipped washbowl I understood why everyone was urging me to wash. My face was indeed extremely dirty. My right shoulder had stiffened badly during the long walk, and when I examined it I could see the beginnings of what was going to be an ugly bruise.

I put myself to rights as best I could, and went downstairs to the taproom.

Supper was not as unpleasant as I had feared it was going to be. Greystone had obviously resigned himself to the inevitable, and when I joined him at a small scarred wooden table set in the corner of the taproom, his smile was rueful. "I fear this is not what you are accustomed to, Kate."

In fact, I had eaten in dozens of places like The Luster Arms, but I did not say that. I picked up my napkin and shot him a nervous look. I was acutely aware of the fact that I was alone with him. "Are *you* going to stay with the vicar, my lord?" I asked bluntly.

"You must remember to call me Adrian," he said with the sort of kind smile he would probably bestow on a frightened child. "After all, I am your brother."

I nodded, a little disarmed by the smile but not entirely reassured.

His eyebrows drew together. "I don't want to leave you alone here, Kate. The landlord seems like a decent sort, but still . . ."

I bit my lip.

"You know, I actually do have a sister," he told me. His eyes glinted with humor. "I promise that you can rely on me to behave."

He could charm the birds out of the trees when he

wanted to, and I felt myself responding with a shy smile of my own.

The fact of the matter is, I played my part to perfection that night. That I did so because I did not know that I had a part to play did not save either Adrian or me from the consequences of my uncle's nefarious plot.

CHAPTER
three

"**Y**OU CAN HAVE THE FLOOR," I ANNOUNCED WHEN FI-nally we stood together in the small bedroom under the eaves. "You were a soldier. You must be accustomed to sleeping on the ground."

Adrian raised his eyebrows in amusement. "I was an officer, Kate. Officers do not sleep on the ground."

My face must have shown that I didn't believe him, for he laughed. "At least let me have one of the pillows. Is it clean?"

I inspected it closely, then lifted it to my nose and sniffed. In a lifetime spent largely in lodging houses, I had learned that smell is as important as appearance. "It is clean," I pronounced with some surprise. "And you can even have a blanket," I added generously. I stripped these articles from the bed and went to spread them out neatly on the floor for him. When I turned it was to find that he had followed me, and I was suddenly and acutely aware of how small I was beside him. I had to tilt my head way back to see his face. The eyes that looked down into mine were dark and unreadable. "Good night, Kate," he said softly.

"Good night . . . Adrian."

I took off my shoes, lined them up neatly beside the bed, and climbed into the bed in my dress. Silence descended. We had left the shutters open, and a line of moonlight slanted in through the window and fell upon the faded patchwork quilt at the bottom of the bed. I lay tensely awake, listening to his even breathing and thinking that I was never going to be able to fall asleep.

The sound of boots pounding on the uncarpeted wooden stairs dragged me back to consciousness. Alarmed, I sat up in bed, and was startled to find myself beholding an extremely broad, white-cambric-covered back. Adrian had stationed himself between me and the door.

Someone put a shoulder to the door and heaved. On the third push the lock gave, the door crashed open, and my uncle stood in the doorway, his face clearly visible in the bright moonlight that was now streaming in the unshuttered window. "Greystone," he pronounced with every appearance of pleasure. Then, silkily: "What are you doing with my niece?"

A shocked male face appeared at my uncle's shoulder. "Damn," it said. "Don't look like we arrived in time after all, Charlwood."

Adrian slowly moved away from me to stand by the window. I felt the loss of his protection bitterly. I didn't understand yet what was happening.

"Come in, gentlemen," Adrian said. I could hear the anger that lay beneath his level tone. He, of course, understood perfectly.

It was when my uncle said, "You will do the gentlemanly thing by my niece, Greystone, or I will blast your name all over London," that I tumbled to what my uncle's presence meant. My breath sucked in so violently that it had to be audible to the men, but no one looked at me.

Adrian was silent. I stared from him to my uncle. Charlwood was smiling, but there was a look in his eyes that caused my stomach muscles to tense in a way that had become all too familiar.

"How did you manage the axle?" Adrian finally asked. His voice held only a detached interest.

"Manage the axle?" I echoed. "Good God, do you think it wasn't an accident . . . ?" My voice petered out. No one was paying the least attention to me.

"You'll marry her, Greystone," my uncle said. "I have a witness who will swear that I found you together in one bedroom. How will the great hero look when that gets out, I wonder?"

He sounded—vengeful.

Adrian leaned his shoulders against the wall next to the window and regarded me as if I were an interesting specimen of insect. "You were very good," he said. "I suspected something when the axle went, but you behaved so naturally that I actually began to think it was an accident."

I looked at my uncle. "Was it an accident, Uncle Martin?" I demanded.

"My poor innocent. Did he tell you the axle broke? It was just an excuse, Kate, to get you to come here with him." My uncle's eyes were bright with pleasure, and I knew that he was lying.

"Nothing happened," I said. I looked from him to his witness-companion, who by now had come all the way into the room. Their presence seemed to suck up all the air, and it was difficult to breathe. "We are both fully dressed," I said.

"Don't matter," the man returned. "You've been compromised, my girl."

My uncle said, "Wayne is right, my dear. You have indeed been most thoroughly compromised." His words were addressed to me, but his eyes were on Adrian.

"No one need know," I protested.

"But they will. I will see to it that they know." His eyes flicked over the small, shabby room, the unmade bed, then returned to Adrian. "I have been hearing rumors, Greystone, that you are interested in pursuing a political career. If that is the case, you have not behaved with a great deal of intelligence tonight. In fact, my boy," he rolled the words out with obvious relish, "you have landed yourself in quite a nasty little dilemma. Marry her, and you have a wife who is nothing more than an Irish gambler's brat. Refuse to marry her, and

I'll spread the story of this night all over London. *That* will effectively finish any hopes of a political career, won't it?"

Charlwood's face was full of smiling violence.

Adrian's face looked as if it had turned to marble.

"What if I say I will not marry him?" I said defiantly.

The sea-green eyes turned to me. "You will do as I say, Kate," Charlwood said softly.

I felt suddenly very cold. No one, before or since, has ever made me feel as physically threatened as my uncle could. Even later, when I was standing at bay with a gun trained at my heart, even then I was not afraid as I was in that bedroom. I realize now that the threat I felt from Charlwood was sexual, but at the time all I knew was that I was terrified. I didn't answer him.

I'll have to run away, I thought. *I cannot possibly stay in this man's power.*

"I'll marry her, of course," I heard Adrian say wearily.

Charlwood laughed. The sound made me shudder, and it was then that I knew I would take the coward's way out.

The men went down to the taproom, leaving me alone. I got back into the bed, huddled under the covers, and tried not to think about the terrible thing I was going to do.

The landlady brought me tea and muffins for breakfast. I drank the tea but couldn't eat. I got back into bed. At noon my uncle came to get me. He had procured a special license, he said, and Adrian and I would be married immediately. I changed the wrinkled dress that I had slept in for a fresh one from the case I had packed for the visit to my uncle's mythical friends, and went downstairs like a sleepwalker.

The ceremony was performed in the taproom, which the landlord had thoughtfully cleared of local customers. It smelled of ale and mud and the manure that some farmer had dragged in on his boots.

It was a terrible place for the Earl of Greystone to be married. I couldn't look at him, I was so ashamed of myself.

When the time came for my response, I whispered "I will," and hung my head.

It surprised me to find that the sun was shining when finally we emerged from the taproom. My uncle was being charming to the minister, his friend Mr. Wayne looked as if all he wanted to do was to find a bed and sleep, and Adrian's face betrayed no expression whatsoever.

His phaeton was in front of the inn; evidently it had been repaired. The bays were harnessed and waiting. I stood in front of the inn, feeling like a package that nobody wanted.

"Get into the phaeton, Kate," Adrian said to me. I glanced up at him nervously. His gray eyes were as dark and cold as the North Atlantic. "I am taking you to my estate of Lambourn," he informed me in a voice that was as cold as his eyes.

I moved toward the carriage, then jumped when I felt my uncle's hand touch my arm. "Allow me to assist you, *Lady Greystone*," he said in a voice full of delighted malice.

"Stay away from her, Charlwood." Two big hands grasped my waist and swung me up to the seat of the phaeton as easily as if I weighed nothing. A moment later Adrian joined me, and the bays trotted briskly out of Luster, moving as if their owner could not wait to leave the little village in his dust.

It was a gloomy ride during which I uttered only two words: "I'm sorry." The look he threw me was contemptuous. I didn't blame him.

We stopped twice to rest the horses and to eat, but I couldn't force a thing down my throat. If I had been the crying sort I would have been bawling my eyes out by the time we reached Lambourn. But, as I believe I have said before, I am not that sort. My eyes were dry and my chin was up as we turned into the long, beech-lined drive of Lambourn Manor, one of the many homes of the Earls of Greystone.

I noticed scarcely anything on that first arrival, but later

I came to know Lambourn well and to love it dearly, so I will tell you a little about it now.

The house was old, and small for a lord's, but its setting on the windswept, rolling Berkshire Downs was beautiful. The turf of the Downs actually came right up to the doors of the house, making it look as if it were part of the landscape. The inside of the house was old as well; the rooms did not look as if they had been painted in the last hundred years. But I thought the faded colors were lovely and restful—every room was soft with pastel shades of ivory, crimson, pink, and blue, all lightly dusted with gold.

Greystone rented out most of his land to tenant farmers, who pastured horses and dairy cattle and sheep on the lush turf and grew barley and wheat and oats in the limestone soil. The manor house was kept going by a small staff of permanent servants, and there were two grooms attached to the stables in order to look after the handful of horses that Greystone kept there.

All this, of course, I learned later. On this first day all I noticed was that the original stone of the house had faded to a lovely silvery gray, and that the servants were not able to suppress their astonishment when Greystone introduced me to them as his wife.

The housekeeper, whose name was Mrs. Noakes, showed me to my room. I learned later that it was small and shabby by the standards of the Earls of Greystone, but to me it was both large and beautiful.

"Since you have not brought your own maid, I will send Nancy to help you dress, my lady," she said.

"I don't have a maid, Mrs. Noakes," I said, "and I am very used to doing without one. Please don't bother Nancy."

She stared at me in amazement. "It is no bother, my lady."

I sent Nancy away, however, and when I was alone I walked around the large room, admiring its comfortable chintz furniture and faded rug, and looking for a connecting door to another bedroom. Aristocratic married couples, I knew, had adjoining bedrooms with a connecting door. There was no such door in this room. My heart lightened a little when I realized that Adrian had not put me in the master bedroom suite.

I went over to the old mullioned window and looked out across a wide expanse of the Downs. There was a window seat tucked into the window bay, and I sat down, folded up my feet, and regarded the peaceful vista of gentle hills and rolling turf. My heart lightened a little more.

I knew I had done a terrible thing, and certainly I was feeling both guilty and ashamed. On the other hand, the horrible, sickening fear induced by my uncle's presence was gone. Guilt and shame were better than fear, I decided ruefully, and went to wash my face in the basin of warm water that Mrs. Noakes had provided.

Greystone and I sat in the pretty dining room, with its carved moldings and beautiful old Persian carpet, and made conversation while dinner was served. Nothing but cool courtesy showed in his face the whole while, and foolishly I began to think that perhaps what I had done was not so bad after all. Lambourn's spell had already begun to trick me into feeling that I was safe.

It was nearly ten o'clock when we finished, and Greystone said to me, "Go upstairs. I will join you after I have had a glass of port."

I felt as if someone had just punched me in the stomach. I could feel my eyes enlarge. He saw my look and raised an inquiring eyebrow. "Y-yes, my lord," I stammered, and fled.

Mrs. Noakes once again offered the services of Nancy, and once again I refused. I waited until she was gone before I ventured out of my room to inspect the rest of the bedrooms on the corridor.

What I saw did not alleviate my alarm. I had not been put in the master bedroom suite because there was no master bedroom suite. The room I had been given was by far the largest on the floor, and with a sinking heart I realized that it must be the bedroom that was used by the earl.

Greystone's brushes were laid out on a bureau in the small room that lay next to mine, but I was under no illusion that he planned to spend the night on the room's chintz-covered chaise longue. This was his dressing room; he was probably planning to sleep with me.

You married the man, I told myself as I stood once more in the center of my pretty bedroom, staring at the wide, comfortable bed. *What did you expect was going to happen?*

The truth, of course, was that I hadn't thought ahead at all. When one is running away from something, one often doesn't take the time to consider what one is running to. This was the uncomfortable reflection that was in my mind when I heard the doorknob turn behind me. I whirled around in time to see the heavy oak door open and Adrian walk in.

The polite mask he had worn for the servants' sake was gone. He was very angry, I realized, and my stomach muscles began to tense. I straightened my back, lifted my chin, and braced myself for what was to come.

He crossed the floor until he was standing in front of me. God, but he was big. I was tempted to throw myself on his mercy, to whimper that I was as much a victim of my uncle's scheme as he was, but I could not get the words to come. They were untrue, anyway. We both knew that I stood to lose nothing by this marriage, while he had lost everything.

He looked down at me, his face hard, his eyes narrowed. My stomach tightened even more. It was not the same feeling my uncle gave me, however, and I realized that I did not feel threatened by Adrian in the same way I felt threatened by Charlwood. This thought gave me a little courage, and I said, "I have told you I was sorry, my lord. I will do whatever you want me to."

His eyes flicked to the bed behind me, then back to my face. "Will you?" he asked.

My heart began to thud. The thought of going to bed

with such an angry male scared me to death. I do not welsh on my bargains, however. I made myself as tall as I could and said baldly, "Yes."

"So," he said, looking me up and down in a way that brought color stinging to my cheeks. "Are you pregnant, then?"

I could only stare at him, stupefied.

His mouth was compressed in a bitter line. "Charlwood would feel that his revenge was truly complete if at the same time he could saddle me with a wife I did not want and an heir that was not mine."

I felt a healthy rush of anger surge through my veins. "I am not pregnant!" I shouted it at him, so furious was I at the suggestion.

"Are you not?" And before I realized what was happening, he had reached out, grasped my arms, and pulled me against him. Instinctively I tried to push against him to get away, but the hands that were gripping my arms held me immobile. The next day I would have bruises where he had gripped me. I opened my lips to protest, but before I could speak his mouth had come down on mine. I felt his temper in its brutal hardness. My own anger flared in response, and I tried to kick him. He lifted me right off my feet and held me against his chest, his mouth still clamped on mine.

He was holding me as if I weighed nothing. I was helpless and furious but—strangely—I was not frightened. I tried ineffectively to kick him once more.

Then, abruptly, something changed in the way he was kissing me. The pressure of his lips became gentler, and his body bent over mine in a way that was possessive without being threatening. I felt the angry resistance in my own body beginning to drain away, felt myself beginning to soften and melt into him.

I have no idea how long we stayed like that. Dimly I was aware of the crackle of the fire, of the sound of the trees rustling gently outside the window. He let me slide slowly down along him until I was back on my feet again, then his right hand moved up to the back of my head, cupping it in his palm, supporting it as he bent me backward. I closed my eyes.

He pushed me away with such abruptness that I stumbled and almost fell.

"No," he said. His voice sounded hoarse and he was breathing as if he had been running. All the pulses in my body were hammering, and I stared at him in bewilderment. I was stunned by what had just happened between us.

"I am not going to make matters worse by consummating this farce of a marriage," he said between his teeth.

He had pulled my hair loose from its pins and it was beginning to slide down my back. My lips were probably bruised and swollen. I backed away a few more steps and said, with as much dignity as I could manage, "I was not the one who initiated that kiss, my lord."

He had gotten his breathing under control. His own hair had become disordered and was hanging over his forehead. I felt a sudden, illicit desire to reach up and run my fingers through it. Like a child resisting temptation, I crossed my arms and tucked my hands under my armpits.

"You will remain here at Lambourn for the time being," he said, ignoring my comment about the kiss. "The marriage will have to be acknowledged—Charlwood will certainly see to that—but he can't make me introduce you to society as my wife."

There was obviously a history of bad blood between my uncle and Greystone, but this definitely was not the time to make inquiries. He was looking as if he expected a reply from me. "That is so, my lord," I said politely.

My submissiveness did not seem to please him.

"I will not be spending the night here," he said. "I am going to ride on to Greystone Abbey."

Greystone Abbey was his chief estate, and I knew it lay near Newbury, some fifteen miles away. It was fully dark by now, but I certainly wasn't going to try to persuade him to stay. "Yes, my lord," I said in the same polite voice as before.

He scowled, and I backed up one more step. As soon as I realized what I had done, I stepped forward again. I uncrossed my arms, stood straight, and looked him in the eye. He looked as if he was going to say something else, but then he turned and strode out of the room. The door closed behind him with a very final thud. I went to the window seat, sat down, and began to shake.

CHAPTER
four

"JUST A LITTLE BIT OF BREAD AND CHEESE, MRS. Noakes?" I coaxed. "I'm frozen and I need food to help me thaw out."

I loved the kitchen at Lambourn. It was always so delightfully warm and cozy, with delicious smells emanating from the great iron stove and a fire blazing in the big stone fireplace. I sat at the well-worn wooden table and watched as the housekeeper, who was also the cook, turned to me with her hands on her ample hips.

"If you had the sense of a booby bird, my lady, you'd know enough not to go out into this weather," she scolded. "Lord knows you don't have enough flesh on your bones to keep you warm in decent weather, let alone in the cold rain we've been having this last week."

I gave her my most ingratiating smile. "I just went down to the stable for a while."

Mrs. Noakes came over to the table and picked up my hands to test their temperature. They were still extremely cold. She clucked—she really did look quite remarkably like a hen—and said, "You'll be getting chilblains if you don't watch out. Fine things for the Countess of Greystone to have on her hands!"

"Even if I do get them, no one will ever know," I said cheerfully, and ignored the look that Mrs. Noakes exchanged with her husband, who was Lambourn's general man of work.

"Mrs. Noakes is right, my lady," the old man said gruffly.

"Willie and George can look after those horses. There's no need for you to go out in such nasty weather." He beetled his bushy gray eyebrows together and added meaningfully, "Particularly in that thin old pelisse of yours."

I sighed. Mr. and Mrs. Noakes were dears, and I had become very fond of them in the eight months I had been residing at Lambourn Manor. I knew they were fond of me too, but for some reason they persisted in treating me like a wayward and not overly intelligent child. They might call me "my lady," but on their lips it sounded more like a child's pet name than a title.

"I just went to visit Elsa," I said now patiently. Elsa was a beautiful bay Thoroughbred mare who belonged to Adrian. When he had first joined the army and gone off to fight Napoleon he had sent her here to Lambourn, where the grass was heaven for horses. She had basically been retired until I arrived and decided to put her back into condition so I would be able to ride. She was sixteen, perfectly sound, perfectly healthy, and delighted to be useful once again. I adored her.

Mrs. Noakes snorted, but she brought me a plate of hot soup as well as a wedge of cheddar cheese and a loaf of fresh bread. I grinned at her, picked up my spoon, and dipped in.

"There was mail for you today, my lady," Mr. Noakes said after a few moments. He was sitting across from me at the table having one of the dozens of cups of tea that he drank during the course of the day.

My head came up alertly. "There was?"

"I put it in the library."

The soup was hot, and I blew on my spoonful before putting it in my mouth. When he did not volunteer anything more, I knew the letter had to be from Louisa. If it had come from either France or Ireland, Mr. Noakes would have said something.

Mrs. Noakes lifted the cover of an iron kettle pot on the stove and inspected the contents carefully. She sniffed, nodded, and turned back to me. "I have told you many times, my lady, that you should invite your cousin to stay with you at Lambourn Manor. It is not right for so young a girl to be alone all the time."

"We have been through this before, Mrs. Noakes," I said as I blew on another spoonful of soup. "I would love to have my cousin to stay with me, but I will not trespass on Lord Greystone's hospitality. Besides," I gave the two old dears an affectionate look, "I am not alone. I have you."

They ignored the compliment. They did not consider themselves worthy companions for me, because they were servants. "His lordship would not mind you sending for your cousin," Mr. Noakes said.

"You don't know that," I countered.

But Mr. Noakes was plowing remorselessly on. "Nor would his lordship mind if you took some of the household money to buy yourself a warm coat, my lady."

I shook my head adamantly. "I will not take his lordship's money. I am living in his house and eating his food, and that is quite enough, I think."

Both old people stared at me, frustration written large upon their honest faces. In truth, if they regarded me as a child, I had rather come to regard them as my grandparents. "Don't fret about me," I told them. "I am very happy with the way things are."

"It's not right," Mrs. Noakes muttered. She turned and banged a pot down on the stove. "It wasn't well done of his lordship to bring you here and then leave you as if you didn't exist."

"I am suite sure he wishes that I did not exist," I said candidly, "and I can't blame him."

I had confided in them both the story of my marriage, and so they knew why Greystone had dumped me so unceremoniously on their doorstep. For some reason, however, they had constituted themselves my champions, although I kept pointing out that I was not the one who had been most wronged.

They hadn't taken my part at the beginning, of course. They thought Greystone walked on water, and when I told them the story of what my uncle had forced him to do, they were quite chilly to me. This lasted for about a month. I understood their feelings perfectly and did my best not to be a nuisance. It was when I got sick that they changed.

I had walked into the village, just for something to do, and on the way home I began to feel unwell. It was a three-mile walk and by the time I got back to Lambourn my legs felt so wobbly that I was afraid I wasn't going to make it.

Mrs. Noakes had met me at the door. "My lady! Where were you? We have been looking for you all over the estate!"

"I walked to the village," I said. I remember that she looked very peculiar, as if I were seeing her through a fog.

She was appalled. "Walked! Why did you walk? If you wanted to go to the village, Willie would have driven you."

"I didn't want to be a bother," I said, and fainted at her feet.

Well, she sent for the doctor, and then she sat up with me all night long, periodically feeding me a horrible-tasting medicine. I was so confused that once or twice I actually thought she was my mother. By the time I was well again, we were friends.

Her change of heart did not surprise me. I have often noticed how attached one can get to a creature one has nursed through an illness. I have felt it myself with horses I have taken care of when they were sick.

I finished my soup and cut myself a slice of cheese. "What's for dinner?" I asked Mrs. Noakes, sniffing appreciatively at the fragrance that was wafting from the biggest pot on the stove.

"Lamb stew. One of your favorites, my lady."

"Yum." I finished the cheese in my mouth and cut another slice. "You are a superlative cook, Mrs. Noakes."

"You are scarcely a judge, my lady," the old woman said

disapprovingly. "From what you tell me, you have spent your entire life eating nothing but wretched lodging-house food."

"It was not always wretched," I replied.

Mrs. Noakes clucked again. Nothing I said could convince her that the life I had led with my father was not disgraceful. She cast one more look over the pots on the stove and came to the table to take her customary chair. I waited for her to make the little sighing noise she always gave when her weight was lifted from her feet. She made the noise and I smothered a smile.

"Mr. Crawford is coming tomorrow," Mr. Noakes said next.

"That will be nice." Mr. Crawford was the Earl of Greystone's man of business. He kept the accounts for all of Adrian's estates. He had been to Lambourn twice before, to check on the estate. I had found him to be a very pleasant man.

"I will serve dinner in the dining room," Mrs. Noakes said.

I knew what she was hinting. "Don't worry, Mrs. Noakes, I won't tell him that I usually eat in the kitchen. I promise."

She compressed her lips and nodded. This business of my taking my dinner in the kitchen with her and Mr. Noakes worried her dreadfully. On the one hand, she could see that I would find it very lonesome eating by myself in the dining room, but on the other hand she hated the thought of the Countess of Greystone eating in the kitchen. I thought she was making a great fuss about nothing, but then I would be the first to confess that I knew nothing about being a countess.

I never told her about the card games that Willie and George and I played in the office at the stable. She would have been aghast.

"I will wear my blue dress for Mr. Crawford and do my best to act like a lady," I said to Mrs. Noakes.

"You *are* a lady," the housekeeper said fiercely.

I gave her my best smile. "You're prejudiced because you like me." I stood up. "Thank you for the soup and the cheese."

I made my way to the library and collected my letter, which Mr. Noakes had left lying next to the clock on the mantelpiece. I read it standing in front of the fire, and when I had finished I refolded it slowly, trying not to feel hurt and disappointed.

Poor Louisa, I thought. Her wretched nieces and nephews had all come down with mumps and her letter had been filled with the woes of taking caring of them.

The one piece of news I had been hoping for had not been forthcoming. *I have heard nothing from a man called Paddy O'Grady,* Louisa had written. *I wrote to the housekeeper at Charlwood, as you requested, and no one of that name has made inquiries about you there either, Kate.*

I bit my lip and stared into the flames. I had spent a good part of the winter thinking about the manner of my father's death, and I badly wanted to talk to Paddy.

I was going to have to think of some way of tracking him down.

I went to the stable earlier than usual the following morning, then I put on my blue dress and waited for Mr. Crawford to arrive.

I suppose I should mention here that my wardrobe was another source of disagreement between me and the Noakeses. After my marriage, Cousin Louisa had sent all my clothes to Lambourn, but I had sent back all of the clothing that my uncle had paid for. I would rather have worn rags.

To listen to Mr. and Mrs. Noakes, you would have thought I *was* wearing rags. This was simply not true. My clothes were in perfectly decent condition. They might not be fashionable, but they were very far from being rags. The blue dress was particularly nice—Papa had bought it for my eighteenth birthday and it had cost him half the price of a nice young mare he had just sold. "It almost matches your eyes, Kate," he had said with his most irresistible smile. "I couldn't find a perfect match—no dye is that vivid a blue."

I remembered his words as I was getting dressed, and they made me smile. It was becoming less painful for me to think of my father. I suppose that old saw about time healing all wounds has some truth to it after all.

When I had worn the dress for Mr. Crawford's first visit I had been so thin that it had hung on me. It fit very well today—a tribute, I thought, to Mrs. Noakes's good cooking.

I was sitting primly in one of the embroidered chairs in the drawing room when Mr. Noakes appeared to announce the arrival of our visitor, who came into the room on his heels.

"My lady." Mr. Crawford was a young Scotsman who took his position very seriously. After Adrian's father had died, Adrian had pensioned off the old earl's man of business and had employed Mr. Crawford. Mr. Crawford was of impeccable lineage, but he was also the middle child in a family of nine. He was intensely grateful for the position and tended to speak of Adrian as if he were the second coming of the Messiah.

"You poor thing," I said as I took in his frozen appearance. "Go right upstairs. There is a fire going in your bedroom and Robert will bring you some hot tea." He gave me a grateful smile, murmured a few polite words about my graciousness, and disappeared up the stairs in the direction of the bedroom he always used.

He looked better when he came into the drawing room an hour later. I was waiting for him and we went into dinner.

Mr. Noakes and Robert served us Mrs. Noakes's delicious wine-sauce chicken. Robert came every day to help Mr. Noakes around the house, but he lived with an aged grandmother in one of the cottages on the estate grounds. The other servant was Nancy, who also lived in one of the cottages. She came to the manor every morning with her father, who saw to the garden.

"I have been in communication with the earl about you, my lady," Mr. Crawford said as he took an abstemious sip of his wine. I had been admiring the large lump Robert was sporting on his forehead due to a fall on some ice, but these words captured my undivided attention.

"About me?" To my chagrin, my voice squeaked. I cleared my throat.

"Yes. He has authorized me to pay you a quarterly allowance. I have the first payment with me."

I could feel my jaw drop. I closed it firmly. "He doesn't . . ." I cleared my throat again. "He doesn't have to do that. I don't need any money."

"Yes, my lady, you do." He was looking at me out of troubled hazel eyes. "If the earl had not been called to Paris so abruptly, he would have taken care of this matter before he left." He was so sweetly serious as he lied to me that I didn't have the heart to contradict him.

Adrian had not rejoined the army, nor had he been called to Paris abruptly. He had gone back to France of his own choice and in a civilian capacity, as I knew from the one terse note I had received from him on the subject. His ostensible reason for this return had been that the Duke of Wellington needed his assistance in dealing with the friction that was constantly breaking out between French citizens and the Army of Occupation. I knew the real reason why Adrian had returned to Paris, however. He had done it to get away from me.

"Is . . . is his lordship remaining in Paris?" I asked anxiously.

Mr. Crawford looked at me with pity. "I am afraid that he is, my lady."

Obviously this poor young man thought he was giving me grievous news. "Oh," I said, afraid to say anything more lest my words betray my delight. I was happy here at

Lambourn, and as long as Adrian stayed in Paris I could go on pretending that it was really my home.

"The Duke of Wellington has found the earl's assistance to be invaluable," Mr. Crawford assured me. "The duke himself is rather . . . blunt. The earl, on the other hand, knows how to be diplomatic. This is of great importance when one is dealing with the French."

This was excellent news. Let Adrian stay in Paris and be a diplomat. However, I still did not want to take his money, and I said so.

"I understand from Mrs. Noakes that you need a new winter pelisse," Mr. Crawford said.

"There is nothing wrong with my pelisse! It may be a little shabby, but it is perfectly warm."

"My lady, the Countess of Greystone cannot wear clothing that is a little shabby."

"No one sees me."

"The tenants see you. The people in the village see you. How do you think it will make the earl appear if his people see his wife wearing shabby clothes?"

"Perhaps they will think I am eccentric." I wasn't willing to give up yet.

"They will blame him," Mr. Crawford said. "It is not fair of you to put him into a position where he will not appear to advantage in front of his own people."

I hadn't thought of it that way. I regarded the gilt edging of my dinner plate, and thought. Then, "Are you certain he wished me to have this allowance?" I asked anxiously.

"Quite certain, my lady." He smiled at me. He was quite a nice-looking young man when he smiled.

"Very well," I said. I swallowed. "Then I suppose I will take it."

"Christmas is coming," Mr. Crawford said. "Perhaps you would like to buy a few gifts?"

I brightened at that thought. In my spare time I had been working on a sampler for Mrs. Noakes, but my needlework was atrocious. If I had some money I could buy her a present in the village. I could buy something for Mr. Noakes and Robert and Nancy and Willie and George, too. I could even buy something to send to Cousin Louisa! I beamed and said, "Yes, I would. Thank you, Mr. Crawford."

He looked embarrassed.

Robert refilled our glasses. The lump on his forehead was certainly sporting an interesting variety of colors. I said, "Are you feeling all right, Robert? That is a truly monumental lump."

He grinned at me. Robert was my age and we liked each other. "I'm good, my lady," he said.

I turned back to my guest and asked, "Will you be going home to Scotland for Christmas, Mr. Crawford?" When he said he would be, I asked him how his family was doing. He said that they were well.

"How lovely it must be to have brothers and sisters," I said.

"You would not think it was lovely if you found a toad in your bed," he replied dryly.

I laughed, and behind Mr. Crawford's back, Robert smothered a smile. "Did one of your brothers do that to you?" I asked Mr. Crawford.

"He did."

"Tell me," I demanded. He told me that story, and then, when he saw how interested I was, he told me more. I was entranced. I had always had the only child's envy of large families.

When dinner was finished and I rose to return to the drawing room, I had another happy thought. I would buy a present for Mr. Crawford too!

I bought the presents, and Christmas was not as bad as I had feared it would be. I missed Papa, of course, but for some reason I was so busy all day that I did not have time to brood. Mrs. Noakes had baked her special Christmas bread and she asked me to take a loaf to each of Adrian's tenant farmers. Everyone invited me in, and gave me punch, and I played with their children. Then, when I returned to the house, I discovered that all my friends had bought presents for me too. I opened them, and then Mr. and Mrs. Noakes and I sat down to an enormous dinner.

It was not a bad day at all.

Two days after Christmas I had the first communication with my husband's family since our marriage. Adrian's younger brother, Harry, turned up on the doorstep of Lambourn Manor and announced that he had come to meet his brother's wife.

CHAPTER
five

THE YOUNG MAN MR. NOAKES USHERED INTO THE LI-
brary that late December morning had the same unearthly fair
hair as his brother, but where the clean bones of Adrian's face
gave an impression of strength, Harry's more chiseled features were so fine that he looked almost angelic. There was
nothing angelic about Harry's spirit, however, as I was soon
to discover.

"Did you come alone, Lord Harry?" said Mr. Noakes,
disapproval oozing from every pore.

"Don't be such an old mutton-face, Noakes," Harry said
blithely. Then, to me, "I must say, I had no idea Adrian's wife
would look like you!"

I glared at him. Harry was not that many inches taller
than I, so he was much easier to glare at than his brother was.
"Apologize to Mr. Noakes this instant," I demanded.

He stared at me in amazement. "Apologize to Noakes?
Whatever for?"

"For calling him a mutton-face."

His mouth dropped open.

"Apologize," I said again.

He closed his mouth. "Sorry, Noakes," he muttered.
"Didn't mean to insult you, you know."

The old man's look of displeasure did not change. "Will
you be staying for dinner, Mr. Harry?"

Harry looked at me once more. "Yes."

Mr. Noakes's frown deepened.

I regarded Harry's riding breeches and boots and asked him what he had done with his horse.

"I know Lambourn is lightly staffed, so I left him at the stable," he replied.

I nodded my approval of such thoughtfulness. "I was just going out for a ride, but I should be happy to offer you some tea first."

His gray eyes, which were considerably lighter than his brother's, flicked downward from my face. Then he said, "Madeira would be better than tea."

I knew what he was looking at. The Noakeses had been scandalized when I had first appeared in the divided skirt I wore for riding. It was a costume Papa had designed himself. "You can't continue to wear breeches," he had said when he presented me with the skirt when I was fourteen. "But I'll be damned if I'll ruin the best seat I've ever seen by making you ride aside."

I had been so pleased by the compliment that I had not even objected to giving up my breeches.

The divided skirt came to my ankles, and I wore it with high boots, so it was perfectly modest, but it had caused a sensation more than once. Everyone usually forgot about it once I was on the back of a horse.

I invited Harry to take a seat in the library. "I don't use the drawing room very much, so there is no fire in there," I apologized as we sat in the two worn blue-upholstered chairs that flanked the fireplace.

"It don't matter," he replied breezily. "This has always been my favorite room at Lambourn."

"It is my favorite room too," I confided, looking around at the mellow book-lined walls, the big polished desk, the large globe, and the two mullioned windows that looked out over the Downs.

Mr. Noakes came in with Madeira for Harry and tea for me. He also served us a plate of Mrs. Noakes's delicious buttered muffins, which he put on a small table between us. I thanked him, and Harry and I helped ourselves to the food.

"So," Harry said after he had finished his first muffin, "tell me all about how you came to marry Adrian."

"What has he told you?" I asked cautiously.

"Nothing. I'm up at Oxford, you know, and he wrote me a letter saying that he had married Charlwood's niece and was going to rejoin Wellington in Paris. He ain't mentioned you since."

I chewed on my lip, regarded the small bronze statue of a dog that graced the mantelpiece, and wondered how much I should tell him.

"Are you really married?" he asked me.

"I am afraid that we are," I said mournfully.

"And you're Charlwood's niece?" His voice sounded incredulous.

"I am afraid that I am."

"Damn," he said, adding belatedly, "I beg your pardon."

I was quite accustomed to hearing men swear. "It is all right," I said, and went on staring at the statue of the dog. It looked like some sort of a mastiff, I thought. Perhaps it was supposed to be one of King Alfred's dogs.

Harry took another bite of muffin, and I could feel him looking at me while he chewed. He brushed some crumbs off his lap and said, "How did it happen?"

I removed my eyes from the dog, looked at Harry, and decided there wasn't any point in not telling him the whole story. He would be bound to hear it from his brother one of these days.

"How rotten for Adrian," Harry said when at last I had finished. He scowled. "Charlwood must have loved putting the screws to him like that."

"I have thought about it a great deal," I said, "and it certainly does appear as if Charlwood planned the whole episode. Otherwise he would never have known to come looking for me like that."

"He planned it," Harry agreed, pouring himself another glass of wine. "He probably paid someone to damage the axle enough to be sure that it would break."

"But why?" This was the question that had plagued me for the last eight months. "This wasn't just a case of Charlwood trying to catch an earl for his niece," I explained. "I saw his face that night at the inn, and he looked positively vengeful."

The angel face opposite me looked grim. "He was after revenge, all right."

"For what?"

He paused for a long moment, his eyes searching mine. "I think I will tell you," he said at last. He put down his glass and lowered his voice. "But it's a family secret."

I leaned toward him, feeling the heat from the fire scorch my cheek. "I swear I'll never tell."

He leaned toward me as well. "It involves my sister, you see. Caroline."

The firelight fell on his hair and for a brief, unsettling moment I had a vision of another man, another face. I shook my head as if to clear it and remembered the time that Adrian had told me he had a sister.

Harry said, "She's married now—happily, thank God. Has two children and lives in Dorset. But ten years ago, when she was sixteen, she eloped with Charlwood."

"What!" The fire cracked as if it were as horrified as I.

He nodded. "It's the truth. She wasn't happy at home—well, I mean to say, none of us were happy at home—and she fancied herself in love with Charlwood. Our fathers had never gotten on, and I think Caroline envisioned herself as another Juliet. At any rate, they actually set off for Scotland. Adrian found out about it, thank God, and went after them. Caught up with them in the early afternoon and got her home before my father knew what had happened."

"Ten years ago?" I said. "Adrian must have been a boy ten years ago!"

"He was seventeen and home for the summer from Eton. He was so furious with Charlwood that he forced a duel on him. Caroline told me about it later. Adrian brought swords and the two of them actually had a duel. Right on the road!"

Harry's voice was full of awe as he recounted this deed. I pictured the scene and shuddered. It was lucky for Caroline that Adrian had won. I said as much to Harry.

"Adrian always wins," Harry said with simple faith.

I sat back in my comfortable chair, ran my hand over the faded arm, and contemplated the information I had just been given. Ten years ago my uncle had been twenty-two. It could not have pleased him to be beaten by a seventeen-year-old.

The fire hissed in the silence and I said, "So Adrian denied Charlwood the wife he wanted, and in revenge Charlwood made Adrian take a wife he did not want."

Harry leaned back and stretched his booted legs in front of him. "That's about it. You must have looked like manna from heaven to Charlwood. It would have been even better for him if you had been ugly, of course, but you served the main purpose. You scotched Adrian's marriage with Lady Mary Weston."

I felt a pang. "Did he love Lady Mary?"

Harry shrugged. "I don't know about love, but he was certainly going to marry her."

"They weren't engaged."

"He just hadn't got around to asking her yet."

"Perhaps she would have refused him."

Harry gave me an incredulous look. "Refuse *Adrian*?"

"It is not inconceivable," I said with dignity.

He didn't even deign to reply, so vapid did he consider that remark.

We finished the plate of muffins in silence. When the last crumb had been devoured, I suggested to Harry that he might like to accompany me to the stable. He agreed and we put on our warm riding coats, left the house through the side door, and walked together along the graveled path that led to the Lambourn stables.

The grounds at Lambourn were almost as simple as the house. Along the path to the stable there were two stone outbuildings that had at one time served as the dairy and the cookhouse and that now, with the family no longer in any regular residence, were filled with odds and ends of furniture that were no longer needed in the house. The path itself was flanked by turf, winter brown now, but in spring it would be richly green.

The stable buildings were constructed of the same stone as the house. There was the carriage house, which at the moment contained only a simple country cart, and the barn. The barn held twelve box stalls, all of which looked out on a cobbled central yard. Five of the double Dutch doors were open at the top to allow their occupants air and sunshine; four of the stalls belonged to Lambourn's equine residents and one to Harry's horse. I started toward the newcomer's stall, curious to see what he was riding.

The open door revealed a bright chestnut Thoroughbred gelding, who was happily munching on a pile of hay. I regarded him critically. "What a nice horse," I said to Harry, who was standing beside me. "He looks as if he has smooth gaits."

Harry looked at me in surprise. "They are smooth. How did you know that?"

"One can often tell by the way the shoulder is set."

The surprise on Harry's face slowly turned to something else. It was a change I had seen dozens of times before. I will never understand why men refuse to think that women are capable of judging a horse.

"Let me show you Elsa," I said, and we moved along to the mare's stall. She was finishing up her own lunch hay, but when she heard my voice she glanced over her shoulder. She didn't nicker—Elsa thought nickering was undignified—but she moved with queenly graciousness to the stall door, where she accepted a lump of sugar and allowed me to rub the white star on her forehead.

Harry's mouth was hanging open, and I smiled. The last few months had seen a dramatic change in Elsa's appearance. Her neck had a lovely crest, her back had filled in, and her quarters were starting to muscle up nicely. In another year she would be magnificent.

"How old is this mare?" Harry demanded.

"Sixteen," I said.

"That's what I thought. What have you done to her?"

"I've been riding her."

He looked at my skirt, this time openly. "You don't use a sidesaddle?"

I shook my head. "I learned to ride astride, and Papa said it would be a shame to make me change."

Willie's voice came from behind us. "Would you like me to saddle her up, my lady, so you can show Lord Henry how she goes?" He sounded so much like a proud father that I had to smile. Both of the grooms at Lambourn really cared about the horses in their charge.

"I'd like to see her go," Harry said. We stood together in the bright cold sunshine and watched while Willie saddled Elsa. On the far side of the barn there were three large fenced paddocks, and I had made a riding ring in one of them by spreading wood shavings over the frozen ground. This is where we took Elsa. The two men watched as I fitted my foot into the stirrup and swung up into the saddle.

I have been riding horses in front of my father's customers for almost all my life, so it didn't make me at all nervous to ride now in front of Harry. He was impressed. He should have been. Elsa was forward and light and absolutely elegant.

"Divorce Adrian and marry me," Harry said when we came to a perfectly square halt in front of him.

I laughed.

"Where did you learn to ride like that?"

"My father. He attended the French cavalry school at Saumur when he was a young man, so he was well grounded in classical equitation."

Harry nodded. "You don't use an English hunting saddle, I see."

"Papa abhorred the hunting saddle," I said frankly. "He said it is responsible for the English being the worst riders in the entire civilized world. He got this old French military saddle for me about five years ago. I wouldn't part with it for anything on earth."

Harry grinned. "Your father would have gotten along great guns with Adrian."

This was not as great a surprise to me as you may think. I had been both astonished and delighted when I first got on Elsa to discover how rhythmic her gaits were, how responsive she was to the lightest of aids. And Elsa had been Adrian's horse.

Harry was going on, "Your father would have been happy to know that one of Adrian's projects in France this last year has been to get the king to restore the cavalry school at Saumur."

Papa would have been more than happy to hear this; he would have been ecstatic. It had pained him deeply to think that the art of classical equitation might be lost forever.

I smiled radiantly at Harry. "That is wonderful news," I said warmly.

Harry blinked.

"Why don't you let Willie saddle up one of the other horses for you and we'll go for a ride together?" I suggested.

By the time we returned from our ride across the Downs, Harry and I were great friends. He would not be going back to Oxford after Christmas, he confided to me as we were sitting in the dining room over Mrs. Noakes's roast beef dinner. He had been sent down for some silly prank—he did not think it was silly, but I did—and now he had to write to tell Adrian the bad news.

"I don't get control of my own money until I'm twenty-five," he told me gloomily. "So for the next four years, I'm dependent upon Adrian. He's going to kick up stiff when he hears that I've been sent down."

"I don't blame him," I said candidly. "Whatever are you going to do with yourself for the next eight months?"

"Damn!" he said. Mr. Noakes gave him a dire frown, but he didn't notice. "Adrian never went to Oxford. When he was my age he was having fun out in the Peninsula. Now that the war's over, there's nothing for my generation to do except go to boring old school."

I smiled at Mr. Noakes to show him that Harry had not offended me. "How thoughtless of Wellington to have ended the war before you had a chance to get killed," I said.

"Dash it all, Kate,"—we had gotten on first-name terms in the first half hour of our ride—"I know war ain't fun. But, don't you see, it's a way of becoming a *man*." He scowled at his glass of wine, picked it up, and drained it off. "Of course, you don't understand," he muttered. "You're a girl."

I understood more than he thought. It could not be easy for an ardent young boy like Harry to have such a paragon for an elder brother. Harry was searching for a way to prove himself as good a man as Adrian, and the only outlet he could find was the harebrained pranks that he knew in his heart were not manly but simply juvenile.

"How did your brother come to go out to the Peninsula?" This was a question that had puzzled me for quite a while. The heir to a great title was not expected to risk his life in battles—that was something a younger son was supposed to do.

We had finished dinner by now, and Harry said abruptly, "Let's go back to the library."

I certainly did not want to leave him alone with a bottle of wine—I thought he had had quite enough already—so I agreed.

"Adrian went to the Peninsula to get away from my father, of course," Harry said when we were once again settled comfortably in the blue chairs in front of the library fire. "The same reason that Caroline let herself get talked into that wretched elopement."

· I thought about this for a while. "Your father was not a . . . kindly . . . man?" I asked.

"He was a monster," Harry returned bluntly. "Used to fly in a rage and use his whip on us."

I was dumbfounded. "He *hit* you?"

"He hit Adrian, mostly." Harry ran his fingers through his hair and regarded me with somber eyes. "He used to take the blame for things Caroline and I did. He was bigger, he'd say. The hitting stopped when Adrian got big enough to hit back, but the fact of the matter was, my father was a bastard to live with."

"But what of your mother?" I asked in horror. "Did she not try to prevent this?"

"My mother died when I was a baby," Harry replied in a matter-of-fact voice. "Things got better for us when Caroline married Ashley. I went to live with Caroline and Adrian went to the Peninsula. When my father died four years ago, we all rejoiced."

I was appalled by this vision of life in an earl's household. I thought of the cold lifeless rooms at Charlwood and wondered if my own grandfather—who, according to Cousin Louisa had been a "hard man"—had presided over the same kind of reign of terror as the one that had prevailed at Greystone.

How lucky I was to have had Papa, I thought fervently. I may have missed having the security of a settled home and income, but I had never once doubted that I was loved.

"Adrian is going to think I acted like a fool, getting myself sent down like this," Harry said now despondently. "And what's worse, he will be right."

This was a boy who needed a mission in life, I thought, looking at his drooping figure. And I had one to offer him.

"I think my father was murdered," I said. "And I'd like you to help me find out why."

Harry had snapped to instant attention at my words. "Murdered?" he said. "What do you mean, murdered?"

I told him how Papa had been shot, and about his dying words. "I mentioned them to your brother," I said, "but he did not take them seriously. He told me that dying men often drift away in their minds. I have no doubt that he is correct, but Papa was not one of those men. He knew very well where he was and what he was saying. He made arrangements for my uncle to be sent for. He . . ." Here my voice wobbled dangerously, but I took a deep breath and steadied it. "He told me that he loved me. He was not drifting away."

"It don't sound as if he was," Harry agreed. "But what did he suspect?"

"I don't know, but I think it has to do with the Marquis of Stade. For some reason, Papa was insistent that he had to show the two hunters we had picked up in Ireland to Stade. He went directly from Ireland to Newmarket, without stopping to see any of his usual customers and without previously approaching Stade to see if he would be interested. This was not Papa's normal way of doing business, Harry. Then, after Papa's death, when I was in London with my uncle, I had a strange encounter with Stade." And I told him about my meeting with the Marquis. "He knew exactly who I was when he stopped Mr. Putnam," I said. "Something is not right. I can feel it."

"Do you think Stade is the one who shot your father?"

"I don't know," I admitted. "But I think he was shot deliberately. Even the local magistrate thought it was odd that someone would have a gun in that part of the woods."

Harry was silent, obviously lost in thought. I got up, went to the fire, rested my booted foot on the grate, and held out my hands to its welcome blaze. I felt chilled to my bones.

Mr. Noakes walked in. "Will you be wanting your horse brought around, Mr. Harry?" he asked.

Harry exploded. "Dash it all, Noakes, why are you so anxious to get rid of me?"

"It is not proper for you to stay alone in the house with Lady Greystone," the old man said repressively.

"She's my sister-in-law!" Harry said.

"She is a very young lady and her husband is away."

"Well, it ain't good for her to be all alone either," Harry retorted. "She needs a little company."

I was beginning to feel as if I were invisible. "Mr. Harry will leave in half an hour, Mr. Noakes," I said as firmly as I could.

Both men looked at me.

"Oh, all right," Harry said.

"Very good, my lady," Mr. Noakes said.

The old man fussed with the fire, asked us if we wanted more lamps lit, and finally left. Harry had looked as if he were gritting his teeth the whole time Mr. Noakes was in the room.

"How do you put up with that?" Harry demanded as soon as the door had closed.

"I am very fond of Mr. Noakes, and I want you to be polite to him," I returned.

"If I am going to help you investigate the death of your father, I am going to have to visit you," Harry pointed out.

"Of course you can visit me. You just can't *stay* here."

"It's damn cold, riding fifteen miles back and forth to Greystone in the middle of winter," he said grumpily.

"You won't be at Greystone very much," I said, "because the first thing you are going to have to do is find Paddy."

CHAPTER
six

WE PLOTTED THE SEARCH FOR PADDY ON HARRY'S subsequent visits. Since horses were the one thing that Paddy knew, I was quite certain that he would try to keep on with Papa's business. This meant that the most likely place for us to find him would probably be at a racetrack. No racetracks were open in January, however, which put a damper on our plans.

"Where did you and your father usually spend January?" Harry asked me one cold afternoon as we sat around a cozy fire in Lambourn's library. His visit had surprised me; he had been to Lambourn only the previous day.

I stretched my toes toward the warmth and wiggled them inside my soft leather shoes. "We frequently spent the winter in Ireland. Papa often bought young horses from small Irish breeders, broke them, and sold them in England for a good profit."

"Do you think that Paddy will have gone to Ireland?"

"I think it's very likely," I admitted.

Harry looked disgusted. "Then we have no choice but to wait until the racing season in the spring to look for him."

I sighed. "I suppose that is so."

Harry puffed out his lips and contemplated his booted feet. I had had the feeling all afternoon that he had something to tell me, and at last he brought it out. "I received a letter from Adrian yesterday," he said gruffly.

I felt myself stiffen. I said nothing.

He looked up. There was a worried look in his eyes. "He's been involved in making the arrangements for the French loan."

Since Mr. Crawford had very nicely arranged for me to receive regularly two of the London newspapers, I knew what Harry was talking about. "The loan with Barings so that France can begin to pay war reparations to the Allies?"

Harry nodded. "That loan."

One of the provisions of the Peace of Paris that had been reached after Waterloo was that France had to pay an indemnity of 700 million francs to the Allies. As the French economy could scarcely support such a payment, the English had arranged a long-term loan from the British bankers Baring Brothers and Hopes.

"The contract for the loan is to be signed next month," Harry went on. The worry in his eyes became even more pronounced. "Adrian is coming to London to make certain everything goes smoothly."

I could feel the blood drain from my face.

"Exactly," Harry said.

I chewed on my lip. "Is he going to stay in London or do you think he will come here?"

"He is certainly planning to come to Greystone Abbey," Harry replied. "In fact, I rather got the impression that he was planning to *remain* in England. He wrote that he has been an absentee landlord for too long."

I looked around the cozy, firelit room and stifled a mournful sigh. It had been lovely to live at Lambourn, but in my heart I had known it could not go on forever.

"If Adrian wants to divorce me, of course I shall agree," I said to Harry. "But I won't go back to my uncle. You have to find Paddy for me, Harry. I can live with him."

Harry was scowling. "Adrian won't divorce you, Kate! Think of the scandal."

"If Lady Mary truly loves him, she won't regard the scandal," I said.

Harry was shaking his head. "Lady Mary don't matter," he said. "Adrian won't divorce you."

Perhaps it had to do with his going into politics, I thought. Perhaps divorce would be a stain he could not live down.

I had been thinking about our problem on and off all winter and now I mentioned the other solution I had come up with. "Perhaps he can arrange for an annulment. I am not certain what the requirements for an annulment are, but we have never had a real marriage. We have never lived together."

Harry said gruffly, "If Adrian has any brain at all, he will hold on to the wife he has. He isn't likely to do any better."

I was touched. "That is very nice of you, Harry. But your brother thinks I was privy to Charlwood's plot, you see, and so he doesn't like me very much."

"I will tell him the truth," Harry said. "Anyone who knows you can see that you would never lend yourself to such a despicable scheme."

I was feeling very low, and his confidence in my honesty was very welcome. "Thank you," I said.

Harry gave me a reassuring smile. "Don't worry, Kate. I'll talk to him. Everything will work out for the best, you'll see. Adrian is an honorable man. He won't abandon you."

"I am not a charity case, Harry," I said irritably.

He didn't reply. Nor did I press the matter. I was a solitary female, with no money and no family. If that didn't constitute a charity case, then I don't know what did. Needless to say, this was not a thought that brought much joy.

"Perhaps I don't want to stay married to *him*," I muttered childishly.

"Don't be stupid, Kate," Harry said.

I scowled but did not reply.

The contract between Baring Brothers and Hopes and the French government was signed on February 10, 1817, with the Earl of Greystone, representing the British government, in attendance. Two days later, the earl left London for his principal seat, Greystone Abbey near Newbury in the county of Berkshire. I knew this because Harry rode over to give me the news that Adrian would be arriving at Greystone the following day.

It took him three more days to come to Lambourn.

As you can imagine, this was not an easy time for me. The weather was good and I rode all of the horses in the stables every day. I couldn't concentrate enough to pass the time by reading. There were no novels in the Lambourn library, so I had spent the winter reading *The Wealth of Nations,* which was not a book one could peruse with a distracted mind.

He came on February 16, at eleven o'clock in the morning. There had been frost that night and I was waiting for the ground to warm up before I went out to the stables, so he caught me in the house. Mrs. Noakes had been nagging me for days about my lack of appetite, and I was hiding out in the library to avoid her. I had been staring blankly into the fire for an hour when Mr. Noakes came into the room and said in a gentle voice that immediately put me on my guard, "His lordship is here, my lady."

I jumped to my feet. Then Adrian walked into the room.

One forgot how big he was. His shoulders filled the doorway. "H-how do you do, my lord," I said in a small, polite voice.

There was a startled pause. I suppose I had sounded as if I were meeting him for the first time. Then, "I do very well, thank you," he replied. "I hope I find you well?"

"Yes." I couldn't think of a single other thing to say. I threw a beseeching look at Mr. Noakes, but he was poised to leave.

"Shall I tell Mrs. Noakes that you will be taking luncheon with us, my lord?"

"Yes, Noakes, thank you."

Mr. Noakes left.

I was alone with my husband.

"Sit down, Kate," he said. "I am not going to eat you."

I sat on one of the blue fireside chairs and he came to sit on the matching one that Harry so often used. He wore a blue coat, buff breeches, and Hessian boots, and his face was ruddy from the cold. He had obviously driven over. I folded my hands in my lap and waited.

"You are certainly not a blabbermouth," he said with amusement.

"I don't know what to say to you," I replied truthfully. I bit my lip. "I have behaved so badly to you, and you have been so nice to me. You make me feel ashamed."

He raised his brows. "You can hardly think that my abandoning you for nine months constitutes being nice."

"You gave me this lovely place to live in," I said. "You even gave me an allowance. We both know the circumstances of our union, my lord. I think you have been very . . ." I paused, searching for a word. "Magnanimous," I pronounced at last.

This time only one eyebrow lifted. The firelight glinted off his hair, as it had so often glinted off Harry's, but Adrian did not induce in me the easy, comfortable feeling I got from his brother.

He said a little abruptly, "Both my brother and my man of business have been urging me to believe that you were not a part of Charlwood's plan, that you were just as much a victim of his plot as I."

I leaned a little forward, anxious to convince him. "Truly, I did not know what my uncle intended, my lord. If I had known, I would never, never have gone with you! But . . ." I could feel the scarlet color sweep into my face. I had been meeting his eyes, but now mine dropped away like guilty things, unable to hold that steady gray gaze.

"But . . . ?" He did not sound angry, merely curious.

I brought it out in a rush. "I should have refused to wed you. I know that. It was cowardly of me to have given in to my uncle's pressure. I am greatly at fault, and I am sorry. I told you once before that I will do whatever you wish me to . . ." My blush grew deeper as I recalled what had happened after that promise, and my eyes flicked upward to see if he recalled as well. His face looked grave. I rushed on, "If you wish to try for an annulment, I shall do all I can to assist you."

"If I do have our marriage annulled, will you go back to Charlwood?" he asked.

"No!" Even I could hear the panic in my voice. I swallowed, and forced my voice to a calm reasonableness. "I have been thinking," I said. "I know you have many houses. Perhaps you might have need of a housekeeper for one of them?" This was an idea I had come up with only two days ago, and I thought it might serve my purposes very well.

"Are you proposing to turn yourself into a housekeeper?" He sounded incredulous.

"Mrs. Noakes has taught me to cook," I announced proudly. "And I have been watching her go about her duties all winter. I could do a good job. I know I could."

"Kate, your grandfather was a viscount. You do not need to learn how to cook!"

He didn't understand. I suppose I really hadn't expected him to. "Well," I said, "if I can find my father's old groom, Paddy O'Grady, I am sure I can stay with him. He has known me since I was born."

"You cannot live with a groom," he said impatiently.

"Paddy is not just a groom," I explained. "He is like my family."

There was a hard look about his mouth. "If we have this marriage annulled, I will make certain that you have enough money to set up your own establishment and live in whatever way you choose," he said.

"I could not take your money," I said, and meant it.

Mr. Noakes appeared in the doorway and announced, "Luncheon is served, my lady. In the dining room."

"Thank you, Mr. Noakes."

As we left the library, Adrian asked me curiously, "Why

did Noakes feel it necessary to say 'the dining room' in such a pointed voice?"

There didn't seem any point in lying to him. "I usually eat in the kitchen," I said, "but Mrs. Noakes doesn't think it's proper."

All the leaves had been taken out of the dining-room table months ago, so even though Adrian and I were sitting at opposite ends of the polished mahogany, we were not that far apart. Mr. Noakes brought in plates of oxtail soup. I took one sip and put my spoon down. My stomach was in too much of a knot for me to eat.

Adrian had almost finished his soup when Mr. Noakes, who was standing against the wall waiting to remove our soup before serving the next course, said in a strangled kind of voice, "My lady, Mrs. Noakes is going to be very upset if you don't eat that soup."

Adrian's head lifted.

"I am sorry, Mr. Noakes," I said. "I am just not hungry."

"Do you always monitor her ladyship's eating habits, Noakes?" Adrian asked mildly.

The old man gave Adrian a wretched look. "I am sorry, my lord. I did not mean to intrude like that. It is just that her ladyship has eaten scarcely anything all week. . . ." His voice trailed away.

"You could never intrude, Mr. Noakes," I said firmly. "And I will try to eat the soup." I swallowed a spoonful to demonstrate my good faith.

The remainder of the meal proceeded quite pleasantly, and I managed to eat enough of the subsequent courses to appease Mrs. Noakes. I asked Adrian about the French loan and he replied with all the good-humored readiness that I remembered from the early part of our disastrous drive, before the axle had broken. For a little while I managed to forget that he probably hated me.

I remembered, however, when we were once again alone in the library. We did not sit down, but stood on either side of the hearth rug, looking at each other. He said, "An annulment is not easy to get, Kate."

"I would testify about my uncle's perfidy," I assured him.

His jaw set. "I'm damned if I want the world to know that Charlwood caught me with the oldest trick in the book."

"It might be a little embarrassing," I conceded. "But surely embarrassment is better than being shackled for life to a woman you don't love?"

Silence. The velvet drapes were open and the sun slanted in through old panes of glass and pooled on the worn Persian rug. I watched the dust motes dance in its bright radiance.

Suddenly Adrian crossed the hearth rug and, taking my chin in his hand, he forced my face up to look at his. It surprised me to feel calluses on those strong, aristocratic fingers. "You are either incredibly naive or quite the cleverest young lady I have ever known," he said softly.

Quite suddenly I was angry. I jerked my face away and he opened his fingers and let me go. I backed up a few steps and glared at him. "I am neither of those things," I said fiercely.

"Are you not?"

"No, I am not!"

He looked at me and his eyes were hard, intent. He said, "Let's go down to the stables and you can show me Elsa."

His change of subject was bewildering, to say the least, but I was more than happy to go along with him. I changed into my winter riding clothes and he put on his driving overcoat and together we walked down to the stable.

The sun had warmed the air considerably while we were at luncheon, and I tilted my face up to feel its heat. We were both silent; the only sound between us was the crunching of our boots on the gravel path.

We walked together up to Elsa's stall and Adrian called her name in a soft, infinitely gentle voice. "How are you, girl?" he said. "Come over here and say hello."

She knew him. She lifted her head and pricked her ears

and then she slowly turned around and came toward him, her muzzle outstretched, her eyes soft. She nickered, then rubbed her nose against his shoulder. He reached up to caress the white star on her forehead.

I think that was the moment when I fell in love with him.

"She looks wonderful," he said to me a few minutes later. He had slipped her leather halter over her ears, buckled it, and led her out of her box. The sun reflected off her gleaming, dark bay winter coat. Adrian looked at me. "Ride her for me," he said.

"I'll get your saddle, my lady," Willie volunteered before I could reply, and he jogged away toward the tack room, leaving Adrian and me standing side by side in the stable yard with the mare between us.

I smoothed my hand along the glossy crest of her neck. "How old was she when you bought her?" I asked.

"She was four and I was fourteen," Adrian said. "She had run a few times at Newmarket, without much success, so I got her at a fairly cheap price. Half a quarter's allowance, if I remember correctly."

"She has such perfect conformation," I said. "Did you never try to breed her?"

"I did, of course. Both of her foals were born dead. I didn't want to put her through that anymore, so I gave up trying."

"You didn't think of taking her to the Peninsula with you?"

"Not this little girl," he said. Amusement and affection mingled in his deep voice. "She isn't really a horse, you know. She's a princess in horse clothes."

I laughed delightedly. It was a perfect description.

Willie arrived with my saddle and fitted it on Elsa's back. Her ears went back when she felt the weight, then pricked forward again when I clucked to her.

Adrian said, "I wouldn't subject her to the rigors of the cavalry, nor would I sell her to some neck-or-nothing fox hunter. That's why I sent her here to Lambourn. She was too young to be retired, of course, but there didn't seem to be anything else for me to do."

Willie had been tightening the girth while we talked, and now he said, "She's ready, my lady."

Adrian looked toward the mounting block, but even though Elsa was almost sixteen hands high, I rarely used it. I put my left foot in the stirrup, swung up, and lowered myself gently into the saddle. I started toward the paddock and Adrian followed, talking easily to Willie.

I started our session off as I always did, with a long, swinging walk to loosen up Elsa's muscles. We then moved into a straight, forward trot, with plenty of impulsion. Next we did circles and changes of lead, and after fifteen minutes of this, I began to collect her frame.

A horse that is ridden in the classical manner will be elastic, forward, and balanced. It will go with its hind legs stepping up well underneath, its supple back acting as a bridge between those active hind legs and the bit. Elsa had responded beautifully to this work. Her muscles had developed, her expression was alert and attentive, and she looked and moved like a horse half her age.

I rode for half an hour, which was enough for this kind of intensive work. Adrian opened the paddock door for us to come out and stood at Elsa's head while I dismounted. I praised her, as I always did, and gave her some sugar. Then Willie led her back to her box and some well-deserved hay.

For the first time Adrian spoke. "I always wanted to ride her that way, but I didn't know how."

"My father taught me," I said. "He studied at Saumur before the revolution."

We left the stable yard together and began to walk back up the path toward the house. My head did not come above his shoulder, and I could see how he shortened his stride to accommodate mine. "I only had books," he said. "La

Guerniere's *Ècole de Cavalerie* was my bible, but I had no one to show me."

"You did very well on your own." Small white clouds were scudding across the brilliant blue sky and the smell of wood smoke floated toward us from the direction of the house. "Frankly, I was surprised when I first got on Elsa to find that she had been so well ridden. The English are usually so heavy."

He did not reply. He had been a cavalry officer, I remembered, and I was suddenly afraid that I had offended him. "I just meant that the English do not ride the classical seat," I added hastily.

"When the Duke of Wellington was a young man, he attended the manège at Angers," Adrian said. "He has always thought the English cavalry was composed of terrible riders."

Papa had thought the same thing, but I thought it was best not to labor the point. "The duke could not have been talking about you," I said.

He looked faintly amused at my defense of his riding ability. "I have improved," was all he said.

We were passing in front of the old dairy, and there was ice on the walk where the outhouse's shadow had blocked the sun. I kept my eyes on the ice to make certain I wouldn't slip and heard him say, "When I was in Lisbon I had a chance to ride at the Royal Manège. It was a revelation."

I looked up and met his eyes. He grinned. It was the first time I had ever seen that particular smile, and my heart gave the strangest flutter. "I brought a Lusitano stallion home with me," he said.

My mouth dropped open. The Lusitano is the national horse of Portugal and, like the Lipizzaners of the Spanish Riding School in Vienna, for centuries it had been bred for dressage. "Here in England?" I squeaked. The Portuguese were notoriously strict about not allowing their horses out of the country.

"At Greystone," he said. "You must come over one day and ride him."

CHAPTER
seven

"**W**AS YOUR BROTHER ANGRY THAT YOU WERE SENT down?" I asked Harry. I had not seen or heard from my husband since his initial visit of five days ago. This was also the first I had seen of Harry.

We were sitting in the library, as usual, and Harry was ravenously devouring one of Mrs. Noakes's buttered muffins. He swallowed and said glumly, "He wasn't angry, Kate, he was disappointed. Anger would have been easier on my conscience."

I understood perfectly.

Harry was going on, "He expects me to go back next term, of course. I am to study with the Rector, so I don't fall behind."

"Do you think you will still have the time to look for Paddy?" I asked anxiously.

"Looking for Paddy is my first priority, Kate," he assured me, and took another bite of muffin.

This was a great relief. I had been worrying about how Adrian's return was going to affect my investigations.

"Seen yesterday's *Morning Post*?" Harry asked around the piece of muffin that was in his mouth.

"No." I was not eating muffins. My appetite had fallen off again these last five days. "I get the papers a few days late."

"Adrian gets 'em bang up on time," Harry said. He swallowed the last of the muffin and lifted one eyebrow in the identical gesture I had obsrved his brother make. It was not a gesture I had seen from Harry before. "There was an interesting bit in the gossip column."

I tapped my toe impatiently on the carpet. "Are you going to tell me or are you going to continue to sit there and smirk?"

"I ain't smirking," he said indignantly.

"Yes, you are."

"No, I'm not."

I closed my eyes and began to count silently to ten. As I reached eight I heard the crinkle of paper. I opened my eyes and found Harry standing beside my chair, holding out a newspaper clipping. I took it from him and saw immediately that it was from the *Morning Post*. I bent my head to read.

The "interesting bit" Harry had referred to was the first entry in the "On Dits" column. It read: *Where is the wife of a certain earl who has recently Returned from Abroad? Are the rumors about a divorce True After All? And if they are, what is going to happen to his Political Career?*

"Oh dear." I looked up from the paper in my hand. "Is your brother frightfully angry?"

"Furious," Harry replied. He returned to his chair and sprawled comfortably, his feet stretched toward the fire. "Adrian don't like having his hand forced, and Charlwood has done it twice now."

"Do you think this," I held up the news clipping, "is Charlwood's doing?"

"Has to be, don't you think?"

"Probably," I replied in a gloomy voice.

"I told Adrian the only one way to fix the bastard was to put a good face on the marriage," Harry informed me with great satisfaction. "And I think he has finally come to agree."

"What do you mean by *put a good face on the marriage*?" I asked warily.

"Make it work, don't you know. After all, Kate, there's no reason why you and Adrian can't agree. You're both

young. You're both good-looking. You're both horse mad."
He gave me an angelic smile. "Why shouldn't it work?"

This truly monumental expression of insensitivity left
me speechless. He must have read my expression, however,
for he waved his hand and said, "Now don't get on your high
horse, Kate. It was you I was thinking of more than Adrian.
You need a home."

I opened my mouth to reply, but he shook his head and
overrode my voice with his. "It's no good your thinking you
can live with this groom, for you can't. You're a lady, and
ladies don't live with grooms. It will be far better for you to
live with Adrian."

I waited to be sure that he had finished, then I said, "It
may be better for me, but what about Adrian? I have no intention of holding him to a marriage he was coerced into making!"

"Best thing that could have happened to him," Harry de-
clared stoutly. "You'll suit him much better than that too-good
Lady Mary."

I strongly doubted this, but it was nice of Harry to say it.
I looked down and reread the words of the gossip column. "Is
it true that a divorce would hurt your brother's political career?" I asked Harry.

"Yes," he said.

"But men have mistresses all the time," I protested.
"Why, even the Duke of Wellington has mistresses! It certainly hasn't hurt *his* political career."

"He ain't getting a divorce, Kate. Mistresses are one
thing; divorce is quite another."

I said hotly, "Well, if that isn't hypocritical, I don't know
what is!"

"It's hypocritical, all right," Harry agreed amiably, "but
it's the way of the world, Kate. You owe it to Adrian to stay
married to him."

I scowled, leaned back in my chair, and stared into the
fire. After a few moments' silence Harry said bracingly,

"Think of this, Kate. It will be much easier for us to investigate your father's murder if we can stay in close communication. If you stay married to Adrian, you will be near at hand to me. Insist on a divorce, and God knows where you will end up living."

I pulled at my lip. "I suppose that is so," I said listlessly.

"Adrian will probably be coming to see you tomorrow," Harry went on, "but I thought I would prepare you for what he's going to say."

"That was thoughtful of you, Harry," I said.

"Now, don't fall into a fit of the dismals," he adjured me. "Adrian is a splendid fellow, Kate. There's nothing to fear. You couldn't find yourself in better hands."

I scarcely slept all night. My mind kept chasing around and around, like a dog after its own tail. The obsessive circle of my thoughts went something like this:

I think Adrian is wonderful and I want to stay married to him.

If we do stay married, and he hates me, I'll be miserable.

I don't want to be married to him if he doesn't want to be married to me.

He already loves someone else. The perfect Lady Mary.

I don't know how to be a countess. I'll embarrass him.

Perhaps I could make him love me.

I think Adrian is wonderful and I want to stay married to him.

Not a very fruitful exercise, as you can see. When finally I arose from my bed in the morning there were dark circles under my eyes. You can imagine Mr. and Mrs. Noakes's comments about that.

The sky was hung with low gray clouds and the air smelled of snow. *No Adrian today*, I thought. I was tucked up in the library, once more trying to concentrate on *The Wealth of Nations,* when his lordship walked in.

There was a sprinkling of snow on the shoulders of his

great coat and melted drops glistened like diamonds on his smoothly brushed hair. I looked at him over the top of my book and didn't say a thing.

Mr. Noakes took his coat and asked if he would have some tea, or perhaps a rum punch.

"Nothing at the moment, Noakes," Adrian replied. "Her ladyship and I want to be private. We are going to have a talk."

"Yes, my lord." The old man's voice was perfectly deferential. He never sounded like that when he talked to me.

The door closed behind Mr. Noakes. Adrian walked over to the fire and held out his hands. "It's starting to snow," he said.

"Yes."

He sighed, then turned to face me. "Kate, I'm afraid that you and I are going to have to hold to this marriage."

The ends of his damp hair had begun to feather in the heat of the fire. I put the bookmark in my book and closed it carefully on my lap. "Why?" I said.

He raised his eyebrow. "I thought Harry hotfooted it over here yesterday with a copy of the *Morning Post*."

"Yes. He did."

The eyebrow rose a little higher. "Then I should think the answer to your questin is obvious. It is in both our interests to hold to our marriage. To be blunt, my dear, you have nowhere else to go, and I do not wish to be made to appear the fool in front of all my friends."

I wanted very much to look at him, then to keep on and on and on looking at him. Afraid that he would read my longing in my eyes, I dropped them. I said stiffly, "My welfare is not your concern, my lord. I can assure you that I am perfectly capable of taking care of myself."

"That was not the impression I received at that inn in Luster," he retorted.

My eyes jerked up in surprise. I sat bolt upright, so that

my back was not touching the back of the chair, and demanded, "What do you mean by that remark?"

His gray eyes were steady on my face. "I mean that you
were obviously terrified of Charlwood. That's why I agreed to
the marriage, Kate. Only a monster would have put you back
into his power."

I was utterly mortified. "I thought you thought I was part
of his scheme," I said in a strangled kind of voice.

"If you were," he replied, "it was because you were
afraid of him." Pause. "What did he do to you, Kate?"

I pressed my hands to my burning cheeks. "He did nothing to me! I was not afraid of him! You did not need to marry
me for *that*. I am perfectly capable of taking care of myself.'

"So capable that when I mentioned that you might go
back to your uncle, you told me you'd rather be a housekeeper," he said.

"I don't like him." I gritted my teeth. "I am not afraid of
him."

This time both blond eyebrows went up, signifying dis-
belief.

I was so upset I jumped to my feet. The book on my lap
fell to the floor. I bent to pick it up, and when I had straightened he was holding out his hand. "What are you reading?"
he asked.

I looked at that muscular, long-fingered, imperative
hand, and slowly relinquished my book.

"Adam Smith," he said with surprise. He looked at me.
"Do you understand this?"

"No," I replied between my teeth. "I just sit there with
my eyes running over the words."

He looked faintly amused. "I'm sorry. I didn't mean to
insult you, Kate. It is just that . . . well, there are not many
young ladies who are interested in economics."

"There weren't any novels in the library," I said.

His look of amusement deepened. "I said I was sorry."

I said evenly, "I do not like to be patronized."

The amusement faded from his face, to be replaced by a thoughtful look. "I will remember that."

I decided that the time had come for me to be frank. I said, "Before we go any further with this discussion, my lord, there are a few things that you must know."

He leaned his shoulders against the dark wood mantelpiece and folded his arms. He inclined his head to me and said, "Go on."

I was still afraid to look at him, so I stared instead at the rug. There were numerous scorch marks on its faded rose-and-blue surface, made when flying sparks from the fire had landed on the rich old wool.

I began: "I must tell you that I have no notion of how to be a countess. That is why my uncle forced you to marry me. He knew that an . . ." I swallowed and forced myself to say the words, ". . . an Irish gambler's brat . . ." I shut my eyes and said silently *I'm sorry, Papa,* before going on, "could only harm your political career." I glanced up quickly to see how he was responding to this, but his grave face was unreadable.

I went back to staring at the rug: "I know nothing of how the wife of such a man as yourself should behave," I said. "I know nothing of how a home such as Greystone should be run. The longest I have ever lived in any one place is the nine months that I have lived at Lambourn; otherwise my home has been nothing but a succession of lodging houses." I looked up, forcing myself to meet his eyes. "I am not suitable to be your wife, my lord. I think you would do better to divorce me."

This speech had been very hard for me to make. I felt as if I was betraying my father. But I had lain awake all night thinking, and I knew the words needed to be said.

His silence frayed on my nerves, and I added, "You are right when you say that I do not like my uncle, but you are wrong when you say I have nowhere to go. Find Paddy O'Grady for me, and I will have a home with him."

When Adrian spoke at last his voice was mild. "I am very sorry I never knew your father, Kate. Not only did he give you a wonderful seat on a horse, but he taught you to be honest. He must have been a fine man."

His face blurred before my eyes. I clenched my fists, willing myself to control. "He was," I said fiercely.

"Everything you have just told me may be true, Kate," Adrian went on, still in the same mild voice as before, "but you are forgetting one thing."

"What is that?" I was afraid to blink lest the tears spill down my cheeks. I stared at him grimly.

"What you don't know, you can learn."

I blinked. The tears, thank God, went away.

"You told me you had learned how to be a housekeeper," he said. "Were you lying to me when you said that?"

"Of course not! I know I could be a housekeeper."

"Being a countess is much easier than being a house-keeper," he said.

I looked at him uncertainly. He pushed his shoulders away from the mantelpiece and held out his hand. "Come here," he said softly.

My heart began to race like a mad thing inside my chest. I took one little step toward him, then stopped. He said nothing, just waited. I took another step, and then another, until finally I was close enough to place my hand in his. His fingers, hard with those surprising calluses, closed around mine. He drew me the rest of the way toward him, closer and closer, until my breasts were almost brushing against him. He smelled like sunshine. I drew in a shaky breath.

"Look at me," he said.

I looked up, and his mouth came down on mine.

There was no temper in his kiss this time. His lips were firm and gentle, not hard and angry, and the effect on me was devastating. My head bent back under that intoxicating pressure, my body lifted upward against his. The seconds passed in increasingly dizzy succession. I felt the heat of the fire on my legs and dimly I was aware of his hands at my waist, the long fingers spread across my lower back to press me to him. I kissed him back with all my heart, and it was heaven.

When he lifted his head and dropped his hands, I was desolate. Then, as reason flooded back, as I remembered that I was in the Lambourn library, with the fire going and the Noakeses waiting in the kitchen, that the man I had been kissing with such abandon had married me against his will, I felt very very frightened.

I backed away from him. I lifted my hand to cover my mouth, as if to shield it from his eyes. I wasn't at all surprised to find that my hand was shaking. I was afraid to look at him, afraid that I would see contempt on his face, afraid that he would think I was truly the trollop he once had called me.

"Kate," he said. "There is nothing to be frightened of."

His voice sounded huskier than usual, but it had held no trace of scorn. Cautiously I raised my eyes.

A lock of hair was falling over his forehead. His eyes, partially screened by half-lowered lashes, looked very bright. He said, "Sweetheart, don't look like that. I won't do it again, I promise."

Part of me was longing for him to take me back into his arms, but another part of me was relieved. I liked to feel in control of myself, and I knew I betrayed myself the moment he touched me.

He said, "Sit down, Kate. We need to talk."

I nodded. I backed up toward my chair and when I felt the frame touch my legs, I sat. He moved to the opposite chair and sat down himself. The chair looked much smaller with Adrian in it than it did with Harry. He thrust impatient fingers through his hair and the errant lock was pushed back into place. He said, "In two days' time you will move to Greystone Abbey. We will stay there long enough for you to learn the things you will need to know as my countess—it shouldn't take long—and then we will go to London for the start of the Season. That should effectively silence all the gossip."

I said, "I thought we were going to talk. It seems to me that all you have done is issue orders."

His eyes narrowed. "Is there something in what I have said with which you disagree?" His voice was polite. Too polite.

"I like to be asked," I said. "I don't like to be ordered."

I was proud of myself. My voice had sounded calm and cool. There was no way he could know that I was terrified. But I had to get this straight between us from the start. I was not going to jump to his bidding every time he snapped his fingers. I had too much pride for that.

Silence stretched between us. I was not going to be the one to break it. Finally he said, "Will it be convenient for you to come to Greystone on the day after tomorrow?" This time his voice was perfectly courteous; his expression was courteous as well.

"No wonder you were so successful in Paris, my lord," I said with genuine admiration. "No one could ever tell from your face that you are probably itching to murder me."

At that he laughed. "I am certainly itching to do something to you," he said, "but it's not murder."

I responded to that comment indirectly. "Is this going to be a real marriage?" I asked.

"That is what I thought I said."

I went back to staring at the carpet. I felt horribly embarrassed and shy asking this question, but I needed to know the answer. "I mean, will we really be husband and wife?" When he did not speak, I clarified even more. "Will we . . . sleep together?"

He said, "Yes."

I said, "Oh."

He said, "Does the thought distress you?"

I said, "I don't know."

He said, "Once we take up residence in the same house, Kate, we will be married in the eyes of the world. If you have serious objections to sleeping with me, then you had better voice them now."

I said, "Are you quite certain that you do not need a housekeeper?"

"Quite certain." He sounded amused. He knew from the kiss, of course, that I would have no objections to sleeping with him. It was probably why he had kissed me in the first place.

I lifted my eyes from the carpet and said with all the dignity I could muster, "Then I will marry you, my lord."

"Thank you." He shook his head as if he were bemused, and got to his feet. "I had better get back to Greystone before this flurry turns into a storm." Without further ado, he strode to the door and shouted for Mr. Noakes.

I trotted after him. "Won't you have something to eat first, my lord?"

Mr. Noakes was bringing his driving coat. "No time, Kate," Adrian said as he thrust his arms into the sleeves and buttoned up the front. He told Mr. Noakes, "I'll go along to the stable myself, Noakes. No need to send anyone."

"Very good, my lord," said Mr. Noakes.

Adrian went to the door and I trailed after him. It had begun to snow in earnest. I opened my mouth to ask him to stay, then closed it again.

"I'll send the coach for you on Thursday," Adrian said to me.

"I don't like coaches," I said.

"The coach is for your baggage. You can ride over on Elsa."

My insides lit up. "I can bring Elsa to Greystone?"

"Certainly."

"It's too cold for you to ride such a long distance, my lady," Mr. Noakes said disapprovingly.

Both Adrian and I ignored him.

"Until Thursday," he said.

"Until Thursday." And I smiled.

CHAPTER
eight

$\mathbf{I}$T WAS HARRY, NOT ADRIAN, WHO CAME TO ESCORT ME to Greystone on Thursday morning. He came into the library for a hot cup of tea while the horses were watered and my meager baggage was put into the coach. When finally the horses were once more ready to go, we all went out to the front of the house. I kissed Mrs. Noakes goodbye, and she cried. Mr. Noakes looked rather misty-eyed as well. I kissed him too.

It was impossible for me to tell them all that they had meant to me. They had given me kindness and stability at a time in my life when I badly needed both. I said merely, "I love you both, and I will be back to visit."

Mr. Noakes blew his nose loudly. Mrs. Noakes said, "God bless you, child."

I nodded, afraid that if I spoke I would start to cry as well. I turned, swung up onto Elsa's back, and trotted away down the drive. Harry followed me on his horse, and the coach came after us both. I looked back once, before we were out of sight, and they were still standing there in the cold. I waved.

Normally I would have enjoyed the fifteen-mile ride to Greystone Abbey, but today I was too apprehensive to pay much attention to the wintry landscape. Harry chatted away, and I suppose I must have answered him, but to this day I have not the faintest recollection what our conversation was about.

Greystone Abbey was located a few miles outside of Newbury. I had been in the town before, but I had never had any occasion to view the home of the Earls of Greystone. I had seen enough great houses in my lifetime, however, to pretty well know what to expect.

We turned in at the gates onto a wide avenue lined with truly magnificent chestnut trees. Except for the chestnut trees it was an avenue not unlike many others that I had seen. Nor, when it came into view, was there anything about the large rambling stone house that looked remarkably different from the other country houses that belonged to the wealthy nobles to whom Papa had tried to sell a horse.

What was different about this house, and what caught my immediate attention, was the huge array of people crowded onto the front stairs.

"Good Lord," Harry said. "Adrian's doing you proud, Kate. He's got all the servants lined up to greet you."

There had to be at least fifty people on the steps. "All those people work here?" I asked Harry faintly.

He shrugged. "They must."

We had entered the curve of the drive now, and I saw someone slip into the house. By the time we had pulled up in front of the great stairs, the earl himself was coming out the front door. The servants parted to let him through, and he came down the stairs to greet us.

"Good show, Adrian," Harry said approvingly as he dismounted.

I swung my left leg over Elsa's back, balanced on my hands while I disengaged my right foot from the stirrup, then slid to the ground. It was a long way down, but I was used to it. Both Adrian and Harry had enough sense not to try to assist me.

"Walters insisted," Adrian said. He turned to me. "Walters is our butler. You had better come and meet him, Kate."

I walked beside him to the bottom of the stairs. I felt very small, with Adrian looming next to me and the horde of servants towering in front of me.

Adrian said, "I should like you all to meet my wife, the new Countess of Greystone." He didn't seem to raise his voice, but it had to be easily audible even to those who were farthest away.

An exceedingly dignified-looking man stepped forward and spoke in measured tones. "On behalf of the staff, welcome to Greystone Abbey, my lady." I gave him credit. His eyes did not once flicker toward my riding skirt.

"Thank you, Walters," I said. The poor man's nose was red. "I suggest that we all go inside out of this cold and you can introduce me to everyone."

He looked startled. "Everyone, my lady?"

"Certainly."

I heard a chuckle from the air above the right side of my head. "You heard her ladyship," Adrian said. He looked at the crowded stairs in front of us and said, "The staff had better go first."

The servants milled around for a while, but finally everyone managd to get indoors. Adrian, Harry, and I followed. I cast a quick glance around the entrance hall of my new home, and was startled to discover that I had been transported to what looked like a medieval monastery.

"Is this where you *live*?" I asked Adrian. My eyes had to be half the size of my face.

"The living quarters are on the second floor," he said. "I'll explain about this," he gestured comprehensively to the vaulted stone ceilings and arched stone doors, "later."

He did tell me about the house later, but this is probably the best place for me to explain why it was that the Earls of Greystone lived in such extraordinary surroundings.

During the Middle Ages, Greystone Abbey had actually been a convent (complete with one hundred nuns, Adrian said). When Henry VIII broke with the Catholic Church, he had confiscated all Church property in England and had either sold it or used it to reward people who had done something useful for him. That is how Greystone came into the hands of Adrian's family. Henry gave it to the first Baron Woodrow in 1539 in payment for services rendered to the crown. (Adrian said that the services rendered were of highly dubious nature, but he would never tell me what they were.)

Anyway, the first baron pulled down the church and moved in upstairs in the main convent building, leaving everything downstairs almost untouched. Later generations of Woodrows had altered and added upstairs, but they also did very little down below. The result was that the first floor of Greystone Abbey was one of the best-preserved medieval sites in all of England.

The vaulted room into which I had first stepped dated from the fourteenth century. There was also a glorious cloister, which was roofed by an exquisite fifteenth-century fan vault. The chapter room, the refectory, the little room that belonged to the nuns' chaplain, the parlor where they talked to visitors from outside, the warming room, all of these were still as they were when the convent had been dissolved by Henry.

All of this I was to learn later. At the present moment, however, my remarkable surroundings were not as important as the people who inhabited them. I turned to Walters, who was a tall, heavyset man with a splendid beak of a nose, and gave him a friendly smile.

"Go ahead, Walters," Adrian said in an amused voice. "Introduce her ladyship to the staff."

We started with the housekeeper, Mrs. Pippen. She had startlingly black hair and was quite stout. Adrian's servants looked as if they ate well. "How do you do, Mrs. Pippen," I said. "I will come to visit you once I have settled in, and we can get acquainted."

She bowed her head sedately. "Yes, my lady."

We then moved to the under-butler and the under-house-keeper and from thence to the chambermaids, the housemaids, the scullery maids, the footmen, and the ushers. I smiled and said something pleasant to everyone, but there were so many of them that I knew I would never remember their names.

"But where is Remy?" Adrian asked his butler. "Did he not wish to greet her ladyship with the rest of you?"

Walters's face turned an alarming shade of puce. "That Frenchie thinks himself above the rest of us, my lord." Walters's voice had dripped with contempt when he pronounced the word *Frenchie*.

"The war is over, Walters," Adrian said briefly.

"Yes, my lord," Walters said. His mouth closed into a straight, disapproving line. "M. Remy chose not to join the rest of the staff, my lord. He said that he was an *artiste*, not a servant."

I looked at my husband. "Is he your cook?" I guessed.

"He is. I brought him with me from Paris, and he is most assuredly an *artiste*."

I turned back to the servants and raised my voice so that everyone could hear me. "I think it was lovely of you to give me such a warm welcome. Thank you."

The sea of faces stared back. I smiled. A few faces smiled tentatively in return.

"Let's go upstairs, Kate," Harry said. "We'll show you the real part of the house."

"Have her ladyship's baggage brought up to her room, Walters," Adrian said.

"Yes, my lord."

"This way, Kate," Harry said, and he led the way to the stone staircase that led to the second floor.

The only aristocratic home I had actually been inside of was Charlwood Court, but I was certain that few houses in England could boast the imposing splendor that greeted me on the second floor of Greystone Abbey.

"My grandfather commissioned Robert Adam to redo the place," Adrian said as he conducted me from the hall to the antechamber to the dining room to the drawing room to the gallery. Harry told me that the Roman-style marble columns in the anteroom had actually been found in the bed of the Tiber and brought to Greystone in 1770. There were also a vast number of noble Roman statues scattered around the rooms, and many imposing Carerra marble mantelpieces. The house was certainly magnificent, but it was not the sort of place where one felt one could put up one's feet and relax. I said as much to Adrian.

"It has never been much of a home," he replied curtly.

I remembered Harry's stories of their childhood, and did not pursue the subject.

The third floor of the house contained the bedrooms, and I was relieved to see that Adam had not been allowed to leave his magnificent mark on these. "My grandfather thought he had spent enough money on the second floor," Adrian said. "Fortunately."

I agreed. My bedroom furniture was upholstered with mauve and blue silk, not with chintz as at Lambourn, but the room, while elegant, was also pretty and welcoming. There were two other doors in the room besides the door to the corridor, both of which Adrian opened for me. One of them led to the earl's bedroom. I glanced in hastily, got a quick impression of a depressing expanse of dark green, then retreated back into my own room. The other door led into a small dressing room, done in the same pretty fabric and colors as the countess's bedroom. "This is lovely," I exclaimed.

"My mother had this room done," Adrian said.

I had noticed once before how his voice softened when he spoke of his mother. "Is your mother dead, my lord?" I asked gently.

"Yes. She died when I was seven. In childbirth." The clipped tones of his voice did not encourage further questions. I had lost my own mother when I was ten, so I understood.

As we were talking, the door opened and two splendidly liveried footmen came in carrying my portmanteaux. They deposited them on the lovely cream-and-blue carpet and backed out.

Adrian looked at my two battered leather cases. "Is that all your baggage?"

"I have always prided myself on traveling lightly," I said.

"Good God, Kate, I carried more baggage than that when I was in the army and on the march."

"I am quite certain that you did not carry your own baggage, my lord," I said austerely. "When I traveled it was just Papa and I and Paddy, and we all traveled lightly."

His silver-blond eyebrows drew together. "I thought I gave you an allowance so that you could buy some clothes. Crawford wrote me the most heartrending letter about your threadbare wardrobe."

I was incensed. "There was nothing wrong with my wardrobe! And I did buy some clothes. But only because Mr. Crawford told me that your tenants would think ill of you if I wasn't dressed properly."

"Crawford was right, but it doesn't look to me as if you took his advice too seriously. Good God, Kate." And he stared again at my two poor portmantaux.

"I am an exceedingly good packer," I said defiantly. "You would be surprised by how much is in those bags."

"I doubt it." His eyes swung back to me. "You were in London last year. What happened to all the clothes you had then?"

We had been standing on opposite sides of a charming powder-blue chaise longue, but now I swung away and went to look out the tall, satin-draped window. The view was of the garden; in the spring and summer it would be a lovely scene, but at the moment it looked barren and rather bleak. "I left them in London," I said. "My uncle bought them, and I didn't think you would want them under your roof."

Silence. When I felt two hands grasp my shoulders, I jumped in surprise. How could so big a man move so quietly?

He turned me so that I was facing him once more. "You were right," he said quietly.

For a moment, envisioning the endless round of dress shops that Louisa had subjected me to the previous spring, I almost wished that I had kept the damned clothes. I was also intensely and uncomfortably aware of the feel of his hands on my shoulders.

Adrian took away his hands and said, "We'll have to get a dressmaker down from London. You can't even go to local assemblies if you aren't dressed properly."

This news cheered me up immensely. "That would be wonderful, my lord," I said thankfully. "You cannot imagine how exhausting it was last year, being dragged through every shop on Bond Street. I must have tried on *hundreds* of dresses."

"I thought women loved new clothes."

"Oh, I like having new clothes," I said. "It is the purchasing that is such a bore. A dressmaker sounds just the thing. She can take my measurements once, then sew me up whatever she thinks it is that I will need."

That amused look was back on his face. I didn't mind it that he found me entertaining. What I did mind was that I didn't know what I had said that was so funny. I gave him a dark look. He didn't seem to notice.

"You will also need a lady's maid," he said. "Shall I have Walters find you someone?"

I opened my mouth to say yes, but then the picture of a young, bruised, tearstained face suddenly presented itself to my mind. I said instead, "There is someone in particular I would like for my maid, my lord. Would it be possible for someone to go to Charlwood to fetch her for me?" Charlwood was only ten miles from Newbury, so I did not think I was asking too much.

"Certainly," he said.

"Her name is Rose," I said. "She is one of the under-housemaids."

He frowned. "I said you needed a lady's maid, Kate, not a housemaid."

"Oh, she was Cousin Louisa's lady's maid while we were at Charlwood," I lied glibly.

His gray eyes searched my face with a shrewdness I did not like. I looked guilelessly back.

"Very well," he said at last. "I will have one of the grooms drive over to fetch this Rose."

I thought about this for a moment. "Do you know, my lord," I said slowly, "I think it would be wise to ascertain whether my uncle is in residence before we send someone there to collect Rose."

"You don't think he would relinquish her?"

"He hates you," I said. "I don't think he would give you a piece of string if he thought you wanted it."

He didn't answer, just looked at me. He knew there was something I was not telling him, of course. I thought it would be good strategy to distract him from the question of Rose. "I would also like to send for Cousin Louisa."

"Married women don't need chaperones," he said.

"The thing is, Adrian," I was so intent upon persuading him that I didn't even notice that I had used his name, "she is in a wretched situation. She is unmarried, you see, and she has no money, so she is forced to live with her brother, who takes advantage of her. Why, she is nothing but an unpaid housekeeper and nursery maid for his wife! And Louisa is good company, even if she is a little bit of a wet blanket."

"Tell me," he said. "How is she a wet blanket?"

"Well, if you must know, I had some lovely schemes for earning my own living and becoming independent, and she squashed them all. You won't believe it, but she found something wrong with every single one of them."

He was looking at me with utter fascination. It was lovely.

"How poor-spirited of her," he said. "Er . . . if I may ask . . . what were these schemes?"

I told him the best one. "I was going to dress as a boy and get a position in a stable. You know how well I ride, my lord. Anyone would have hired me."

His face was perfectly grave. "*I* should certainly have hired you."

"See?" I said triumphantly.

"Dare I ask what Cousin Louisa said that caused you to abandon this enormously clever plan?"

"She said that I would certainly have to share a room with other men. If that was the case, of course, it would be difficult to maintain my disguise."

His lips twitched. "True."

I looked at him suspiciously. "Are you laughing at me?"

"I must admit that I agree with Cousin Louisa's assessment of your scheme, but I am not laughing at you, Kate. In fact, I admire your courage." He gave me one of those heart-shattering smiles of his, and all my suspicion withered away. It really wasn't fair for a man to have a smile like that.

I pulled myself together and went back to my original point. "May I send for Louisa, my lord? She would be no trouble, and she can help to show me how I should go on in society."

"Send for her by all means," he said. "God knows, there is enough room in this house for half of Wellington's army."

"Lambourn is much cozier," I agreed.

He sighed. "I have been an absentee landlord for too long, Kate. There's nothing for it but to stay here for the next few months so that I can get on terms with the local gentry and the tenants."

"We need some dogs," I said.

Silence. "Dogs?" he repeated.

"Certainly. A few dogs would make the house seem much homier. Haven't you ever had a dog, my lord?"

The muscles in his face tightened. "I would not have brought a dog into the same house as my father." His eyes were bleak. "He did not admire animals."

I hated to see him look like that, but I knew I couldn't show him that I had noticed anything. I said briskly, "I have never had a dog either. We traveled too much. But I've always wanted one."

"Then you shall have one." His face relaxed and he smiled again. Everything inside me softened. It really *wasn't* fair. He looked once more at my portmanteaux. "I'll have Mrs. Pippen send one of the chambermaids to unpack for you," he said. "Dinner will be in two hours." And he was gone.

CHAPTER
nine

IN FASHIONABLE HOUSES IN LONDON, DINNER WAS served at eight or even nine o'clock, but in the country one still got one's dinner at six. I wore my only evening dress, a blue taffeta I had bought in Lambourn with my allowance, and arranged my hair into a bun on the crown of my head. Fashion called for an array of ringlets to fall artistically out of the topknot, but I was not skilled enough to create ringlets, so I just pulled it all smooth.

My hands were freezing as I waited in my sitting room to go down to dinner, and I walked over to the fire to warm them. I knew very well that my cold hands were not due to the temperature in the room, which was quite comfortable, but to the fact that I was terrified.

Will we sleep together?

Yes.

That simple conversation was going around and around in my head. I was here in his house. He had introduced me to his servants as his wife. He was going to make the best of an unpleasant situation. We were going to stay married.

Will it be tonight?

I shivered and looked at the elegant gold clock that was set upon the charming white painted mantelpiece. It was time to go down.

My husband and his brother were before me in the drawing room. They were both dressed in formal evening attire: single-breasted black tailcoats, white shirts and neckcloths, white waistcoats, buff-colored pantaloons, and white silk stockings. They made me feel shabby.

"I say, Kate," Harry said, "I've never seen you in an evening dress before. You look bang up to the mark!" His frankly admiring look made me feel better. I turned to my husband, hoping he would echo his brother's compliments.

Adrian said, "Let us go into dinner." He came to offer me his arm, and I laid my fingers rather tenatively on its immaculate black surface. With Harry trailing behind, we paraded across the magnificent marble floor and into the dining room.

It was an imposingly beautiful room, done in creams, pale greens, and golds. The only darker color in the room was the four deep-green alcoves that lay along the left wall, and the darker color effectively set off the striking white marble statues that filled them. The wall opposite to the alcoves contained four tall windows, which led out to the terrace. An immense crystal chandelier hung from a ceiling that was decorated with painted cream-and-gold medallions. The oblong mahogany table, laid with service for three, had twelve gilt chairs with pink upholstery pulled up to it. Extra chairs were lined up against the wall.

Adrian seated me at one end of the table and went to take the seat on the opposite end. Harry's place was exactly between us. The men sat, and we regarded each other over a huge expanse of highly polished dark wood. Footmen in royal blue-and-gold livery brought in the first course and placed it in front of us. It was some sort of soup I didn't recognize. The fine bone china was edged in cobalt blue and gold and had the Greystone crest imprinted in the design. I picked up my spoon and took a very small taste.

From the far end of the table Adrian remarked that the mulligatawny soup was excellent. Perhaps it was.

Harry said, "One thing about the Frogs, they know how to cook."

I took another delicate sip. It was a little spicier than the food I was accustomed to.

My footman—I say *mine* because he was stationed directly behind my chair—asked if I wanted wine. I usually had water or lemonade with my dinner, but tonight I said that I would take wine.

Adrian said, "That is claret, Kate. Have you ever had claret before?"

"Certainly," I replied with dignity, and took a small sip. It was actually quite nice. I liked it better than the soup. I took a second sip.

The soup was removed, and I devoutly hoped that Adrian's chef wouldn't come storming upstairs demanding to know why I hadn't finished mine. The second course was brought in—chicken in some kind of a sauce, served with at least eight side dishes. It was good, but I wasn't very hungry. I managed to get some of the chicken down, but I never touched the side dishes that littered the table. I started on a second glass of wine.

Adrian said to me, "Tomorrow I will introduce you to Euclide, my Lusitano stallion."

I opened my mouth to reply, then closed it. He was sitting on the other side of a sea of side dishes, at least fifteen feet away from my own seat. I heard my voice remark, "I think this is ridiculous."

Adrian raised his eyebrows. After a quick glance at his brother, Harry followed suit. From behind their chairs, their footmen also looked at me. I took another sip of my wine. "Do you dine like this every night?" I asked.

"How else should we dine?" Adrian inquired politely.

"Well, if we must sit in this damned palatial room, the least we can do is put all our chairs together at one end of the table. I'm getting a sore throat from trying to make myself heard."

Harry said, "How can you have a sore throat? You've been mum as a church mouse all evening, Kate."

"That is because I do not like to shout at my dinner companions," I replied with dignity.

"I think it's because you've been too busy gulping down the wine," Harry said.

I glared at him. "That is not true! And you are hardly one to talk about gulping wine, Harry. You practically inhale it!"

"Children, children," Adrian said soothingly.

Both Harry and I turned our glares on him. He was looking amused.

I said, "If you don't wipe that very superior expression from your face, my lord, I fear I will be forced to do something dangerous."

He looked interested. "And what would that be?"

I took another sip of my wine. "You will have to wait and find out."

"You'd better get that wine away from her, Adrian," Harry remarked.

I closed my hand around my glass. "Ladies drink wine. I was in London. I saw them do it."

"Ladies also eat their dinners," Adrian pointed out. "Wine on an empty stomach is not good for anyone."

"I always eat when I drink wine," Harry said righteously.

I thought about this. "Muffins," I said.

Adrian looked bewildered.

Harry said, "Exactly. Why do you think I ate all those muffins, Kate? It was to soak up the wine I was drinking."

I looked at my plate. There seemed to be quite a lot of chicken left. "But I'm not hungry."

"Try," Adrian said.

I picked up my fork and took a bite. A large hand reached out next to me and removed my wineglass. I yelped, turned to my footman, and demanded, "Put it back."

"Walters is getting you a nice glass of lemonade, Kate," Adrian said. "It will be much better for your sore throat than wine. Now take another bite of chicken."

"Traitor," I said to my footman. He was a fair-skinned

young man, and he blushed. I turned back to my chicken and took another bite.

"I still think this is ridiculous," I said.

Adrian surprised me by agreeing, "You are quite right, Kate. I will have them set the table differently tomorrow."

"All the chairs together?"

"All the chairs together."

"There isn't any sort of a family dining room?" I inquired. "I can see that this is a splendid room for entertaining, but it is rather . . . overwhelming . . . for intimate family gatherings."

"You are perfectly right," he said. "Perhaps I'll have a new wing built—one that will be just for the family."

I looked at him suspiciously, but he was not wearing that amused expression that so enraged me. He looked serious.

"That's a splendid idea, Adrian," Harry said. "I've always hated this house."

"It does not hold happy associations for any of us," Adrian agreed bleakly.

"I have finished my chicken," I announced.

Walters came into the room with a pitcher of lemonade for me. The footmen removed our plates and all the side dishes that I had not eaten and brought in the dessert. It was apricot tart, and I ate it all.

It was nearly eight when I arose from the table and left the gentlemen to their wine. Walking very carefully, I went back to the drawing room and stared at the fire in the magnificent green marble fireplace. There seemed to be two of them. A footman came into the room and inquired if he could get me anything. I asked him his name and where he came from. It was going to take me a long time to get to know all of the servants in this house, so I thought I might as well make a start.

His name was James and he had grown up in one of the cottages on the Greystone estate. We were chatting away about his little brothers and sisters when Adrian and Harry came into the room.

"That was quick," I said.

"We didn't want you to get lonesome by yourself," Harry returned, giving poor James an extremely arrogant look.

"I have been having a very enjoyable conversation with James," I told Harry. "I was not lonesome at all."

"Dash it all, Kate," Harry said indignantly, "this is not Lambourn, you know. You can't get all cozy with the servants here!"

"Thank you, James," Adrian said quietly. "That will be all."

James marched out, relief evident in every line of his back.

"You hurt his feelings," I accused Harry.

He shrugged. "Who cares?"

"*I* care," Adrian said, still in that same quiet voice.

I looked at him in surprise. He was watching Harry. "We have an obligation to those who depend on us for their livelihood, Harry," he said. "Great privilege also means great responsibility. I would like you to remember that."

Harry looked a little sulky. "I wasn't going to ask you to fire the bloody footman, Adrian."

"There is a lady present," Adrian said. "Watch your language."

I looked around for the lady.

Harry hooted. "He means you, Kate."

"Oh." I felt extremely stupid, and to disguise my discomfort I went to the fireplace and stared into the two flames.

Adrian said, "What would you like to do, Kate? Do you play cards?"

"I play whist," I said, "but you need four players for that." I blinked, trying to clear my vision so that there would be only one fire. "To tell you the truth, my lord, I don't think I could concentrate on cards just at the moment. I feel strangely light-headed."

"You're foxed, Kate," Harry said. "It was the second glass of wine."

"Do you think so? It's not at all an unpleasant feeling, Harry. Perhaps that's why gentlemen drink so much."

"Very likely," Adrian said. He came over to me, took my hand, and placed it firmly on his sleeve. "Come along, Kate," he said, "I am going to take you up to your room. A good night's sleep will cure your light-headedness."

I walked with him to the door. "Good night, Harry," I threw over my shoulder just before we went out.

His response floated after me into the great hallway, and for a moment I felt a cowardly urge to turn and run back into the shelter of Harry's presence. The man beside me was not a safe brother but a very unsafe husband. I heartened myself with the memory of his remark about my getting a good night's sleep, however, and when we reached the door of my room, I bade him good night in a reasonably steady voice.

To my relief he did not come in, saying only, "I'll send for someone to help you undress."

I wasn't too foxed to undress myself, but I wasn't at all averse to acquiring the reassuring presence of another female. "Thank you, my lord," I said.

In five minutes the maid who had helped me to dress appeared to help me undress. Her name was Nell, and we chatted away while she took the pins out of my hair. She was from Newbury, she told me, and her father was a blacksmith.

Finally I was in my nightgown and in my bed and Nell was gone. The fire was still blazing, and I contemplated my snug warmth with pleasure. In most lodging houses the bedroom fires were out by eight o'clock, and here it was almost ten and the fire was roaring away.

There was no sound from the room next door. I put my arms around my pillow and went to sleep.

"Kate."

Someone was calling my name, and I struggled to fight

my way out of the comfortable soft darkness of sleep and into the light.

"*Kate.*"

The voice came again. Not urgent, just steady, calm, and immensely authoritative. I opened my eyes and found myself looking at Adrian. I blinked, and he was still there.

"I was beginning to think you were never going to wake up," he said.

"You told me to have a good night's sleep," I said crossly. I yawned. "Why are you waking me up in the middle of the night?"

"It's not yet midnight, sweetheart. Hardly the middle of the night."

I struggled to sit up against the pillows. My head felt fuzzy. "What are you doing here?" Then I registered the fact that he was wearing a dressing gown. My lips parted in a soundless *O*.

He sat on the side of the bed and looked down at me gravely. "If we are going to make this a real marriage, then this is something we have to do, Kate."

My mouth made the same soundless *O* as before.

He smiled and reached out to smooth a strand of hair away from my face. I felt his fingers brush against my cheek. "It will help if you're still a little foxed," he said. His voice was soft and warm, the voice I had heard him use to Elsa. He had put a candle on the rosewood table beside my bed, and its light picked out the cleanly chiseled bones of his cheeks, nose, and jaw. A lock of pale gilt hair had slipped over his forehead, and it gleamed in the candlelight. This was the first time I had seen him without a cravat, and the bare column of his neck looked very strong.

It was a cold night, but the room was warm. I looked over his shoulder and saw that the fire was still blazing. He must have made it up. Even though I was wearing a warm flannel nightdress, I shivered. I brought my eyes back to his and said bravely, "I know how horses do this, my lord, but I'm not quite certain about people."

He laughed softly. "Don't worry, Kate, I'll show you." And he bent his head and kissed me.

It was more intoxicating than any wine could ever be. As he felt me respond he deepened the kiss. I felt my lips parting, felt his tongue asking to come inside my mouth. He leaned me back against the pillow and I opened my mouth to him, lifting my hand to the back of that strong neck, to caress his skin with my fingertips.

His kisses were making all my senses reel. I moved my hand higher and buried it in the thickness of his impossibly fair hair. It had the texture of heavy silk, and I let it slide through my fingers, buried my hand and let it slide through again.

His own hand moved, coming between us to cover my breast, and I was shocked by the spasm of pleasure that touch sent all through me. He moved his mouth from mine and began to kiss my throat. His hand moved caressingly on my breast, his thumb stroked my nipple. A pulse began to beat between my legs. Of its own volition, I felt my body lift toward his.

"Sweetheart," he said in a voice that sounded decidedly unsteady, "let's get this nightgown off."

"Off?" I repeated. I sounded as if I were in a daze.

He was pulling my gown up even as I spoke, and I raised my arms obediently and let him lift it off of me completely, baring me to his eyes. The most amazing thing about all of this is that I wasn't embarrassed. I wanted him to touch my naked flesh. I had never dreamed that a man's touch could feel this wonderful.

He stood for a moment to shed his own dressing gown, and I stared in wonderment at his body, at the broad chest and shoulders, the narrow waist and hips, the long, muscled legs. I saw that he was aroused, but it didn't frighten me. He was too beautiful to be frightening.

He came back to the bed and I reached up to touch lightly the crisp silvery hair on his chest. My touch made him shiver, and that pleased me. He said, "God in heaven, Kate, but you are beautiful."

I almost said "So are you," but before I could speak he was kissing me again.

He kissed me and kissed me, until I felt I was drowning in a sea of intoxicating sensations, sensations that rolled through my entire body, drawing me to him with the same ineluctable power with which the moon draws the advancing tide. The pulse between my legs beat more and more insistently. Then he touched me there, and the intense pleasure of that touch made me whimper, partly in wonder and partly in fear. I did not quite know what was happening to me.

"It's all right, sweetheart," he said. "Trust me, Kate. It will be all right."

I lay there, utterly open to him, my heart racing, my breathing quick and shallow. The whole lower part of my abdomen was filled with a relentlessly rising tension, a tension that was being fed by Adrian's stroking finger. I was completely concentrated on that feeling, reaching and reaching for something I desperately needed, when the explosion hit me. I gripped his shoulders and held on as a wave of intense pleasure flooded through my body, radiating out from that single epicenter. When he parted my legs and moved between them, I wanted him there. I arched my back and waited.

It was all right at first. He was filling my emptiness. Then he muttered, "Hold on, sweetheart," and drove.

The pain was a complete surprise. My breath sucked in and I must have made a sound, for he said breathlessly, "I know, Kate. I know. Just hold on and it will be all right in a minute."

The pain got worse, but I clamped my teeth together and was silent. I did not try to push him away. He had said that this was something we needed to do, and I accepted that. I endured.

At last it was over. He withdrew, but before I could feel used and abandoned, he had gathered me close in his arms. He was breathing as if he had been running, and I could feel his heart hammering against my shoulder. I was glad. He had done such a stupendous thing to me that I felt it was only fair that I should make an impact upon him. I pressed my cheek into his sweaty shoulder, shut my eyes tightly, and let him hold me.

"It will be better the next time, Kate," he said after a while. His voice sounded normal again.

"It won't hurt?" I whispered.

"No, sweetheart." He touched his lips to the top of my head. "It always hurts the first time. I'm sorry."

I felt so cherished there in his arms—so safe. I said sleepily, "Does it hurt men their first time?"

"No, it doesn't." I could hear the amusement in his voice, but I was too drowsy to protest.

"Not fair," I said.

"I suppose it isn't."

I thought about saying something else, but before I could manage it I went to sleep.

CHAPTER
ten

I WAS AWAKENED THE FOLLOWING MORNING BY A chambermaid coming into the bedroom with a tray of hot chocolate and muffins. The room was warm and I was all alone in the big bed. I had a vague recollection of Adrian waking me in the dark to put my nightgown back on, but I thought he had stayed with me. I sat up against the pillows and drank my chocolate while the maid added a new log to the fire. It had obviously been made up once already, and I asked her for the time.

"Nine o'clock, my lady."

I almost spilled my chocolate. "Nine o'clock! It can't be nine o'clock! I never sleep until nine o'clock!"

The maid did not reply to this singularly inane comment. Obviously, I had slept until nine o'clock this morning. No wonder Adrian had gone. I took a small bite of the muffin and chewed. It was delicious. While I ate my muffins and drank my chocolate, I discovered that the maid's name was Lucy, that she was the daughter of a Newbury apothecary, and that she had two older sisters, one married and one not.

Lucy went to the window to open the curtains and the sun came pouring into the room, making a pool of light on the rich cream-and-blue rug. I felt energy running like spring sap through my veins and longed to be outdoors in the crisp, clear air, but I knew I ought to begin my career as Countess of Greystone in a more fitting manner. Feeling extremely virtuous, I put on a morning dress and went downstairs to interview the housekeeper.

Mrs. Pippen had a sitting room all to herself, and it was far cozier than the rooms the family was forced to inhabit. She invited me to sit in a comfortable, cushioned chair before the fireplace and sent one of the maids to fetch tea. Then she settled her stout figure into the chair on the opposite side of the fire and regarded me politely.

I smiled at her. Her hair was black as ink and oddly lightless. I wondered if she dyed it. I began, "Have you been at Greystone a long time, Mrs. Pippen?"

She was reticent at first, answering questions but volunteering nothing. I talk so much, however, that eventually people have to start talking back, just to maintain their sanity. By the time we were on our second cup of tea, she was gossiping away. When I confided that I knew very little about the way a house this size functioned, and was depending on her to be my guide, she became positively voluble.

I spent an hour in the housekeeper's room, and by the time I left my outside was overheated from sitting too close to the fire and my inside was awash in tea, but I felt it had been time well spent. Mrs. Pippen had none of the motherly qualities of Mrs. Noakes, but she seemed to be a decent, competent sort of woman. We parted friends.

I passed through the green baize door that separated the servants' part of the house from the family's and almost ran into Walters.

He apologized profusely, then told me he had been coming to seek me out. "His lordship has been looking for you, my lady. He is in the library."

I thanked him and went along the high-ceilinged, portrait-hung corridor in the direction of the library. I am not usually a shy person, but suddenly I felt absurdly shy of meeting Adrian. How could one act normally with a man after one had done *that* with him? I pushed open the library door and peeked in.

It goes without saying that the library was an enormous

room, but the books that covered three of its walls from top to bottom made it seem much warmer than the rest of the house. Adrian was sitting behind a large desk placed in front of one of the windows that were set into the fourth wall. The desk's surface was covered with stacks of paper, and he was writing. He looked up as I came in. "There you are, Kate," he said. He put his pen back in the inkwell. "Where have you been hiding yourself?"

"I was talking to Mrs. Pippen," I replied. Slowly I crossed the carpet, a brilliantly colored affair of scarlet and blue. The sun coming in the window behind him lit his head like a halo, and suddenly my chest felt constricted and my breathing quickened.

He smiled at me, but his eyes were grave. "How are you feeling this morning?"

"Fine," I croaked.

"I expect you're too sore to feel like riding, but I'd like to show you Euclide."

I felt color flood my face at his mention of my soreness. "That would be nice." Between embarrassment and other, more violent emotions, I was terser than I usually am.

He looked concerned. "Are you certain you are all right?"

I struggled to find my normal voice. "Of course I am all right, my lord. And I would love to see you ride Euclide."

He made a comical face and stood up. He was wearing country morning dress: a riding coat and top boots without spurs. "Can you possibly know how reluctant I feel to ride in front of you?" he asked.

"Nonsense." The talk of horses was helping me enormously. I could always talk about horses. "The Portuguese would never have given you one of their precious stallions if you were not an extremely fine rider."

"I have learned to be a decent rider," he said. He came around the desk to stand beside me, and his closeness affected my breathing again. I was both annoyed and alarmed by this phenomenon. How could I hide my feelings from him if I went all breathless every time he came within two feet of me? He looked down at me. "But I am not the rider you are, Kate."

"Papa was an excellent teacher," I managed to say. I had the most dreadful desire to put my arms around his waist and lean my body against his. I crossed my arms firmly in front of my chest to keep them from doing anything silly.

He said, "Shall I have Euclide brought to the house, or would you like to see the stables?"

"I'd like to see the stables. But first . . ." My voice trailed off as I wondered if he would think that the request I was about to make was presumptuous.

A single eyebrow lifted. "Yes?"

"I was just wondering about your collection of Saxon artifacts," I said diffidently. "I didn't notice it on the house tour you gave me yesterday."

He regarded me for a moment in silence. I was beginning to think that I *had* been presumptuous when he asked, "Would you like to see it?"

"Yes," I said, "I would."

He took me to one of the small bedrooms in the nursery suite on the third floor. The room was furnished with ancient-looking oak furniture and a threadbare rug, but I only noticed these later. What you looked at when you first came into this room were the walls, which were hung with a dizzying display of spears and swords and shields and daggers and battle-axes. There were other, less bloodthirsty artifacts also. Reposing on what looked like a handmade shelf over the narrow box bed were two garnet-encrusted golden drinking cups. A scarred sideboard held an assortment of other items, and I went over to examine them. Displayed on the open shelves were a silver drinking horn, a jeweled belt buckle, a bronze bowl, a bridle bit, and two gold armbands.

"How old is that bit?" I asked.

Adrian laughed. "Why did I know you would ask me

first about the bit?" He lifted the bronze bit from the shelf and put it into my hands. "It dates from Roman times," he told me.

I looked it over carefully. Then I said, "Tell me about the rest of these things."

It took us an hour to look at everything. He knew all the different kinds of swords and spears, which ones belonged to the early Saxons, which to the Vikings, and which to the later Anglo-Saxons. After we had examined each of the weapons, he lifted a saxe dagger from the wall and held it balanced between his fingers. "When I was seven I found this dagger up on the Downs," he said. "I wanted to know where it came from, and my mother helped me to trace it. When I discovered that it belonged to the early Saxons, I wanted to know about them." He shrugged. "One thing led to another, and that is how I became a collector."

I looked around the small, crowded room. "Was this your bedroom when you were a boy?"

"Yes."

"It doesn't look as if there was much space left in here for you."

He shrugged again. "There was nowhere else to put the things."

I thought of this enormous house. I thought of the bright, eager, curious child he must once have been. I said, "When you build the new family wing, you must set aside a room just to display this collection."

A voice spoke from the doorway. "I've been looking all over for you two! Have you shown Kate that Lusitano of yours yet, Adrian?"

Adrian said, "No, Harry, I have not."

"We're going just as soon as I change," I added.

"Good," Harry said cheerfully. "I'll come too."

The Greystone stables were half a mile from the house, on the far side of a small park of carefully planted chestnuts, beeches, and limes. There had been a thaw during the last two days, but the path from the house was graveled, so we did not dirty our boots with mud.

"I hope Adam didn't do the stables, too," I commented dryly as we passed under the bare branches of the lovely trees.

Harry said, "No fear of that, Kate," and Adrian laughed.

The stables were actually like scores of other noblemen's stables that I had seen. The outside of the barn was the same stone as the house; inside there were wooden boxes for the horses, dirt floors, a separate tack room for saddles and bridles, and a huge loft for hay. The carriage house, also built of stone, held four vehicles and had a large separate room for harnesses. Behind the buildings there were ten large, fenced paddocks. I saw that Elsa was turned out in the one nearest to the stable. She and the gelding in the next paddock were eyeing each other over the fence. Then she squealed, kicked up her heels, and galloped along the fence line, her head held high, her mane and tail streaming. The gelding followed eagerly. I smiled.

One thing that made the Greystone stable different from any other I had seen was the oblong of sand enclosed by a low wooden rail that lay behind the carriage house. It was a riding ring.

"Not quite the riding school in Lisbon," Adrian said ruefully, "but I've had the surface leveled and the sand is firm."

"Papa told me that all the great European manèges are housed in buildings that look like palaces," I said. "The one in Vienna is supposed to be as magnificent as your drawing room!"

"I have never seen the Spanish Riding School in Vienna, but I can assure you that the Royal Manège in Lisbon is every bit as magnificent as my drawing room," Adrian said. "The school had to disband during the war, but now that we have peace again I hope it will re-form. It is too valuable a resource to be lost forever."

While we were speaking a groom was leading a saddled horse out of the stable. He was a dark bay, about fifteen and a half hands high, with a powerful arched neck and even more powerful quarters. Adrian nodded to the groom to hold him while we walked around him so I could admire.

"I have grown so accustomed to looking at English Thoroughbreds," I said. "I had almost forgotten that horses could look like this."

"Have you seen any of the European manège horses before?" he asked.

"I owned a Lipizzaner for a few years," I said.

He whistled.

"He was old when Papa got him, but he was my best teacher, after Papa himself, of course."

"Where did your father manage to lay his hands upon a trained Lipizzaner?"

I looked up at him and grinned. "He got him from an Austrian who was running away from Napoleon."

He looked back at me, his expression unreadable. "And how old were you when you were riding him?"

I thought for a few minutes. "Thirteen and fourteen. He was twenty-four when I lost him to colic. He was a wonderful old horse—one of the Conversano line."

"I am more reluctant than ever to get into the saddle," Adrian said.

Harry chuckled. "I don't blame you. The first time I saw her ride I asked her to divorce you and marry me."

I like praise as much as the next person, and I could feel myself beginning to glow. "Euclide is splendid," I said to Adrian. And he was. Lusitanos are more compact than Thoroughbreds. Their necks and backs are shorter, their legs sturdier, with wide, strong hocks that enable them to bring their hind legs under their bodies with relative ease. The English had created the Thoroughbred to run, but the Lusitano had been created to fight. The breed has changed little from the days when the Romans came to the Peninsula and founded stud farms and remount depots for their cavalry. At that time it was important that the hind legs be engaged in order to do the highly collected battle movements. The Portuguese have kept the engagement in order to perform the high school dressage movements of the manège.

"Get on," I said to Adrian, and he did.

He was an excellent rider. His upper body was so big and strong that he could balance his horse just by sitting upright, and his legs were so long that he could influence with very little pressure. Harry and I leaned against the fence and watched him and Euclide for half an hour, and a number of times I had to blink tears away from my eyes. They were so beautiful together, so light and happy in their work. They had the kind of partnership that I think is one of the greatest treasures of the world.

"I understand perfectly why the Portuguese gave you Euclide," I said when at last Adrian had come to a halt in front of me.

"Aye," said a voice behind me, "that was a very pretty sight. I did not expect to be seeing high school dressage in the stable yard of an English lord."

I recognized the voice and the accent instantly, and spun around. He was standing not six feet away from me, and his weathered old face was one of the most beautiful sights I have ever seen. "Paddy!" I shrieked, and ran to throw myself into his arms.

He hugged me, then held me away and looked at me for a long moment. Finally he nodded, as if he approved of what he saw, and said, "I'm after hearing that you're married?"

I felt Adrian come up behind me. "Yes," I said, "I'm married to the Earl of Greystone, Paddy." I turned to Adrian. "My lord, may I present Mr. Patrick O'Grady."

Adrian held out his hand. "So you are 'Paddy,' " he said with the easy, genial charm that was so attractive. "I am very pleased to meet you."

Paddy put his work-worn hand into Adrian's large clasp. "Thank you, my lord."

Harry came up on my other side. "I say, Kate, is this your Paddy?"

"Yes, it is." I turned back to Paddy. "This is my lord's brother, Paddy—Mr. Woodrow." Adrian rated a formal introduction; Harry did not.

Paddy nodded his salt-and-pepper head in Harry's direction before turning back to Adrian. "That's a beautiful horse you have there, my lord," he said. "Miss Cathleen's father would have liked him fine."

"He's a Lusitano," I told Paddy.

"I can see that he's a Lusitano, girl," Paddy said. "And trained to the high school, too."

"Her ladyship will ride him tomorrow," Adrian said. "Then we both will be able to see how good he really is."

Paddy smiled and said, "That is so, my lord."

I tugged on his sleeve and demanded, "Where have you been all this time? Why have you never come to see me?"

"I was in Ireland for the winter, girl," Paddy said. "I returned to England a week ago and went to Charlwood to find you. That was when I discovered that you had married his lordship here."

Adrian glanced at the sleek chestnut mare that Paddy had ridden into the stable yard. "I'll have one of the grooms see to your mare, Paddy," he said. "Come along up to the house with us. My wife will want to talk to you."

For the first time Paddy looked uneasy. He was perfectly comfortable with earls as long as they remained in the stables. An earl in his own house was something else.

"Come along with you, now," I said in a good imitation of his own accent. "You and I both know that an Irish groom is every bit as good as any English earl could ever be."

Paddy's washed-out blue eyes twinkled at me. "Is that so, now?" he said, and let me take his arm and walk him up the graveled path to the house.

Paddy was predictably amazed by the medieval convent, but when we reached the upstairs drawing room his expression hardened into something approaching the grim. He stood beside me in the drawing room and took in the crimson-silk-hung walls, the immense Persian rug, the gold-medallioned ceiling, and the excruciatingly uncomfortable silk-upholstered gilt chairs that were arranged in an enormous circle around the marble fireplace.

Adrian looked at Paddy's face and said easily to me, "Why don't you take Paddy to the library, Kate? I'll have Walters bring you tea. I have several appointments this afternoon that I must attend to."

I gave him a grateful look.

"I'll come with you, Kate," Harry said.

"You have appointments also," his older brother told him.

Harry looked surprised. "No, I don't."

"You do now," Adrian said.

Harry looked mutinous. Then he met Adrian's gaze. "Oh, all right," he muttered, and kicked his foot like a disappointed schoolboy.

I herded the old groom down the corridor to the library, immensely grateful for my husband's recognition of my need to have Paddy to myself.

Paddy looked around at the high, book-lined walls as he followed me into the room. I aimed for the two chairs that were placed in front of Adrian's desk. "It's a grand house you've got yourself here, Miss Cathleen," he said. He took the chair I pointed him to. "Mr. Daniel would be proud."

I took the second chair and turned it to face him.

"He seems a good man, the earl," Paddy said. "Did you marry him for himself or for the Lusitano?"

I sighed and told him the whole story of my marriage. "So you see," I ended, "poor Greystone is simply making the best of a painful situation."

"I'm thinking it's not many men who would find it painful to be married to you, girl," he said. He looked at me shrewdly. "You don't look too unhappy yourself."

I could feel the treacherous color staining my cheeks. My eyes slid away from his. "I'm not."

"I should not have left you with Charlwood," Paddy said. A grim note sounded under the soft Irish accent. "It was what Mr. Daniel wanted, and at the time it seemed the right thing to do, but I should not have done it."

"You couldn't know he was a villain," I said.

"I checked up on you, Miss Cathleen," he said. "I went by Charlwood a month after Mr. Daniel's death, and the lads in the stable said you were living there with a female relative. I saw you once and you looked all right to me."

"You saw me! Why didn't you let me know you were there?"

"You were grieving, girl. I could see that. I did not think you needed a reminder of your old life just then."

For the first time I let myself acknowledge how hurt I had been by his neglect. It was good to know that he had not just abandoned me, that he had cared enough to check that I was all right.

Paddy was going on, "When I returned to Charlwood in the spring, they told me you had gone up to London to be presented to society. I thought that was a fine thing. Just what your da would have wanted for you."

I made a face, which he ignored.

"When I came back from Ireland two weeks ago I went to Charlwood once again, hoping to see you. That was when I first learned you were married to the Earl of Greystone."

"What made you seek me out this time?"

"It was time," he said simply. "I've missed you, Miss Cathleen."

"I've missed you too, Paddy," I said. "I thought you'd forgotten all about me."

"I would never do that. But your father wanted you to take your place among your mother's people, and I did not want to interfere."

We smiled at each other, both a little misty-eyed. Then I

said, "Paddy, I think Papa was murdered and I think that Lord Stade had something to do with it." And I told him all about my encounter with Stade in London.

He leaned forward in his chair as I talked, listening intently. When I had finished, he said slowly, "I have long thought there was more to Mr. Daniel's death than a hunting accident. After you left Newmarket with Lord Charlwood, I went around asking questions on my own, but I could find out nothing."

"It has to do with Stade," I repeated. "Remember how determined Papa was to show the marquis those two hunters we picked up in Ireland? He could have sold those hunters anywhere, Paddy. Why did he insist on going to Newmarket to see Stade?"

"Aye," Paddy said. "I remember it well. And we got those hunters in Galway."

We looked at each other. Galway is on the west coast of Ireland and Newmarket is on the east coast of England. It was a long way to bring two decent, but certainly not extraordinary, hunters.

I said, "If Stade killed Papa, then I want to make him pay for it."

Paddy agreed. Well, I knew he would. He's Irish.

He said, "But where do we start? I'm thinking the trail, if there is one, will be cold by now, girl."

"I think we should start with the hunters," I said. "We could make some inquiries at the farm where Papa bought them."

"He got them off James Farrell of Inishfree Farm." Paddy never forgot a name.

"I know you've just come from Ireland, Paddy, but do you think you could go back? I've got some money now. I can pay your expenses."

Paddy scowled. "Didn't I just sell a handsome young gelding to a fine army captain for five hundred pounds? I'll not be taking your money, Miss Cathleen. I have plenty of my own."

I had hurt his pride. I widened my eyes and said respectfully, "Five hundred pounds!"

"Aye." He grinned at me, that gap-toothed grin I had known since babyhood. "And he never noticed that the horse was under at the knees."

We laughed. Then the thin, weathered face opposite me sobered. "Mr. Daniel was more to me than my own blood could ever be. If someone did him dirty, then that someone is going to pay."

I nodded my solemn approval of these sentiments.

"I'll leave for Galway tomorrow, girl," he promised.

"You'll let me know what you discover?" I asked anxiously.

"I'll come back like the wind as soon as I have something to report."

"It was Stade," I said. "I know it."

"I will see what I can find out, Miss Cathleen," he said. "Then we will plot our revenge together."

CHAPTER
eleven

I INTRODUCED PADDY TO MRS. PIPPEN AND ASKED HER to feed him and find a room for him in the servants' part of the house. As far as I was concerned, Paddy rated higher than the king, but I had enough sense to realize that he would be extremely uncomfortable in the palatial surroundings that prevailed on the family side of the baize-green door. Well, I thought the servants' quarters were cozier myself.

I left Paddy with Mrs. Pippen and was passing through the corridor on my way upstairs to change my clothes, when Walters appeared. He was followed by a tired-looking young man in riding clothes, who walked with a noticeable limp. "My lady," Walters said, "here is a messenger for his lordship from Lord Castlereagh."

Lord Castlereagh was the Secretary for Foreign Affairs in the present government. "Is it urgent?" I asked the messenger.

"I believe it is, my lady," the young man replied.

"I do not know where his lordship is at this moment," Walters confessed. He looked as if he considered this failure to be a cardinal sin.

"He said something about having appointments this afternoon, Walters," I volunteered.

"Perhaps he is in the estate office, then," Walters murmured. "I will send a footman to inquire."

"Do that, Walters. In the meanwhile I will attend to Lord Castlereagh's messenger."

Walters said, "He can wait in the antechamber, my lady. There is no need for you to trouble yourself."

"It is no trouble at all," I replied, and motioned the limping young man to follow me into the aforementioned antechamber, which functioned as a waiting room for those who were not quite exalted enough to be invited into the drawing room yet were too elevated in rank to be consigned to the kitchen. Lord Castlereagh's messenger followed me obediently, and when I turned it was to find him staring at his surroundings with a countenance that could only be described as awestruck.

There was reason for his expression. The Greystone anteroom might be smaller than most of the other rooms in the house, but it was no less magnificent. The floor was composed of rich, varicolored marble, and dark green marble columns—the ones that had been rescued from the Tiber—flanked both the door and the fireplace. Gilded statues topped the columns, and the ceiling was gilded as well. I might add that there were no chairs in the room to encourage those waiting to make themselves comfortable.

I rang the bell and a redheaded footman appeared. There was only one redheaded footman on the staff, so I remembered his name. "Charles, will you bring two chairs to the anteroom, please?"

Surprise flickered across the footman's face when I called him by name. Then he bowed and murmured, "Right away, my lady."

I motioned to the visitor to join me in front of the fire. "I'd take you to a more comfortable room, but there isn't any," I said. "I'm sorry, but I don't know your name."

"Lieutenant John Staple, my lady."

I looked at his travel-stained, plain blue riding coat. "Are you still with the army, Lieutenant Staple?"

"Yes, my lady. I was injured at Waterloo, and for the last year I have been assigned to messenger duty at the Foreign Office."

"Cavalry or Foot?" I asked.

His chin went up proudly. "Foot, my lady."

"My husband was also at Waterloo," I said.

An attractive smile flitted across the young man's tired face. He said, "Yes, my lady, I have firsthand cause to know of Lord Greystone's presence at Waterloo." I gave him an encouraging look and he added, "I was with Pack's brigade when Marshal Ney attacked our left center."

I had done some reading up on the Battle of Waterloo over the winter, so I knew what Lieutenant Staple's words meant. Pack's brigade had been part of Wellington's second line of defense in the left center, and when the Dutch and Belgian troops that composed the first line had fled in the face of a heavy French attack, the English had been badly undermanned to face the strength of the oncoming French.

"There were three thousand of us, and four times that many of them, my lady, but we charged them," Lieutenant Staple told me with quite justifiable pride. "They were so surprised that they fell back in confusion, but we all knew it was only a matter of minutes until they re-formed and came back at us. That was when Lord Greystone came to our rescue."

All of England knew the story. Wellington had put Adrian in charge of the heavy cavalry because their regular commander had been killed in action two days before, and once Adrian had seen what was happening on the left center, he had ordered a charge. The cavalry had smashed into the lines of French infantry, sending them staggering back from their powerful hillside position, cutting them down by whole battalions.

The charge had completely wrecked the French columns, and the English cavalry captured two eagles as well as two thousand prisoners. Not content with this coup, Adrian had then led his horsemen even deeper into enemy territory, sabering the artillerymen of Ney's artillery and severing the traces of the artillery horses. Without horses to pull them, the seventy-four guns had been rendered useless to the French throughout the remainder of the day.

The pièce de résistance had come out after the battle, when Wellington learned that Adrian had been wounded by a musket ball in the fighting on June sixteenth and had fought the entire engagement at Waterloo with two broken ribs! He had concealed the injury so as not to be put out of action in the bigger battle he knew was coming.

At this moment, Charles came into the room carrying a chair. He was followed by another footman bearing a second chair. They set them in front of the fire. I sat in one and motioned for Lieutenant Staple to take the other. I noticed how one leg stretched out in front of him awkwardly as he lowered himself, his hands braced on the chair's arms. His eyes closed briefly with relief as the weight came off his leg.

I thought that the people at the Foreign Office ought not to have asked him to make so long a ride, but I had enough tact not to share that thought with him. I understood very well how annoying it can be when people tell you that you have undertaken a task that is too much for you.

I encouraged him to tell me all about the gallant defense of the left center and Adrian's heroics. He was still chatting away when Walters appeared in the anteroom doorway. "Lord Greystone is indeed in the estate office, my lady," he announced. Then, turning to Lieutenant Staple, he said, "If you will follow me, sir, I will take you to his lordship."

I was in my room about to change into my blue taffeta evening dress when the connecting door to Adrian's room opened and he came in. My heart gave such a jolt when I saw him that I thought he was certain to have heard it. I reached out a hand to the bedpost to steady myself.

He looked at the dress laid out on the bed and said, "I came to ask you not to get dressed for dinner, Kate. I've asked Staple to dine with us, and he will have to sit down in his riding clothes."

"I can wear the dress I had on this morning," I said. "Will that be all right?"

"A morning dress will be fine." He spoke absently, as if he had something else on his mind.

"I hope Lieutenant Staple did not bring bad news?" I asked hesitantly. I did not want to pry but, frankly, I was dying of curiosity.

He sighed, came farther into the room, leaned his shoulders against the wall beside the fireplace, and regarded me broodingly. "Castlereagh writes that the unrest in the country is growing worse. The government is talking about suspending habeas corpus and instituting 'gag' laws against seditious meetings and literature."

I frowned. The problem of social unrest in England had been growing ever since the booming wartime economy had collapsed after Waterloo. One of the biggest causes of dissent was the Corn Law, which had been passed the previous year. The purpose of this law was to protect British landowners by halting the import of cheap foreign corn into the country. The result had been a half-starved, underemployed population, so outraged by its poverty and suffering that in January the Regent had been stoned on his way to open Parliament.

"Suspending habeas corpus will not solve anything," I said angrily. "The problem is that people are hungry and there aren't enough jobs."

"I know," he agreed. "Things have come to such a pass that four thousand petitioners have met on St. Peter's Field, Manchester, and are planning to march on London. The government is terrified. Castlereagh wants me to come to London immediately."

I blush to confess that my first reaction to this news had nothing at all to do with the poor starving souls in Manchester. "You're leaving?"

His eyes lifted to mine. "Yes."

"What, for heaven's sake, does Castlereagh expect you

to do?" I glared at him. "Lead a cavalry charge against those poor men?"

He looked at me for a moment in silence, then he said, "I hope you have not been listening to Staple with too credulous an ear."

"Why not? He was very flattering about you, my lord."

Adrian shook his head. "I happened to be the man in command, that's all. The English cavalry has always been famous for its charges. They go tearing into battle with exactly the same fervor with which they go tearing after a fox." A gleam of amusement shone in his eyes, as if he was inviting me to share a joke. "The fact is, they couldn't stop their horses even if they wanted to."

I did not agree. "You managed to stop them long enough to capture two of Napoleon's eagles," I pointed out.

The amusement died. "Stupidest thing I ever did," he replied shortly.

It had been the capture of the eagles, of course, that had caused him to be written up in Wellington's dispatches. That, along with his previous injuries, had been sufficient to make a hero out of Adrian.

"Don't you like being a hero?" I asked curiously. Most men would have adored it.

"I think it's ridiculous," he said bitterly. He turned to stare into the fire, affording me an excellent view of his back. "The real heroes of Waterloo are all dead, Kate." He kicked at a log and sparks shot up in a cascading spray of red-gold. "There were fifteen thousand English casualties at Waterloo, and seven thousand of our Prussian allies were killed as well. God knows how many of the French were slaughtered. To talk about someone still living as being a hero is nothing short of sacrilege." He gave the logs another kick.

I gazed at him in silence. He had leaned his hands on the mantelpiece and was still staring into the fire. His back looked rigid. "Is that what you said to Lieutenant Staple?" I asked.

He shook his head wearily. "The whole experience was

such a nightmare that men need something to help them romanticize it so they won't have to remember the reality. I just happened to be one of the unlucky fellows they chose to lionize. Believe me, I didn't do any more than thousands of other soldiers on that field."

"Why are you telling me all this?" I asked.

He turned away from the fire and looked at me. "Because I don't want you having any false ideas about my being a hero," he said. The candle in the wall sconce shone behind his head like a halo. "I'm not."

I smiled and did not reply.

Dinner was a pleasantly informal affair that evening. From somewhere in the house Mrs. Pippen had unearthed a small table, and Adrian had caused it to be installed in the dining room. It was made of old-fashioned oak, would sit ten people at the very most, did not suit the room at all, but it was much more conducive to conversation than the splendid table that it superseded.

"I'll order a small mahogany table when I'm in London," Adrian said when Harry commented on the new addition. "Kate's right; the other table is much too large for family dining."

"Where did you put the other table?" I asked.

"I have no idea. Mrs. Pippen tucked it away somewhere. We can drag it out if ever we have a dinner party."

I smiled at Lieutenant Staple, who was sitting on my right, and told him a comical story about trying to dine with someone who is seated half a mile distant from one. He had looked a little overwhelmed when we first sat down, but my story made him laugh. I embroidered my theme a little, and he was much more relaxed when the first round of footmen entered the room bearing food. I glanced at Adrian and found him watching me with approval in his eyes.

To my horror, I immediately thought about bed.

I turned to Harry, gave him a brilliant smile, and said

something utterly inane. He laughed. The first course, a pleasant-tasting soup made with chicken, was served, and we all tucked in.

Adrian was leaving with Lieutenant Staple the following morning. "I don't want Staple riding all the way back to London," he had told me before we came down to dinner. "I'll drive the curricle and he can accompany me."

I had agreed that the obviously weary lieutenant should not make such a ride again. Then I had asked Adrian if he knew how long he would be staying in London and he had said he didn't, but that he would let me know when he did. He had said nothing at all about tonight.

I drank lemonade instead of wine, ate my dinner, and listened to the men talk about the problems in the country, contributing a comment here and there when someone looked my way. The candles glimmered in the great overhead chandelier, which was almost as large as the oak table. The fire crackled in the fireplace. The footmen's feet made scarcely a sound on the thick rug. There was the muffled sound of rain pattering against the glass of the long windows.

"It's raining," I said.

The men stopped talking to listen.

"If it's still raining tomorrow, we'll take the chaise," Adrian said to Lieutenant Staple.

The fire cracked again, drowning out for a moment the sound of the rain. When I heard it again it was drumming harder than before.

I refused dessert and said to Adrian, "I'm going to go and say good night to Paddy."

He nodded, and the three men got to their feet as I left the room.

I found Paddy tucked up in the housekeeper's room with Mrs. Pippen and Walters. They were all drinking tea.

"I just came to say good night to Paddy," I told them. "Please, sit down."

The old groom came across the room to give me a good

hard hug. "You are not to be fretting yourself, girl," he ordered.

"I'm not."

"Hmm." He gave me a shrewd look. "I'll be seeing you in the morning before I leave."

Everyone would be leaving me in the morning, I thought dismally. I managed a smile. "Sleep well." I turned to Paddy's companions. "Good night, Mrs. Pippen. Good night, Walters."

They were still on their feet. "Good night, my lady," they chorused. I nodded and retreated to my room.

Lucy was there waiting to help me undress. I thought, *I must remember to ask Adrian if he sent anyone to Charlwood to look for Rose.*

Then I thought that it might be weeks—months even— until I saw Adrian again. I probably wouldn't even see him again tonight. He probably would rather talk to Lieutenant Staple than make love to his unwanted wife.

I had worked myself into a fine state of gloom by the time I was in my nightgown and in my bed. I dismissed Lucy and picked up *The Wealth of Nations,* which I was now reading for the second time. It seemed to me that Adam Smith had an important message and that I had missed half of it on my first go-round.

I looked at the pages of my book, but what I was really doing, of course, was listening for sounds on the other side of the connecting door. Lucy had drawn the drapes across the bedroom window, but I could still hear the rain drumming against the glass panes.

I had read one page over at least four times when my listening ears picked up the murmur of voices from next door. Adrian, talking to his valet. My heart began to slam and the book trembled in my grasp. I looked down at the page, but it was a blur. I kept looking anyway, but all my senses were focused intently on that connecting door. He had to come.

And at last, he did. I heard the door open. I looked slowly up from my book. He was closing the door behind him. He said, "If you are not feeling up to it, Kate, I can go away." He was wearing a dressing gown.

"Don't go away," I said.

He came toward the bed. I closed my book and put it on the table next to me, hoping that he would not notice how my hand trembled. He sat on the bottom of the bed and looked at me. "I have some bad news," he said.

I couldn't imagine what he was talking about. "Bad news, my lord?"

"Just before we went into dinner the groom I had sent over to Charlwood returned. It seemed that the girl you wanted to have as your maid is dead, Kate."

I blinked, trying to adjust to a topic I had not expected. "Dead?" I echoed. I frowned. He was looking very grave. "What happened?" I asked sharply.

"She tried to get rid of the child she was carrying," he said. "She bled to death."

I pressed my knuckles against my mouth. "Dear God," I breathed.

"I'm sorry, my dear. It is not a pretty story."

I slammed my fist into the mattress. "Damn him, Adrian!" I slammed it again. "Damn him! Damn him! Damn him!"

His big hand settled over mine, stilling my futile pounding. I took a long breath to steady myself and told him about the time I had seen Rose come out of my uncle's bedroom.

He listened, and when I had finished there was a white line around his mouth. He said in an unusually clipped sort of voice, "Charlwood has never had any sense of honor."

My husband is one of the few men I have ever known who can use the word *honor* and you know it means something.

"Harry told me he tried to elope with your sister," I whispered.

"Yes," he said, his enunciation still very clipped. "Charlwood Court is but ten miles from here, and the summer Caroline was sixteen, Martin came down from Oxford. He persuaded her to meet him secretly. She was unhappy at home and it was easy for her to fancy herself in love with him. It ended up in an attempted elopement."

He was looking at his hand, which still covered mine on top of the blue wool blanket.

"Harry said you stopped it." I was still whispering.

"Yes. I would never trust my sister's happiness to a man like that." He raised my hand, turned it over, and kissed the palm. His eyes met mine. "You were right to be afraid of him, sweetheart. But now you are safe with me."

I felt the touch of his lips all the way down in my stomach. His mouth moved to my wrist and lingered there. He had to be able to feel the hammering of my pulse. He lifted his lips and fingered the ruffle at the edge of my nightgown sleeve. "This," he said, "is a nuisance."

"Perhaps I ought to remove it, then," I said unsteadily.

"Mmmm." His hands were already at my throat, undoing the first of three pearl buttons.

He lifted my nightgown off, tossed it to the floor, then stood to strip off his own dressing gown. The bedside lamp was still lit, and in its glow I could see the puckered red scar that lay along the right side of his rib cage. I thought of the injury he had concealed at Waterloo, and when he came back to the bed I leaned toward him to trace the line of the scar, first with my forefinger and then with a rain of little kisses all along its length.

He said my name and I lay back upon the bed and lifted my arms to him.

"It will be better this time," he murmured in my ear. "I swear it will be better." He kissed my ear, my temple, my cheek, and then, finally, he reached my lips. A hot drenching surge rose within me, and I opened my mouth to him. His hand caressed my breasts, and when the nipples were standing up hard, it moved lower to my stomach and my hips. He kissed me, and I quivered in his hold as his hand moved lower still. The fire crackled, the rain beat against the windows, and I surrendered my body completely to mindless desire.

It was so wonderfully sweet, so hot and sweet, my blood, my juices all running hot and molten under his touch. Everything between us felt so natural, so *right*, but when at last he started to enter me, my body remembered last night's burning pain and tensed in anticipation.

"Relax, sweetheart," he murmured. "Relax and it won't hurt."

I tried. I shut my eyes, willed my thigh muscles to relax, lay perfectly still, and let him in. Deeper and deeper he came, so slowly, so carefully, and there was pressure but no pain. I let out my breath shakily and looked up into his hard, intent face. He said huskily, "All right?"

I nodded, and lifted my legs, and my body closed around him.

As if from a long distance, I heard the rain begin to drum heavier against the window. Then he drove, coming up into me like a powerful surge of water, wave after wave of it, irresistible, and my body shook with his coming, racked with shocks of such intense pleasure that I think I actually cried out.

It wasn't until long afterward, when we were lying together quietly, my head pillowed in the crook of his shoulder, that the fear moved in. This emotion that I felt for him was too strong, too all-encompassing, too powerful. It wasn't safe for either of us.

He went to sleep still holding me, and I lay quietly so I wouldn't disturb him. His skin was warm against my cheek, his chest rose and fell with reassuring regularity, but these physical things could not brighten the bleakness of my thoughts.

I love him, but I must not make the mistake of expecting him to love me. This was the anguishing thought that was tearing at my insides and keeping me awake this storm-tossed night.

Now you are safe with me.

He had said that, and he had meant it. He was a man whose instinct would always be to protect those who were weaker than he. He had shielded his younger brother and sister from the rage of their father. He had married me because he had seen that I was afraid of my uncle. He had been kind with his lovemaking because of this protective instinct that was so much a part of his nature.

I was safe with him. The question was: was he safe with me?

This feeling that I had for him was not tepid. It was passionate and it was possessive. If ever I gave it free rein it would smother him, and destroy me.

He had blown out the bedside lamp before he went to sleep, and the room was dark. I lay awake for hours, listening to his breathing and to the sound of the rain, the storm that raged in my heart fiercer by far than the storm outside the window. When finally the rain ceased just before dawn, I had accepted what it was that I must do.

I could not burden him with a love he had not asked for and could not want. I must hide my feelings from him; I must leave him free.

I thought painfully that it would be much easier to do this if I were his housekeeper and not his wife.

CHAPTER
twelve

ADRIAN DEPARTED EARLY THE FOLLOWING MORNING with Lieutenant Staple, and I saw him off with a resolute smile. Paddy left shortly thereafter, with promises to report back to me as soon as he had some information.

I felt deserted after they both had gone, and to distract myself I went down to the stable and rode Euclide. Harry came with me, and he and several of the grooms hung on the fence while the stallion and I went through some exceedingly pretty canter pirouettes and a *passage* that would be magnificent when he got a little stronger. He was a wonderful horse.

After I finished with Euclide, I had Elsa saddled up and Harry and I went for a ride. He took me on a tour of the estate, and as we rode I told him about my conversation with Paddy. "He has left for Ireland to see what he can discover," I concluded.

"Hmm." Harry's brow was puckered. "Have you told Adrian about this, Kate?"

"No." I was looking directly through Elsa's ears at the road ahead. "There wasn't time."

"Hmm," Harry said again. I felt him looking at me, but I refused to turn my head. Instead I lifted my eyes to the clean blue sky.

It was as if last night's storm had washed away the last of winter, so clear was the sky, so fresh and pure was the air. I drew in a deep breath and looked at the empty winter fields that lay on either side of the dirt lane. Harry said, "A few days of weather such as this and the farmers will be getting out their plows."

I had never lived in one place long enough to follow the farm year, so it was with real interest that I asked him what crops were planted on the estate.

Harry, who had grown up here, replied easily, "Mainly corn, of course—barley, oats, and wheat. The land you are looking at is leased, along with the cottages. Most of our tenant families have leased the same land for generations."

We had been riding gently uphill for the last half mile, and now we reached the crest of the hill and started down the other side. Fields stretched out before us on both sides of the path, separated by neat lines of hedgerows. Midway down the hill, to the right of the road, was a small cottage with a thatched roof. As we drew closer I could see that it had a fenced-in yard next to it, with a shelter that was obviously meant for a pig. A man was hammering at the shelter's roof. Last year's pig had doubtless been slaughtered the previous autumn for winter eating, and the accommodations were being readied for this year's resident.

"Hi there, Blackwell," Harry shouted jovially as we came abreast of the yard.

"Mr. Harry." An unremarkable-looking man, of middle age, middle weight, and middle height, came to the fence. "Feels like spring," he said amiably.

"That it does." Harry turned to me. "Kate, this is one of our tenants, John Blackwell." He looked back to the farmer. "Blackwell, make your bow to her ladyship, the new Countess of Greystone."

The man did not look at all surprised. Probably nothing that happened at Greystone was long a secret from the earl's tenants. He smiled at me, showing a badly chipped front tooth, and tugged at his forelock. "Pleased to meet you, my lady. Welcome to Greystone."

"Thank you, Mr. Blackwell," I said.

"His lordship went to London this morning, Blackwell,"

Harry said. "He asked me to tell you that he will find an eye specialist while he's there and make an appointment for your daughter."

"Thank you, Mr. Harry," the man said fervently.

"Not at all. I'll let you know as soon as I've heard from his lordship."

The man thanked Harry again, profusely, and Harry replied amiably and then we rode off.

"What is wrong with his daughter's eyes?" I asked when we were out of earshot.

"She's almost blind," Harry said. "Blackwell asked Adrian recently if he knew of a doctor Blackwell could take her to."

"How old is she?"

He shrugged. "About nine or ten, I should say."

A thrush flew up suddenly from the field on my right and Elsa jumped in surprise. I patted her neck and asked Harry, "Why hasn't her father done something before this?"

Harry shrugged again. "A man like that has no way of finding a specialist, Kate. And while my father always kept the cottages in good repair, he was not the man to concern himself with a tenant's daughter's eyesight."

I thought of Adrian's comment about privilege and responsibility and wondered where he had learned that particular lesson. Certainly it had not been from his father. I opened my lips to ask Harry some questions about his mother, and remembered in time Adrian's remark that she had died in childbirth when he was seven. She must have died while giving birth to Harry. I said instead, "Well, it seems that the Greystone tenants will be much better off under your brother than they were under your father, Harry."

He nodded a little curtly.

I said, "I'll race you to the bottom of the hill."

The days passed. The workers' march that had so worried Lord Castlereagh petered out before it reached London, but Adrian wrote that there were things for him to attend to pertaining to funds for the Army of Occupation and that he would have to remain in London for a few more weeks. I tried not to wonder if Lady Mary Weston was in town, but of course the more I tried not to think about that, the more I did.

I distracted myself by riding Euclide and Elsa, by visiting the Noakeses, and by buying three adorable spaniel puppies. I also turned my dressing room into a sitting room so I would have someplace comfortable to inhabit.

The biggest distraction of all proved to be the arrival of Cousin Louisa in the Greystone coach, complete with a dressmaker and multitudinous rolls of satin and tulle and velvet and muslin and kerseymere and silk.

I happened to be in the house when my cousin arrived, and I raced down the front steps to give her a hug. "Louisa! Why didn't you write to let me know you were coming?"

She hugged me back. "There was no time," she said. "Greystone arrived at my brother's house two mornings ago and told me to pack. By early afternoon we were on our way to London. I hired Miss Runce the next day—yesterday, Kate!—and Greystone saw us off this morning." There was color in her cheeks and her green eyes were shining.

I was actually a little surprised by how glad I was to see Louisa. I took her into the house, handed Miss Runce over to Mrs. Pippen, and gave Louisa a tour of the medieval convent and the Adam palace. Then I brought her upstairs to my sitting room, where we were attacked by the puppies. I waved Louisa to a chair and went into the corridor, where I spied a footman going into one of the bedrooms carrying Louisa's bag.

"George!" I called when he had come out into the corridor again. "I think these puppies need to be taken outside."

"Yes, my lady."

I looked at his elegant livery. "You had better get Matt and Tom," I said. "You can each take a puppy. Do not return them until they have performed!" Just yesterday Hasty had had an unfortunate accident on my sitting-room rug.

George grinned. "Yes, my lady."

Once the puppies had been removed, Louisa and I settled ourselves in the comfortable faded-chintz furniture Mrs. Pippen had collected for me, and I said, "Now we can be comfortable."

"My dear," Louisa said with awe as she brushed some puppy hairs off her skirt, "this *house*."

"Isn't it dreadful?" I asked cheerfully. "Adrian said he was going to build a new wing for the family, and I think I shall hold him to it."

"Ah," Louisa said. *"Adrian."*

I flushed.

She took pity on me. "He is a perfectly splendid man, Kate. It was such a pleasure to see the way he handled my brother."

"Put the rotter in his place, did he?"

"Yes," Louisa said with satisfaction, "he did."

I said a little awkwardly, "I would have asked you to join me sooner, Louisa, but Adrian was in France and I did not feel I had the right to add to his household without his permission."

Louisa said, "I perfectly understand, my dear." I had told her the brief story of my marriage when I had written to her last spring asking her to send my clothes to Lambourn, so I knew she did understand.

"Greystone was perfectly charming to me, Kate." Louisa smiled a little mischievously. "He congratulated me on talking you out of posing as a boy and getting a job in a stable."

"I don't see why you both seem to find that idea so amusing," I said crossly.

My cousin said with sudden soberness, "It is because we neither of us have your purity of heart, my dear."

"You mean you think I'm naive," I grumbled.

My cousin shook her head and something on her lap

caught her eye. She carefully picked off a single, long, white puppy hair, which she dropped delicately onto the rug. Then she looked at me. "Charlwood's scheme was utterly despicable," she said. "He wished only harm to both you and Greystone. The best revenge you could have on him, Kate, is to have a happy marriage."

I sighed. "That may be asking too much, Louisa."

She widened her eyes in exaggerated surprise. "You don't like Greystone?" she inquired.

"Don't be an idiot," I snapped.

"Then where is the problem, my dear? I thought he seemed quite fond of you."

Fond of me. I almost shuddered. What did I want with his fondness? One was fond of puppies. I picked up a piece of paper one of the puppies had been chewing on and threw it into the fire. It flamed up immediately and I watched it grimly, refusing to look at Louisa.

Louisa was going on, "He thinks enough of you to want to present you at court."

"What!" My head jerked around and I stared at her.

She gave me a smile that I can only describe as smug. "You heard me correctly, Kate. One of Miss Runce's tasks is to make you a court dress. Greystone is going to get his sister to present you."

I was stupefied. A Court Presentation had been as far out of my reach as the moon when I was merely Miss Cathleen Fitzgerald.

"I told you he was fond of you," Louisa said.

If she repeated that word again I was liable to throw something at her. I knew very well why Adrian was going to the trouble of arranging a Court Presentation for me, but I wasn't about to confide his motivations to Louisa. I changed the subject and asked her about her journey.

The sunny, windy weeks of March passed slowly by, and Greystone was a peaceful and a productive place. The spring plowing went on in the fields and the seed was sown. I rode Elsa around the estate and made the acquaintance of all the tenants and their children. Adrian had asked me to ride Euclide for him, so I spent about an hour each day working the stallion. I visited the Noakeses. Mrs. Blackwell and her daughter went to London in Adrian's chaise to see a specialist, and they returned with a pair of eyeglasses that improved Mary's sight considerably. Miss Runce sewed and sewed and sewed and my wardrobe actually began to look respectable. Cousin Louisa began to help out with the local Poor Relief Society and soon became a bosom bow of the Rector's wife. On orders from Adrian, Harry dutifully spent several hours a day reading Latin with the Rector, and in the afternoons he would ride with me or go out with a gun.

It was the sort of life I had always longed for, and I tried very hard to be content. In fact, I was afflicted with restlessness. At the beginning of March there had been an extremely unpleasant incident in Paris between an English and a French officer, and Castlereagh had asked Adrian to go to France to try to win Wellington's agreement to further reduce the size of the Army of Occupation. Adrian wrote that he did not expect to be back in England until the end of the month.

I tried not to dwell on the fact that it was his continued absence that was ripping up all my peace.

On March 21, the first official day of spring, Louisa and I went into Newbury to collect some books we had ordered from the bookstore. We took the phaeton that was kept at Greystone, and I drove.

The day was fine, with high white clouds dotting the clear blue expanse of the sky. The grass margins on the side of the road were sprinkled with early wildflowers. I was driving a pair of exceedingly pleasant grays. April was nearly upon us. I was almost happy.

Our errand in town proceeded smoothly enough. Louisa collected her novels from the bookstore and then she told me she had promised Miss Runce to bring back a few yards of blue ribbon to trim a dress she was sewing. Louisa went into the dry-goods shop and I waited outside, keeping an eye on the grays and on the young man who was holding them. He was the son of the shop owner, and I didn't know him well enough to trust him.

There was little traffic in the street and the grays were standing placidly. I had just about decided to join Louisa in the shop, when I felt someone come up behind me. I turned, and found myself transfixed by the clear sea-green gaze of my uncle. I felt the color drain from my face.

"Kate," he said with grotesquely exaggerated pleasure, "how lovely to see you, my dear." He made no attempt to hide the malice in his voice.

"I regret that I cannot return the compliment," I said.

He was amused by my churlishness. "You should be grateful to me, baggage. It is because of me that you are now a countess." His eyes glittered with enjoyment. "I hear your husband has gone back to France, leaving you to enjoy the pleasures of Greystone alone. Such a pity."

The best revenge is to make your marriage a happy one. Cousin Louisa's words came back to me, and I looked at my uncle's wickedly satisfied expression and knew Louisa was right.

I smiled brilliantly. I said, "Yes, Adrian is in France at present, but he will be returning to England in time for the Season. His sister is to present me at court, and then we will set up housekeeping in Grosvenor Square."

All the smugness was swept from my uncle's face. "Caroline?" he said. "Caroline is presenting you at court?" There was a note in his voice when he said her name that I had never heard from him before. Evidently I had hit a nerve.

"Yes." I let my smile grow a shade more brilliant. "Louisa has joined me at Greystone, and she will be coming to London also. It looks as if my second Season will be far more enjoyable than my first ever was, Uncle." I looked over his shoulder. "Ah, here is Louisa now."

As soon as she saw the color of his hair, Louisa knew whom I was talking to, and her own smile was firmly in place as she came up to us. "Charlwood," she said agreeably, "what are you doing in Newbury?"

"I had business here," he answered. The muscles of his face were tense. I had never seen him betray so much emotion.

A hay wagon went by on the street and the grays turned their heads and looked after it. Louisa lifted her package. "I have the ribbons, Kate. We must be going."

"Yes." I looked back to my uncle and found that he had recovered his usual cloudless expression.

"Perhaps I will see you in London, Kate," he said. "I am going up for the Season also."

"Don't expect an invitation to dine," I said bluntly, and he laughed.

He remained on the pavement and watched as we climbed into the phaeton. He didn't move until I had picked up the reins and begun to turn the grays into the street. Then, with an abrupt motion, he swung around on his heel and strode away.

Neither Louisa nor I spoke until we were out of the town. Then she said, "Why was Charlwood so angry, Kate?"

The secret of Caroline's elopement was not mine to share, so I said simply, "I don't think he was happy to see me looking so prosperous."

Louisa sighed. "It is too bad that Martin has turned into such a hard, cold, unforgiving sort of man."

I clucked to the gray on the right, who was lagging, and he stepped forward. "What was my uncle like when he was a child?" I asked Louisa curiously.

"He adored your mother," Louisa said. "Their own mother—your grandmother, Kate—was an invalidish sort of a woman who had little time for her children. Lizzie was older than Martin and she always mothered him. He was utterly stricken when she ran away with your father."

I thought about this. "That must be why he hated Papa,"

I said. "I don't think Papa ever realized that. If he had known my uncle's true feelings, he would never have left me to his guardianship."

"I'm sure that is true," Louisa agreed.

Against my will, I felt a pang of pity for the stricken and abandoned child my uncle had once been.

On March 22 I received a letter from Adrian saying that he would be back in London within the week. I was to remove to London as soon as possible, and bring with me enough staff from Greystone to run the townhouse.

I exploded into action. Mrs. Pippen would stay at Greystone, of course, but Walters, Remy, and a host of footmen, chambermaids, housemaids, and grooms would have to be moved to London if the house in Grosvenor Square was to function properly. Wellington himself could not have moved all of these people as quickly and efficiently as I did. The day that they all left for London, I rode Elsa over to Lambourn to say goodbye to the Noakeses.

The old dears had been ecstatic when I first told them about my proposed Court Presentation, and Mrs. Noakes still could not hear enough about my dress. I had to describe it for her once more, right down to the last ostrich plume.

Mr. Noakes listened politely, but he was far more interested in what Adrian was going to do about the unrest in the country.

"I don't know what he *can* do, Mr. Noakes," I said candidly, "apart from voting for the repeal of the Corn Law, of course."

"I never thought I'd see the day that England would be overrun by rabble," he grumbled. "If the government don't do something, we'll have a revolution just like the Frenchies did."

"People are hungry, Mr. Noakes, and there are not enough jobs to go around."

"The problem is that too many people have left the land to go to the cities," he said.

"Many of them were forced off the land, Mr. Noakes," I pointed out. "And since the war has ended, a huge number of soldiers and sailors have been forced out of the military. There is no room for them on the land, and so they too have gone to the cities. And there are just not enough jobs!"

The old man growled.

"Enough of politics," Mrs. Noakes said briskly. "I hope you brought your appetite with you, my lady, for I've made your favorite tart."

I assured her I was exceedingly hungry, and the rest of my visit passed happily. The next day Louisa, Harry, and I left for London.

CHAPTER
thirteen

THE MOVE TO LONDON WAS ACCOMPLISHED WITH RE-markably little fuss. I arrived at the Greystone townhouse in Grosvenor Square to find the horses settled in, the servants settled in, fresh flowers in all of the rooms, and Remy preparing one of his famous ragouts for dinner. I made the acquaintance of the London housekeeper, Mrs. Richards, and she gave me a tour of the house, which was spacious and elegant without being intimidatingly palatial.

The following day Louisa dragged me around all of the shops on Bond Street. It was completely unnecessary, but she enjoyed herself hugely and I didn't have the heart to destroy her pleasure. As I watched Louisa ogle bonnets in a store window, it occurred to me that she didn't have any of her own money to spend. I decided that I would give her half of my own enormous allowance and tell her that the money was a stipend from Adrian.

The second day we were in London, I took Elsa for a noontime ride in Hyde Park. I was a little concerned that she would spook at the noisy London traffic, and so I asked Harry to accompany me. He rode a sedate gelding with whom Elsa was friends, and between Monarch's unruffled demeanor and my own encouraging pats and comments, she made it to the park with only a few minor shying episodes.

I heaved a sigh of relief as we passed through the gates. If anything happened to Elsa, Adrian would kill me.

"That mare hasn't seen traffic like this in her entire life,"

Harry commented as we trotted side by side under the trees. Their leaves had turned that particular pale green that one only sees in the springtime, and I regarded them with pleasure. Spring was my favorite season. Harry went on, "I was afraid she might put you under the wheels of a cart, but she was as steady as an old campaigner."

"She has a great deal of sense," I replied, "and she trusts me."

The speedwell-blue sky above the trees was dotted with high white clouds, so perfectly arranged that they looked as if someone had painted them. I was still looking upward, reins loose, completely inattentive to my horse, when a squirrel scuttled out of the trees and ran across the bridle path. Elsa jumped, bucked twice, and I came off.

I was so surprised, and so unprepared, that I lost the reins, a cardinal sin that would have enraged my father. I landed on my seat so hard that the breath was knocked out of me.

Elsa, thank God, was as surprised by my abrupt departure as I was. She didn't run away, but instead stopped dead, pricked her ears, and looked at me with a puzzled expression on her face. It said as clearly as any words could have: *What are you doing down there?*

"It's all right, girl," I said breathlessly. I glanced at Harry, but he had been smart enough to hold up his hand to stop the two riders who were behind us. Strange horses coming by would most certainly have spooked the riderless Elsa into flight.

I got slowly to my feet, talking to her all the while. When at last my fingers closed securely around the hanging reins, I shut my eyes and breathed a prayer of thanks.

"You all right, Kate?" Harry asked.

"I'm embarrassed," I returned.

He chuckled and kept his hand up to hold the oncoming horses until I was once more safely in the saddle.

The party that had witnessed my humiliation now came

trotting up to us. "Is everything all right here?" one of the men asked.

"The only thing that is hurt is my self-esteem," I returned with a smile. "Thank you for stopping. If my mare had run away I really would have been in trouble."

The two men smiled back. Then the youngest one said, "I say, aren't you Harry Woodrow?"

Harry recognized the young man in return, and after a brief conversation he turned to me. "Kate, may I present George Marsh. He was at my college and came down last year."

In his turn, Mr. Marsh presented his companion, a sallow-faced man in his mid-forties named Chalmers. There was something about Chalmers that looked naggingly familiar.

"Have we met before, Mr. Chalmers?" I asked as we chatted, while Harry made plans with George Marsh to go out that evening.

"I have not had that pleasure, Lady Greystone," he returned with a practiced smile. "Believe me, if I had met you, I would remember it."

I didn't believe him, but at the time it didn't seem important whether or not I had ever met Winston Chalmers. We all would have been saved a great deal of trouble had I remembered that afternoon.

When Harry and I returned to Grosvenor Square, we were greeted at the door by Walters himself, who announced majestically, "His lordship has returned."

My heart began to slam. "He's here?"

Walters was too polite to comment on that stupid remark. "You will find him in the red salon, my lady," was all he said.

"How nice," I replied feebly. My eyes fixed on Harry, who had begun to make his way cautiously toward the stairs. "Where do you think you're going?" I demanded.

"You won't want me intruding on your reunion with Adrian, Kate," he replied with one of his most angelic smiles.

"I'll just go along upstairs out of your way and you can explain to him about my being in London."

I shot forward and put my hand on the sleeve of his riding coat. "Oh no you don't, Harry. If you think you're going to leave the explanations up to me, you are much mistaken." I closed my fingers more tightly on the blue superfine. "You are the one who insisted that Adrian wouldn't mind you coming to London with me. If there is any explaining to do, you are the one who's going to do it."

Harry scowled. We both knew that Adrian had expected Harry to remain at Greystone to work on his studies with the vicar, who was a classics scholar. I had let him come to London, partly because I understood his restlessness, but mainly because I did not want to be alone with my husband. "Come along, now," I said briskly, keeping a firm hold of his coat, "it won't be so bad. Adrian doesn't yell."

Harry said, "Adrian might not yell, but that don't mean he can't make himself dashed unpleasant when he wants to." He was looking exceedingly gloomy, but I had no intention of letting him off. I began to walk down the hall toward the red salon, ruthlessly towing him along beside me.

When I reached the room the door was closed. I took a deep breath to steady myself and pushed it open.

My eyes found him immediately, standing before the windows with a paper in his hands. The door hinges were well oiled, and the door had opened soundlessly, but he looked up almost instantly, and his eyes locked with mine.

No one spoke. My heart was pounding so hard, I was certain that Harry must be able to hear it. Something flickered in the dark gray gaze that was holding mine, and I had the strangest sensation that he had touched me. I pressed my feet into the floor to keep them from flying to him, and said breathlessly, "Welcome home, my lord."

"Thank you." He slowly folded the paper, put it on a small piecrust table, and began to cross the rich Persian carpet in my direction. He looked as if he was going to kiss me, and I knew I couldn't let him do that. If he kissed me, I wouldn't be able to stop myself from flinging my arms around his neck and kissing him back passionately. I would completely give myself away.

I panicked, and extended my hand.

He stopped in his tracks, looked at me, and slowly raised an eyebrow. I felt my cheeks grow scarlet, but I didn't move my hand. At last he took my fingers into his, bowed over them, then returned them gently. Next he looked at his brother.

"Hallo, Adrian," Harry said nervously. "Good to have you home."

"I did not expect to see *you* in London, Harry," Adrian replied.

"I thought Kate would appreciate some company," Harry said.

Adrian glanced at me briefly. "Louisa did not come with you, Kate?" His voice was quite unnervingly courteous, and I understood perfectly what Harry had meant when he said that Adrian could be dashed unpleasant.

"Yes, she did." I gave Harry a quick look. His angelic face was marred by an unusually sullen look, and that was not the way to deal with Adrian. I said quickly, "But I did think it would be nice to have Harry's company, my lord. He has brought his books with him, and he has promised me he will study every day."

"That is certainly admirable of him, Kate. Did you bring the vicar with you as well?"

I bit my lip. Of course he knew we had not brought the vicar with us. "No," I said.

"I see. Well then, Harry, since your intentions are so scholarly, do you wish me to engage a tutor for you?"

Harry's expression had grown increasingly sullen as we discussed the vicar. "I don't see the point of studying all that Greek and Latin anyway," he muttered in the general direction of the carpet. "It's nothing but a bloody bore."

I saw Adrian's lips tighten at the swearword, and said hastily, "It's all right, my lord, I don't mind." I knew that poor Harry was suffering because I had put Adrian out of temper, and I cast about vainly for something to say that would lighten the atmosphere.

Harry raised his eyes from the carpet. "*You* never had to study this boring old stuff," he said, making bad worse. "I'm twenty years old, Adrian! I don't want to be a schoolboy anymore. When you were twenty, you were an officer in the Peninsula."

"I was in the Peninsula watching men get killed," Adrian agreed. "And you are kicking up larks and getting yourself sent down from Oxford."

A dark flush highlighted Harry's high cheekbones. "I got sent down because I was bored." His eyes slid away from Adrian's face and he went back to staring at the carpet. "Oxford is so . . . so futile."

Silence as Adrian looked at his brother's bent head. "What do you wish to do with your life, then, if you don't wish to return to Oxford?" he asked at last. The tone that had set my teeth on edge was gone; he sounded genuinely interested.

Harry shook his head violently. "I don't know."

"Do you want a cavalry commission?"

"There is nothing for the cavalry to do in peacetime, Adrian. It would be as boring as Oxford."

A baffled look passed over my husband's face as he regarded his surly young sibling. There was silence in the room as he walked over to the fireplace and stood with bent head looking down into the flames. Then, evidently having made up his mind, he kicked one of the logs into place and turned to face us. In the light of the flame his hair looked more gold than silver. "All right," he said, "you may take a vacation from your studies and remain in London, Harry. Caroline will be arriving shortly, and it will be nice for the three of us to be together again."

The sulkiness lifted from Harry's face and he grinned. "Thank you, Adrian. You're a great gun."

Adrian said, "We'll discuss your future again in the summer, before you go back to Oxford."

Harry's grin faded and he sighed. Then he mumbled something about going upstairs to change his clothes, excused himself to me, and left the room. The door closed firmly behind him.

There was a faint line between Adrian's brows. "I hope I haven't made a mistake," he said. "I haven't the time just now to look after him, and an untried boy loose in London can get into a great deal of trouble."

I said, "He admires you tremendously, my lord. He wants to be like you, but he doesn't know how."

The line between the silver-blond brows sharpened. "He shouldn't want to be like me," my husband said. "He should want to be like himself."

"He has to find that out."

He was still standing in front of the fire and I was standing by the door. He looked at me, and I knew that he was waiting for me to make the next move. Part of me wanted to run away like Harry, and part of me wanted to throw myself into Adrian's arms. I knew I could do neither, so I took a few cautious steps farther into the room and said brightly, "You won't believe what just happened to me. I came off Elsa!"

"Did you?" His eyes looked me up and down in a way that made every nerve in my body tingle. "Are you all right?"

I conjured up a wall of words to throw between us. I told him all about Elsa; I told him about Euclide; I told him about Louisa and the Poor Relief; I told him about my court dress; I even told him about Mary Blackwell's new glasses. The only item of information from the last month that I neglected to mention was my meeting with Charlwood.

Adrian listened to this long and remarkably silly speech with an expression that was both serene and impenetrable.

When I finally ran out of chatter, he said, "I am glad to hear that you have been so busy, Kate."

"I have always wanted to have a home, you see," I said idiotically.

His head moved fractionally and his eyes grew a shade darker. "Greystone was never a home," he said. "Perhaps you will change that."

I did not know how to answer him.

He moved away from the fireplace, and I hastily stepped out of his path. He walked to the door, stopped, turned, and gestured to the paper that he had been looking at when I came in. "My sister writes that she will be arriving in London either tomorrow or the following day. Her husband will be accompanying her, as well as their two small children. Will you tell Mrs. Richards to have their rooms ready?"

"Of course."

He gave me a courteous smile. "If you will excuse me, then, my dear, I too have an appointment."

I said again, "Of course."

He turned without another word and disappeared into the hall.

The long-anticipated meeting was over and I had not given myself away. Why, then, did I feel as if I wanted to cry?

There was only one master bedroom in the Grosvenor Square townhouse. It was extremely large and had attached dressing rooms that opened off either side of it. The countess's dressing room contained several wardrobes for clothing, a long mirror, a dressing table with another mirror, two upholstered chairs, and a chaise longue. The earl's dressing room contained wardrobes, a shaving mirror, a long mirror, and another bed.

I was thinking about that bed as I bade good night to my new lady's maid, a French girl Walters had found for me, and climbed into the huge four-poster that I had slept in alone for the past two nights. Adrian had not been home since the afternoon. He had sent word that he had met a friend at the House Guards and would be dining out. It was now eleven-thirty, and still he was not home.

I was miserable. I had repulsed him this afternoon and he had not liked it. I knew what that raised eyebrow had meant when I had offered him my hand and not my lips.

Where was he going to sleep? This was the question that was exercising my mind at the moment and keeping me awake.

It would be better for me if he slept in his dressing room. I knew that. He had captured my heart already. If I slept with him, and continued to sleep with him, I would become so entangled with him that I would never be able to let go. I would suffocate him and in the process destroy us both.

I knew all this, and still I did not want him to sleep in his dressing room.

I waited and waited, but all was quiet next door. I could see a crack of light under the connecting door and I knew that Rogers, his valet, was waiting for him too. Finally, at about one in the morning, I fell asleep.

I came awake as soon as the dressing-room door opened. I didn't move, however, just half-opened my eyes and watched as Adrian entered. He was wearing a dressing gown and his feet were bare. He crossed silently to the empty side of the bed and put the candle he was carrying on the bedside table. He took off his dressing gown, went to drape it across the back of a chair, then returned to the bed. I opened my eyes more widely and watched him come. He walked lightly, like a giant cat, and his muscled body glimmered in the candlelight. He was beautiful.

He bent to blow out the candle, then saw that I was awake. Our eyes met.

"You're late," I said softly.

"Yes." He didn't speak again, just regarded me out of eyes that looked dark and heavy. I had seen that look often enough on my father to know what it meant. *He's been drinking,* I thought.

I said, "You'd better come to bed before you catch a chill."

"I never catch chills," he said gravely. His enunciation was perfect. He wasn't drunk, then. But he had been drinking.

He folded back the quilt and got in beside me.

"Aren't you going to blow out the candle?" I whispered.

"No." He shook his head. "I want to see you."

I gazed up into his dark, heavy-lidded eyes. His hair, which had grown longer while he was in France, framed his head like a silver helmet.

"I missed you," I said. I couldn't help it.

"Did you?" he murmured. And then his lips came down to mine.

I could taste the wine that he had been drinking. I buried my hands in his hair and held him to me. His mouth moved from my lips to my breast, and the treacherous sweetness began to spread through my loins. I whimpered with pleasure.

When we were together like this, I couldn't hide from him what I felt. His weight pressed me down into the feather mattress and I felt myself open for him as a flower opens to the warmth of the sun. I stared up at the tapestry canopy over us and felt him enter me, and it was like sunlight pouring into me, hot, irresistible, life-restoring. The feather bed was soft beneath my back and I arched to meet him, his powerful thrusts filling my womb with wave after wave of stunning pleasure. I locked my arms around his neck and said his name, over and over, like an incantation, like a prayer.

The following day, Caroline arrived. Looking at her, I had no further doubts that my uncle had been in love with her. She was twenty-six, a year younger than Adrian and six years older than Harry. She gave me a charming smile as she turned from greeting her brothers. "At last," she said, "I have a sister!"

I had been nervous of meeting her, but her words disarmed me completely. I grinned and held out my hand. She ignored it and came to give me a kiss and a hug. She had Harry's fine-boned, angelic face and was not very much taller than I. She turned to her elder brother and said, "I'm glad to see you have upheld the family tradition for good looks."

"You have not yet greeted Miss Cranbourne, Caro," Adrian said pleasantly, and as Caroline turned to speak to Louisa, Adrian introduced his brother-in-law to me.

Lord Ashley was in his mid-thirties, a pleasant-looking man with a humorous mouth and intelligent hazel eyes. He shook my hand and said, "I hope you will not be too put out by my family, Lady Greystone. We are a noisy lot, I'm afraid."

He had to raise his voice to be heard, since the baby in the nurse's arms was wailing and the toddler whom a nanny had in charge was announcing loudly that he was hungry. I said to Adrian's brother-in-law, "Please call me Kate." Then I beckoned to Mrs. Richards and said to the harried-looking nurse and nanny, "If you will go with Mrs. Richards, she will show you to the nursery and make sure you have all that you need."

Both women gave me a grateful look and followed Mrs. Richards to the staircase.

"Thank you, Kate," Caroline said. "They are tired."

"There's nothing wrong with their lungs, that's for sure," Harry said.

Lord Ashley said fervently, "I could use a glass of port, Adrian."

"Did you all travel in the same chaise?" Adrian asked with amusement.

"Edward rode the entire way," Caroline announced. "I cannot imagine why he should be in need of a glass of port. It is I who need sustenance."

"Come into the drawing room," I said, "and we will all have some refreshment."

A bottle of port was brought for the gentlemen, and I ordered tea for the ladies. While the men ranged themselves in front of the fire, Caroline, Louisa, and I retired to the striped satin sofa.

"Tell me," Caroline demanded as soon as she was seated, "what are you wearing to the Presentation?"

I described my dress to her as I poured the tea.

"Of course, you will wear the Greystone diamonds," Caroline pronounced when I had finished.

Adrian had said nothing to me about the Greystone diamonds, but before I could stop her Caroline had called to her brother, "Adrian, don't tell me you have not yet given Kate the diamonds?"

He was listening intently to something his brother-in-law was saying, and did not hear her. I thought that perhaps he did not want to hear her, and said firmly that I would rather not discuss the diamonds. Caroline ignored me, raised her voice, and repeated her question. His head finally swung in our direction and he answered, "The diamonds? They are at Rundle and Bridge's being cleaned. Don't worry, Caro. Kate will have them in time for her Presentation."

"Good." Caroline turned back to me. "You won't be able to wear the tiara, because of the ostrich plumes, but the necklace and earrings and bracelets will look well."

"It sounds like a great deal of jewelry," I managed to say faintly.

"Every woman at the drawing room will be simply *hung* with jewelry, Kate," Caroline assured me. "The idea is to look as laden as is humanly possible." She thought for a moment. "Perhaps we can get the tiara on you, after all. We can fix the ostrich plumes around it."

"Do you know, I am rather nervous about this Presentation," I confessed to Adrian's sister. "I have nightmares that I will trip on my dress or do something else that is horridly gauche."

Caroline's slate-blue eyes lit with laughter. "I felt the same way," she confided. "Everyone does, I think."

"Yes, but if I make a cake of myself it will reflect upon Greystone," I said gloomily.

"I keep telling you that you have nothing to worry about, Kate," Louisa said. She turned to Caroline. "Her curtsy is perfect. She could hold it for an hour if she had to. She will do beautifully."

"I wish that it was over with!" I said.

"In a few days it will be." Caroline smiled at me. "I have been looking forward to this season ever since Adrian wrote to ask me to present you," she said. "We are going to have such fun, Kate. Wait and see!"

I looked at her lovely, sparkling face and thought once more about my uncle.

CHAPTER
fourteen

My Presentation WENT OFF AS SMOOTHLY AS everyone had promised it would. Adrian and I, along with Caroline and Lord Ashley, were taken to St. James Palace in the Greystone carriage, which was decked with three footmen garbed in elaborate livery. I wore the obligatory ostrich-plume headdress along with the Greystone diamond tiara, three different kinds of skirts draped over a huge hoop, diamonds at my throat, in my ears, and on my wrists and fingers. The cost of the dress alone would probably have fed a village for an entire year. The diamonds would have fed all of Ireland.

Caroline and I left the men in the huge reception room and crammed ourselves into the presentation chamber anteroom along with about twenty other girls and matrons, all of whom were encased in hoops and hung with diamonds. Actually making my curtsy to the queen was almost an anticlimax. She was old and wrinkled and most unprepossessing. Caroline and I curtsied, she beckoned us forward, and for the next ten minutes she proceeded to ask us questions about Adrian!

The reception room was packed when we returned, but Adrian's head topped even that sea of tall men and ostrich plumes. We had almost reached him when I saw that he was talking to a slender girl whose honey-colored hair was piled elegantly high under her waving plumes. My heart plunged. It was Lady Mary Weston.

Caroline must have felt me hesitate, because she turned

to look at me. Then her eyes went back to her brother. "Who is that talking to Adrian?" she asked.

"That is Lady Mary Weston," I answered in what I hoped was an unemotional voice.

Caroline didn't reply, but I saw that she recognized the name. We squeezed our hoops through the remaining crush until we reached Adrian. He greeted us with a smile. "The deed is done?" he asked.

"Kate was magnificent," Caroline assured him.

"Kate is always magnificent," he replied. I shot him a suspicious look, but his face was unreadable. He proceeded to introduce Lady Mary to us both.

Caroline smiled and made a polite reply.

I said soberly, "Lady Mary and I have met."

"But not since you became Lady Greystone," said the girl who had expected to achieve that title herself. "I have just been wishing Greystone happy; allow me to offer the same sentiments to you."

Her expression was as serenely lovely as always, but she had paled a little when she saw me. "Thank you, Lady Mary," I said.

"Where is Edward?" Caroline asked her brother.

"He was talking to someone about breeding cattle, I believe," Adrian said.

Caroline groaned. "If Edward has found someone to talk to about breeding cattle, we will never get him out of here."

"Are you ready to leave?" Adrian asked. "If you are, I'll find him for you."

"If we can leave without being rude, I'd like to," I said. "The smell of all these different perfumes mingling together is not particularly appetizing."

"Mmm," my husband said. His eyes were scanning the room. "There he is." He looked down at Lady Mary, excused himself, and pushed off into the crowd, which parted before him as it always did.

I saw the expression in Lady Mary's eyes as she looked

after him. If I had ever had any doubts about her feelings for Adrian, that one, naked look laid them to rest.

Damn, I thought. *Damn. Damn. Damn.*

A distinctly chilly, feminine voice said, "Mary, my dear, I have been looking for you."

Lady Mary turned. "I am sorry, Mama," she replied quietly. "Allow me to present Lady Ashley and Lady Greystone."

If looks could kill, the Duchess of Wareham's glare would have struck me through the heart. I looked back into her haughty, aquiline face and *I* grew a little pale. I am not accustomed to people looking at me like that.

As the duchess and her daughter moved off, Caroline murmured in my ear, "If I were you I wouldn't stand in front of any open windows when the duchess is nearby."

I tried to produce the smile she expected. Then Adrian returned with Edward, and we made our escape.

The Presentation over, my second London Season officially began. It was very different from my first. Doors were opened to the Countess of Greystone that had remained firmly shut to Miss Cathleen Fitzgerald. I went from being a satellite on the outer reaches of the *ton* to being one of its stars.

I won't deny that it was far more pleasant being part of the inner circle, but what I enjoyed the most about this time in London was being part of a family. Caroline was so kind to me that I soon began to feel that she really was my sister, and I adored her children. For an only child to find herself suddenly blessed with a brother, a sister, two nephews, and a cousin is a wonderful thing.

Of course, I also had a husband. Ironically, I would have been a happier wife if I had loved him less. I would not have felt such anguish that he did not love me back.

Sometimes I pretended. At night, lying in his arms, feeling his passion, I would pretend to myself that he loved me. He wanted me, that was certainly clear enough, and it wasn't hard to make the leap in my mind from wanting to loving.

But the morning inevitably came, when the sun rose and the passion was spent. I wasn't a green girl; I knew that men could want where they did not love. He was always beautifully courteous to me, always thoughtful and kind. But he kept me at a distance. I hated it, but there was nothing I could do to change it. The circumstances of our marriage were always vividly present to my mind. I had no right to ask for his love; I had no right to burden him with mine.

Hiding my feelings from him was the hardest thing I have ever done. Just seeing him walk into a room was enough to make me dizzy. It was easiest just to avoid him if I could, and I soon discovered that the intense social whirl of the Season made avoiding him fairly easy. In the *ton,* married women were not expected to make a couple with their husbands. Those times that Adrian actually escorted me, he was also escorting Caroline and Louisa, and often it was Edward, or even Harry, who accompanied us on our round of social engagements.

The only time Adrian and I were alone together outside the bedroom was on the mornings that we took the horses to the park. Adrian had sent to Greystone for Euclide, because he did not want to leave him unworked for weeks, and on these mornings we would leave the house at six o'clock to ride through the slowly wakening London streets to Hyde Park.

The park was always deserted at this hour, and the air smelled as fresh and sweet as it did in the country. The grass and the flower beds glistened with dew and the thrushes sang as if they were in Berkshire, not in London. The air had a nip to it, and we would let the horses warm up their muscles in a long, stretching, side-by-side canter.

I loved these mornings. It was the only time we were really easy together—two people who were happy in each other's company because we were intent on a common goal. We had found a fairly flat grassy spot near the lake and we would work the horses there, me on Elsa and Adrian on Euclide.

To ride classical dressage requires total concentration by both horse and rider, and we worked quietly, only aware of the other so that we would not get in the way. It was a perfectly happy time. The warmth of the early-morning sun on my bare head, the peace that perfect communication with an animal can always bring, the steady rhythm of Elsa's trot as she extended it, snapping out her forelegs with wonderful brilliance—I wanted to hold on to that time, to stretch it out and make it last forever.

On the way home we would discuss the session, how each horse had gone, what the problems were, how to correct them the next time we rode. At these times there was no distance between us, no sexual tension to muddy the clarity of our relationship. We passed ideas back and forth, feeding off the other's insights, perfectly comfortable, perfectly in tune.

Then the house would loom before us, and grooms would take away the horses, and we would go back to being Lord and Lady Greystone. It was unutterably depressing.

Such was the situation in the Greystone household when Paddy returned from Ireland.

I had coaxed Harry into taking me to see Madame Tussaud's wax-figure museum that morning, not because I was so anxious to see it but because I thought he had been unusually quiet recently and I wanted to see if there was anything wrong. I gave him plenty of opportunity to talk to me, but he was not forthcoming, and when we reached home again Walters informed me that Paddy had arrived. Caroline and Edward had taken little Ned to the Tower to see the royal menagerie, Louisa had gone to return a book to Hookham's library, and Adrian was meeting with some government official or other, so Harry and I had Paddy to ourselves.

I ordered some refreshment, ushered everyone into the morning room, sat on the edge of a yellow silk chair, stared at Paddy, and said expectantly, "Well?"

Paddy took a long drink of beer. His pale blue eyes were very sober. "I think I have found out why Mr. Daniel was killed," he said.

Harry gave a sharp exclamation of surprise and excitement. I leaned even farther forward on my chair and said nothing. Paddy looked at me and began his tale.

"You were right to think that it began with the hunters, Miss Cathleen, although it was not the hunters themselves that set Mr. Daniel off." Paddy took a sip of beer. "I talked to Farrell, the man who was after selling the horses to your da, but I learned nothing from him. I was a wee bit discouraged, but I decided to stay in the area for a while—to see if I could pick up on anything—and that is how I came to be there for the Galway races."

My eyes narrowed as my thoughts turned inward. "We saw racing in Galway that time we bought the hunters," I said slowly.

Paddy nodded emphatically. "So we did, girl. And this time I saw what Mr. Daniel must have seen two and a half years ago."

He paused to take another drink of beer. The Irish all have a great sense of drama.

Harry hissed impatiently. Paddy ignored him, took another swallow, and picked up his story.

"Do you remember the horse that won the Galway Cup at those races?" he asked.

"Yes." I rarely forget a horse, and this one had been particularly memorable. "He was a bay, with an amazingly powerful stride."

Paddy smiled, obviously pleased with me. "God bless you, Miss Cathleen, you're just like your da," he said.

I smiled back at him.

"What does this bay have to do with Kate's father's death?" Harry demanded. He had all the English impatience with storytelling; they always want to go straight to the point.

Paddy gave him a fatherly look. "I saw him again a few

weeks ago, Mr. Harry. That was when I noticed that he runs just like the bay colt that Stade won the Guineas with." Paddy turned back to me. "As you noticed yourself, girl, it's a very distinctive stride. You cannot mistake it. The three-year-old Stade is running this year has it as well."

I was puzzled. "I'm afraid I don't understand, Paddy. What is the connection?"

"I did not see that myself until I started asking around." Paddy set his empty glass down on a side table, stared for a long, thoughtful moment at his scarred old boots, then lifted his pale blue eyes to mine. "It was then that I made an interesting discovery," he said. "I looked up the Stud Book and found that the Irish colt's sire was a stallion named Finn MacCool. Now this Finn MacCool had been a grand runner in Ireland, but he was hurt as a four-year-old and retired to stud. It was then that his true brilliance began to come out."

Harry and I were staring at Paddy the way the sultan in the *Arabian Nights* must have stared at Scheherazade. Paddy went on, "It seemed obvious to me that Stade's colts must have the same bloodlines as the horse that had won the Galway Cup, so I paid a visit to the horse's owner, Frank O'Toole, and I learned a very interesting thing."

Paddy paused. Harry looked as if he wanted to scream, but he managed to restrain himself.

"Five years ago there was a fire in Finn MacCool's barn," Paddy said. "O'Toole said he and his men got all the horses out and safely turned into a paddock—or so they thought. They were too busy trying to keep the fire from spreading to check the horses for the rest of the night, and when they finally got back to the paddock the following morning they found that a part of the fence was down and the horses had gotten out. They rounded up all of the others, but Finn MacCool had disappeared."

He paused. Significantly.

My mouth opened. "Oh my God," I said.

Paddy nodded. "They never got him back. The general feeling in Galway is that he got trapped in a bog and sank."

"Was Finn MacCool a dark bay?" I demanded.

Paddy nodded. "Unmarked."

I inhaled, then said flatly, "Alcazar."

"That is what I am thinking, Miss Cathleen. And I would wager all my earthly goods that that is what Mr. Daniel thought as well."

Harry said in an injured voice, "I would very much appreciate it if someone would tell me what you are talking about. I realize I must be stupid, but I haven't tumbled to it yet."

I turned to him and said, "The Marquis of Stade has a stud named Alcazar."

No matter what he might claim, Harry wasn't stupid. His breath sucked in audibly as he realized what we suspected. "Good God, Kate," he said. "Are you saying that Stade's horse, Alcazar, is really Finn MacCool?"

"Alcazar was a very undistinguished runner," I said. "Papa could never understand how so mediocre a horse could sire such a splendid runner as Castle Dawn, the horse that won the Guineas two years ago in record time. Since then, Alcazar has produced a number of other winners. And they are all unmarked bays, with a driving, powerful stride."

Harry's eyes began to glitter with excitement. "Do you think your father challenged Stade about Alcazar's identity, and so Stade had him killed?"

"No, I don't think that was what happened. Don't you remember that I told you that the last words that Papa spoke were *I didn't think he suspected that I knew*?"

"I'm thinking that Mr. Daniel would have wanted to take a private look at Alcazar before he accused anyone," Paddy said. "Someone must have seen him."

We sat in silence and a wave of depression swept over me. This was it, then. Papa had been killed because he had suspected Stade of stealing a successful stallion and substituting it for his own mediocre stud.

"Stade is as rich as Golden Ball," Harry burst out. "Why would he resort to something so underhanded? He don't need the money."

"It is not winnings that Stade is after," Paddy said. "I'm thinking it is the prestige of owning such a grand stud that attracted him. Stade has wanted to be admitted into the Jockey Club for years, but his membership was always rejected. With a stud like Finn MacCool, the prejudice against him would eventually crumble."

Harry had another objection. "Then why wouldn't he just have bought this Finn MacCool if he wanted him so badly?"

"I found out that some rich Englishman was after trying to buy the stallion," Paddy reported. "O'Toole wouldn't sell. Said he'd waited his whole life for a horse like that. Wouldn't have sold him for all the rubies in India. It made the horse's loss even worse, of course, because O'Toole ended up with neither the horse nor the money. All he had left was a few foals—one of which was the horse I saw race last month."

An energizing burst of anger swept through me, blowing away my depression. I gritted my teeth. "Well, Stade is not going to get away with it," I said grimly. "He killed my father, and he stole Mr. O'Toole's horse, and I am going to make him pay."

"That's the spirit, Kate," Harry said.

Paddy nodded his own agreement, but warned, "Before we can do anything, we need proof."

I asked Paddy, "Were you able to talk to Finn MacCool's groom?"

He smiled approvingly. "That I was, girl. And didn't it come out that Mr. Daniel had talked to him as well?"

Harry whistled.

"The groom also told me that Finn MacCool had a small mole on the right side of his sheath," Paddy said.

"No matter what his color or his markings might be, every horse is different," Harry said. "The more I think about it, the more impossible it seems to me that Stade could pull off a switch like this. Alcazar's grooms would know if another horse was substituted for him. Grooms always know their own horses."

"I'd be willing to wager that we'll find Alcazar's grooms were fired before the new horse was brought in," Paddy said.

Harry lifted his brows in Adrian's own gesture.

I spoke into the silence, "I think we're all in agreement that the next logical step is to look at Alcazar ourselves."

Paddy said, "And haven't I brought Finn MacCool's old groom from Ireland with me so we can do just that?"

The cold hand of fear squeezed my stomach. I said, "First we must make certain that Stade is not in residence."

Harry turned to me. "What we need to do is get Adrian to take us to Newmarket for the running of the Guineas. Stade will be sure to be at the racetrack that day, and that will give us the perfect opportunity to take a look at this Alcazar."

I regarded Harry with admiration. "That is a splendid plan, Harry."

He looked pleased with himself.

Paddy said, "It is a good plan so long as Sean and I are the ones who are doing the looking."

Harry scowled.

"We can lay our exact plans when we are actually at Newmarket," I said hurriedly. "What we need to do first is to convince Adrian to take us there. And that might not be so easy."

"I know," Harry said. "He is so busy these days, and so . . . abstracted."

"I don't think he is very happy with the government's repressive new laws," I said.

"Of course he ain't happy with them," Harry said. "The way Liverpool is acting, you'd think barricades were going up in Pall Mall."

"It's disgraceful," I agreed.

"Tell Adrian that you always went to Newmarket for the Guineas with your father, and you want to go to the meet for old times' sake," Harry suggested.

I bit my lip. "All right."

"I'm after thinking that there is no need for either of you to come to Newmarket at all, Miss Cathleen," Paddy said. "I will wait until the day of the running of the Guineas, and then Sean and I will go to look at the stallion. Afterward I will come back to London to tell you what I have seen. It will be better if we do it so."

"You had better resign yourself to the fact that we are coming, Paddy," Harry snapped. "There is no way on this earth that I am going to be left out of this adventure!"

Paddy gave him a disapproving look. "We're after seeking justice," he said. "This is not a schoolboy's adventure, boyo."

Harry's face took on a stern expression that I had never seen it wear before. He looked suddenly older. "I understand that, all right. I'm sorry. Adventure was the wrong word."

I said only, "I am coming." Harry might talk of adventure, and Paddy of justice, but what I wanted was simpler. I wanted revenge.

At that moment, Louisa walked in with her library books. She stopped when she saw us and color rose in her cheeks. "I'm sorry, Kate. I did not know that you were engaged."

I smiled to show her it was all right. "Put your books down, Louisa, and come meet a dear friend of mine," I said. "This is Paddy O'Grady."

Louisa gave a delighted smile and came forward to offer her hand. "I've heard so much about you, Mr. O'Grady," she said. "Kate is very fond of you."

Paddy bowed over her hand with a grace that surprised me. "Thank you, ma'am," he said in his softest voice.

"Miss Cranbourne was the 'female relation' who was

staying with me at Charlwood Court," I explained to Paddy. "She is my mother's cousin."

"Is it so?" Paddy said.

"Is Mr. O'Grady staying with us, Kate?" Louisa asked.

My reply of "Of course he is" clashed with Paddy's "The grooms can put me up in the stable."

"Nonsense," Louisa said firmly. "You cannot stay in the stable, Mr. O'Grady."

"Louisa is right," I said. "This house isn't half as intimidating as Greystone, Paddy. You can have a quite ordinary bedroom on the second floor with the rest of us."

Paddy looked down at his boots. "I cannot be staying here like a guest," he protested. "I have not the manner nor the clothes for it, girl."

I waved my hand. "Harry can take you out tomorrow and buy you some clothes." Then, as he was about to protest again, "Please, Paddy? For me? You are all I have left of Papa, and I *want* you to be near me." I gazed at him beseechingly.

He sighed. "I cannot refuse you when you look like that, Miss Cathleen, and you know it."

Of course I knew it. I smiled.

Louisa said, "If you like, Kate, I will take Mr. O'Grady to Mrs. Richards and she can show him to a room."

I nodded, and Louisa and Paddy left the room together. Harry and I looked at each other. "We'll get the bastard, Kate," he promised.

I could feel my jaw set. "Yes," I said. "We will."

CHAPTER
fifteen

THE DAY AFTER PADDY'S ARRIVAL THE COUNTESS OF Bridgewater had her annual ball. Since the Earl of Bridgewater was an important figure in the government, Adrian had to go, and of course I went with him. It was almost the only time we had gone out socially by ourselves, and I was nervous.

He came into my dressing room just as Jeanette was fastening a lovely strand of pearls around my throat. Adrian had given them to me on the night I first went to Almacks, and I loved them. I looked at his reflection in the mirror and smiled a little tensely. "I am almost ready, my lord," I said.

"There is no hurry," he replied, "I have not yet sent for the carriage." He sat down in a chair that was too small for him and looked as if he was prepared to wait for another hour.

A little flush had crept into Jeanette's cheeks when Adrian walked in. She was usually a very self-possessed girl, but Adrian's presence always seemed to affect her that way. I had caught her several times gazing at him as if he were some sort of a god. It was a little annoying.

"Is my hair finished, Jeanette?" I asked. Even to myself, my voice sounded cool.

Her cheeks grew a fraction pinker. "Not quite, my lady. I must just poot ze combs in." She picked up two pearl combs and deftly tucked them into the artful tumble of curls she had arranged on the top of my head. She really was very talented.

I had to admit that my hair had looked much nicer since she came.

I stood up carefully, so as not to disturb her handiwork. Adrian stood up as well, and as I turned to face him I said, "You may send for the carriage now, my lord. I am ready."

He didn't move, just stood there regarding me out of unreadable gray eyes. Adrian always looked splendid, but in a black evening coat he was enough to break your heart. I shot a quick look at Jeanette out of the corner of my eye and caught her doing it again.

"You look lovely, Kate," he said at last. "Very regal."

"Regal?" I said doubtfully, looking down at myself. My dress was a relatively simple affair of white net worn over a Clarence blue satin slip. It had been very expensive because the net was sprinkled with pearls, but it did not have any of the lace or bows or elaborate embroidery that I knew I would see adorning most of the women's dresses this evening. Louisa had said I was too small for such excessive trimming, and I agreed with her.

"Yes," he said, "regal."

I shook my head in disagreement. "I'm too short. You have to be tall, like Lady Mary Weston, to be regal."

He didn't disagree with me, he simply said he would go and order the carriage.

"Damn," I muttered under my breath as I watched him leave the room. I had wanted him to tell me that I was far more regal than Lady Mary.

We got caught in a line of carriages outside the Bridgewater house in Berkeley Square and had to wait for a half an hour before we finally reached the front door. I used the time to tell Adrian about my desire to go to Newmarket for the Guineas.

We were sitting side by side in the carriage, facing forward. He had stretched out his legs as far as they would go, and I had spread my skirts carefully so that they wouldn't wrinkle. The skirt made an effective barrier between us and I looked straight ahead as I talked, trotting out my prepared story about how Papa and I had always seen the Guineas together and how much I longed to return this year for old times' sake. When I had finished he didn't answer immediately, and I sat in silence and thought glumly about how silly I had sounded.

Not for the first time, I wondered if I should tell him the whole story. When recently I had suggested to Harry that we do this, he had objected violently. "Adrian's got too much on his mind just now, Kate. Castlereagh is pushing him to come aboard at the Foreign Office, and of course that is exactly what Adrian always planned to do. But he don't like this repressive course the government has taken in domestic affairs. This is not the time to worry him about Stade and a ringer stallion."

I had felt an unpleasant flash of jealousy that Adrian would confide these problems to Harry and not to me, but I had to admit that what Harry said made sense. It would not be fair to burden Adrian with my problems at a time when he was dealing with problems of his own.

"If it would be too inconvenient for you to accompany me, then perhaps I could go with Harry," I ventured.

"No."

I bit my lip.

"It will not be inconvenient for me to take you to Newmarket, Kate," he said. "In fact, it will be a relief to get out of London for a while." I turned to look at him, and he gave me a rueful smile. "I'm beginning to think that I don't have the temperament for politics after all."

"It's not you that doesn't have the right temperament, my lord," I said hotly. "The country would be much better off if you were prime minister instead of that frightened worm, Liverpool."

"They're all frightened," Adrian said, "Liverpool and Sidmouth and the rest of the Tory leaders. I don't understand them at all." He sounded genuinely bewildered. "They have dusted off some old unrepealed Act which gives magistrates the power to send to prison any persons they think likely to commit an act prejudicial to public order." A current of anger ran beneath his voice as he turned toward me. "Can you imagine what that means, Kate? It means that red-faced squires all over the country will be throwing into jail every poor soul who passes a rude comment in the local pub!"

"It is disgraceful," I said.

"I cannot understand them," he repeated forcefully. "Everywhere I look in London I see demobilized soldiers and sailors who can't find employment. These are the men who defeated Napoleon, Kate! They deserve better than that their government should be afraid of them."

He did not understand that Liverpool and Sidmouth and their ilk were narrow-minded little men who thought only of the welfare of their own class. Unlike Adrian, they did not feel it was their duty to protect those less fortunate and less powerful than they.

"I know your family have always been Tories," I said slowly, "but perhaps the Whigs would be more to your taste?"

The coach crept forward a few more steps.

He sighed. "The Whigs are hopelessly divided into factions, Kate."

I did not understand. "Factions?"

He held up one finger. "First, we have the Grenvillites, who are just like the Tories, only they think Lord Grenville should be prime minister and not Liverpool." He held up a second finger. "Then we have the Foxites, who are supposedly in favor of reform but who have no use for economics. Economics, of course, is the whole point of reform," his eyes glinted, "as any intelligent reader of *The Wealth of Nations* should know."

I nodded intelligently to show him that I did indeed know.

A third finger went up. "Then there are the radical reformers, people like Whitbread and young Grey and

Brougham. But they all disagree with each other as well as
with the Grenvillites and the Foxites."

"Good God," I said. "The Whigs sound as if they're as
disorganized as the Irish."

He gave an unwilling laugh. "The Irish at least can always agree to oppose the English. The problem with the
Whigs is that they can discover nothing with which they can
agree to unite in opposition."

The carriage inched forward again.

"It sounds dismal," I said.

"It is. I will be happy to escort you to Newmarket."

The carriage stopped and a footman holding a torch
opened the door. Another footman stepped forward to assist
me to alight. We had arrived at the Bridgewater ball.

The ball was notable for two things. The first was that
Adrian danced with Lady Mary Weston.

This fact did not appear to be at all earth-shattering to
anyone else in attendance. I was already on the floor with another partner—a young cavalry officer who held a position at
the Horseguards—so it could not be said that Adrian had neglected me for a previous love interest. Nor was there anything about their demeanor that was at all remarkable. They
conversed gravely and decorously while waiting for the music
to start, and they performed the waltz with perfect correct-
ness.

But it was a waltz. He had his arms around her. She was
looking up into his eyes. He was looking into hers. I wanted
to pull her away from him and scratch her face off. Jealousy
is a very ugly emotion.

Then, when I went into the supper room with my escort,
whose name I can't remember, I saw Adrian sitting with three
other people, one of whom was Lady Mary.

"Are you feeling quite the thing, Lady Greystone?" my
escort asked me. "You have gone quite pale."

My face might be pale, but I was seeing red.

"I'm fine." I forced a smile. "I see my husband over there. Why don't we join him?"

The man agreed with alacrity. Everyone always wanted to have a chance to get close to Adrian.

When I approached Adrian's table, the men rose and someone went to bring two more chairs. There was a general shuffling about as they made room for us, and Adrian introduced me to Mrs. Hampton, a handsome young woman whose husband had been on Wellington's staff in the Peninsula. Apparently she was the one whom he had taken into supper, not Lady Mary. I felt marginally less furious.

Lady Mary asked me if I was enjoying the dance. Her supper companion was a haughty-looking young man whose shoulders must have been padded, they looked so extravagantly wide in contrast to the rest of him. I tried not to stare at them as I told her I was indeed enjoying the dance.

"You seem to have captivated poor old Charles Prendergast," Adrian said.

Sir Charles Prendergast was a burly gentleman of at least sixty. He had danced with me twice and talked my ear off about a hunter that my father had once sold him that had been "the best damn horse I've ever ridden."

"Papa once sold him a horse that he liked," I said.

Padded Shoulders said, "I am quite certain that Sir Charles found more to admire in you than your father's horse, Lady Greystone." He lisped.

I stared at him in amazement. Adrian coughed and turned his face away. "No," I said, "he really liked the horse."

"Lady Greystone's father was well-known for his excellent horses," Lady Mary said to her escort. Her cheeks were a little flushed.

"I say—was he some kind of a dealer, then?" Padded Shoulders gave a giggle to show that he was joking.

I answered him but kept my eyes fixed on Lady Mary. "Yes, in fact, he was." If I had not already guessed how she felt about Adrian, her comment would have told me. Mary

Weston was not usually the sort of girl who made remarks like that.

Padded Shoulders, realizing he had committed a gaffe, huffed and puffed and tried to change the subject. Mrs. Hampton came to his rescue with a comment about the lobster patties. Then a footman came up behind Adrian's shoulder.

"Lord Castlereagh would like a word with you, my lord," he said. "He is in the library."

"Very well," Adrian said. "If you will excuse me, Mrs. Hampton, Lady Mary," his eyes met mine, "Kate."

We all chorused that of course we would excuse him. The supper table broke up shortly after he left, and for a moment Lady Mary and I were left alone together.

I had been in London long enough to have learned what code governed the marriages of most aristocrats, and faithfulness was not included in the rules of the game. Men were always free to play where they desired, while a woman's duty was to ensure that her firstborn son was her husband's child. After that she could have as many lovers as she liked, as long as she was discreet.

I knew that I had no claim to Adrian's fidelity. I had sworn to myself that I would not burden him with my feelings. I looked into Lady Mary's serene and lovely face, narrowed my eyes, and said, "Find someone else to love, Lady Mary. Greystone is taken."

She stared at me in stupefaction. Finally she managed a faint "I beg your pardon?"

"It's quite simple. I am telling you to leave my husband alone."

"I don't know what you are talking about, Lady Greystone," she said.

She knew perfectly well what I was talking about, but I was not averse to spelling it out. "I am talking about the fact that you are in love with Greystone. I don't blame you for that. I realize that you knew him before I did. But fate was not on your side, Lady Mary." I moved a step nearer to her so that our faces were quite close. "Greystone is now married to me, and I take my marriage very seriously." I narrowed my eyes even more. "*Very* seriously, Lady Mary, if you take my meaning."

The color returned to her face in a rush of blood. "Are you trying to frighten me, Lady Greystone?" she asked incredulously.

"Yes," I said.

"This is incredible," she said.

"I know how to use a gun," I said.

Her mouth dropped open. "Are you threatening to shoot me?"

At that moment Sir Charles Prendergast came puffing up with a sightly-less-elderly companion in tow. He hailed me triumphantly. "Lady Greystone!"

I turned away from Lady Mary, satisfied that she had received my message. "Sir Charles," I said graciously, "is this the gentleman who is in search of a new hunter?"

When I had been speaking to Sir Charles previously, I had taken the opportunity to try to stir up some business for Paddy.

Sir Charles beamed at me. "Indeed it is," he said. As he made the introductions, Lady Mary walked slowly away.

If Lady Mary dancing with Adrian was the first notable thing that happened at the Bridgewater ball, the second was the appearance of my uncle.

He arrived quite late, while I was at supper, and I did not know he was there until I returned to the ballroom and saw him taking the dance floor with Lady Charlotte, the Bridgewaters' youngest daughter.

I looked around immediately for Adrian, but he still must have been closeted with Lord Castlereagh, because he was nowhere in sight. The gentleman to whom I had promised this dance was escorting me to the floor, and he must have felt me falter. He stopped, looked down at me with concern, and asked, "Are you all right, Lady Greystone?"

"I'm fine," I replied. "I was just surprised to see my uncle—Lord Charlwood—at this particular ball. I did not know he was politically inclined."

My escort smiled cynically. "He's not here because he's politically inclined, Lady Greystone. He's here because he's wealthy and unmarried. The Bridgewaters are trying to marry off Charlotte this year, and Lady Bridgewater has set her sights on Charlwood. The betting in the clubs is that he's finally met his match."

I regarded the unremarkable-looking girl who was standing next to my uncle. "In Lady Charlotte?" I asked.

"In Lady Bridgewater," came the dry reply.

We reached the floor just as the orchestra began to play. It was a quadrille, and we went to join a set that was on the opposite side of the room from my uncle.

I had become quite adept at the quadrille these last weeks, so I did not have to concentrate on my steps quite so intently as I once had. Consequently, I was aware of the moment when my uncle first noticed me.

He saw me, and instantly his eyes began to search the room. I thought he must be seeking Adrian, and my own eyes made a quick circle to ascertain if he had surfaced yet. He had not.

The music played on, and I turned and curtsied and was handed from partner to partner, and all the while I worried about what was going to happen when my uncle and my husband finally met.

At last the dance ended. I accompanied my partner off the floor, agreeing distractedly to whatever it was that he was chatting about. "The next dance is a waltz, Lady Greystone," he said as we came to a halt in front of some gilt chairs. "Dare I hope that you are free?"

A smooth voice from behind me said, "I'm afraid, sir, that my niece has promised this dance to me."

"Uncle Martin!"

I whirled to face him and he bestowed upon me that familiar, fraudulent smile, the one that did not touch his eyes. "You are looking even lovelier than I remembered, Kate," he said. "Marriage must agree with you."

"It agrees with her extremely, Charlwood." Adrian's voice was cold. "And my wife has promised this dance to me."

I jumped and exclaimed, "Adrian!"

The men looked daggers at each other over my head. I backed up until my shoulder was touching the safety of Adrian's arm. I saw Charlwood give one more quick glance around the room, and finally I realized who it was he was looking for.

Caroline.

She's not here. If Adrian had not been standing right behind me, I would have said it. But I knew he would be furious if I mentioned his sister to Charlwood, so I held my tongue. Uncle Martin would realize it without my help soon enough.

The strains of the waltz lifted through the immense, crowded, candlelit room. Adrian put his hand on my bare shoulder and said, "Kate?"

I tilted my head back and smiled up at him. For a fraction of a moment his fingers tightened. The icy look on his face warmed into a return smile. Together we turned our backs on my uncle and walked out to the dance floor. Adrian held out his arms and I went into them as if there was nowhere else in the world that I would rather be.

As, indeed, there was not.

CHAPTER
sixteen

HARRY WAS IN TROUBLE. I HAD SUSPECTED IT FROM the way he was acting, and suspicion turned into certainty when I finally remembered—two weeks too late—where I had seen Mr. Chalmers before. I had met him at the racetrack, and he was a gambler.

"He's a bad lot, Kate," Papa had told me. "One of those bloodsuckers that makes his living from draining green youngsters who have more blunt than sense."

When I remembered this I had a sinking feeling that my brother-in-law was one of those green youngsters Chalmers had sunk his teeth into. Harry seemed excessively nervous of late, and his angelic countenance was looking decidedly drawn.

I was not the only one in the family to notice Harry's state. I heard Caroline tell him that he was looking dreadful and that he had better start to keep earlier hours. And Adrian took a long look at him on one of the rare evenings that we were all dining at home, and recommended that he stop trying to burn the candle at both ends.

He had been keeping late hours, of course, but so were all of us, and we did not look like something that one of my puppies at Greystone had chewed into a limp rag. Harry was getting as many hours in his bed as were the rest of us, and even Louisa, who was *much* older, had brighter eyes and healthier color than he did.

Something was preying on his mind, and I was dreadfully afraid that he had gotten into the clutches of that worm Chalmers. Every time I tried to broach the subject to Harry, however, he slipped out of my grasp, pleading some engagement or other that required his immediate departure.

He was so slippery, in fact, that finally I was forced to set a trap for him. Edward and Caroline had taken little Ned to see the show at Astley's Amphitheatre, and Caroline had come home raving about the equestrian exhibition and the simulated Great Fire of London. After listening to Caroline, I had the idea to ask Adrian to get tickets to Astley's for me and Harry, telling my husband that I knew we would both enjoy this performance, which would doubtless bore his much more sophisticated sensibility.

I had to add the latter comment because when I first broached the subject, Adrian sounded as if he would enjoy coming to Astley's with us. As I was quite certain that Harry would keep his lips closed tight as a clam if his revered older brother were present, I had to squash this inclination, much as I would have enjoyed my husband's company.

Adrian got us seats in the box that provided the best views of the stage and the sawdust ring where the horses performed. I fully intended to take advantage of the time that Harry was cooped up with me to get to the bottom of whatever it was that was bothering him, but I ended up so enraptured with the show that I did nothing for the first hour and a half but ooh and aah at the lavish performance.

Harry was as entranced as I was, and the two of us hung out of the box together, cheering on the pony races and wildly clapping for the dancing horses.

It was while they were preparing the stage for the Great Fire that I recollected the reason for my attendance at this marvelous performance. If I was not to miss the finale, I would have to work fast.

"All right, Harry," I said, "I know you are in trouble. I know all about the despicable Chalmers. Tell me, how much do you owe him?"

He started guiltily. Then he mumbled, "I don't know what you're talking about, Kate." He wouldn't meet my eyes, however, but sat staring intently at the workers on the stage, who were setting up for the Great Fire finale.

"Yes, you do know," I countered. "My papa once told me that Chalmers was the kind of bloodsucker who preyed on green youngsters with more blunt than sense. That sounds to me like a good description of you."

"Damn it, Kate!" He turned to glare at me. "If you knew Chalmers was a bad'un, why didn't you tell me?"

"I didn't place him until a few days ago," I confessed. "I had this feeling that I had seen him before, but I couldn't remember where."

Harry brought his open hand down on the balustrade with some force. "Damn it!" he said again.

"I gather he's got his teeth into you?" I asked sympathetically.

"Yes." Harry sat back and looked at me with desperation written all over his face. "I don't know what I'm going to do, Kate. I owe him twenty thousand pounds!"

I felt my jaw drop. "Twenty thousand?"

"Yes."

This was an appallingly large sum, completely out of the reach of anything I could help him with. "What happened, Harry? How did he do it to you?"

He rubbed his hands over his face in a tired gesture. "He took me to a gaming hell, Kate. I was flattered. He seemed such a man of the world, and I was actually flattered that he would bother with a boy like me." His eyes shut. "God, I was so bloody stupid."

It went without saying, but I said it anyway. "You lost."

"I lost. When I didn't have the money to continue, they very graciously accepted my IOUs. I went back a few more times, hoping that the luck would change, you know? When I finally had the sense to stop, I owed twenty thousand pounds. I didn't have the money to cover my vowels, of course, so

Chalmers kindly agreed to loan me the money. He gave me a week to pay him back."

I said a word I had heard Papa use sometimes when he was really angry with someone.

"Yes," Harry said bleakly. "Exactly."

While I thought about Harry's problem, I watched the men who were shoveling a few piles of manure out of the sawdust pit beneath us. The rich aroma came drifting to my nostrils. I sniffed appreciatively and said, "What I don't understand in all this, Harry, is how Chalmers can come out ahead. He actually stands to lose his money if you can't repay him."

"I've been thinking about the whole scheme, Kate, and what I think is that Chalmers is in partnership with the owner of that hell he took me to. The gig probably is that Chalmers lures in the victim, and in return he gets a commission on what the dupe loses."

"But nobody makes any money if you can't repay them!"

He gave me an anguished look. "They know who I am, Kate. If I don't repay them, they'll go to Adrian."

I didn't say anything. I knew without him telling me that Harry would give everything he owned to prevent his brother from finding out how he had been gulled.

The little boy in the box next to us began to whine, "When is it going to *start* again, Mama?"

"Soon, dear," came the soothing reply.

Harry averted his face and said, "God, Kate! What is he going to think of me if he finds this out? First I pull that bloody stupid stunt and get sent down from Oxford. And now—*this*."

I did my best to reassure him. "He might not be as horrified as you think, Harry. He was actually worried that something like this might happen. He told me that an untried boy loose in London could get into a great deal of trouble, and he didn't have the time to look after you properly."

Harry's mouth tightened. "So that was his opinion of me."

"Not just of you, Harry! Of any untried boy thrown on London without proper guidance."

He turned his head and looked at me, and his expression was bleak. "Would this have happened to Adrian had he been thrown on the town when he was twenty?"

This time I was the one to look away. We both knew that it would not.

"I don't want Adrian to know about this, Kate," Harry said with quiet desperation.

I understood. I sighed. "Well, then, we are going to have to find a way to come up with twenty thousand pounds to pay off that worm Chalmers."

We looked at each other gloomily. The chances of either of us being able to lay our hands on twenty thousand pounds was remote, to say the least.

In the box next to us, the impatient little boy began to bang on the balustrade.

Harry said, "I was thinking of trying to steal back my IOUs. If they don't have the vowels, they have no proof that I owe them anything."

"Harry, what a brilliant idea!"

He gave me a wry smile. "The idea may be brilliant, but the execution is going to be somewhat more difficult."

"Who has the vowels? Chalmers?"

"I think so." He ran a nervous hand through his hair, making the carefully disordered locks his valet had arranged earlier look even more natural. "The first time I borrowed from him, I had the cash to pay him back. I went to his lodging the following morning, gave him the blunt, and he returned my vowel. He took it out of a locked desk drawer. I watched him."

"Then we must break into his lodging, shoot the lock off the drawer, and steal the vowels." I beamed at him. "What could be simpler?"

He gave a shaky laugh. "You're a great girl, Kate, but I can't involve you in this. Adrian would kill me if he ever found out that I had put you in any kind of danger."

"Adrian would probably be glad to get rid of me so that he could marry that saintly Lady Mary Weston," I said darkly.

"Don't be stupid," Harry said. "Of course he wouldn't. Who would want to marry a tedious girl like that after he'd been married to you?"

I gave him a grateful smile. "That is nice of you, Harry."

"It ain't nice, it's the truth."

At last the orchestra began to play. Harry and I both whipped around toward the stage, which seemed to ignite before our very eyes! The Great Fire of London had begun.

All the way home in the carriage, Harry and I traded ideas about how to break into Chalmers's lodging house. I finally managed to convince him that one of my schemes would work perfectly.

Harry was to introduce Chalmers to me, and I would tell the worm how much I loved to wager and ask him to take me to a gaming hell. I would accompany him to the hell, and then, while Chalmers was safely engaged with me, Harry would break into his lodging and steal back his vowels.

"You'll probably even win," Harry told me. "I did, the first time I went. I think it's part of the scheme. Then, once you start losing, you go on playing because you know you've won once, and you keep thinking you're bound to start winning again."

It seemed to me that Harry had figured out the scheme pretty well and, if only he could get his IOUs back, the experience would be nothing but beneficial. By the time we reached home he was looking decidedly more cheerful.

Caroline and Edward were dining with friends, and Paddy and Louisa were out too, but Adrian was home, and as we ate one of Remy's chicken fricassee dinners, Harry and I told him all about the show. When I finished describing the

Great Fire, Adrian said dryly, "It was probably a finale like that that burned the last amphitheater down."

I laughed and agreed. "But it was splendid to watch."

I had noticed that Frank, the young footman who was standing behind Adrian's chair, had been listening to my description with breathless attention, and now I said to him, "If you and some of the other footmen and the maids would like to see the show, Frank, I'm sure his lordship would be happy to get you tickets."

Harry said, "Kate, don't you know by now that you ain't supposed to chat with the footmen while you're eating!"

I was annoyed. "Of course I know that, Harry, but it's only the family here tonight."

Adrian turned his head slightly. "I would be happy to procure tickets for you, Frank," he said. "Just let me know how many, will you?"

Frank had gone beet red. "Yes, my lord," he said. "Thank you, my lord." He looked at me. "Thank you, my lady."

I grinned at him. "You'll love it," I said.

Harry shook his head. Then he asked, "Where have Paddy and Louisa gone tonight?" We had been seeing less and less of Louisa and Paddy of late; they always seemed to be busy doing something together.

I said with great satisfaction, "I believe they ate earlier so they could go to the theater. Kean is doing *Richard the Third* at Drury Lane, and Paddy loves that play. It makes the English look so bad."

Adrian chuckled.

"Why are you looking like that?" Harry asked me.

I opened my eyes wide. "Like what?"

"Like the cat that ate the cream," Adrian said.

I was feeling like the cat that ate the cream, but I didn't want to say why. I smiled mysteriously and helped myself to one of the side dishes. It was green beans.

"Doing some matchmaking, Kate?" Adrian asked.

My eyes flew to him. "How did you know?"

"You are not exactly inscrutable," he said with amusement.

"I know that Paddy is not of Louisa's class," I said defiantly, "and of course he is much older than she, but he is a very fine man and he has an excellent eye for a horse."

"How old do you think Paddy is?" Adrian asked curiously.

"He must be sixty," I replied.

"He's fifty-three," Adrian said.

"You're joking me!"

He shook his head. "I asked him."

"Fifty-three! But that means he's only ten years older than Louisa."

Adrian took a drink of his wine. "So it does."

Harry said, "Paddy and Louisa can't possibly get married, Kate."

"You are such a wretched snob, Harry!" I said furiously.

"It ain't snobbery," he defended himself. "I think Paddy's a great gun, but a lady like Louisa can't live constantly traveling from one horse farm to the next."

"My mother lived like that, and she was a lady," I said even more furiously than before.

"Your mother was young," Harry said. "Louisa's old."

Well, this was true.

"If Paddy and Louisa do decide to marry, we just shall have to find them a home," Adrian said. "While I would not call Louisa old, she is most certainly not ready to begin a new life racketing around the countryside, and Paddy's business would benefit from having a home stable as well."

I gave him a delighted smile. "What a perfectly splendid idea, my lord!"

Harry also nodded his approval. "Will you buy them a horse farm in Ireland as a wedding gift, Adrian?"

This comment dashed my spirits a little. It made great sense, of course, but Ireland would put them both so far away from me.

Adrian said, "Actually, I was thinking I would give them a good lease on Lambourn."

"Oh," I whispered. "That would be perfect." I gazed at him, and I knew my heart was in my eyes, but I couldn't help it.

"Yes, I think it would be," he agreed. "I know you love them both, Kate, but I really don't want them living with us for the rest of their lives."

Harry said innocently, "I can't understand why."

"Then I am not going to explain," Adrian said, and Harry chuckled.

I said, "But the decision to marry must be Louisa's and Paddy's. If they don't love each other, then we must not force them. Marriages made like that always end in misery."

Absolute silence greeted this pronouncement. It took me a moment to make the connection, and then I turned fiery red. I looked down at my beans and thought miserably that I must have the world's loosest tongue.

"As usual, Kate, you are right." I heard Adrian's chair being pushed back. "If you will both excuse me, I have an engagement."

Harry and I sat in silence as he left the room. After the door had closed behind him, Harry said to me, "Damn, Kate! How could you have said such a stupid thing?"

"I don't know, Harry," I said miserably. "I wasn't thinking of us at all! I was just making a . . . a generalization."

"Well, you made Adrian angry. A man don't like having his wife fling into his face the fact that he was forced to marry her."

"I know, I know," I wailed. "Truly, Harry, I didn't mean it!"

He sighed. "Don't look so wretched, Kate. He'll get over it."

"Would you like more lemonade, my lady?" my footman asked solicitously.

I looked at him. "I think I'll have some of that wine instead, George," I said.

Harry said uneasily, "Is that a good idea, Kate?"

"Probably not, but I'll have some anyway. I'm not going anywhere tonight. I think I'll just sit here with you and get foxed."

I had three glasses of wine, and when I stood up the room tilted alarmingly. Harry had to give me his arm to get me upstairs. "Get into bed and sleep it off," he advised me.

"Do you think he's going to hate me for what I said, Harry?" I asked pitifully.

"No." He looked at Jeanette. "Her ladyship ain't feeling quite the thing," he said. "Better get her straight into bed."

"Yes, Meester Harry," Jeanette said. She closed the door, steered me into the room, stood me in front of the fire, and unbuttoned my dress. She was very efficient. I was in bed in less than ten minutes.

I fell instantly asleep and knew nothing until many hours later, when I felt Adrian get in beside me.

He was very quiet, and the feather mattress didn't give him away, but I always woke when he came in. I opened my eyes but, except for a crack of moonlight coming in through the half-closed drapes, the room was dark. It must be quite late, I thought; the fire had burned down. He didn't look at me but pulled the quilt up over his shoulder, turned on his side, punched the pillow into the shape that he liked, and settled himself to sleep. I lay quietly and regarded his quilt-covered back.

"Adrian?" I finally asked in a very small voice.

Silence.

"Adrian, are you awake?"

"Yes, I'm awake, Kate." He definitely sounded reserved.

"I'm sorry about what I said tonight," I said.

"Don't worry about it."

"I didn't mean that I thought *our* marriage would end in misery."

"I understand. Good night, Kate."

I sniffled.

Silence.

I sniffled again.

"Are you crying?" he asked dangerously.

"No. I never cry. I am just somewhat foxed, I think."

Finally he turned over so that I was no longer talking to his back. *"Foxed?"*

"I had quite a few glasses of wine after you left. My head still feels fuzzy."

"What was Harry thinking of, to let you have several glasses of wine?" he demanded.

"He didn't really want me to."

"No, I imagine he didn't." Now he sounded resigned.

I said earnestly, "Adrian, I am very, very sorry about what I said tonight. The thing is, you are always so nice to me that sometimes I forget all about the circumstances of our marriage. That is what happened tonight. I wasn't thinking about us at all!"

He said, *"Nice* to you. God, Kate, you can be so dense."

The reserved note I hated was gone from his voice, and I wasn't even insulted that he had called me dense. He could call me anything he wanted as long as he didn't talk to me as if I was a stranger.

"I don't mean to be dense," I said. "I want to be a good wife, Adrian. Truly I do."

He sighed. "I know you do, sweetheart. I'm sorry if I upset you. Now go back to sleep. It's very late."

"Would you mind holding me for a little?" I asked.

I could tell that he didn't want to, but I was desperate. Finally he reached out and gathered me into his arms. His hold was careful and much too impersonal. I didn't care. I snuggled my cheek against his shoulder and let my body relax into his. "The bed is too cold when you're not here," I whispered.

"Mmmm?"

"Did you really have an appointment, or did you go to your club and drink wine like I did?"

I felt the chuckle rumble through his chest. "Kate, you're diabolical." The arms that encircled me lost their stiffness and pulled me closer. The relief I felt was so intense that I shut my eyes. "How did you know?"

"I'm a witch," I murmured into his shoulder. I was really feeling sleepy now. Warm and sleepy and safe.

"I think you must be," I heard him say. And then I must have drifted off, because I don't remember anything else.

CHAPTER
seventeen

TWO DAYS LATER, HARRY ESCORTED ME TO THE HOUSE of Lady Marsham. I had never before had the pleasure of meeting Lady Marsham, as she was not received by the better hostesses of the *ton*. Lady Marsham, it seems, was addicted to games of chance, and her afternoon "salon" was nothing more than a gambling house. Harry took me because it was a house that Chalmers often frequented, and we hoped to cross paths with him there.

My hostess received me with overwhelming enthusiasm. "My dear Lady Greystone! How lovely to meet you! How lovely to have you grace my humble salon! Do let me introduce you to a few people! Dare I hope you will join me in a game of cards!"

She wore a purple turban and enormous earrings, and I thought I detected the smell of wine on her breath. Her large salon had brown velvet drapes on the windows and all the drapes were tightly drawn so that not a single decent ray of sunlight was able to peer inside. The room was lit by lamps, and green-baize-covered tables were set up everywhere. People were playing cards with the kind of intense concentration that denotes the serious gambler. Only a few bothered to look up when Harry and I came in. Chalmers was nowhere in sight.

"I like whist," I said. "Perhaps Mr. Woodrow and I can play whist together."

I knew that Harry was an excellent whist player—it was

the one thing he was actually better at than Adrian. Thanks to Papa, I also could play a decent game. Harry and I had agreed before we came that whist would be safest.

Lady Marsham flashed a set of yellow teeth at me, and at the same time she beckoned to a man who was lounging against the fireplace. He came to join us, and Lady Marsham introduced him as Captain Horatio Burr.

He was a middle-aged man with a dissipated-looking face, and he spoke with an Irish accent. I knew his type immediately. Papa would not have approved of my associating with him.

I nodded graciously. "How do you do, Captain Burr," I said.

"If you would like to play whist, Captain Burr and I will be happy to oblige you," my hostess said.

"That would be lovely," I said to Lady Marsham's raddled face.

The four of us repaired to an unoccupied table near the window. I sat, making certain that my skirt did not touch the brown velvet drapes, which looked decidedly unclean, and glanced around the room while Captain Burr dealt the first hand. I did not see anyone I recognized. Thank God.

Captain Burr turned up the last card. "Spades are trump," he said. "You have the first bid, Lady Greystone."

I opened my hand, assessed my cards, and said, "One heart."

We had been playing for perhaps half an hour when Chalmers finally came in. I had been getting excellent hands, which Harry expertly led into every chance he had. We were winning, which is always a very pleasant sensation.

I had just taken a trick and was scooping up the cards when I felt Harry's foot press mine under the table. I glanced toward the door and saw Chalmers.

We finished the game, and out of the corner of my eye I could see Chalmers crossing the stained Turkish carpet in our direction. When the last trick had been taken, and Harry was adding the money to the pile already in front of him, Lady Marsham affected to notice the man who was standing by our table.

"Mr. Chalmers," she said. "La, you startled me, sir!"

"Oh, Harry," I said with girlish enthusiasm, "is this your friend Mr. Chalmers?"

"Indeed it is, Kate," he replied, and proceeded to introduce us.

"We have met once before, Lady Greystone," Chalmers said gallantly. "Don't you remember? In Hyde Park? You had just had an . . . accident . . . with your horse."

I laughed gaily. "Oh my, yes. I fell off, you mean. It was so embarrassing." I turned to Lady Marsham and recounted the incident.

Captain Burr stood up. "Would you like to take my place, Chalmers?"

The worm gave a toothy smile. "Thank you, Burr." He sat down and the Irishman took himself off. "You are playing whist?" he asked.

"Yes." I gave him a big-eyed look. "Harry is so good at whist."

Lady Marsham said, "You are the one who has been drawing the cards this afternoon, Lady Greystone."

"I have always been a very lucky person," I said, and watched from under my lashes as Chalmers and Lady Marsham exchanged a satisfied smile.

Harry and I ended up winners on the afternoon, though the cards began to flow more evenly after Chalmers had sat down with us. The three of us exited together, and Harry left me alone with Chalmers while he went off to summon a cab.

"You appear to be a man of the world, Mr. Chalmers," I said. "I wonder if you might know any place in London where I could play E.O.?"

E.O., or Even-Odd, was an illegal game of chance in which bettors placed wagers as a wheel was spun. Wheel games were not available in any reputable club; to play E.O. one had to go to a hell.

The worm's eyes positively glittered. "Do you like to play E.O., Lady Greystone?" he asked.

"I've never played it before," I confessed, "but I really am a very lucky person, Mr. Chalmers. I am certain that I would win at E.O."

His teeth flashed. They were slightly pointed—just like in the picture I had once seen of a shark. He said, "I am afraid that in order to play E.O. I would have to take you to a place where ladies don't usually go."

I gave him my most dazzling smile. This was a mistake, but I didn't realize it until later. "How exciting," I said. "Can we go tomorrow night?"

"Of course," he replied. "I should be delighted to be your escort, Lady Greystone."

"You won't tell my husband, will you, Mr. Chalmers?" I pouted. "Greystone is such a bore about gambling."

He couldn't promise me fast enough that he wouldn't breathe a word of the adventure to Adrian. He was such an obvious villain that I wondered how Harry could possibly have been taken in by him.

We made hurried arrangements for the following evening, and then Harry returned with a cab. Chalmers bowed over my hand. Harry handed me into the cab. Chalmers left. Harry got in after me and I told him triumphantly, "We're on!"

The reason I did not ask Chalmers to take me to the hell that very evening was that I was engaged to go to Almack's with Caroline. Almack's was the club from which I had been so firmly excluded the season before. I had been immensely gratified when Caroline told me she had procured vouchers for me, but in truth the august assembly rooms had turned out to be something of a bore.

Caroline loved to go. "You know I adore Edward," she

said to me that evening as the Greystone coach rumbled out of Grosvenor Square on its way to King Street, where Almack's was located, "but I must confess, Kate, that it has been delightful meeting so many of my old beaux! Last night Freddie Brixton quite assured me that I had broken his heart when I married Ashley."

"Did you really break his heart?" I asked.

Her light laughter rippled through the enclosed space. "Of course not! It's a game, Kate. That's why it is such fun."

I leaned my head back against the blue velvet seat cushion and looked at her out of the side of my eyes. "What about Charlwood?" I asked. I had never before broached this subject with her, but the opportunity was just too inviting to ignore. "Was it a game with him, Caroline?"

All the laughter left her face. "No," she said abruptly. "No, with Charlwood it wasn't a game."

"He's in London." I turned my head slightly so that I could look at her. "I saw him the other night."

Her white-gloved hands gripped each other in her lap. "I did not know that." She was staring straight ahead, at the empty seat opposite us. "Where did you see him, Kate?"

"At the Bridgewater ball."

"Did . . . did Adrian see him, too?"

"They met. Sparks flew, but no one got hurt. There were a lot of people looking on."

She said despairingly, "Dear God in heaven, what a sorry mess this has turned out to be." She turned her head slowly, as if it ached, and looked at me. "I assume you know the story?"

"I know that you once tried to elope with him and that Adrian brought you home. I know that Charlwood has never forgiven Adrian, and that is why he forced Adrian to marry me."

Caroline drew a deep breath. "Yes . . . well . . . that's about it."

"I think Charlwood still loves you, Caroline," I said.

She was looking very distressed. "It's been so long . . . he can't."

"I think he does."

The coach wheel went over a stone in the road, and we both bounced. When we had righted ourselves, Caroline said, "He has never married?"

"No."

She was quiet.

I asked, "Did you love him, Caroline?"

She closed her eyes and I didn't think she was going to answer. But finally she sighed and said, "He was such an unhappy boy, Kate. There was no one at all who cared about him. He was angry and bitter, and he struck out at other people because he was so unhappy himself. I understood that, you see, because I was unhappy, too."

I said, "From what Harry has told me, your own home life was scarcely more pleasant than Charlwood's."

"My father was a monster." Her voice was deeply bitter. "But no matter how bad things got, Harry and I always had Adrian. Martin was not so fortunate. He adored his sister, but she ran away to get married and left him behind."

I tried to defend my mother. "She could not have taken him even had she wanted to."

She shrugged. "I suppose not."

"Did you love him, Caroline?" I repeated.

She sighed again. "Not enough. I ran away with him because I felt so sorry for him, but we hadn't gone very far before I began to wish I hadn't done it. I have to confess that I was very glad when Adrian took the decision out of my hands."

"You were only sixteen," I said.

"Yes. I wanted to be happy, Kate. I didn't want to take on Martin's unhappiness as well as my own." She stared out the window at the empty street. "I made my come-out when I was seventeen, and when I was eighteen I married Edward." She turned back to me. "And I have been happy. I don't want to see Martin again, Kate. I don't want to be made to feel guilty."

I said awkwardly, "You shouldn't feel guilty, Caroline."

"I know I failed him."

"You were too young. You shouldn't feel that way."

She shook her head in denial. "He has turned into a very bitter man, and I could have saved him from that. He loved me, you see. He was older than I was, and he loved me more than I loved him."

The carriage horses slowed to a walk. I looked out the window and saw that we were approaching the turn into King Street. I asked Caroline the question that had been on my mind for a while. "But why did Charlwood have to elope with you, Caroline? Surely he was an eligible match—certainly every matchmaking mama in London thinks that he is! Harry once told me that your fathers didn't get on, but certainly economic interest would have prevailed, given time."

She shook her head. "Our fathers hated each other, Kate. One of them was a bigger bastard than the other, and they had argued years before over some stupid thing or other. My father would never have allowed Martin to marry me." There was a distinct note of pain in her voice as she added, "Martin fancied us as Romeo and Juliet, but I am not the stuff that heroines are made of."

"Juliet was a tragic heroine, and you wanted to be happy," I said. "Don't blame yourself for that, Caroline."

There was another coach in front of the sanctified doors of Almack's, and we had to wait. I said, "Perhaps if Adrian realized that Uncle Martin truly loved you, he would not be so harsh on him." The carriage before us had evidently emptied out, because we began to roll forward. "In fact, considering the similarity of their home lives, I should have thought that he would have had some fellow feeling for Uncle Martin."

"My brother is incapable of understanding a temperament like Martin's," Caroline replied as the carriage came to a halt. She gave me a half-smile as she gathered her shawl around her shoulders. "Adrian is so splendidly, competently male. Not even my father could tarnish him. He could never understand the deep insecurities of a man like Martin."

A footman opened the carriage door and put down the portable steps. Caroline made a graceful exit from the carriage and I came after her, my brain humming with all the new information I had just received.

There had been a debate in the House of Lords that evening about once more scaling down the Army of Occupation, and when the session broke up at about ten-thirty a whole wave of husbands, fathers, and brothers descended upon Almack's. Caroline's husband, Edward, was the one who came for us. Adrian, he said, had gone along to White's with a few of Wellington's other old aides to discuss the session.

"There's a whole section of the Lords that wants to keep on grinding French noses into their loss," he told us, "but there seems to be enough peers who realize that the expense of keeping so many men abroad is prohibitive. Adrian is optimistic that things will go our way."

I nodded, but I have to confess that my attention was on something else. The Marquis of Stade had just walked into the room.

"Do you know Stade?" I asked Edward.

He looked surprised at this abrupt change of subject, but answered readily enough, "Not very well. I know you despise me for it, Kate, but I really am far more interested in cows than I am in horses, and Stade is definitely a horse man."

"Of course I don't despise you, Edward!" My eyes hadn't left Stade. "Is that Barbury he is with?"

"I think so."

Sir Charles Barbury was the perpetual president of the Jockey Club, the inner circle of men that virtually ran horse racing in England. It was a very prestigious group. Papa had once said it was easier to marry an Italian princess than it was to be admitted into the Jockey Club.

"I wonder what they're doing at Almack's," I muttered. Almack's, with its pallid offerings of lemonade and tea, seemed far too tame a place for the sport and gaming-mad gentlemen of the Jockey Club.

"Sir Charles has a *tendre* for Mrs. Welton," Caroline said. "And Mrs. Welton is always at Almack's, because she is launching her husband's niece this season."

Well, that effectively explained the presence of Barbury. Stade, I supposed, was here because he had accompanied Barbury. Stade was *not* a member of the Jockey Club, although everyone knew that he longed to become one.

As I watched, Barbury's eyes alighted upon a dark-haired woman wearing a pale blue satin dress. He said something to Stade, then moved to join the woman, who welcomed him with an extremely cordial smile. Stade looked around the crowded room. His eyes found mine and stopped. For a long moment we stared at each other across the room.

Murderer, I thought.

A voice at my ear said, "I wonder if I might have this dance, Lady Greystone?"

It was Mr. Cruick, a very wealthy middle-aged gentleman who had a stud farm near Newmarket. He had, in fact, come to my father's funeral. He was also a member of the Jockey Club.

I smiled. "Mr Cruick! How lovely to see you. But whatever are you doing in a boring place like Almack's?"

"Pushing off my daughter, my dear," he said with a sigh. "We had her ball at the start of the Season, but then my best broodmare was due to foal, so of course I went home. The wife insisted that I come back, however, so here I have been, wasting all these days of good weather in London. I'll be going back to Newmarket for the Second Spring Meeting, of course. Told the wife I didn't care if I missed Bella's marriage, that nothing would stop me from watching the running of the Guineas."

I nodded sympathetically, and he looked with apprehension toward the dance floor. "I hope this isn't one of these newfangled waltzes, my dear. I don't want to step all over your toes."

I grinned. "Would you like to sit this one out with me, Mr. Cruick? I see two chairs over there that we could nobble."

He beamed. "Just the thing, Lady Greystone!" We moved together toward the chairs and he said, as if he were confiding a great secret, "Dancing ain't my strongest suit."

We sat, and as I arranged my skirt, I said, "I just saw Stade come in with Sir Charles Barbury. His colt, Castle Rook, is sure to be the heavy favorite to take the Guineas this year."

Mr. Cruick looked gloomy. "I'm afraid so, Lady Greystone. I have a colt running myself, and he's one the best I've ever bred, but those Alcazar colts are simply outstanding."

"They have certainly been doing well."

"Can't figure it out," Mr. Cruick muttered. "Horse was mediocre at best when he was running."

The music started, and it was indeed a waltz. I watched the elegantly twirling couples and said innocently, "I didn't realize that Stade was a member of the Jockey Club."

"He ain't," came the swift reply. "He's been up for membership twice and been blackballed twice."

I showed well-feigned surprise. "Blackballed? Good heavens, he's a marquis!"

"A title alone don't mean a man ain't a bounder," pronounced Mr. Cruick, whose grandfather had been a duke.

I could feel Stade still watching me from across the room. Ignoring him, I asked, "Is there anything known to his disrepute?"

"He was almost barred from racing a few years ago," Mr. Cruick confided. "There was an incident where a horse of his lost a race he should have won and then came back the next day to beat a well-backed favorite handily. The favorite was a horse of mine, as a matter of fact. Questions were raised. The official verdict was that the jockey was to blame, not Stade."

"But enough people had doubts to get him blackballed?"

"Precisely, my dear."

"He and Sir Charles Barbury seemed very friendly," I said tentatively.

"I know." My partner looked gloomy again. "It takes two blackballs out of nine to reject a membership application, and Barbury and I have been the two who have consistently blackballed Stade."

"Oh."

"I've heard he promised that Barbury could breed one of his top mares to Alcazar," Mr. Cruick went on.

We looked at each other. Nothing more needed to be said.

All in all, I found my conversation with Mr. Cruick extremely satisfying. It confirmed my own belief that once the truth about Alcazar came out, the Jockey Club would ban Stade from racing. They could do it. A few years ago they had run the Regent himself off the turf. Stade would be a bagatelle after that.

It would destroy Stade, and give me my revenge for Papa. Papa would have loved it.

The waltz ended and my partner for the next set, a very tedious young man who had decided to be in love with me, made his appearance and dragged me away from my fascinating conversation with Mr. Cruick.

We left Almack's early, as Caroline had developed a headache. I felt a pang of guilt that I had brought it on with my questions about Uncle Martin, but on the whole I thought it was for the best that she be prepared for the meeting that I knew must be in her immediate future.

CHAPTER
eighteen

"What does one wear to a gambling hell?" I asked Harry late the following afternoon.

He groaned. "Something that disguises you, Kate. Ladies aren't supposed to *go* to gambling hells."

I was annoyed. "I will be as discreet as possible. I certainly don't wish anyone to recognize me, Harry." I ran over my wardrobe in my mind. "I have an extremely plain rose-colored evening dress. Would that be appropriate?"

"Do you have a cloak with a hood?"

"Yes."

"Wear that," he recommended. "And keep the hood pulled up so that no one can see those eyes of yours."

I asked sweetly, "You don't think that people will remark upon a cloaked and hooded lady playing E.O.?"

"They may remark upon you, Kate, but as long as they don't know who you are, we'll be safe. We don't want somebody running to Adrian with the tale of having seen his wife in a gambling hell."

I shuddered at the thought. "We certainly don't."

"Wear the cloak," Harry advised, and I said that I would.

Needless to say, Mr. Chalmers could hardly come to the house to call for me, so I arranged to meet him at the theater. Harry told Adrian he was taking me to see Kean do *Richard the Third*, and Harry and I did actually sit through the first act of the play before we slipped out to meet Chalmers in the vestibule. Then I got in a cab with Chalmers, and Harry got in another cab to go and steal back his IOUs.

From the moment that I got in the cab, I had qualms about the evening. For one thing, the worm sat much too close to me. I kept sliding toward the door, and he kept following, and by the time we finally arrived at the hell on St. James Square, I was pressed up against the side of the cab. I couldn't slap him and tell the cab to take me home, because I had to keep him occupied while Harry robbed his desk. I got out feeling distinctly flustered.

Chalmers gave me his shark smile and offered his arm. I hated to touch him, but it was for Harry. I took his arm and let him lead me to the freshly painted door of a perfectly innocuous-looking brick building. For some reason, the clean paint on the door made me feel better.

Chalmers knocked and the door was opened by one of the most enormous men I had ever seen in my life. He was as tall as Adrian, but he was wide all the way up and down. He was *huge.* "Good evening, Mr. Chalmers," he said in a voice that came directly from the London streets.

"Good evening, Jem. I hope the E.O. wheel is well-oiled tonight, for I've brought someone who wants to play."

The huge man grinned at me. He had no teeth.

I pulled the hood of my cloak farther forward, and we went in.

The first thing I noticed was the unappetizing smell of mingled gin and beer and wine and male sweat. I shot a swift glance around the room, which was filled with men in green eyeshades playing at cards or dice around green-baize-covered tables, and saw to my dismay that there were only three other females present, and I could tell from their dresses that they were not ladies. One of them looked at me and sneered. The whole thing was even worse than I had imagined.

"Damn," I muttered under my breath. Adrian would murder me if he ever found out about this.

"The E.O. table is this way, my dear," Chalmers said

smoothly. I resented the "my dear," but I could hardly demand that he call me Lady Greystone.

"What time is it, Mr. Chalmers?" I asked.

He took out his watch. "Nine-thirty."

Harry was supposed to come and get me after he left Chalmers's lodging. We had figured that he should be able to make it to St. James Square by ten-thirty. "Just play E.O. for an hour, Kate, and then I'll fetch you home," he had said.

I squared my shoulders and said bravely, "I can hardly wait to play."

It took me exactly one half hour to lose all the money I had come with. I bet odds eight times in a row, and evens came up eight times in a row. Then I switched to evens, and what came up? Odds!

The men gathered around the table commiserated with me on my bad luck.

"I'm afraid I haven't any more money," I said to Chalmers.

He looked surprised. I suppose what I had lost seemed paltry to him, but it represented all the money Harry and I had won the previous afternoon at whist, plus the remainder of my quarter's allowance.

Chalmers's surprised look was quickly followed by one of his shark's smiles. "Allow me to procure you some re-freshment, my dear," he said. "The luck is sure to change."

I accepted the offer of refreshments, because I had an-other half an hour to waste until I could look for Harry to res-cue me. I was not happy when Chalmers escorted me down the hall and into a small, deserted salon, but neither did I want to spend any more time than was necessary in the view of the denizens of that disgusting hell.

"You can take off your cloak now, Lady Greystone," Chalmers purred. "Make yourself comfortable and I will pour you some wine."

The only seating in the room was two small sofas, which faced each other on either side of the fireplace, with a table between them. I left my cloak on, sat squarely in the middle of one sofa, and folded my hands. "I do not drink wine, Mr. Chalmers," I said. "I would like some tea."

"This isn't Almack's my dear," he said. "We don't serve tea." I found that "we" very interesting. Evidently Harry had been right when he surmised that Chalmers was in partnership with the owners.

"Well, lemonade, then." It cost me some effort, but I did not twist my hands nervously in my lap.

He shrugged and went to the bellpull. After a minute, a thin, pimply-faced boy came into the room, and Chalmers ordered lemonade for me. Then he poured a glass of wine for himself.

The lemonade came, the boy left, and Chalmers closed the door behind him. We were alone.

Damn, I thought. *Now I'm really in the soup.*

He put the lemonade down on the table, sat next to me on the sofa, and lifted a hand to push back the hood of my cloak. "I can quite understand that you don't want anyone in the room outside to recognize you, Lady Greystone," he said, "but surely there is little point in hiding your lovely face from me?"

"I'm cold," I said.

The worm actually touched my cheek. It took heroic self-control on my part to keep from flinching away from him. "You don't feel cold to me," he said.

I began to inch toward the end of the sofa.

"If you would like to continue to play E.O., Lady Greystone, I will be happy to advance you the money," he said.

"That is very nice of you, Mr. Chalmers," I moved a few more inches, "but I am afraid that I would be unable to pay you back. I've gone through all of my quarter's allowance, and I can't possibly ask my husband for more money."

"You'll win," he said confidently. He moved after me.

"But what if I don't?"

His eyes narrowed in a manner I didn't like at all. "There is another way you could pay me back, my dear," he said, "and your husband wouldn't have to know a thing about it."

By now he had me pressed up against the arm of the sofa. He reached an arm in front of me, neatly trapping me in the corner. "Let me up, Mr. Chalmers," I said warningly.

He leaned forward so that his face was very close to mine. "Kate," he said huskily. "You are so beautiful. You can play E.O. to your heart's content, my dear, and all you have to do in return is be kind to me."

I couldn't believe what I was hearing. His face was coming even closer, and I realized he was going to kiss me.

Revulsion galvanized me into action. I put the palm of my hand under his chin and shoved hard. I may be small, but I am strong. One cannot regularly ride a thousand pounds of horse in a collected frame without developing back muscles.

The worm was thrown off balance, and I slipped under his arm and ran to the door. I heard him curse as I lifted the latch. I slammed the door closed behind me and gave a quick look up and down the corridor.

I thought briefly about trying to escape out the back way, but then I heard Chalmers rattling the latch. I decided that safety lay in numbers, and raced up the hallway to the playing room.

As I entered on one side of the room, the door on the opposite side was opening to admit a new patron. *Please God,* I prayed, *let it be Harry.*

The new patron had fair hair like Harry, but he was considerably larger.

It was Adrian.

Jem, the huge, toothless doorkeeper, took one look at him, growled, "Not tonight, my lord," and stepped into his path. Adrian pushed him aside as if he weighed no more than little Ned. Across the smelly, crowded room, his eyes had found me.

"It's Greystone!"

The name flew around the tables, and even the hands of the dealers stilled. Every eye watched as Adrian strode across that polluted room like the Archangel Michael blazing through the legions of hell. From close behind me I heard a sharp intake of breath, and then the sound of feet hastily retreating in the opposite direction. The worm had wisely chosen to make himself scarce.

Adrian stopped in front of me and said softly, "What the bloody hell are you doing here?"

His nostrils were white. His gray eyes were glittering. He was furious, and I couldn't say I blamed him.

"I'm ready to leave," I said.

"You're damn right you're ready to leave," he said.

He never swore in front of me. He had to be absolutely livid.

"Come on," he said. His voice was still too soft to be heard by anyone but me, but he seemed to be talking through his teeth. "And pull up that bloody hood!"

I pulled the hood up hastily, and he grabbed my hand, put it on his arm, and held it there, as if he was afraid I was going to escape. Then he strode back toward the door, forgetting to moderate his stride to mine. I half ran, half skipped beside him, trying to keep up.

Jem was waiting beside the door. He opened it, and as Adrian dragged me out into the street, I distinctly heard him chuckle.

There was a cab waiting for us outside. Adrian opened the door, practically threw me in, and gave our address to the driver. Then he followed me, closing the cab door firmly behind him. The driver clucked to his horse, and the cab began to move.

I was alone with my furious husband.

I desperately tried to think of some reason to account for my presence at the hell that would not involve Harry. I am usually inventive, but at the moment I couldn't think of a thing.

The best defense is a good offense, Papa had always said. I took his advice and launched the first shot, demanding, "How did you know I was there?"

"Bonds saw you getting into a cab with Chalmers outside of Drury Lane." He was still talking through his teeth in that ominous fashion. "He came to White's to tell me. Thought I should know that my wife was getting into bad company."

I had met Mr. Bonds. He was an old friend of Adrian's from Eton.

"I had my hood up," I said suspiciously. "How did he know it was I?"

"He knew you were my wife, just as all the men in that bloody hell knew you were my wife!"

I was infuriated. "They didn't know until you came charging in there like an enraged lion and dragged me out! I had my hood up the whole time I was there!"

"You didn't have your hood up when I saw you!"

I remembered how that had come about. "That Chalmers is a very nasty man, Adrian," I said. "You won't believe what he said to me."

"Oh, yes, I would."

"No, listen to this." I leaned toward him earnestly. "I lost all my money in the first half hour I was there, you see, and so I told him I couldn't play any more. He offered to loan me money if I wanted to continue to bet."

He said grimly, "Kate, that is the oldest trick in the book."

"I know that! I had no intention of taking his money. I told him I couldn't, that I had no way of paying him back. And then he said that I could lose as much money as I wanted, so long as I was kind to him. Can you believe that, Adrian? The disgusting worm wanted me to sleep with him!"

Just remembering that interview made me indignant. "He has teeth just like a shark," I added.

There was a short silence. It was too dark inside the cab

for me to see his face, so I didn't know how he was taking this revelation.

"And what did you do after he made this disgusting proposition?" he asked finally. I thought his voice sounded slightly less grim than it had before. Still, I thought it would be wise to omit the part about Chalmers trying to kiss me.

"I ran away," I said. "I had just come back into the gaming room, when you arrived." I made my voice as conciliating as possible. "I must say, my lord, that I was extremely glad to see you."

Silence.

"I'll never go there again," I said. "It was a horrible place."

He grunted.

"Do you think the despicable Chalmers has made that proposition to other women?" I asked.

"I have no doubt that he has. And been accepted, too."

I shuddered.

His anger appeared to have abated somewhat, and we finished the drive in silence. The night footman opened the door for us, and I was beginning to hope that perhaps Adrian was satisfied that I was properly repentant and would not pursue the matter further, when he said, "Come into the library, Kate. I want to talk to you."

My heart sank.

I trailed behind him down the corridor to the teak-paneled library, where a fire was burning and the lamps were lit. He gestured me to one of the comfortable old green velvet chairs in front of the fireplace, and as I sat down he went to pour a glass of wine for himself. I looked at the decanter a little wistfully. I could have used a little wine myself.

"Would you like tea?" Adrian asked me courteously.

I shook my head. It was probably better to get this over with as quickly as possible.

He came to sit in the other chair, took a sip of his wine, and regarded me out of hooded eyes. "What you have not told me, Kate," he said, "is why you went to that hell in the first place."

I bit my lip and nervously smoothed my taffeta skirt. I still couldn't think of a reason that wouldn't involve Harry.

Adrian went on, "You told me you were going to the theater with Harry and instead you met Chalmers and went with him to a gambling hell. You obviously had an assignation with him. Was it the excitement of going somewhere illicit that drew you, Kate? Or were you so eager to gamble that you had to go to a place where you thought I would not hear about it?"

His words cut me to the heart. It wasn't fair to let him think that he was married to a woman who had so little regard for his name; a woman who was nothing but a reckless gamester, a sensation-seeker. He had been so good to me; he didn't deserve that. I was going to have to sacrifice Harry.

I bent my head, drew a deep breath, and told him what had happened.

When I finished the only sounds in the room were the crackling of the fire and the beating of my heart. When Adrian spoke at last, his voice was ominously quiet: "So Harry let you go alone to that hell with Chalmers."

I flew to poor Harry's defense. "It was only for an hour, Adrian! Harry said I would probably win, because that's what they do to lure new pigeons into continuing to play once they start to lose. It was only because I lost all my money so quickly that I got cozened into being alone with Chalmers." A thought struck me, and I frowned. "Do you think he fixed it so that I would lose?"

"Of course he fixed it, Kate." The grim note was back in his voice. "He couldn't wait to get his hands on you."

"Well, Harry wasn't to know that," I said hastily. "And I got away from Chalmers and would have waited safely in the gaming room for Harry to arrive. It all would have gone perfectly smoothly if that wretched Mr. Bonds had not seen me and come tattling to you!"

He got up and went over to the decanter to pour himself another glass of wine. I said to his back, "Adrian, Harry only went along with my scheme because he was so anxious to keep the tale of his stupidity from you."

"I did not think I was such an ogre," my husband said.

"No!" I jumped to my feet. "You don't understand, Adrian! It is precisely because he loves you so much, and admires you so much, that he did not want to look small in your eyes. Don't you see? Can't you understand what it must be like to have *you* for an older brother?"

"If he loves me so much, then he should have trusted me not to think badly of him." Adrian turned to look at me, his face very somber. "And he should never, never have let you go to that hell."

He didn't understand.

Suddenly the door opened, and Harry was there on the threshold. His hair was ruffled, his neckcloth was disordered, and there was dirt on the knees of his beige breeches. His eyes flew to me. "Kate, are you all right?"

I tried to smile, but it was not very successful. "I am fine, Harry."

His eyes moved slowly to his brother. I could see him brace himself. "You brought her home, Adrian?"

"Bonds saw her getting into the cab with Chalmers and came to tell me," Adrian said.

Harry closed the door and stepped forward into the lamplight. He was very pale.

"Did you get your vowels?" Adrian asked.

Harry swallowed. "Yes." His eyes flicked briefly to me and then back to his brother.

I said, "I'm tired. I'm going up to bed."

Neither man said a word as I walked to the door. I felt absolutely wretched. I had only been trying to help, but my clever scheme had made all of us miserable.

I lay awake for most of the night, but Adrian never came.

CHAPTER
nineteen

WHEN I SAW HARRY THE FOLLOWING MORNING AT breakfast, he was very subdued. I tried to apologize for having peached on him to Adrian, but he just shook his head and said that I had been right to do as I did.

He looked so miserable that I tried to cheer him up. "Well, at least you got your vowels back," I said brightly. "The evening wasn't a complete loss."

He drank some coffee, gave me a pale smile, and agreed.

Breakfast was always set out on the sideboard so that people could help themselves, and I took a muffin and a cup of coffee and went to sit across the table from Harry. "If it wasn't for that nosey parker Bonds, everything would have gone perfectly," I said.

"No." He shook his head. "Adrian was right, Kate. I should never have allowed you to be alone with Chalmers. I don't know what I was thinking of."

I was beginning to get annoyed. "The two of you act as if I were a helpless child! I am perfectly capable of taking care of myself, Harry."

"Adrian told me that Chalmers wanted you to sleep with him," Harry said bluntly.

"Well, it's not as if I was going to do it!"

"I know that. But it can't have been pleasant for you, Kate."

It hadn't been, but I had survived. I sighed and looked

with some distaste at my coffee and muffin. The smell of the food was making me feel faintly nauseated.

I said, "I was only trying to help you, Harry, and instead I've made the situation between you and Adrian worse. I am so sorry. Was he very angry with you?"

"He wasn't angry. Considering the circumstances, he was quite restrained." Harry's voice held a note that I couldn't immediately identify. "He told me that in the future, if I came up against something I couldn't deal with, that I was to come to him; that he would help me and I wasn't to worry about him making judgments about my competency."

I placed the note now. It was bitterness.

"Oh dear," I said.

"He was very understanding," Harry said.

Damn.

"If you'll excuse me now," Harry said, "I have an appointment." Men always had an appointment when they didn't want to talk to you anymore.

I watched him leave the breakfast room and thought grimly that if Adrian kept on being this understanding he was going to drive Harry into doing something dangerous.

I was tired and depressed and in no mood for a garden party, but that was what was on the afternoon's agenda for me and Caroline. Every year the Marchioness of Silchester had a garden party at her home on the Thames, and all the most fashionable people in the *ton* attended. Since the Countess of Greystone must always be counted as one of the most fashionable people, I had been invited. After Harry had gone out I thought briefly about crying off, but since my own company promised to be pretty dismal, I decided it would be better if I kept myself occupied. I went.

Silchester House was only a few miles outside of London, but the atmosphere was distinctly countryish. Fortunately the day was warm and sunny, so we were able to be outdoors on the Irish-green lawn that had been landscaped into three distinct terraces, the last one reaching right to the river's edge. There was even boating available if one so desired.

Caroline and I were escorted by Edward, and at the last minute Louisa decided to accompany us, as Paddy was spending the day at the Tattersall horse sales. Adrian was supposed to have come as well, but he left word with Walters that something unexpected had come up and we would have to go to the garden party without him.

Another of those convenient appointments, I thought mournfully.

We alighted from the carriage at the front of the house, then walked through to the drawing room where the French doors were standing open. The Marchioness was receiving her guests out on the stone terrace.

"I always have a beautiful day for my garden party," the Marchioness said smugly as she greeted us. "It is part of the Silchester tradition."

We smiled, and murmured polite compliments, and walked across the flower-banked terrace and down the stone stairs to join the people on the first stretch of lawn. It wasn't long before Edward had found someone to talk to about cows, and Caroline someone to trade baby stories with, and Louisa and I drifted along together, nodding vaguely to people we knew and not saying much.

I was wearing a bonnet, but the sun soon began to give me a headache. I said as much to Louisa.

"You don't look well, Kate," she replied sympathetically. "There is a rose garden at the side of the house. Why don't we go and sit under a tree?"

I agreed. It was true that I hadn't slept well, but this was not the first morning that I had woken up feeling unusually lethargic. I had actually taken a nap the previous afternoon before venturing out to the gaming hell. I hadn't napped since I was two!

"Was Paddy looking to buy something today, Louisa?" I

asked idly as we took seats on a pretty but not very comfortable stone bench that was placed beneath the shade of a spreading beech tree. The small garden was filled with all different varieties of rosebushes, and their scent perfumed the air.

"No," my cousin returned. "He merely wanted to get an idea of the prices that Tattersall was getting at his auctions."

I nodded, picked up a single pale pink petal that had been lying on the gravel at my feet, and smoothed it between my fingers.

"It's important that Paddy keep abreast of the market so that he knows what to ask for his own horses." Louisa sounded very knowledgeable. "He can't expect to get as much as Tattersall's does, of course, but on the other hand, he doesn't want to give his horses away."

I said with amused affection, "You have got it down wonderfully, Louisa."

Her cheeks flushed the same pretty pink color as the rose petal in my hand. "I . . . well, I have grown quite fond of Paddy, Kate," she said. "I know most people would consider him socially beneath me, but I really think he is the most . . . solid . . . man I have ever met."

"He's a wonderful man," I said. "He's loyal and affectionate and honest and kind . . ." I was running out of adjectives. "I have always considered him part of my family." I shot her a look. "I can see that he is very fond of you, Louisa."

I thought she would be pleased, but instead she looked downcast. "I think he is, too, Kate. But I am afraid that nothing will ever come of it. He says his way of life is not suitable for a lady like myself."

"Well, it probably isn't," I said honestly.

"I would like it a lot better than spending the rest of my life drudging away for my sister-in-law!" Louisa said spiritedly.

She certainly had a point there.

I opened my mouth to tell her about Adrian's offer, but

then closed it again. He was so disappointed with me that he might not want people as closely connected to me as Louisa and Paddy living at Lambourn. I contented myself with saying merely, "I will talk to Adrian. If we can arrange some place permanent for Paddy to base his business, would you marry him?"

"Yes," Louisa said. She glowed.

I smoothed the rose petal between my fingers and repeated, "I will talk to Adrian."

We sat in the rose garden for another hour, and a great number of people stopped and talked to us as they drifted in and out. Finally I had to bestir myself to go to the house to use the ladies' withdrawing room. I was on my way into the house through the French doors when I ran into my uncle. He was coming out.

He saw me, and stopped as suddenly as if he had run into glass. "You," he said.

There didn't seem to be any appropriate reply to this, so I just nodded and asked rather feebly, "How are you, Uncle Martin?"

He came all the way out onto the terrace and stood beside me next to a great stone pot that was filled with azaleas. He said, "Is Greystone here with you?"

I sent up a brief prayer of thanks for Adrian's appointment. "No."

Charlwood's crystalline eyes glittered. "Is Caroline here?" he demanded next.

It took me but a split second to make up my mind about how I should answer him. "Yes," I said, "she is."

He turned away without another word, crossed the terrace to the stairs, and stood there, his eyes searching the people spread out below him, his auburn hair blazing in the bright sun. Then he ran down the stairs, disappearing from my view. Slowly I crossed the terrace to the stairs and looked below myself.

I saw my uncle weaving his way in and out of the crowd of people, heading for the second flight of stairs that led down to the next terrace. I looked at the second terrace and saw the straw bonnet with blue ribbons that I knew Caroline was wearing.

She had to meet him sometime, I thought, and at least Edward was with her today. I went slowly back across the terrace and into the house to find the ladies' withdrawing room.

Caroline was very quiet on the way home in the coach, and Edward looked distinctly grim around the mouth. Louisa stared dreamily out the window next to her, probably looking forward to a blissful future with Paddy. It was a silent ride.

When we reached home, Caroline said to me in a low voice, "I'll come up to your dressing room with you for a moment, Kate, if you don't mind."

"Of course I don't mind," I replied instantly. I might be tired and depressed, but I wasn't dead. I was dying to know how her meeting with Charlwood had gone.

She followed me into my dressing room and waited patiently while I told Jeanette that I would ring when I needed her. As soon as the door had closed behind my maid, Caroline collapsed into a chair and said, "I met Martin."

I moved to the chaise longue and perched on the edge of it. "I thought you might have," I said.

"Did you see him too?"

"Briefly."

She shut her eyes. "He's changed, Kate," she said.

"Has he?"

"Yes." She opened her eyes and gave me a very troubled look. "He . . . he almost frightened me."

My attention sharpened. "What happened?"

She frowned. "It wasn't anything very dramatic, Kate. He came up while I was with a group of other people and asked if he could speak to me. We walked down to the edge of the river, threw bread to the ducks, and talked." She chewed on her lip. "It wasn't even what he said that frightened me; it was more the way he looked."

I slipped off my shoes and flexed my tired feet. "What did you talk about?"

"Oh, he asked me if I was happy. I said that I was very happy, that I had two wonderful children." Her eyes met mine. "Then he asked me about Edward."

I nodded slowly.

"He asked me if I loved him."

"And what did you say?"

"I said that I loved him very much." She grimaced painfully. "Martin didn't say anything, Kate, but he looked . . . oh, frightening, somehow. So then I said all kinds of banal things about time healing all wounds, and that he would find someone to love as much as I loved Edward if he would only let himself. I babbled on and on, because he made me so *nervous.*"

I nodded. I knew exactly how nervous Charlwood could make one feel.

Caroline said, "I told him that he had to forget about me and go on to live his own life. That he had to let go of the past."

"That was exactly the right thing to say," I assured her.

"He said that he thought of me all the time, Kate, that he has never stopped loving me, and that he never would."

"Oh dear," I said feebly. I wasn't surprised.

Caroline was actually wringing her hands. "We were *children,* Kate! It isn't healthy for him to feel like this. It's as if he's become . . . warped."

"He is warped," I said sadly.

"It's all my fault," she wailed.

Slowly, I shook my head. "No," I said. "It's not your fault, Caroline. I have been thinking about Uncle Martin for a long time now, and there is really no excuse for his behavior."

Tears were dripping down Caroline's face. "He had such a wretched childhood . . . he was so unhappy . . ."

I said, "Think about this, Caroline. Adrian's childhood was just as terrible as Charlwood's—maybe even worse." I pushed down the rage I always felt when I thought about this, and said somberly, "Harry told me that your father used to beat him."

She nodded and sniffled loudly. "I think my father hated Adrian," she confided. "No matter how hard Papa tried, he could never make Adrian afraid."

I leaned a little forward. "And has Adrian turned out to be a bitter, hate-filled man?"

She shook her head, sniffled again, and began to search for a handkerchief.

I continued my interrogation. "If Adrian's elopement had been foiled, would he have sought revenge the way Charlwood has?"

Caroline blew her nose and said with absolute conviction, "Adrian would never have eloped. He would never have left Harry and me."

I pushed away the unpleasant thought that my mother had eloped and left *her* brother and said instead, "There is the difference between the two men. Adrian thinks of others. Charlwood thinks only of himself."

Caroline blew her nose once more and looked at me. A single teardrop clung to her lashes and shone like a diamond in the lamplight. "You don't understand, Kate," she said. "Martin *loved* me."

"He wanted you," I corrected. "If he loved you he would not have persuaded you into a clandestine elopement that could only have resulted in a terrible scandal. For God's sake, Caroline, how did he think you were going to live? His father was still alive. Your father was still alive. Under the circumstances, neither one of them would have given you an allowance! How was Uncle Martin planning to support you?"

"I don't know," Caroline said in a very small voice. "I never thought about those things."

"Of course you didn't. You were sixteen years old. But

Charlwood was twenty-one—a year older than Harry is now. And even Harry would not try anything so harebrained as eloping with a girl when he had no money!"

There was silence as she thought about this.

I said with conviction, "Uncle Martin may not have been dealt the best hand in life, but he has not played well with the cards he was given."

"Everything you say is true, Kate. I can see that." Another tear rolled down her cheek. "But that doesn't mean I still can't feel sorry for him."

I swung my shoeless feet up on the chaise longue, rested my head against the cushion, folded my hands on my chest, stared at the ceiling, and thought that Caroline's heart was kinder than mine.

CHAPTER
twenty

I WAS SO EXHAUSTED THAT NIGHT THAT I FELL DEEPLY asleep as soon as I put my head on the pillow, and I didn't awaken until late the following morning. I saw from the rumpled pillow next to me that Adrian had been to bed also, but I had been sleeping so deeply that I hadn't heard him come in or get up. I rolled into the big depression in the feather mattress that his body had left, curled up, and felt miserable. I hadn't seen or talked to him since the night he had brought me home from the gambling hell.

If only I didn't love him so much.

Impossible to keep the thought from running again and again through my mind. If only I didn't care, and we could have the kind of polite, discreet, undemanding marriage that I saw so many other aristocratic couples had. If only I could laugh at our misunderstandings and go blithely on my way, unencumbered by this painful baggage of passionate love.

I rubbed my temples, which ached as if I had drunk too much wine. It wasn't wine that was making me feel so wretched, however, it was depression. I shut my eyes and wondered if I would ever be truly happy again.

I was so depressed that I didn't even want to get up, and I asked Jeanette to bring a cup of tea to the bedroom for me. Most fashionable ladies had their breakfast in their rooms, but I had always thought this custom terribly degenerate. This morning, however, I just couldn't stomach the smells of the grilled kidneys and bacon that Harry and Adrian fancied in the morning.

The day crept by. I got Harry to accompany me to the park so I could exercise Elsa. Adrian and I hadn't had the horses out in four days, and she needed the exercise. The fresh air made me feel better too. I spent the afternoon playing cricket with Ned in the garden, and his childish good spirits helped to cheer me up.

We were engaged to go to a ball that evening at the Castlereaghs', and I knew that this was one party that Adrian would not excuse himself from attending. He might be deeply unhappy with the government, but he had real respect for Lord Castlereagh. Added to that was the fact that Lord Castlereagh's wife was one of the patronesses of Almack's, and to shun her ball would be a catastrophic mistake.

I paid a great deal more attention to my appearance that evening than I usually did. "I look so pale," I complained to Jeanette as I stared at myself in the dressing-table mirror. I leaned forward and pinched my cheeks. This was a great improvement. Now I looked as if I had just broken out in two giant measles.

"If you like, my lady, I will poot a leetle rouge on your cheeks," Jeanette said. "It is true that you are vairy pale."

"I'm indoors too much," I said crossly. "I look like a death's-head." I waved my hand. "Go ahead, Jeanette, and paint me up."

She took out a rabbit's foot, dipped it into a pot that she whisked out of one of the dressing-table drawers, and began to brush some colored powder onto my cheeks. "You are really wonderful, Jeanette," I said with admiration when she had finished. "I look so natural and healthy. One would never know that it was paint."

Jeanette didn't smile—she never smiled—but she looked pleased.

The door from the corridor opened and Adrian looked in.

"The rest of us are ready, Kate," he said. "Shall I send to have the carriage brought around?"

"Yes. I will be downstairs in a moment, my lord. You can send for the carriage."

He closed the door, and we listened to the sound of his footsteps as he ran lightly down the stairs. Now that the god had gone, the pretty sparkle died out of Jeanette's eyes, and she went to the wardrobe to get out my blue velvet evening cloak. I stood up, she put it around my shoulders, and I was ready to go.

Caroline and I were both silent during the drive, pretending to listen as the two men talked about some bill or other that was due to come up in front of the Lords that week. I sat next to Adrian and felt an ache in my heart so fierce that I wanted to cry. I was so close to him that when we rounded a turn my body actually touched his, but never had I felt so strongly that we were separated by a chasm I could not bridge.

We did not have to wait for very long to get into the Castlereaghs' house. Other hostesses measured their ball's success by the number of people who attended, but Lady Castlereagh was so arrogant and so powerful that she only invited the social crème de la crème to attend her own functions. And the chosen few always came.

We alighted. We relinquished our cloaks. We were greeted by the Castlereaghs. We were announced by the majordomo. We entered the ballroom.

The first person I saw was my uncle.

Adrian felt me falter, and his hand tightened under my elbow. He bent his head close to mine and murmured, "Are you all right, Kate?"

"Yes," I said. "I just did not expect to see Charlwood here."

"Bachelors with a title, an unencumbered estate, and a good income are invited everywhere," Adrian said dryly. "Even to the Castlereaghs'."

His hand was warm on my elbow, his head was still bent close to mine. I hadn't been this near him in days. I looked up at him and found that his eyes were on his sister.

"Caroline met him yesterday, at the Silchester garden party," I said a little flatly. "She'll be all right."

"I hope so." There was a worried line between his brows. I felt a stab of jealousy, and was ashamed of myself.

A voice said, "Greystone, you dog, surely you don't plan to monopolize your beautiful wife for the entire evening?"

We both looked around. It was Mr. Bonds, the busybody who had told Adrian about my appointment with Chalmers. I gave him a cold stare. He and Adrian exchanged a look over my head. I hated it when people did that.

"I'm sure that Kate will be happy to give you this dance, Jack," Adrian said.

I didn't want to dance with the perfidious Bonds, but I could hardly say this to one of my husband's oldest friends. "Of course, Mr. Bonds," I said in my chilliest voice. I would dance with him, but I didn't have to be nice to him.

Unfortunately, it was a waltz, so I had to talk to him. He started off by saying immediately, "I can perfectly understand that you are out of temper with me, Lady Greystone, but I was extremely worried when I saw you get into that cab with Chalmers. He has a very nasty reputation."

"That is quite all right, Mr. Bonds," I said frostily.

He looked sad. "You *are* out of temper with me."

I stared at his chin, which had a dimple right in the middle of it, and did not reply. We swept around the corner of the dance floor and began to waltz down the long side.

"Is there anything I can do to make amends?" he asked plaintively.

"You can keep your nose out of my affairs in the future," I said hotly.

"All right." His voice was meek. I glared up at him. There was a distinct twinkle in his hazel eyes. It reminded me that I had quite liked him before his nasty betrayal. "If I promise not to peach on you again, will you cry friends?"

"I knew exactly what I was doing," I said furiously. "Everything would have concluded perfectly smoothly if you had not gone running off to Adrian. Harry got his IOUs back and was at that disgusting hell not ten minutes after Adrian and I had left."

"The next time I will realize that you have matters under control," he said. "But I did not know what a formidable lady you are, and I panicked."

I sniffed.

"Most women would not have had the bottom to carry out so clever a scheme," he said.

"Well . . . I suppose I will forgive you this time," I said.

"I will be very grateful if you do."

I smiled at him. He really did have very nice eyes.

"Friends?" he asked.

"Friends," I agreed.

Stade was not at the ball, but Lady Mary Weston was there as well as Charlwood. The presence of two out of my three nemeses was more than enough to keep me occupied, and I worked hard trying to keep track of the whereabouts of both my uncle and Lady Mary while at the same time endeavoring to be civil to my own partners.

Fortunately, Adrian disappeared for a large gap of time during the middle of the ball, so he was not available for Lady Mary to get her claws into. I watched the door like a hawk, and as soon as he and Lord Castlereagh appeared on the edge of the dance floor, I snared Adrian. Lady Castlereagh was doing the same to her husband, and from the look on her face I gathered that she was not pleased that he had done a disappearing act for most of his own ball.

Adrian lifted his eyebrows. "I fear I am in Lady Castlereagh's black books," he said. "Are you angry with me too, Kate?"

I could hardly say that I was much happier that he had spent his time with Lord Castlereagh than with Lady Mary, so I just smiled and said, "I will forgive you if you'll dance this waltz with me."

"With pleasure," he replied, and led me to the floor.

It was heaven to be in his arms once more, and I floated as if on a cloud until I was assailed by the treacherous dizziness that I had been experiencing at odd moments of late. He noticed how my hand tightened on his shoulder, looked down at me, and asked if I was all right.

"It's warm in here and I feel a little dizzy," I confessed.

"You're pale." We were by the French doors that led out to the terrace, and he asked, "Would you like to get a little air?"

I nodded gratefully, and he put his arm around my shoulders, grasped my elbow, and steered me to the door and out into the blessedly cool night air. I inhaled deeply.

"Better?" he asked after a minute.

"Yes," I said. His arm was still around my shoulders, and I turned and leaned into him so that the full length of my body lay against his. I put my arms around his waist and rested my head against his chest. His heart beat steadily under my cheek, and I knew the exact second when it began to accelerate.

Thank God.

The relief I felt was so intense that my knees actually buckled with it. At least there was one way I could still reach him. I tilted my head back so that I could look up at him. His face wore the hard, unmistakable stamp of desire.

"Don't be angry with me, Adrian," I whispered. "I am so unhappy when you are angry with me."

"Sometimes, Kate," he said through his teeth, "I would like to kill you." And then he bent his head to mine.

His hands were pressed hard against my spine, holding me to him; his thumbs caressed the underside of my breasts. I was pressed so close to him that I could feel every line of his body, as he could feel mine. His mouth was hard, demanding, erotic, and I opened to him. We stood there on the Castlereaghs' terrace, not ten feet from the dancing couples in the ballroom, and kissed like lovers who were but a step away from tumbling into bed.

He lifted his head. "My God, Kate," he said. His voice was raw. "Let's go home."

My body ached for him. I nodded, and then, over his shoulder, I saw the man who was standing just outside the French doors, staring at us. The ballroom light shone through the glass panes, affording me a clear look at his face. It was white and shrunken-looking, and the eyes blazed in a way that was utterly terrifying.

Charlwood.

"What is it?" Adrian asked, and he put me aside so that he could swing around himself to see what I was looking at. But all he saw was my uncle's back as he retreated into the ballroom.

"It was Charlwood." I managed a reasonably normal tone of voice. "He caught us kissing."

Adrian made an impatient gesture and urged me toward the French doors. At the moment, Charlwood was not what was on his mind. But all the time that he was telling Caroline that I was not feeling well and he was taking me home and would send the carriage back for her and Edward, I kept seeing Charlwood's face as it had looked when he came upon me and Adrian.

The marriage he had forced upon Adrian had not turned out as Charlwood had envisioned. I was not a social pariah. If anything, I had turned out to be an asset to Adrian. I liked people, and in turn they tended to like me. The way was clear for Adrian to embark upon a great political career, if that was what he wished. And now Charlwood had come upon evidence that Adrian was not even personally unhappy in his marriage; that there was passion between him and his unwanted wife.

I wished very much that Charlwood had not seen us on the terrace. I had a foreboding that the scene he had witnessed just might be enough to push him into doing something that would not be to the benefit of any of us.

The ride home was mostly silent, but it was not the silence of discord. On the contrary, Adrian and I were cuddled next to each other in the corner of the carriage and he had his right arm around me, pressing me closely to his side. The dizziness that I felt had nothing to do with the air temperature and everything to do with the internal heat of desire that was steadily mounting inside my body.

It seemed an endless amount of time that we were enclosed together in the privacy of the dark carriage. As the horses trotted through the nighttime city streets, Adrian held me with his right hand, while his left slipped inside my velvet cloak and caressed my breasts. His fingers slid beneath the ivory silk of my bodice and rubbed gently back and forth across first one nipple and then the other. I could hear how ragged my own breathing sounded in the dark, and I couldn't stop myself from leaning forward to meet his touch.

By the time we got home I could feel the wet heat throbbing between my legs. His condition wasn't any better than mine, and we swept into the house and up the stairs to our bedroom in record time.

"Shall I call Jeanette to undress me?" I asked him as he closed the door behind us.

"No," he said. "Come over to the fire and I'll undress you myself."

Since the dress I was wearing had a long row of tiny pearl buttons, this task proved to be far more excruciating than he had anticipated. He cursed as his big fingers fumbled with the delicate fastenings. "Good God, Kate, a medieval chastity belt couldn't have provided any more protection than these beastly buttons!"

One of the buttons came completely off the dress and rolled across the blue rug. I laughed unsteadily.

"That's the last of them." He turned me around and pulled the dress down to my waist.

"I'll do the rest," I said.

"Don't bother with a nightdress." His eyes were glittering as his hands went to his own throat. He ripped off his neckcloth and started on his shirt.

I was trembling violently as I finished undressing. My clothes lay in a heap on the rug and my skin was flushed with the heat from the blazing fire. Adrian shed the last of his own garments, stepped toward me, and lifted me up against him. He kissed me, opening my mouth, and as I pressed my body along the length of his, the heat between us was scorching. My bare feet were swinging clear of the ground, and he carried me to the bed and laid me down, following after me, his hand moving to touch me where I most wanted to be touched.

"All right?" he asked, his voice hoarse.

"Yes," I said, and opened my legs to receive him.

He entered me, and I locked my arms around his neck and lifted my legs to encircle his waist. Great waves of sensation washed over me as I felt the powerful thrust of him inside me, intensifying the feeling, lifting me higher and ever higher still, until I thought the need might kill me. Then he reared back a little and drove once more, deep into the heart of me. The last wave splintered into a dazzling shower of starlight, and shock after shock of pleasure poured through me, and at the same time I felt the hot flood of his seed pour into my womb.

We lay locked together for a long time, waiting for our breathing to slow, for our heartbeats to return to normal. At last I let out a long, heartfelt sigh.

Still keeping us connected, he rolled onto his side so that his weight came off me. After a while he said, "Did that feel good?" I could hear the smile in his voice.

My eyes were heavy, and I closed them. "Um," I said drowsily.

"Tired?"

"Um," I said again.

He moved carefully within me, and I felt him grow bigger. His face was lying just inches away from mine on the pillow, and I lifted my lashes and looked into his eyes. He moved again, and I could feel my mouth open in surprise.

"Adrian?" I whispered.

His eyes were very dark. "How good does it feel, Kate?" he said. "Tell me how good it feels."

He moved again, and I felt the first wave of sensation begin to roll up through me. His eyes had narrowed. A strand of hair had caught in his lashes, and I puffed gently to blow it away. Another wave washed through me.

"Tell me," he said again. "How good does it feel?"

"Very good," I breathed. "It feels very good."

"God," he said. "I think I could do this all night, Kate."

"Just once more," I said. "I think that's all that I can stand."

He woke me early to see if I wanted to take the horses to the park, but when I sat up the room began to spin and I had to lie down again. "I haven't been feeling very well in the mornings lately, Adrian," I admitted. "Perhaps we could go later?"

"I have to be at the Horseguards for most of the day," he said.

"Oh." I lay back on my pillow and gazed at him. There was a pale golden stubble on his cheeks and chin, and his hair was ruffled and hanging in his eyes. I badly wanted to go with him and I tried to sit up again, but it was no good. The room swam before my eyes and my stomach heaved.

Damn.

"What's wrong, Kate?" He sounded alarmed.

I closed my eyes and faced the truth. "I think I am with child, Adrian."

He didn't say anything. I opened my eyes a little and peeked at him.

"You don't sound very joyful," he said quietly. His own face looked grave.

I wasn't joyful. I didn't have time to be sick right now. I had too much daughterly business to complete before I could begin to turn my attention to being a mother. However, I could hardly say this to Adrian.

I shut my eyes again and said, "It's hard to be joyful when you are feeling sick." I sniffed. "And I really wanted to go riding with you this morning."

"We'll find another time to do our riding, sweetheart," he said gently. I felt his lips touch my forehead. "I promise."

I looked up at him. "Are you happy?" I asked.

"I am happy about the baby," he said. "But I'm not happy that you are feeling ill."

I managed a smile. "I'll get better. The morning is the worst."

"Have you seen a doctor?"

I shook my head.

"I'll get the name of someone good and have him come and call on you," he said.

Of course he was concerned. If this baby was a boy, he would be Adrian's heir. I would have to see this doctor. "All right," I said listlessly.

"Go back to sleep, sweetheart," he said.

I looked toward the window to see if I could judge the time, and my eyes fell upon two telltale piles.

"Adrian! Our clothes!"

He turned to look. "Yes. What about them?"

"We can't leave them there. How will it look?"

His eyes glinted, but his voice was grave. "Not good, Kate," he said.

"Will you please pick them up?" I said urgently. "I

would do it myself, but if I try to get out of this bed I will be sick."

"That would look even worse," he said. The glint in his eyes was even more pronounced than before.

"It's not funny, Adrian!" I said. "I do not want my maid finding my clothes thrown on the floor like that. She will know exactly what happened last night. She's French."

He grinned.

"Adrian! Pick up those clothes!"

He stood up. He was not wearing any clothes at all, and he looked marvelous. If Jeanette could see him now, she would really think he was a Greek god.

"Don't upset yourself, sweetheart," he said soothingly. "I will pick up the clothes."

And he did. He even folded them neatly and piled them on a chair before going next door to his dressing room to get ready for the day.

CHAPTER
twenty-one

IT WASN'T UNTIL I WOKE AGAIN AT TEN O'CLOCK THAT it occurred to me that I had made a mistake in telling Adrian about the baby. We were due to leave for Newmarket in three days. What if he thought I shouldn't go?

Aside from an upset stomach when I awoke, feeling tired, and occasional bouts of dizziness, I was perfectly fine. I told this to Dr. Adams, the young doctor who called to see me that very afternoon at Adrian's request.

Initially, I had not been pleased by Dr. Adams's youth. He was a slim, almost boyish-looking man, and it was terribly embarrassing having to talk to him about such intimate matters as my sex life with Adrian and my monthly flow. I felt I would have been more comfortable with an older, more fatherly kind of man.

However, Dr. Adams was so cheerful and brisk and matter-of-fact that it was not as bad an ordeal as I had feared it would be. And my worst fear—that he would ask me to take off my clothes—did not come to pass. He simply talked to me, told me that I was probably not quite two months pregnant, that I was perfectly healthy and could continue with my normal life as long as I made certain that I got enough sleep.

"I can go to Newmarket later this week for the races?" I asked.

"Certainly," Dr. Adams replied. He gave me a very nice smile. "I don't think I would recommend Derby Day at

Epsom, but Newmarket should be perfectly safe, Lady Greystone."

As I saw him off, I actually felt glad that Adrian had chosen a young, modern doctor who did not have antiquated notions about the dangers of pregnancy.

He had also chosen a doctor who obviously knew something about Newmarket. The other major racetracks in England—Epsom, Ascot and Doncaster—all had grandstands and catered to crowds of all classes. Epsom on Derby Day regularly boasted an attendance of over 100,000 people, and with the beer tents doing a brisk business, it could get rather rowdy. I knew because I had been there. Nor was racing the only attraction for the spectator at these tracks. Dicing, gaming, wrestling, and boxing were going on in various tents all over the racetrack grounds.

The track at Newmarket, on the other hand, was exclusively for racing and exclusively for the upper-class owner and spectator. The biggest crowd, such as the one that would gather on Guineas day, wouldn't number more than five hundred people. There was no grandstand. The men watched the races on horseback; the women from carriages. There was no chance of my being dangerously jostled at Newmarket. I knew that, and I was thankful that the doctor knew it also.

"Dr. Adams says that I am perfectly fine and there is no reason why I cannot go to Newmarket" were the words with which I greeted Adrian when he came home at five o'clock to change his clothes. I had been waiting for him in the red salon and had given Walters strict orders to ask his lordship to see me as soon as he came in. Ned had been keeping me company, and we were playing kit-cat-cannio together when Adrian walked into the room.

"I win, Aunt Kate! I win!" Ned shouted. We were both sitting cross-legged on the red Persian rug in front of the fireplace, with a pad of paper and some pens between us. We turned at the same moment to watch Adrian crossing the floor.

He looked down at the row of three *X*s Ned had made diagonally across the grid of squares. "If you are the one with the Xs, then it certainly looks as if you have won, Ned," he said.

"Aunt Kate and I have discovered that the one who has the X always wins, Uncle Adrian," Ned confided. He drew another grid of nine boxes. "See. If I put my first X here," Ned proceeded to put an X in the upper right-hand box, "and then I put my next X here," another mark was made in the lower left-hand box, "then the O person can't stop me!"

Adrian looked at the grid intently, and then he nodded. "You're right, Ned," he said. "It was very clever of you to figure that out."

"Aunt Kate helped," the little boy said generously.

"Good for you, Aunt Kate," Adrian said.

Ned's nurse appeared in the doorway. "Time for dinner, Master Ned," she said.

Ned gave me a longing look.

"Go along with Miss Pettigrew and have your dinner," I said. "I'll come to see you later and tell you a story."

The little boy stood up. "Oh, good," he said. "I like your stories, Aunt Kate."

Adrian put out his hand to me and I let him pull me to my feet. A current of awareness passed between us at the touch of our hands.

Ned reached the door, turned, and gave us a sunny smile. "Bye for now, Aunt Kate. Bye for now, Uncle Adrian."

"Bye for now, Ned," we chorused in return.

After the little boy had gone, I told Adrian about what Dr. Adams had said.

"Did you tell him about the dizzy spells?" he asked.

"Yes. I told him everything, Adrian." I could feel my cheeks flush. "He certainly asked me everything!"

"Very well," he said after a moment. "Then there seems to be no reason why we can't go to Newmarket."

"There is no reason at all," I said, and my smile was as sunny as Ned's had been.

*   *   *

The day we left for Newmarket, the sky was gray with the promise of rain. We took two coaches; one contained Louisa and me, and the other contained all of our baggage as well as Jeanette and Rogers, Adrian's valet. Paddy had left the previous day with Sean MacBride, Finn MacCool's old groom, so it was just Harry and Adrian riding beside the carriage.

It was one of those cold, damp spring days that can chill you to your very marrow. Adrian had provided us with rugs inside the coach, and I huddled under one, grateful for the warmth of the wool. Next to me, Louisa did the same.

"It's a pity Caroline could not come," she said as the horses trotted briskly out of Berkeley Square.

"I know. It's unfortunate that the Race Meeting is the same week that they were invited to visit Holkham. But you know Edward! Once he heard about how Mr. Coke had improved his livestock herd, I don't think God Himself could have detained Edward from taking a look. He certainly couldn't be put off for a mere horse race."

Louisa chuckled. "Lord Ashley is as devoted to his cows as you are to your horses, Kate."

"He seems to be. Isn't it amazing?"

The chaise hit a bump and we both bounced. I pulled the rug more securely around my waist and wiggled my toes. They were cold already. I wished I had allowed Walters to give us a few hot bricks.

Louisa said, "Do you know anything about where we will be staying, Kate?"

We were to be the guests of Sir Charles Barbury himself. Adrian had met him for the first time only a few weeks ago, and lo and behold, here we were, invited to the home of the permanent president of the Jockey Club for the week the most prestigious of Newmarket's races was run. And Sir Charles probably felt himself honored that Adrian had accepted his offer of hospitality!

"Sir Charles's estate lies between Newmarket and Mildenhall," I said. "I'm afraid that's all I know, Louisa. Papa and I certainly never rated an invitation to visit Sir Charles. When we went to Newmarket, we stayed in a lodging house."

I thought of the lodging house where we had stayed on our last visit, and of what had happened while we were there. Unbidden, unlooked for, the image of my father's face appeared before my mind's eye. It was not his face as it had looked after he had been shot, but as it had been for the rest of my life: vivid with the sheer joy of living.

Oh, Papa. My lips moved to form the words, but no sound came out. I felt such terrible sadness. He had been only forty-six years old. It wasn't yet time for him to die.

I felt the cushion under me move, and then Louisa was close beside me, reaching over to cover my cold hands with hers. "He must have been a very fine man to have had such a wonderful daughter," she said softly.

I didn't trust my voice, so I blinked and nodded.

"I felt so sorry for you, Kate, that winter at Charlwood," my cousin said hesitantly. "If I seemed ... uncaring ... it was that I did not wish to intrude upon your grief. You did not know me, and I thought any attempt of mine to console you would be unwelcome." Her fingers tightened briefly, and then she took her hand away and sat back. "I just want you to know that it was not lack of concern on my part that kept me silent."

My throat muscles felt too tight. I said, "I understand, Louisa." My voice sounded thick, and I swallowed. I could feel tears pressing behind my eyes.

What is the matter with me? I thought. *I never cry.*

Silence fell between us until we were out of London and on the road north. At last I was able to say in my normal voice, "Paddy is a lucky man."

Louisa had been looking out the window of the coach, but at my words she turned, her expression both surprised and bewildered. I explained, "You are a woman who knows how to be silent. Papa always said such a woman is worth her price in rubies. Unfortunately, it's a virtue I never managed to acquire."

Louisa laughed.

I said in a rush, "Louisa, Adrian said he would lease Lambourn to Paddy if the two of you should ever decide to marry."

The first drops spattered against the carriage window. "Say that again," my cousin said.

I repeated my words, adding, "You can be sure that Adrian means the lease to be very reasonable. It's a perfect place, Louisa. Lambourn's wonderful for horses, and it's only a few miles away from Greystone. We could see each other all the time."

"Oh, Kate." Now it was Louisa's turn to fill up.

The rain against the window sounded as if it was coming down more steadily.

"It wasn't even my idea," I said. "Adrian came up with it all on his own."

She said shakily, "It's such a blessing that you found a man like Greystone, Kate. And I am not saying that because of Lambourn."

I gazed at my lap, refusing to meet her eyes. "Of course Adrian is wonderful," I said. "Everyone thinks so."

"He's strong," Louisa said. "He's strong without being a bully. Married to you, most men would either end up letting you do their breathing for them, or they would feel they had to master you. You were fortunate to find a man who is strong enough to let you be what you are."

I wasn't at all sure that I liked what I was hearing. "You make me sound like a headstrong mare, Louisa," I said with undisguised annoyance.

At that moment, the chaise began to slow down. The men had decided to get in out of the rain, and Louisa was saved from having to give me an answer.

*　　*　　*

Harley Hall had been in Sir Charles Barbury's family for several generations, and perhaps it was its proximity to Newmarket that had caused Sir Charles to become involved in racing at the early age of twenty-one. The rain had stopped by the time we arrived, and as I peered out the window as we progressed up the drive I saw a typical stone Jacobean manor house with mullioned windows and tall chimneys.

"Thank heaven we have arrived," I said to Louisa. "The bouncing of this chaise is enough to make anyone feel sick to the stomach."

"It has been wearisome," my cousin agreed.

The chaise came to a halt in front of the great stairs. The men had gone back to their horses as soon as the rain had stopped, and it was Adrian himself who opened the chaise door for us. He leaned his head and shoulders inside and asked, "How are you doing?"

The question was politely directed to both of us, but I knew he was really talking to me. I said, "If I don't get out of this chaise immediately, Adrian, I am going to scream."

"The steps are coming," he said.

I slid off my seat and walked unsteadily toward him. "I'll jump."

He gave me a sharp look, then put his hands on my waist as I reached the doorway and lifted me down to the ground. I breathed the cool, damp air into my lungs. My stomach had been uneasy for the last hour of the trip, and I was feeling distinctly grumpy.

The steps came, and Louisa descended with dignity. We were joined by Harry, and together the four of us ascended the front stairs of Harley Hall. We were greeted at the door by the butler, who told us that Sir Charles had taken a few of his other guests to see his racehorses, which were stabled in a training barn near Bury. The butler then passed us on to the housekeeper, who took us to our rooms.

I could not believe how tired I was feeling. I had done nothing all day but sit in a carriage, yet my legs did not feel strong enough to hold me up. I scarcely glanced at my surroundings, but went directly to the big wooden rocking chair that stood in front of the fireplace, sat, and stared into the flames.

The door opened and a footman came in carrying our portmanteaux. The footman was followed by Jeanette, who said she would unpack for me. I listened as Adrian told her that I was feeling fatigued and that she should come back later. At last the door closed.

"Why don't you take a little nap, Kate? You'll feel better after you've had a rest," Adrian said gently.

"I don't want to nap," I said. Actually, I believe I whined. "There is no reason for me to feel fatigued. I have done nothing all day but sit."

"You have made a long trip in an enclosed carriage and you are in the early stages of pregnancy," he said. "You have every reason in the world to feel fatigued."

"I hate feeling this way," I said. "I hate not having my usual energy."

"You will feel better after you have had a rest," he repeated.

I was actually dying to crawl into that bed, but I didn't want to admit it. "All right," I said with a martyred air. "If it will make you happy, I will take a nap."

"Thank you, sweetheart," he said.

I stood up. "I don't want to lie down in my clothes, and you sent Jeanette away."

"Do you want me to ring for her again?"

"No. I don't want her."

"Then what *do* you want, Kate?" If he had sounded exasperated, I would have forgiven him. I was exasperated with myself. The fact that he sounded amused made me furious.

"I want you to go away," I said. "How can I nap with you looming over me?"

"Can you unbutton that dress by yourself?"

"Of course I can unbutton my own dress! Do you think I am an imbecile?"

He walked to the door. "Would you like me to have the housekeeper send you up some tea?"

"No," I said.

"Then I will leave you to your rest." He didn't even slam the door, but closed it quietly behind him.

I slept for two hours, and when I awoke I felt much better. Sir Charles had returned, and when I had dressed and gone downstairs I found my host and the rest of the company assembled in a large room with a vaulted ceiling that must have been the Great Hall of the original house.

The first person I saw as I walked into the room was the Duchess of Wareham. The second person I saw was her daughter, Lady Mary Weston.

I felt my hands close into fists at my sides. The colossal nerve of the girl almost took my breath away. She had actually gotten herself invited to the same house party as Adrian! Probably she was hoping that she would be able to steal some time alone with him.

Over my dead body, I thought.

"Lady Greystone, I am so pleased to welcome you to Harley Hall." I removed my eyes from Lady Mary's face and looked at the woman who was addressing me. She was middle-aged and pale, but her eyes were kind. "I am Lady Barbury," she said.

Of course, I knew that Sir Charles had a wife, but no one had ever seen her. She did not share his passion for racing. I forced a smile and managed some kind of a reply. She then proceeded to take me around the room to introduce me to the company.

Papa had sold horses to about half the men present, so there were plenty of familiar faces. I did not know any of the women, except, of course, the perfidious Lady Mary.

I was somewhat mollified by the fact that Adrian was

standing with Sir Charles and another man in front of the fireplace, at least halfway across the room from Lady Mary and her mother. Adrian gave me a warm smile as I went to join them, and I felt a little better.

But I was not happy. I had too much else on my mind right now to have to worry about Lady Mary getting her claws into my husband.

CHAPTER
twenty-two

WE ARRIVED AT HARLEY HALL ON MONDAY AND the racing wasn't due to start until Wednesday, with the Guineas being run on Friday. Consequently, my coconspirators and I had three days to wait until we could make our first move, which was to determine for sure whether or not Alcazar was indeed Finn MacCool.

Paddy had taken his usual lodgings in town, and he had Sean MacBride, the stable lad from Ireland, with him. On Friday morning, when we could be certain that Stade was at the racetrack, Paddy and Sean would ride out to Stade's estate near Bury to check the stallion's identity. And then we would know.

On Tuesday morning Sir Charles took the gentlemen over to Newmarket Heath to watch the horses exercise. The Heath, like the racecourse, was owned by the Jockey Club, and over four hundred horses were trained in the stables based around Newmarket. The picture of all those splendid Thoroughbreds, galloping like the wind under a powerful East Anglian sky, was to my mind one of the most beautiful sights in all the world.

The ladies were left to Lady Barbury's care, and she gave us a tour of the famous Harley Hall gardens. The grounds were extensive and varied. To the west of the house was a wide grassy ride lined by double rows of horse chestnuts, and small flower-filled gardens were tucked away in hidden places all along the ride's expanse. To the south of the house there were wide lawns studded with islands of willows, elder, and privet. There was an extremely pretty stream whose banks were lined with planes, alders, elms, sycamores, and willows. The lawn closest to the house featured classical statues and stone urns.

The grounds were really exceptionally lovely, and I admired them with the utmost sincerity and never once let on that I would rather have watched the horses on the heath.

The gentlemen returned to the house shortly after noon, and a light luncheon was put out in the breakfast room. Harry and I filled our plates at the laden sideboard and went to sit at the table together. I glanced around the cheerful, busy room and immediately registered the fact that Lady Mary was missing.

"Where is Adrian?" I asked my brother-in-law suspiciously.

"Some fellow from the Home Office grabbed hold of him at Newmarket," Harry said. "He said he would return to Harley Hall by himself later in the afternoon."

Of course, I was relieved to know that Adrian wasn't with Lady Mary, but I felt a stab of resentment that he couldn't even attend the races without some petty government official demanding his attention.

At this point, Lady Mary herself walked into the breakfast room. A dark-haired young man who walked with a slight limp was right behind her, and it looked to me as if they were together. "Who is that with Lady Mary?" I asked Harry.

"You were introduced to him as well as I," Harry complained. "Why do you always have to ask me who people are?"

"Don't be such a pain," I said. "Who is he?"

"His name is Richard Bellerton." Harry proceeded to spread mustard all over his beef and then to cut himself a huge bite. He stuffed it in his mouth and began to chew.

I gave him a cold stare. "And just who is Richard Bellerton?"

Harry continued to chew.

I kicked him under the table, and he jumped.

"Stop it, Kate," he hissed at me. His cheeks had gone quite red.

I gave him a smile that was almost as angelic as his own. "I want to know who this Bellerton is, Harry."

He swallowed the last of his beef and demanded, "Why are you so interested in Lady Mary's beaux?"

"Ah, then he is a beau!"

We both looked at the couple who were filling their plates at the sideboard. Mr. Bellerton was not much taller than Lady Mary, but he was broad of shoulder and slender of waist. I thought that they made an exceptionally handsome pair.

"Before we left town, a bet was entered in the book at White's that they'd be engaged by the end of the Season," Harry admitted.

I felt as if a stone had just rolled off my heart. I beamed. "How perfectly lovely."

"He's Aldershot's nephew," Harry went on. "Since the old buzzard never married, Bellerton stands to inherit both the title and the money. I'd say the fact that the duchess is here with Lady Mary makes it pretty clear that she approves of the match."

This was sounding better and better. "Is this Bellerton a racing man?" I asked. "I've never seen him before."

"He's Lady Barbury's cousin," Harry said.

Lady Mary began to approach the table, saw me watching her, and faltered. I gave her a friendly grin and her eyes widened in surprise. She wiggled her lips at me a little, then moved swiftly to a seat at the opposite end of the table. Mr. Bellerton carried his plate to the chair beside hers.

I turned back to Harry. "This Bellerton limps," I said.

"Yes. He was wounded at Waterloo."

I was delighted. Lady Mary had found a hero for herself and now presumably could be trusted to leave mine alone. I looked at Harry, who was busy devouring another slab of beef, and my own appetite stirred. For the first time all day, I

felt hungry. I picked up my knife and cut myself a small bite
of cold roast beef.

The Race Meeting opened on Wednesday, and all the
men of Sir Charles Barbury's house party, as well as Louisa
and I, were present to watch the first race go off. The men
watched from horseback, while Louisa and I had a good view
of the finish line from Sir Charles's high-perch phaeton. The
day was sunny, but there was a bit of a wind blowing, and
Adrian had tucked rugs around the both of us before we left
Harley Hall.

I loved the races because I loved to watch the sheer
beauty of Thoroughbreds running, but men went to the racetrack to bet. Papa had been a great gambler, and his gambling
had accounted for most of the ups and downs of our economic
life. He made a great deal of money selling horses, and he lost
a great deal of money betting on them.

Adrian had been abroad for so long that he was almost
completely unacquainted with English racing, and the previous night I had made a list for him of all the horses he should
bet on when the men put their money down with the "leg"
who did business with Lord Barbury.

These "legs" were professional gamblers who accepted
bets at varying prices on every horse in a race, a system they
called "making a book." They were heavily patronized by
racegoers, but I thought they were a scourge. Poisoning a
horse's drinking water or slipping him an opium ball were
common tricks legs used in order to stop a favorite. The
Jockey Club was supposed to try to keep legs honest, but they
were not as successful as they should have been.

Adrian started off the day beside us, but then—as
usual—he was claimed by first one man and then the other
and we saw him only in snatches during the remainder of the
day. But Louisa and I were scarcely neglected. Many old
friends stopped by to chat and to tell me how nice it was to
see me at the track again.

It should have been a perfect day. The sun continued to shine and by early afternoon the breeze had died down and the weather was pleasantly warm. The races all went off smoothly, and if the favorites did not always win, at least they put up a good enough show to make one feel that they had not been poisoned. Four of the horses I had recommended to Adrian came in first, and he congratulated me on my astuteness, which pleased me.

It was the world I had grown up in: the thundering Thoroughbreds; the smells of leather and horses and manure; the exuberance of the winners; the downcast faces of the losers. All of these things had been part of my life for eighteen years, and I loved them.

But Papa wasn't there. For some reason, I hadn't expected to miss him the way I did. He had been dead for a year and a half, and I had thought that my grieving was done with, but it seemed that it was not.

The ache inside me grew more and more painful as the afternoon went by, and I became quieter and quieter. When the last race was finally over, I said to Louisa, "I want to stop by Papa's grave before we return to Harley Hall."

Louisa had twice asked me during the course of the afternoon if I was feeling well, and now she began to search the crowd. "I don't see Lord Greystone at the moment, Kate."

"He is probably settling up with the leg," I said to Louisa. "It may take some time, and I told him I was going to leave directly after the last race."

Louisa frowned worriedly. "I think you should wait to go visit the grave until he can accompany you."

But the need had been growing inside me all afternoon long, and I didn't want to wait. I said, "Papa is buried in the churchyard just outside of town. It will not take me long to pay a quick visit, Louisa."

I lifted the reins to back the horses out of our spot, but my cousin put a restraining hand on my arm. "Wait one moment, Kate." I threw her an impatient look, but she was sig-

naling to someone. I followed her eyes and saw Paddy thread-
ing his way through the crowd of men and horses. He had
been by to talk to us several times during the course of the
day, and the sound of his soft Irish voice had made me feel
even more bereft.

"Are you ladies after leaving?" he asked as he rode his
pretty chestnut mare up to the side of the phaeton.

"Kate wants to stop by her father's grave before we return to Harley Hall," Louisa said. "Will you come with us,
Paddy?"

"Surely," he returned, his light blue eyes on my face.

"I haven't been to his grave since the day of the funeral,"
I said.

"I stop by every time I am in Newmarket," Paddy told
me gently, "and I know a few of the lads who stop by when-
ever they are in town."

Papa had always had the gift of making himself loved.

I smiled a little tremulously. "Well, then, shall we go?"

"Drive on, Miss Cathleen," he said, and moved his horse
out of my way.

Someone had planted bluebells on Papa's grave. They
were the exact color of his eyes, and they broke my heart.

Stade will pay. I was dangerously close to losing control
of my emotions, and these were the only words I could find to
keep myself from falling apart. I clenched my fists.

*Don't worry, Papa. I won't let him get away with it. I will
make him pay for what he did to you.*

The ache in my throat was unbearable; the bluebells
were a blur of blue against the white stone.

Oh God, Papa. Oh God. Papa . . . Papa . . .

The wind had picked up and it was blowing across the
graveyard with a chilling bite. A sparrow pecked in the grass
nearby, searching for a worm. I couldn't see Papa's name anymore.

"Come along with you now, Miss Cathleen," Paddy said, and I felt his arm come around my shoulders.

I felt so alone. I was so terribly cold. I needed comfort so desperately. "I want to go home," I said.

He was guiding me toward the phaeton. "We're too far from Greystone, darlin'," he said. "I'm going to take you back to Harley Hall."

"I don't want to go to Greystone," I said. I could feel the tears start to roll down my cheeks, and I blinked ferociously to chase them away. "I want to go home."

"Up you go," Paddy said in that heartbreakingly soft voice, and he lifted me to the seat of the phaeton. A moment later, Louisa followed.

I reached for the reins and wondered if I would be able to keep the horses on the road. Louisa said, "Wait a moment, Kate. Paddy is tying his horse to the back of the phaeton. He will drive us back to Harley Hall."

I didn't even object. The three of us squeezed together on a seat that was meant for two, and Paddy drove us all the way to the front steps of Harley Hall.

Adrian was standing on the graveled drive talking to Richard Bellerton. We drew up and I heard his voice say, "Has something happened, Paddy?"

I was squeezed in the middle of Louisa and Paddy, and it was Louisa who answered, "We stopped by the grave of Kate's papa and it upset her."

"Ah," he said. Then, quietly, "Let me help you down, Louisa."

Louisa disappeared from the phaeton's seat and I slid over to take her place. Then Adrian was reaching his arms up for me. I put my hands on his shoulders and felt him lift me from the phaeton, out into the air, and then down to the ground in front of him. To my utter dismay, I felt a sob rising from deep in my chest.

"Oh, Adrian," I said. "Oh, Adrian."

He didn't reply, he simply picked me up as if I were a

child and carried me up the front steps of Harley Hall. I buried my face in his shoulder so that no one could see my tears. The butler let us in. I heard his voice, and then we were going up another flight of stairs. Adrian bent a little to open a door, and at last we were safely inside in our own room. He kicked the door shut behind us and carried me over to the rocking chair in front of the fireplace. He sat down with me in his lap.

"It's all right, sweetheart," he said gently, "now you can cry."

And I did. I sobbed as I had never sobbed before, deeply, uncontrollably, and he held me until the storm was over and I was limp with exhaustion.

I lay against him, and listened to the steady beat of his heart against my cheek, and felt the strength of his arms cradling me, and knew that at last I had come home.

I said in a voice that was still woefully unsteady, "I'm sorry. I don't know what happened to me. I never cry like that."

"There is nothing to apologize for in crying, Kate," he said.

I didn't agree. "Crying doesn't change anything," I said. "All it does is waste energy."

"That's not true," he said.

"Yes, it is."

He was silent.

"*You* don't cry about things, Adrian," I said.

I felt his chest expand and contract as he took a deep breath. He did it again. Then he said, speaking very slowly, as if the words were being dragged out of him, "Do you know how many men I killed in that famous charge of mine, Kate?"

I was so surprised at this change of subject that I lifted my head. "You took out the whole of the French left center," I said.

There was an oddly strained look on his face, and suddenly the strangeness of his phraseology struck me. "Do you know how many men *I* killed," he had said.

"Did you lose a lot of your own men, Adrian?" I whispered.

He said, "*I* made the decision to push on well beyond the British position. *I* made the decision to go for the guns. And on the way back we were caught by a company of French lancers. Our losses were severe."

He looked so bleak. I hated to see him look that way. "No one blames you for that, Adrian."

He shook his head impatiently. That wasn't what he wanted to hear.

I ran my finger between his brows, trying to smooth away the tense line that had appeared there, and wondered why he was telling me this story. He began slowly to rock the chair in which we were sitting, and once more I rested my head against him.

He said, "When at last the battle was over, I decided to ride back across the field to the place where we had been caught—to see if there was anyone left alive whom I could help." I could feel the tension in his voice and in his body as he faced the horror of this memory. "How can I describe the sight of that field? There were thousands of dead men lying there, and thousands more of the wounded, calling out in agony. It was like a vision of hell, Kate." I felt his mouth touch the top of my head, and his breath stirred my hair as he said harshly, "I cried. I could scarcely see where I was going for the tears that were pouring down my face."

The rocking chair continued its slow, regular, soothing rhythm. I lay against his warmth and strength, and thought about what he was telling me. He said, "So you see, I *do* cry, Kate. And I am not ashamed of it. Just as you should not be ashamed of crying for your father." He put a finger under my chin and tipped my face up so he could look at me. "There are some things that deserve that kind of emotion," he said.

He was a man of incomparable generosity. I loved him so much. I gazed back into his eyes and almost blurted out just how I felt. I don't know what stopped me. Well, actually, I suppose I do know. It was pride.

It was inevitable that I would tell him one day, but not just now.

I said instead, "Thank you, Adrian." I rested my head back against his chest. "You have made me feel much better."

We continued to rock.

CHAPTER
twenty-three

FRIDAY MORNING DAWNED BRIGHT WITH THE PROMISE of another brilliantly clear spring day. The Guineas would go off in perfect weather over a perfectly conditioned track. Louisa and I drove to Newmarket under an almost cloudless sky, and all along the road the early-blooming cherry trees were a froth of white, and bluebells and violets were sprinkled through the grass at the edges of the road.

Louisa chatted cheerfully as the phaeton rolled along, and I knew that Paddy had not told her about his projected business. I answered her as best I could, but my own mind was not easy. I could not forget what had happened the last time someone had tried to ascertain the real identity of Alcazar.

Dear God, keep Paddy safe, I prayed. *Please, please, keep him safe.*

The racetrack was as crowded as I've ever seen it, and all the talk was about the Guineas and the chances of Castle Rook. Stade's colt was the overwhelming favorite, a situation that was a perfect setup for a leg to try to nobble him. Much as I hated Stade, I didn't want to see anything happen to the colt, and I hoped Castle Rook had been well-watched these last twenty-four hours.

I looked for Stade all morning, but I didn't see him until after the second race had finished, and then I spied him in the company of Sir Charles Barbury.

Harry saw him at the same time I did. "There's the

bounder now," he muttered. Harry had not gone off with friends as he had the previous two days, but was sticking close by the side of my phaeton.

"I haven't seen Paddy yet," Louisa remarked.

Harry and I exchanged a look. Then Harry said casually, "He mentioned something to me yesterday about going to see a horse this morning."

"Goodness," said Louisa. "I hope he is back in time to watch the running of the Guineas."

I forced a laugh. "You sound like an inveterate racing buff, Louisa. One would never know that this was your first meet."

Louisa looked pleased. "It's fun," she said.

"Have you won any money, Louisa?" Harry asked.

My cousin shook her head. "I haven't bet."

I felt a pang of guilt as I realized that the probable reason Louisa hadn't bet was that she hadn't any money. I had planned to share my allowance with her, but before I could do so I had squandered it all at that wretched gaming hell.

"Broke like Kate and me, eh?" Harry said sympathetically.

To my surprise, Louisa shook her head. "I have scarcely touched the allowance Greystone made me," she said. "I just think it's foolish to put money down upon a horse."

Adrian rides to the rescue again, I thought ruefully.

"If people didn't bet, there wouldn't be any racing," Harry said.

I sighed. "Unfortunately, that is true."

A man on a bay Thoroughbred mare was picking his way through the crowd, and I remarked to Harry, "Isn't that a pretty mare, Harry? She reminds me a little of Elsa."

Harry grunted.

"I hope she will be all right cooped up in that stable in London," I worried.

Harry hooted. "Cooped up! I heard the orders you were barking before we left." He imitated what he thought was my voice: *"Now make sure she is hand-walked for an hour at least three times a day, Georgie. And don't forget to give her her treats."* He snorted. "Between your orders for Elsa, and Adrian's equally extensive orders for Euclide, the grooms won't have time to see to any of the other animals."

I gave an unwilling grin.

"Here comes Adrian now," Harry said, and we all turned to watch the bareheaded rider on the big chestnut gelding as he maneuvered his way through the crowd in our direction.

Castle Rook won the Guineas. He got caught behind a wall of horses when he tried to go inside, and his jockey had to drop back and bring him around the outside. A groan had gone up from the crowd when this happened, as most of the people there had visions of their money going down the sewer. But once the colt had open track in front of him, he ignited.

It was a monumental performance. The dark bay colt's powerful driving strides seemed to eat up the ground beneath him. He passed first one horse and then another as if they were standing still. He swept into the lead at an eighth of a mile from the finish, and by the time he passed in front of us at the finish line he was ten horse-lengths ahead of the colt in second place.

Chills were running up and down my spine as I watched him run.

Pandemonium reigned among the spectators.

Adrian's eyes were blazing. "What a magnificent performance!" he said to me. "Have you ever seen anything to equal that, Kate?"

I could only shake my head. I had never seen anything like it before. No one had.

The intense blue sky of East Anglia looked down upon the splendid bay colt as he was ridden in triumph back up the track. The spectators cheered themselves hoarse as he went by. The Marquis of Stade, his owner, was hidden from sight by the congratulatory crowd that had mobbed him.

Let him enjoy his moment in the sun, I thought grimly. He was going to find his face in the mud soon enough.

By the end of the day, Louisa was fretting at Paddy's absence. I was more than fretting; I was terrified that something had gone wrong. At least half the spectators had left the course by the time Paddy finally put in an appearance. Louisa and I were so glad to see him that we almost fell out of the phaeton into his arms.

He spun Louisa a charming tale about a horse that he had almost bought, and then Harry dragged him away from the phaeton to have a private word. I had my eyes glued to their faces, and when I saw Harry break into a smile, I knew that Paddy had been successful, that Sean had identified the stallion as Finn MacCool.

I had to wait until the following morning before I was able to hear for myself what had transpired. Harry arranged for us to meet Paddy and Sean near a little bridge that went over the stream at a spot halfway between Harley Hall and the village. The morning was still not a good time of the day for me, but I was getting a little better. I thought that perhaps the country air was agreeing with me.

Fortunately, Adrian had gone out ahead of me to take the hounds for a run with Sir Charles, so I did not have to make up an excuse for him as to why I wanted to be out so early.

Harry and I reached the appointed place first, and we dismounted and let the horses graze as we waited on the stream's flat, grassy bank. Behind us the bank grew steeper, and the green grass was liberally sprinkled with cuckooflowers and marsh orchids and cowslips. It was another impossibly beautiful spring morning. I watched as a few sheep grazed their way across the hillside. Cuckoos were shouting somewhere in the distance, and from the steep, wooded bank on the other side of the stream there came the steady tapping sound of a woodpecker busily at work.

We waited for perhaps fifteen minutes, and then we were joined by Paddy and the small, wiry, black-haired man whom I knew to be Sean MacBride.

"That stallion is Finn MacCool himself," Sean said. "He was stolen away from Mr. Farrell during the fire." The man's greenish eyes were blazing with anger. "I'll have him back," he said. "I'll have him back in Ireland, where he belongs."

"That you will, boyo," Paddy said. "We must just decide now how best to do it."

"And stud fees!" Sean said fiercely. "He will be owing stud fees for all those mares he bred to our stallion!"

I hadn't thought about stud fees. I nodded emphatically. "You are right, Sean. Mr. Farrell is certainly owed stud fees."

"Sean took a good look at the Marquis of Stade yesterday while he was peacocking around after he won the Guineas," Paddy said. "Sean identified him as the man who tried to buy Finn MacCool before the fire."

This was getting better and better. I almost rubbed my hands.

"Lord Barbury is the president of the Jockey Club," I said. "I think our next step is to lay this evidence before him."

"Stade will deny it," Paddy said. "And I'm after thinking that the word of an Irish stable lad will not count for much against the word of a fine English marquis."

I disagreed. "There has been a great deal of speculation about the amazing success of Alcazar as a sire," I said. "They will have to investigate these charges."

"And how will they be doing that?" Sean asked.

"Someone from the Jockey Club will have to go to Ireland to take a look at Mr. Farrell's horses. He must still have some of Finn MacCool's get in his stables."

"That he does," Sean said with satisfaction. "There is Conchubar, and hasn't he won the Galway Cup the last five years running?"

"If he's the horse I saw run two years ago," I said, "you cannot miss the resemblance to Castle Rook."

"They're all the image of their da," Sean said. "He throws true, does Finn MacCool."

"What about Mr. Daniel?" Paddy said. "Is there no way we can charge Stade with his murder?"

Something of what I was feeling must have shown on my face, because Harry put his arm around my shoulders. I leaned against him gratefully. "I don't think there is, Paddy," I said. "Of course, we can mention our suspicions to Lord Barbury, and I think that they will weigh with the Jockey Club, but we have not enough evidence to bring Stade to public justice."

"It is not enough that he should just suffer the banning of the Jockey Club," Paddy insisted. "He should be made to pay for Mr. Daniel. A life for a life."

"I agree," I said. "But I don't think we can bring it off."

Harry had been uncharacteristically silent this whole time. Now he said, "Paddy, for a man like Stade to be ostracized by his own kind, well, that is an even worse punishment than death. He will be a pariah."

"In the racing world he will be a pariah maybe," Paddy said. "But what will the rest of the world care about such a thing when even the Regent himself has been banned from the track by the Jockey Club?"

"The offenses are not the same," I said. "The Prince was suspected of telling his jockey to stop a horse. Once. And a great number of people think that the jockey most likely acted on his own. Stade stole a valuable stallion and quite probably killed a man to keep from being found out. Harry is right. He will be a pariah. He will never be able to show his face in good society again."

Paddy looked unconvinced.

I said passionately, "Paddy, don't you think I would like to see him drawn and quartered? Don't you think I would like to see his head stuck up on London Bridge?" I drew a deep, unsteady breath. "But I do not think we have the evidence."

No one spoke. The woodpecker had fallen silent, but the cuckoos were still calling to each other from the woods on the other side of the stream. Two ewes followed by their lambs had made their way down from the hillside and were taking a drink from the stream. The sweet-smelling early-morning breeze stirred the hair at my temples and rippled through the grass.

The world looked so very beautiful. It wasn't fair that Papa could no longer see it, and that Stade could.

Paddy sighed. "I suppose you are right, girl. But it's a strange kind of justice."

Sean returned us to the business at hand. "We will be getting back Finn MacCool?"

"That you will, lad," Paddy said grimly. "That you will."

Sir Charles, Adrian and two other gentlemen were having breakfast when Harry and I returned to Harley Hall. Adrian looked surprised when he saw me walk into the breakfast room. Since my morning-sickness problems had begun, I had been taking tea in my room like all the other ladies.

Harry said to Sir Charles, "After you have breakfasted, I wonder if we might speak to you for a moment, sir."

Sir Charles looked mystified, but he replied with perfect courtesy, "Of course." He drained his teacup. "I am finished now. Come and we'll go into my office."

I could feel Adrian's eyes on me as we followed Sir Charles out of the room.

Sir Charles's office was off the library and contained a mahogany secretaire and two chairs. The bookshelf part of the secretaire was filled with assorted copies of the *Racing Calendar, Baily's Racing Register, The Turf Register, Sporting* magazine, and, of course, the Stud Book; the desk part contained a pile of papers, a quill pen, a Sheffield plate wax jack for melting sealing wax, and a pair of spectacles. Sir Charles and I took the chairs and Harry leaned against the carved mahogany mantelpiece. Sir Charles moved his spectacles a few inches, then looked at us inquiringly.

Harry didn't mince words. "We would like you to convene a meeting of the Jockey Club as soon as possible, sir," he said. "We have charges to bring against the Marquis of Stade."

Sir Charles looked thunderstruck. *"What?"*

Harry repeated himself.

"What are these charges?" Sir Charles demanded. He did not seem pleased with us.

Harry and I exchanged glances, and then Harry proceeded to relate to Sir Charles all that we had discovered.

When Harry had finished his saga of greed, theft, and murder, the Jockey Club president said, "It is possible, of course, that this Irish groom is lying, that he is hoping to steal a great stallion for his master."

This made me angry, and I spoke for the first time. "Sir Charles, I saw Mr. Farrell's horse run in Ireland. He is unmistakably of the same blood as the horse that won the Guineas yesterday. If you, or any other of the Jockey Club stewards, will travel to Galway, you will see this for yourself. Furthermore, I suggest that you try to trace Alcazar's old grooms. I think you will find that they will confirm the fact that the horse Stade is trying to pass off as Alcazar now is not the same horse that they were looking after."

A ray of sunlight slanted in the room's single window and glinted off the glass lenses of the spectacles lying on Sir Charles's desk. He said slowly, "One has always wondered how the mediocre Alcazar could produce such magnificent offspring."

"I know my father wondered," I said. "And that is why he suspected a switch. That is why he tried to take a look at Alcazar." I stared steadily at the spectacles on Sir Charles's desk and said flatly, "And that is why he was killed."

"That may be so, Lady Greystone," Sir Charles said,

"but that is not something that the Jockey Club is competent to judge."

I lifted my eyes. "I understand that, Sir Charles. I am only asking for a hearing so that this information may be made known to the stewards. It will be up to the stewards then to take what action they deem fitting."

"Most of the stewards are presently in Newmarket for the running of the Guineas," Sir Charles said. He rubbed his right temple as if it was paining him, then he sighed. "Very well. I will notify the stewards and we will hold a meeting at the Jockey Club Headquarters in Newmarket tomorrow. You will please be there, Mr. Woodrow, at eleven o'clock. And bring with you the two Irish gentlemen to testify."

"I am coming too," I said.

Sir Charles looked at me in surprise. "That will not be necessary, Lady Greystone. I would not subject you to such a stressful experience."

I said, "I wouldn't miss it for all the rubies in India, Sir Charles." I could feel my mouth set. "I have been waiting a very long time to confront the man who killed my father."

Sir Charles looked a little taken aback at my blood-thirstiness. "Mr. Woodrow?" he said. "Surely you will be able to convince Lady Greystone of the inadvisability of her attending."

Harry, bless him, said, "I think she should come."

Sir Charles looked annoyed.

I stood up. "That is settled, then," I said. "Tomorrow morning at eleven."

Sir Charles also rose to his feet. "Will Lord Greystone be accompanying you?" he asked.

Harry and I exchanged looks.

"I don't know," I said. "I'll have to ask him."

I went upstairs to our bedroom and was not overly surprised to find Adrian there waiting for me. The maids were busy in the room next door, and I said to him, "Come for a walk in the garden and I will explain to you why Harry and I wanted to see Sir Charles."

"I would like that," he said in an expressionless voice.

I shot him a furtive glance as we went down the stairs and out through the French doors onto the terrace, but his face was as expressionless as his voice had been. No one was better than Adrian at keeping his thoughts to himself.

We met Lady Mary, her mother, and two other ladies on the terrace. We all smiled, and commented on the beautiful weather, and then Adrian took my arm and we began to make our way toward the two stone lions in the center of the lawn that I knew guarded the entrance to a circular yew enclosure.

We were silent until we were within the privacy of the hidden garden. There were a few stone benches placed on the lawn so that one could view the ten Corinthian columns of Portland stone that the yews framed, and Adrian guided me to one of them. Then he waited.

I had not seen that reserved look on his face since I had told him about the baby. My stomach sank as I realized—too late—that I should have told him of my suspicions about Stade long before this.

Damn, I thought unhappily. *Why do I always do the wrong thing when it comes to Adrian?*

I had wanted to tell him, I remembered, but Harry had said that we shouldn't bother him, that he had too much else on his mind. At the time Harry's advice had seemed sensible. I saw now that it had been disastrous.

I made my voice as steady as I could and told him everything. He listened in absolute silence.

"I wanted to tell you ages ago, Adrian," I finished, "but Harry said that you were so preoccupied with political problems that it wouldn't be fair to burden you with this."

"I see."

"You *have* been very busy," I said in my own defense. He was staring straight ahead, not looking at me. The bones and planes of his face were as perfect, and as still, as the classical statues in Lady Barbury's garden.

"Harry said . . ." I began again.

"Yes, you told me what Harry said." He turned his head so that he could look at me. His eyes were very dark. "You and Harry are thick as thieves, aren't you?" he asked.

I was so surprised by the comment, and by the sudden bitterness in his voice, that my mouth dropped open. Finally I pulled myself together enough to say, "Harry is like my brother."

He stood up. "We had better get back to the house, Kate. I told Bellerton that I would take a gun out with him, and I'm late."

Another one of those appointments. I stood up as well. I knew I had mucked this up badly, but I didn't know how to retrieve the situation. I felt awful. He had been so wonderful to me yesterday, and now he was hurt.

Damn.

We walked back toward the lions, our steps in harmony but our spirits wildly out of tune. When we reached the great stone statues, I said in a small voice, "Will you come to the meeting of the Jockey Club with us, Adrian?"

"Oh, I don't think that will be necessary, Kate," he said. "You have managed well enough without me up till now."

"I'd *like* to have you come," I said.

"You have Harry," he replied. And that is the note on which we parted.

CHAPTER
twenty-four

WE MET AT ELEVEN O'CLOCK THE FOLLOWING morning in the New Rooms in the town of Newmarket, where the headquarters of the Jockey Club were located. The room into which Sir Charles escorted us smelled strongly of leather and dog and horse, and I thought that I was probably the first female ever to cross its hallowed threshold. As we walked in I shot a quick glance at the sober faces of the eight men who were before us. The eyes that looked back at me did not seem particularly friendly.

"My dear Lady Greystone," someone said, and I turned to see Mr. Cruick approaching. He smiled kindly as he greeted me and shook Harry's hand. Seeing the face of a friend in this all-male bastion made me feel a little better.

Sir Charles asked us all to take seats around a large, mahogany table, and I sat with Harry on one side of me and Paddy on the other. The rest of the men in the room took chairs around the table as well. The light hum of polite conversation kept the silence from becoming awkward as everyone waited for the arrival of the accused.

Five minutes later, Stade walked in. I was glad to see his confident swagger falter when his eyes fell upon me. He looked at Paddy sitting next to me, and knew his game was up.

He gave it his best effort, however. He heaped scorn on the "Irish trash," who were obviously hoping to steal his prize stallion. He professed pity for the "poor girl, clearly deranged by grief"; that was I. Harry he termed my "innocent dupe."

It was Mr. Cruick who called for the evidence that I knew would weigh most heavily with the stewards—the Stud Book. All the men in the room were serious horsemen, and they knew the paramount importance of heredity in horse breeding. *Breed the best to the best*. Finn MacCool would speak for himself through the records in the Irish Stud Book.

The volume was produced and Sir Charles put on his spectacles and located the entry for Finn MacCool. The room was utterly silent as he began to read.

" 'Sire: Skylark.' "

A rustle of surprise ran around the entire room. Skylark was an English horse who had belonged to the Earl of Egremont. He had been extremely successful both on the track and as a sire.

I was watching Stade, and I saw his jaw clench as the men of the Jockey Club reacted to Skylark's name.

" 'Dam: Royal Maeve,' " read Sir Charles. The name of the Irish mare was not familiar to the assembled Englishmen, but when Sir Charles looked up Royal Maeve's track record, it was found to be impressive.

The last track record to be considered belonged to Finn MacCool himself. Sir Charles read the statistics aloud in a dry, uninflected voice. Victory after victory was cited. In his entire career, the horse had lost only one race, and that was the race where he had incurred the injury that caused his retirement.

There was absolute silence in the room when Sir Charles had finished. The stewards did not need to look up Alcazar in the Stud Book. His mediocre breeding and career were already known to everyone present.

Sir Charles closed the Stud Book quietly and removed his spectacles. Paddy spoke into the continuing silence, "All we are asking of the stewards is that someone travel to Inishfree Farm to look at the horses that are Finn MacCool's get. It is the request that Mr. Fitzgerald would have made, if he had not been murdered first."

The faces of the men around the table were looking exceedingly grim. Stade's unwinking brown gaze was fixed with hatred upon Paddy. "You Irish scum all stick together," he said.

Paddy's pale blue eyes did not drop before the Marquis's aggressive stare. "And you, sir, are a lyin', thievin', murtherer," he returned in the soft, gentle voice that horses loved.

Stade cursed, and began to rise from his chair, his head lowered bull-like on his thick neck.

"Sit down, Stade."

My eyes snapped around toward the door expecting to see Adrian standing there. The door was still securely shut, however. It was another moment before I realized that the clipped, authoritative voice had not issued from Adrian's lips at all, but from Harry's.

Stade sat down. Everyone in the room stared at Harry, whose angelic face looked quite amazingly formidable. He said in the same incisive voice, "This is not a matter to be settled by name-calling, Sir Charles. This is a matter to be settled by evidence." Harry's cold eyes circled the faces around the table. "Will you allow me to recapitulate what you have learned this morning, gentlemen?"

Sir Charles nodded gravely, giving him permission to continue.

Harry steepled his fingers together and said, "You have listened to the testimony of Sean MacBride, Finn MacCool's old groom, who has told you that the horse that is being passed off as Alcazar is in fact Finn MacCool himself. You are all horsemen, and thus you know that no one knows a horse as intimately as the man who grooms him.

"Fact number two, you have perused the evidence that is in the Stud Book. You are all breeders, and thus you know how loudly the bloodlines of these two stallions speak."

Across the table from me, Lord Sussex nodded in agreement.

Harry's voice continued dispassionately, "You have learned from Sean MacBride that the Marquis of Stade tried to buy Finn MacCool and that after his offer was refused, there was a suspicious fire in Finn MacCool's barn."

The man who was sitting next to Stade shot him a look that I can only describe as disgusted. Harry went relentlessly on, "You have been told of the puzzling disappearance of Finn MacCool and the subsequent astonishing improvement in Stade's breeding program." Once again his eyes slowly circled the table. "And then there is the fact that immediately after the fire at Inishfree Farm, all of Alcazar's grooms were dismissed."

The room was completely silent. All of the Jockey Club stewards, who were much older than he, were regarding Harry with attention and respect. He placed his hands flat on the table in front of him, gave me a compassionate look, and said softly, "Then there is the death of Daniel Fitzgerald."

The men who had been leaning forward all sat back. No one wanted to contemplate Papa's death, but Harry was not going to let them off. "Mr. Fitzgerald was shot not far from the estate of the Marquis of Stade," he said. "The man who fired the gun was never found and the local magistrate ruled that the shooting was accidental, but you gentlemen of the Jockey Club must know that there has not been such an accidental shooting in the Newmarket area in a hundred years."

I saw a muscle twitch in the corner of Stade's left eye.

At last Harry looked at him. "You either had him killed or you shot him yourself, Lord Stade," he said.

The marquis's menacing brown gaze fixed upon Harry. "You can't prove that," he said.

"Probably not," Harry returned regretfully. "But we can prove that you switched the stallions."

Stade knew that we could. You could see it in his face. The rest of the men in the room could see it too.

The noontime sun was slanting in through the slats of the open venetian blinds. Lord March coughed and someone else cleared his throat. Next to me, Paddy made a restless move and then was quiet. We all stared at the neat, regular features of Sir Charles and waited.

Sir Charles picked up his spectacles and began to polish them with a cambric handkerchief. My own hands were clenched together in my lap. *He has to believe us,* I thought fiercely. *He has to.*

Sir Charles replaced his spectacles on the table in front of him and put away his handkerchief. He looked at Harry and said, "We will have one of our members travel to Galway as you suggest, Mr. Woodrow. We will also institute a search for Alcazar's old grooms."

A faint sigh went around the room, as if everyone present had been holding their breaths and then had released them at the same time.

At last Sir Charles turned his eyes to the angry, defiant face of the Marquis of Stade. "I am in little doubt, however, as to what we shall find," he said. "And if these investigations do indeed show the truth of what has been alleged here today, I tell you now, Lord Stade, that should you ever again enter a horse in any race in England, no gentleman will run against you."

Paddy put his rough, work-worn hand over mine. We had won.

Once Stade had stormed out, it took a little while for the rest of the room to clear. Mr. Cruick grabbed my ear and I had to listen one more time to his recital of how Stade had once cheated him in a race. Paddy and Sean were talking to Sir Charles, and I knew that they must be discussing the return of Finn MacCool to his legitimate owner. A number of the other men had surrounded Harry.

I commiserated with Mr. Cruick, then accepted the condolences of several gentlemen who came up to express their horror about Papa's murder.

"Wish we could prosecute the bounder," Mr. Cruick said.

"Well, well, there's no sense in dragging our dirty linen out into the public view," Lord Henry Groton said. "Stade will be ostracized not only from the racetrack but from good society as well. Punishment enough, I should say." He patted my shoulder. "Your father's death may have been an accident after all, Lady Greystone."

All the men around me nodded.

"It wasn't," I said.

Lord Henry looked a little put out. I was not playing the game properly. Aristocrats did not, as Sir Charles had said, "drag their dirty linen out into the public view." Even if more evidence had been available, the gentlemen of the Jockey Club would not like to see a marquis put on trial for such a sordid act as the murder of an Irish horse dealer.

"I am afraid we will never know," Lord Henry said pompously.

"That is so," agreed Mr. John Plimpton, who had known Papa well. "You must be content that you have successfully finished your father's investigation, Lady Greystone. Finn MacCool will be returned to Ireland, and Stade will be banned from English racing. I know that is what Daniel would have wanted."

"Yes," I said listlessly.

At that moment Harry turned around, and I caught his eye. He started toward me immediately. "Ready to leave, Kate?" he asked.

"Yes," I said.

The gentlemen of the Jockey Club gallantly bowed me out, doubtless wondering why I had insisted on coming in the first place.

As Harry tooled the phaeton back toward Harley Hall, I wondered myself. I felt none of the triumph that I had expected I would feel at the defeat of Stade. Instead I just felt . . . empty.

"You're awfully quiet," Harry said.

I sighed. "There isn't much to say, Harry." I turned to look at him. "Except to tell you how magnificent you were. I was so impressed! And so were the stewards. You were a veritable Cicero, Harry!"

He looked pleased.

"You should go into Parliament," I said. "You would be wonderful speaking in the House of Commons."

He shook his head. "Adrian is the one in the family to go into government, Kate."

A flock of sheep had ambled onto the road ahead of us, and Harry had to stop the horses. "Stupid creatures," he said disgustedly.

"Adrian sits in the Lords," I said. "That doesn't mean that you couldn't have a splendid career in the Commons."

The milling sheep had evidently decided they would take a little stroll up the road instead of returning to their pasture. Harry shouted at them to move, but they ignored him. His loud voice startled our own horses, however, and then he had to quiet them. When they were once more standing still, he was able to return his attention to me. "Do you think so?" he said.

I nodded emphatically. "Yes. I do. Just look at how important Charles James Fox was in the Commons. And Edmund Burke. And . . ."

I could hear the excitement he was trying to disguise as he held up his hand and said, "All right, Kate. I take your point."

He clucked to the horses, then began to walk them forward in the hope of encouraging the sheep to vacate the road.

"You bowled them over at the Jockey Club," I said. "You were so cool and logical, Harry. Didn't you see how all those powerful men were hanging on your every word?"

"Ba . . . a . . . a . . . a . . . ba . . ." The sheep finally noticed the horses and began to scurry around, trying to find a way off the road. They really were the most colossally stupid animals.

"I still have to finish Oxford," he said.

"Yes, but after you finish I am sure that there is a family seat you could have."

"There is, of course."

The House of Commons was nominally elected by the commons of England, but what usually happened was that the common people in a particular district voted as their local lord decreed.

"I'll talk to Adrian about it," Harry said. The suppressed excitement was now bubbling in his voice. "I think I might quite like to go to the Commons."

We were finally through the sheep, and the horses once more picked up a trot. I thought of the way Adrian's face had looked when Harry and I had left the house this morning, and I realized the major cause of my dejection. I might have just triumphed over my enemy, but I would never be truly happy as long as I was at odds with Adrian.

Adrian was not at Harley Hall when I returned, and I learned from Mr. Bellerton that he and several of the other men had gone to look at one of the large stud farms in the area. I waited all afternoon for him to return, hoping that a few hours of looking at beautiful Thoroughbred mares and their foals might have put him in a better temper. I wanted very much to tell him about what had transpired at the Jockey Club meeting. But the afternoon hours slipped relentlessly by, and still there was no sign of Adrian.

Lady Barbury had invited a crowd of people from some of the other house parties in the area to come to Harley Hall for an informal dance that evening, and when Adrian did finally make an appearance I was sitting in front of my dressing-table mirror having my hair done.

I swung around to look at him, causing Jeanette to pull

the strand of hair she was working on rather sharply. I yelped, and she apologized profusely.

"Never mind," I said. "It was my fault."

"I'm sorry I'm late, but we stayed rather longer than we intended," Adrian said to me. "It won't take me long to change." He disappeared in the direction of his dressing room, where his valet had been waiting for the last hour.

He had not smiled, and his voice had sounded distinctly wintry. He was still angry with me for keeping secrets from him.

Damn.

I stared resolutely in the mirror while Jeanette fiddled with my hair.

This is all my fault, I thought. *I hurt his feelings by not confiding in him.*

My pride didn't seem important any longer. In fact, at this point nothing seemed more important than having Adrian smile at me again. The first chance I got, I was going to tell him that I loved him.

CHAPTER
twenty-five

A T SIX-THIRTY SIR CHARLES'S OWN HOUSE PARTY, augmented by a few extra guests, sat down to a formal dinner; the other guests would not begin arriving for the dance until nine. I was seated on Sir Charles's left, directly opposite the Duchess of Wareham, who as the ranking female guest was honored by the place at her host's right hand. The duchess had not been precisely friendly to me during this visit, but at least she was no longer shooting dagger-looks every time she saw me. Lady Mary's attachment of Mr. Bellerton had evidently gone a long way toward reconciling the duchess to the fact that her daughter had been cheated out of Adrian.

Sir Charles and I discussed the races, his horses, his hounds, and the weather. An unspoken mutual agreement kept us from mentioning the Marquis of Stade or the morning's meeting. When Sir Charles politely switched his attention to the duchess, I turned to the gentleman on my other side and we talked about the races, his horses, the weather, and, finally, Adrian's future in the government. I was enthusiastic about the first three topics, and noncommittal on the last.

"You will have to speak to my husband about his plans, Lord Denham," I said sweetly. "I am afraid that I can tell you nothing."

"He is making far too great a thing of these government sanctions," Viscount Denham, who was in the Home Office, assured me earnestly. "We are simply concerned for the public safety."

I tried to keep my lip from curling cynically. *Public safety, hah,* I thought to myself. *You are concerned for your own privileges, my lord.*

I smiled and said with big-eyed innocence, "I know that my husband feels great concern for the welfare of the many veterans who have fallen upon hard times with the peace they fought so gallantly to secure."

Lord Denham, who might have been handsome if he had owned a chin, shook his head sadly, "I fear many of these ex-soldiers and -sailors have turned into nothing but a lawless rabble, Lady Greystone," he told me.

"It is hard to be law-abiding when the law is making you go hungry," I replied.

Making a visible effort, he smiled benignly. "I was hoping that you would use your influence with your husband to persuade him to join Lord Liverpool's government, Lady Greystone. It is the natural place for a man of Greystone's stature and talents." He leaned his head a little toward me and said with great significance, "After all, Lord Liverpool won't be prime minister forever."

I stared at him in profound surprise.

He favored me with a look that he managed to make both humorous and condescending. "I know you are thinking that the Duke of Wellington would be the natural successor to Lord Liverpool, but there are those of us who think Greystone might be a better choice."

In fact, I had not been surprised at the suggestion that Adrian might one day be prime minister. I probably wouldn't have been surprised if he had said that one day Adrian might be king. It was something quite else that had startled me.

"Whatever makes you think that I would have any influence with Greystone on a matter such as this, Lord Denham?" I asked in amazement.

His smile became even more condescending. "Beautiful young wives always have influence with their husbands, Lady Greystone," he said.

I did not reply immediately, but took a bite of the stuffed venison on my plate. Lord Denham took several sips of wine and watched me over the rim of his glass. After I had swallowed the venison, I said gently, "The only thing that influences my husband is his conscience, Lord Denham. You may rest assured that he will do whatever it may dictate."

The viscount did not look as if he liked this answer at all.

After dinner the ladies withdrew to freshen their toilettes, and by the time I came back downstairs the guests had begun to arrive. A thought struck me, and I turned to the lady who had come down just behind me and asked, "Do you happen to know who has been invited to this dance, Lady Mary?"

She nodded gravely. "My mother and I helped Lady Barbury write out the invitations."

The implication, of course, was that the duchess and her wonderful daughter had been perfect guests, while I had done nothing but drive off to the races every day. Well, I had been *invited* for the races, damn it.

I said, "Was the Marquis of Stade invited?"

"Yes," she said. "He has the Marlons staying with him, and the Stoningtons."

It seemed as if the dance would be thinner of company than Lady Barbury had expected, I thought. Not even Stade would have the nerve to show his face after what had transpired at the Jockey Club this morning.

The dance was an informal affair. The drawing-room rugs had been taken up, the chairs pushed back, and three musicians stationed in front of the fireplace. The atmosphere was much jollier than anything I had attended in London. No Almack's patronesses, with their gimlet eyes, were present to put a blight on people's sense of fun.

Adrian avoided me. He didn't do it obviously; he even danced a country dance with me. Adrian would never publicly humiliate me; but he knew and I knew that he was avoiding me.

I tried not to let this worry me. I even told myself that Adrian must care about me a little if he was so upset by my keeping secrets from him. I would have him to myself tonight, and if all else failed, I knew I could effect some kind of a reconciliation in bed.

At ten-thirty, the musicians struck up a waltz. I had been sitting out the previous dance with Mr. Bellerton, who had not danced all evening, and now I said, "Please won't you dance this waltz with me, Mr. Bellerton?"

He smiled and shook his head. "I'm afraid that Napoleon put an end to my dancing days, Lady Greystone. But don't let me detain you. There are at least a dozen men present who would love to dance the waltz with you."

But I had seen the wistful glances he had cast toward the dance floor earlier, and I was not about to let him off. "If you step on my toes, I won't say a word," I promised him. "And there is so much dipping in a waltz that no one will notice your limp."

He laughed, and once more tried to get out of it.

"Do you *know* how to waltz, Mr. Bellerton?" I demanded.

He set his jaw. "Yes, Lady Greystone, I do. The last time I waltzed was in Brussels, on the night before Waterloo."

"I think you are giving up too easily," I informed him. "You have been looking longingly at that dance floor all evening. I think it's cowardly to let a little limp keep you from doing something that you so clearly enjoy."

I could see that he was getting angry. I have found that calling a man a coward is usually guaranteed to produce this result. "This is the perfect place for your return to the dance floor," I continued annoyingly. "An informal atmosphere, a small group of friends," I waved my hand comprehensively, "what could be better?"

Poor Mr. Bellerton was in a quandary. He could not tell me to go to the devil, which he clearly wanted to do; nor could he get me to give up. He finally said grimly, "Very well,

Lady Greystone, I will attempt the waltz. But you must promise to allow me to retire if I cannot do it."

"Done," I replied. I took his hand and almost pulled him out to the floor before he could change his mind.

His steps were tentative at first, and they were certainly a little uneven, but he kept time with the music and I had no trouble following him. We waltzed down one side of the room, executed the corners with commendable expertise, and went back up the other side. A few of the men on the floor grinned when they saw him and said things like "Good show." Mr. Bellerton displayed no signs of wanting to sit down. In fact, he was smiling.

When the dance was finished we stood together for a moment at the edge of the floor. He looked down at me, a faint smile still on his lips. I grinned and said, "I told you so."

He laughed.

Lady Mary's voice said, "Richard! You were dancing!"

Astute of her to have noticed.

We both turned to look at her. Her expression was not pleased.

He said, "Lady Greystone bullied me into it." His eyes were sparkling as he turned to me once more. "Do you always know what's best for people, Lady Greystone?"

"Well . . . perhaps not *all* the time."

He laughed again, and Lady Mary gave me an extremely nasty look. She stared at her beau and complained, "You would never dance with me!"

"He wouldn't dance with me, either, until I forced him to," I remarked. "Men are so sensitive about how they look."

"Thank you, Lady Greystone," Mr. Bellerton said with amusement.

I looked at Lady Mary's face and understood how she must be feeling. She had been being so careful not to hurt Mr. Bellerton's feelings, so sympathetic to his fear of being humiliated, that she had gone along with his refusal to dance.

And now she found him waltzing with me—and loving it! When she gave me another nasty look, I couldn't blame her.

A roar of laughter came from the other end of the room, and when I looked I saw that the noise was coming from a small group of people surrounding Adrian in front of the terrace doors. His face was bright with amusement, and I wanted so badly to walk over and join him, but at that moment Mr. Cruick appeared at my side and asked me to join him for supper. Suppressing a sigh, I agreed.

When we came back from supper I immediately scanned the drawing room, but Adrian was nowhere to be seen. He had not been in the supper room either, and I wondered if perhaps Lord Denham had dragged him off somewhere to talk politics. As my eyes made one more quick circle of the room, I saw the terrace doors opposite us open, and then Adrian came in with Lady Mary. He closed the door behind them, turned to her, and lifted her hand to his mouth. Their eyes met, and she smiled. I felt stabbed to the heart.

As if from a long way away I heard Mr. Cruick's voice asking, "Are you all right, my dear? You just went deathly pale."

I don't know what I answered him. I don't know how I got out of the drawing room. I only know that I was standing all by myself at the bottom of the stairs when a footman came up to me bearing a note upon a silver tray.

"I was asked to give this to you, Lady Greystone," he said.

I took the note. I opened it and stared at the strong, black lines of script that seemed to jump up at me from the cream-colored paper. The words cleared my brain immediately.

If you desire to receive information that will connect the Marquis of Stade to the death of Daniel Fitzgerald, come immediately to the kitchen garden gate. Alone. It was signed *A Friend.*

In defense of myself, I must say here that I was so upset by the scene that I had just witnessed between Adrian and

Lady Mary that I was not thinking clearly. I like to think that under ordinary circumstances I would not have been such a fool. However, nothing I say can disguise the fact that I proceeded to lift one of the guest's cloaks from the small salon where they were all piled, and to slip unseen out one of the side doors of the house.

The night was very clear and chilly. I hugged the borrowed velvet cloak close around my bare shoulders and arms as I made my way along the graveled path that led to the back of the house, where the kitchen garden was situated. The almost-full moon was hanging in the sky above the trees, illuminating the world with an eerie white light.

I reached the garden gate and stood for a moment, watching and listening. The only movement in the moonlit night was the gentle swaying of the boughs of the apple trees on the far side of the stone wall that separated the garden from the part of the drive that tradesmen used. Slowly I opened the gate and moved into the garden.

Somewhere a nightingale was singing. I tripped on the edge of my too-long borrowed cloak and halted, my attention caught by the shadow of the shed that lay against the wall in the corner of the garden. The apple trees rustled softly in the breeze, and I stared at the line of light that showed under the front door of the garden shed. From the far side of the wall came a jingling sound, and I recognized the noise a harness makes when a horse shakes its head.

Danger.

I realized in a rush of panic that I had been a fool to answer this mysterious summons alone. My heart began to pound, and then I heard behind me the sound of a footstep crunching on gravel. I whirled around, hands extended to protect myself, just as a heavy blanket was thrown over the entire upper part of my body, catching my hands helplessly within its folds. Strong hands wrapped the blanket tightly around me, lifted me like a sack, and began to carry me, even though I fought as ferociously and uselessly as a trapped cat.

We did not go very far. I was still struggling when I was flung to the ground. I landed hard and lay still for a moment, the wind knocked out of me. As I struggled to catch my breath, a hand grasped the end of the blanket, gave it a vicious jerk, and tumbled me out of it onto the hard-packed dirt floor of the garden shed.

"Get up." The voice fairly vibrated with hatred and fury. The line of light that had caught my attention earlier had come from the lantern that, when I raised my eyes, cast enough light in the shed for me to see the Marquis of Stade standing over me—with a pistol pointed at my chest.

Oh my God, I thought. *Oh my God.*

My heart was hammering as I cast a quick look around the shed, trying to see if there might be some way out of this.

"You little bitch," he snarled. "Get up." He called me other unspeakable names as I got unsteadily to my feet, my eyes now riveted on that pistol. The rage poured from him in waves that were almost tangible.

I gained my feet. My mouth was so dry I didn't know if I could speak, but I had to try. "You won't get away with this, Stade," I managed to croak. "You got away with killing Papa, but you are a suspect now. You won't get away with killing me."

His neck muscles were swelled like a bull's. "Yes, I will," he said. "They may suspect me, but they won't be able to prove anything. No one has seen me this time either."

My hands had involuntarily spread themselves in front of my stomach in a futile gesture of protection.

My baby, I thought. *I can't let him kill my baby.*

Once again my eyes desperately searched the shed. There were some garden tools leaning against the far wall, but I would never have the time to get to them.

"You won't get away with this," I repeated.

"I'm going to kill you," he said, and raised his pistol so that it was once more trained on my chest.

At that moment the door behind him swung open. He

heard it and started to swing around, but he had already begun to squeeze the trigger. His hand jerked, and the shot boomed out and buried itself in the wooden wall behind me.

Through the black smoke given off by the pistol, I saw Harry standing in the doorway, a fireplace poker in his raised hand. He was in the act of bringing it down on Stade's head when Stade once more got his double-barrel pistol pointed. It went off at the same moment that Harry's poker connected, and both men fell crashing to the ground.

"Harry!" the bloodcurdling scream of Harry's name came from me. There was blood streaming from Stade's forehead as he lay sprawled motionless on the ground. I stepped on his stomach as I frantically scrambled to get to Harry.

There was blood all over his shoulder, but his eyes were open and his voice was clear as he said to me, "You all right, Kate?"

"Oh my God, Harry," I said, "you've been shot!"

I thought I heard Stade beginning to move, and I turned around to check on him.

Another voice spoke from the doorway. "Kate! What in the name of God is happening here?"

It was Adrian.

"Thank God!" I said. "Adrian, Harry has been shot!"

He was down on his knees next to his brother in an instant. I looked around for a weapon in case I needed it, and grabbed a spade as the most useful tool available. I stood next to Stade, ready to bash him again if he started to wake up.

Adrian had pulled off his neckcloth and was using it to stanch the blood from Harry's wound. I felt intense relief when I heard Harry groan. At least he was still alive.

"You took a nice pop in the shoulder, lad," Adrian was saying to his brother. His voice was perfectly calm. "It's going to hurt like bloody hell when the sawbones gets at it, but you'll survive."

"You got . . . the note?" Harry gasped.

"I did. Thank you, Harry. You did everything right."

They were such simple words, and they were spoken simply too, but I know that my throat closed down with emotion, and I saw the way Harry's fingers closed around his brother's hand.

CHAPTER
twenty-six

ADRIAN SENT ME BACK TO THE HOUSE TO FETCH help and to send someone for a doctor. I waited in the hall, and when they carried Harry in the front door on a hurdle, it brought back with a flash of painful intensity the day my father had died.

I huddled against the wall, looked at Harry's white face and closed eyes as he was carried by, and prayed. *Please God, not Harry too. Please, please, please. Not Harry. Don't take Harry. Please* . . .

The four stalwart footmen who were carrying Harry's makeshift stretcher headed for the stairs. Adrian came over to me and put his arm around my shoulders. "He isn't going to die, Kate," he said quietly. "It's just a shoulder wound."

I pressed into his comfort and his strength. "You're not just saying that?" I whispered.

"I am not just saying that. Now, I want you to come along upstairs with me. You've had a terrible shock and you need to rest."

I let him move me toward the stairs. When we reached the first step I stopped and said, "They carried Papa in like that after Stade shot him."

"Your father was shot in the chest," he said in that same quiet voice. "Harry's injury is in his shoulder."

Slowly we began to climb the stairs. Four steps up, I stopped again and looked searchingly into his face. "Are you sure he is going to be all right, Adrian? You are not just saying that to make me feel better?"

He returned my look, his dark gray eyes level and grave. "Trust me, Kate. I have seen all kinds of wounds, and you may believe me when I say that Harry is not going to die."

I did believe him. My eyes closed and my knees buckled with the intensity of my relief. He felt me sway, lifted me off the stairs and into his arms, and carried me the rest of the way to our bedroom.

"Take care of her ladyship," he said to a startled Jeanette as he deposited me on the bed. He looked down at me. "I'll come back after the doctor has seen Harry," he said, and departed to see to his brother.

I let Jeanette undress me and I told her to make up the fire before she left. Then I wrapped myself in a satin quilt from the bed and curled up in the big rocking chair in front of the fire. I prayed for Harry.

It was several hours before Adrian returned. His first words when he saw me peeking around the back of the rocker were "You should be in bed."

"I couldn't sleep until I heard what the doctor had to say."

He crossed the room slowly and leaned his shoulders against the mantelpiece so that he was facing me. He looked so very weary, and my heart went out to him. "The doctor dug the bullet out," he said. "Harry was very brave. I gave him rather a lot of brandy and he's sleeping now. I'm going to change my clothes and spend the night in his room in case he wakes and needs something."

I said in a rush, "Adrian, I am so sorry. It's all my fault that Harry was hurt. If I had not been so stupid this would never never have happened."

He looked at me out of shadowed eyes. "It *was* a stupid thing to do, Kate. How could you have been so foolish as to go tearing off on your own like that?"

"I'm afraid I wasn't thinking very clearly," I said
small voice. "How did Harry know where to look for me?'

Lines of weariness bracketed his mouth; he looked lik
man who has not slept in days. He said, "You took M.
Ellsworth's cloak. She and Harry were going to go for a stroll
in the gardens, and when they went to get her cloak, it was
missing. In its place Harry found Stade's note. Apparently
you put it down when you picked up the cloak. It is nothing
short of a miracle that Harry read it."

My eyes clung to his face. "Why did he?"

He shook his head slowly. "We'll have to ask him that
when he is feeling better. The information I have given you
thus far I garnered from Miss Ellsworth."

"So when Harry read the note, he grabbed a poker and
came racing to my rescue?"

"Yes. And he instructed Miss Ellsworth to take the letter
to me." The shadows around his eyes and the lines around his
mouth seemed to deepen. "Thank God he did not take the
time to look for me himself, Kate. If he had, we would have
been too late."

I said, "Stade just wanted revenge, Adrian. He wanted to
hurt me because I had exposed him to the Jockey Club." I
clutched the quilt closer against the sudden chill that made me
shudder. "What an evil, evil man he is."

"Yes," he said bleakly, and was silent.

I longed, with an ache that was almost physical it was so
intense, for him to hold me. But the distance between us was
more than just physical. My thoughtless stupidity had almost
killed his brother. How could I ask him to comfort me? How
could I dare presume to offer comfort to him?

I tightened my grip on my quilt until my knuckles were
white and said again, "I am so sorry."

He frowned at me. "What I cannot understand is why in
God's name you did not send for Harry as soon as you got
Stade's note."

As upset as I was, I didn't fail to notice that he had not

questioned as to why I had not sent for him. The gulf between us was yawning wider and wider.

"I just didn't think, Adrian," I said wretchedly. "Once I was in the garden I realized I had made a mistake, but Stade caught me before I could return to the house for help."

"He took you into the garden shed, I gather?"

"Yes." My voice got a little stronger. "He was going to shoot me, Adrian. He did actually squeeze the trigger, but Harry came in behind him and made him miss. Then Harry hit him over the head with the poker, but Stade managed to get a shot off before he went down. That was the shot that hit Harry. They both fell to the ground at the same time."

Silence. He rubbed his hand over his face.

"I am so very very sorry." I said, repeating myself like a parrot that knows only one phrase.

He lowered his hand and gave me a strained smile that did not touch his eyes. "Well, at least one good thing can be said to have come out of this night," he said.

"And what is that?" I asked in utter bewilderment.

"I believe you once told me that Harry wanted to be a hero," Adrian said. "Well, he most certainly was that tonight, Kate. He saved your life."

I blinked. "I had not thought of that, but you're right, Adrian. If Harry had not come along when he did, I would most certainly be dead."

"He was even wounded. Give him a day or two and he will be delighted."

I stared into his unsmiling eyes. "Harry isn't going to die, is he, Adrian?" I could not keep my voice from cracking.

"No, he isn't going to die, Kate." He pushed his shoulders away from the wall. "I am going to sit up with him tonight, however. I wouldn't be at all surprised if he developed a fever."

"I would be happy to keep you company," I offered tentatively.

He rejected me without a moment's hesitation. "Go to

bed, Kate. You look like a ghost. You've had a terrible shock, and you don't want to run the risk of miscarrying the child."

"No, of course I don't want to do that," I said woefully.

"Then get into bed," he repeated. "You may safely leave Harry to me."

When Harry awoke just before dawn, he did have a fever. The doctor came back and prescribed some kind of a brew for him to drink. He suggested bloodletting, but Adrian wouldn't allow it.

The day dragged by interminably. I went in to sit with Harry for two hours in the afternoon, while Adrian caught some sleep, and Harry's fever-bright eyes and flushed skin frightened me badly. His brain was clear, however. He knew me, and he even made a joke about all the attention he was getting.

"I feel so bad that you were hurt, Harry," I said. "It was all my fault. But I am so grateful to you. You saved my life."

"The bastard was going to shoot you," he said.

"He certainly was. I was never so glad to see anyone in all my life as I was to see you." I repeated, "You saved my life."

His eyes glittered. He said, "Could I have some water, Kate?"

"Of course."

I sat beside him, and held his hand, and talked softly of this and that, but after a while his attention wandered. I saw his eyes going again and again to the door.

When at last it opened and Adrian came in, the relief on Harry's face was unmistakable.

"How are you doing, lad?" Adrian asked as he came to stand on the opposite side of the bed from me.

"Good," Harry said. "Kate is taking good care of me."

"I thought she would, but you are going to have to put up with me for a while. Kate is going to go for a walk in the garden with Lady Mary."

Walking with Lady Mary was absolutely the last thing I wanted to do, but I said, "That will be nice," and got to my feet. Adrian put a competent hand on Harry's forehead.

"I'm still hot," Harry said.

"This kind of fever very often accompanies a gunshot wound," Adrian said. "I've seen it hundreds of times. You'll be right as rain in a few days, Harry."

Harry's eyes were clinging to Adrian's face. Adrian grinned at him. "Don't complain, little brother. You are in a nice warm house, in a nice warm bed, with a beautiful woman to tell you what a hero you are. Let me tell you, it's a great deal better than a muddy tent in Spain!"

"I wasn't aware that I was complaining," Harry retorted.

Adrian glanced at me and nodded his head toward the door. I bent to kiss Harry's forehead; it was too hot. "I'll look in on you again later," I said.

He nodded.

"Time for another dose of medicine," Adrian said.

Harry groaned.

I went out.

Lady Mary was indeed waiting for me at the head of the stairs. I decided it would be too much trouble to try to think up an excuse as to why I couldn't walk with her, so I went. We were joined on the terrace by Mr. Bellerton.

"Did you have a fever after you were wounded, Mr. Bellerton?" I asked him as we walked along one of the multitudinous gravel paths that wound through Lady Barbury's gardens.

"I certainly did, Lady Greystone," he replied.

I felt a trifle better. "My brother-in-law has a fever and it worries me," I confided. "He seems so sick."

"Where was he shot, Lady Greystone?"

"In his right shoulder."

"Did the bullet lodge itself inside him?"

"Yes. The doctor had to dig it out."

"That's why he has a fever," Mr. Bellerton said. "It happens every time a bullet is dug out."

"But the patient always recovers?" I could not hide my anxiety.

"Usually," Mr. Bellerton said.

I stopped walking. "Usually? My husband told me that he was certain Harry would recover."

"If Greystone told you that, then you have nothing to worry about, Lady Greystone," Mr. Bellerton said. "He has seen enough wounds in his time to be a judge."

That, of course, was what I kept telling myself. But I had seen the worried line between Adrian's brows when he looked at his brother. I was not sure.

"I am certain that many of the deaths in the Peninsula resulted from lack of good nursing care," Lady Mary said. "That will not be the case with your brother-in-law, Lady Greystone."

Much as I hated to accept comfort from her, I had to admit that her comment was comforting. I nodded and walked slowly forward once again.

"What precisely did happen last night, Lady Greystone?" Lady Mary asked. "We have heard all sorts of rumors today. Do you know that they carried in Lord Stade after Mr. Woodrow?"

I was outraged. "Is Stade still in the house?"

"No," Mr. Bellerton said. "He went home by chaise this morning."

They did not press me again, but they were both looking at me so hopefully that I had to ask, "The rest of the household really doesn't know what happened?"

They shook their heads.

I reflected that it would probably be better for people to know the truth. If we tried to maintain secrecy, all kinds of speculation was likely to ensue.

"Well, I wasn't trying to elope with Stade," I said tartly.

Lady Mary and Mr. Bellerton exchanged glances.

Damn, I thought. People *were* speculating!

"Of course no one thinks *that*, Lady Greystone," Lady Mary said.

Hah.

"I think I will tell you exactly what happened," I said, and proceeded to do just that. Their eyes were popping by the time I finished my tale.

"What a villain," Mr. Bellerton said feelingly.

"I hope they hang and draw and quarter him and stick his head on London Bridge," I said.

"I don't blame you," Lady Mary said. If I hadn't seen Adrian kissing her hand last night, I would have quite liked her.

"I don't believe we do that to criminals anymore," Mr. Bellerton murmured with amusement.

"Too bad," I said.

"Rest assured that he will be called to account for his attack on you, Lady Greystone," Mr. Bellerton assured me. "Thanks to that piece of viciousness, he will be looking at a much more severe punishment than a simple banning by the Jockey Club."

That news would have made me happy, if only I were not so worried about Harry.

As the day waned, Harry's fever rose, and Adrian spent yet another night sitting by his side. The doctor came with more potions and another offer to bleed Harry, which Adrian once again refused.

The following morning, Harry's fever broke. His brow was cool and he was sleeping soundly when I came into his room at seven in the morning. Adrian, who had spent the night in a chair drawn up close to Harry's bed, was sleeping too, his feet resting on an ottoman. His hair was rumpled, there was stubble on his cheeks and chin, and he was wearing a coat but not a neckcloth. He did not look comfortable.

I took advantage of his unconscious state to bend and

kiss him on the forehead. His eyes flew open. "Kate," he said groggily.

"Yes. Harry's fever has broken, Adrian! Feel him—he's cool."

"I know. It broke about two hours ago." He struggled to extricate himself from the knitted blanket he had wrapped himself in. A piece of the wool was caught on one of his buttons, and I disengaged it for him. He didn't stir until I had removed my hands. Then he got up and walked to the bed. He nodded with satisfaction at what he saw, turned back to me, started to say something, and was interrupted by a huge yawn.

"This means that he will be all right, doesn't it?" I asked anxiously.

"Yes." He rubbed his hand up and down over his face, obviously trying to wake up. "It's just a matter now of waiting for the wound to heal." He rubbed his head, further rumpling his hair.

"Adrian," I said gently, "go to bed. I will remain here with Harry until he wakens."

"I'm all right," he said. "I got some sleep in the chair."

"You look exhausted," I told him.

He shook his head, and yawned again.

I walked to the door and opened it. "Go to bed, Adrian," I said.

He tried vainly to stifle another yawn. "Perhaps I could do with a few hours' rest," he admitted.

I looked at his stocking feet. "Where are your boots?"

He looked vaguely over his shoulder. "By the fire?"

I went and fetched his Hessians, put them in his hand, pointed him toward the door, and gave him a gentle push.

He resisted long enough to say, "Be sure and call me when the doctor comes."

"I will," I promised. He went out into the hall. I softly closed the door behind him and went to sit beside Harry.

*   *   *

He awoke at nine o'clock grumbling that he was hungry. I ordered him some broth and fed it to him, since he could not manage the spoon. Then he went back to sleep.

He woke again shortly before noon, when the doctor was due to arrive to change his bandage. When I told him about the doctor's projected visit, he scowled.

I bit my lip and said, "I feel so guilty when I see you suffering like this."

The scowl disappeared. "There's nothing to feel guilty about, Kate," he said gruffly. "It's just a pop in the shoulder. I'll be right as rain in a couple of weeks."

I rested my elbows on the edge of the bed and said earnestly, "If you hadn't come in when you did, Harry, I would be rotting in the ground by now."

He pretended to shudder. "You have the most descriptive vocabulary."

"Well, it's true." I leaned my head closer. "Adrian told me that you found the note Stade had sent me on top of the pile of cloaks. We have been wondering—whatever induced you to read it, Harry?"

"I saw your name on it," he replied slowly. "I don't usually read missives that are not addressed to me, you know, but I got the strangest feeling when I saw that note. I didn't even think about it. I just picked it up and read it."

"And then you decided to come after me?"

He nodded. "I gave the note to Miss Ellsworth and told her to find Adrian, then I picked up the first heavy object I could find and ran like hell. I got a very bad feeling when I read that note, Kate. A *very* bad feeling."

At that, I stood up, leaned down to him, and kissed him lightly on his mouth. "Thank you," I said.

Bright color washed into his pale cheeks.

"You saved two lives that night," I informed him.

"Two?" He looked up at me, clearly bewildered.

"I hope you will stand godfather."

Understanding dawned. He gave me a radiant smile and

reached his good hand up to me. "That's wonderful news, Kate!"

I put my hand into his, held to it tightly, and said, "I have been so worried about you, Harry. . . ." The tears that seemed to come so easily to me these days brimmed in my eyes.

"I'm perfectly all right, Kate," he assured me hastily. "No need to get sloppy, you know."

I blinked, made a heroic effort, and got ahold of myself. "You look dreadful," I informed him. I sniffled. "You're even starting to show a beard. I didn't know you had a beard, Harry," and I ran my fingers curiously across the silvery down on his cheek.

But Harry's eyes were on the doorway. "Adrian!" he said. "I have been wondering where you were."

Adrian's hair was brushed, his cheeks were smooth, his clothes unrumpled, but there was a peculiarly tense look on his face as he came into the room, as if all the muscles under his skin had tightened. His voice was expressionless as he said, "How are you feeling, Harry?"

"All right," Harry said. "Kate has been talking my ear off, which has helped to keep my mind off the pain in my shoulder."

Adrian's back was to me so I couldn't see his face, but his voice was even as he replied, "Kate is very inventive."

"You didn't need to return so soon," Harry said. "You must be exhausted, Adrian. I don't think there's been a time in the last two days when I opened my eyes and you haven't been here."

"I grew accustomed to catching sleep when and where I could in the army," Adrian replied. "You would be surprised by the amount of sleep I managed to snatch in this chair."

"Well . . . I must own that I was very glad you *were* here," Harry said in a low voice. "Thank you."

"It is I who must thank you," Adrian replied. "After all, Harry, you saved the life of my wife."

CHAPTER
twenty-seven

THE DOCTOR CAME AND CONFIRMED THAT HARRY WAS much improved. Then the men sent me out of the room so the doctor could change Harry's bandage, and I went downstairs to inform our host and hostess of the good news.

Most of the houseguests had departed the day before, since the race meet was finished. The only people left besides my family were Mr. Bellerton, Lady Mary, and her mother. Everyone was very concerned about Harry, and Sir Charles Barbury told me that Stade would be brought up before a grand jury if I would be willing to testify.

"I am afraid it will be rather a public ordeal for you, my dear," he said apologetically.

"I should be delighted to testify," I said firmly. "And I'm certain that Harry will testify as well."

Sir Charles sighed. "Yes. Well, I am afraid that it will have to be done. Stade cannot be allowed to go free. Stealing a horse was one thing, but trying to kill the Countess of Greystone is something else."

I wondered how Sir Charles would have felt about the matter if I had been plain Miss Fitzgerald and not the Countess of Greystone. I decided it would be wiser not to ask.

Adrian came down to join us for luncheon.

"My brother is sleeping," he answered Sir Charles's concerned question. "Changing the bandage is always something of an ordeal."

Poor Harry.

Adrian gave his host a rueful smile. "I'm sure you did not expect to have us as guests for so long a period, Sir Charles. But I do not think I will be able to move my brother for several more days."

"My dear chap!" Sir Charles was waving his hands in his anxiety to reassure Adrian. "I assure you, it's nothing but a pleasure to have you gracing my home. Please do not think of leaving until you are perfectly comfortable with the state of Mr. Woodrow's health."

"You are very kind," Adrian replied.

"Not at all! Not at all! You are to regard Harley Hall as your home! Do not hesitate to ask for whatever you might require, Greystone. It is an honor to have you here."

Adrian replied politely to Sir Charles's effusions, and we all went into luncheon.

The next few days crept slowly by. The stronger Harry grew, the more bored he became, and I found myself spending most of my time in his room trying to keep him amused. We played endless hours of piquet, and I believe my total losses were something in the neighborhood of three million pounds.

Adrian and I lived together like strangers who were forced to share the same quarters and were doing their best not to get in each other's way. My brave resolution to tell him that I loved him had been quenched the instant that I had seen his lips tenderly touch Lady Mary's hand.

Added to that, he was clearly disgusted with the mindless impetuosity with which I had almost gotten his brother killed. He was far too generous to keep harping on the subject, but I could read his contempt in the coolness of his eyes when he looked at me, in the indifferent tones of his voice when he was forced to address me about some matter that affected us both.

I was fair-minded enough not to blame him for being annoyed with my stupidity—I was annoyed with it myself—but

I could not forgive him for Lady Mary. To make matters even worse, she and the duchess remained at Harley Hall for the entire duration of our stay. This enabled me to torture myself with the picture of my husband and Lady Mary walking and talking and riding together in the bright spring sunshine, while I sat inside and played hour after hour of piquet with a decidedly crabby Harry.

When Harry finally rebelled and demanded that the doctor allow him to return home, I supported him enthusiastically. The doctor relented and said we could leave the following morning. I went down to dinner that evening with a heart lighter than it had been in many days. After all, it was the last meal that I would have to spend being polite to Lady Mary.

Lord Barbury greeted me in the drawing room with unwelcome news. The Marquis of Stade had slipped away from his home the day before and could not be located. It was generally believed that he had fled to the Continent. Apparently his yacht had been seen in the harbor at Aldeburgh.

Lord Barbury conveyed this information in a tone of elegiac regret that absolutely enraged me. "Do you mean to tell me, Lord Barbury, that Stade was never arrested?" I demanded.

Lord Barbury took instant alarm at the tone of my voice and glanced nervously at Adrian, who was standing behind me. "Remember, he was injured, Lady Greystone," Lord Barbury said.

"I did not know that a blow on the head constituted a pardon for attempted murder," I returned.

Lord Barbury sent another glance toward Adrian, but when my husband remained silent, Lord Barbury had to answer me.

"Of course his injury doesn't pardon his actions, my dear. What I meant was that the authorities thought he was too badly hurt to need further confinement."

"And no one thought to keep his house under surveillance?" I went on relentlessly.

"Well . . . no," Lord Barbury said.

I felt someone move to my side and knew from the familiar fragrance that wafted to my nostrils that it was Louisa. Another thought struck me and I said to Lord Barbury, "Does Stade usually keep his yacht in the Aldeburgh harbor?"

Lord Barbury looked unhappy. "Well . . . no," he said again.

"And no one thought it suspicious when his yacht made a surprise appearance in the harbor just when Stade was due to be arrested?" I demanded.

Lord Barbury was silent.

Mr. Bellerton said gently, "Stade will never be able to return to England, Lady Greystone. He will be forced to live out the remainder of his life in permanent exile. That is a formidable punishment in its own right, you know."

"It is not enough," I said.

Support came from an unexpected and not overly welcome source. "I agree with Lady Greystone," Lady Mary said. "It seems to me this whole business has been sadly bungled."

"I agree," Louisa said firmly.

At last Adrian spoke. "I believe Lady Barbury would like us to go into dinner," he said.

I was in a foul mood all through dinner. It was obvious to me that the authorities had connived at Stade's escape, and the more I thought about it the more infuriated I became. When I announced after dinner that I was going to retire, Lord Barbury visibly sighed with relief.

I looked into Harry's room, hoping to find him awake so that I could tell him what had happened, but he was sleeping soundly. Disappointed, I trailed down the hall to the room that I was sharing in such civil discord with Adrian. I didn't send for Jeanette but began to pace restlessly up and down in front of the fireplace.

I was still pacing an hour later when Adrian came in. I swung around to face the door as soon as I heard his step. "They let him go deliberately, Adrian," I said.

He closed the door behind him and came slowly into the room. "Yes, I'm afraid that they did, Kate," he replied.

"But *why*?" This was what I could not understand. "No one questioned his guilt. Why did they let him get away like that?" I had pulled the pins out of my hair when first I came in, and now I hooked the loosened mass behind my ears to keep it out of my way. "I don't understand," I said.

He sighed. "You appear to be the only person who doesn't understand, Kate. It's quite simple, really. Stade's escape was facilitated in order to save the nobility of England the embarrassment of a trial in the House of Lords."

I stared at him and didn't reply.

He went on, "Perhaps you did not realize that, as a Peer of the Realm, Stade would have to be tried in the Lords?"

"I don't care where he is tried," I said. "I want justice, Adrian!"

He shrugged. Shrugged! "Everyone wants justice, Kate," he said, "but precious few of us ever get it. And what Bellington said is true. Stade will be punished enough by permanent exile."

"Are you *defending* their actions?" I asked incredulously.

"What actions? No one helped Stade to escape," he said. "He acted on his own."

"There are crimes of omission as well as comission, Adrian," I returned angrily. "Don't try to tell me that there was no collusion involved in Stade's escape."

He said, his gray eyes bleak as a winter sky, "Tell your troubles to Harry, Kate, not to me. I'm too grown up to still harbor dreams of a perfect world."

His face swam before my eyes in a haze of red. I balled my hands into fists to keep from hitting him and said between my teeth, "Are you calling me a child?"

"You do not appear to be able to grasp the realities of the situation," he replied.

"Stade killed my father." I could hear the harshness of my own breathing. "I don't want him living comfortably in Paris, Adrian. I want him *dead*."

"He tried to kill you. He tried to kill my brother. I have no pity for Stade either, Kate. But I think this is the best solution."

He was holding himself as straight as he always did, but there was a suggestion of weariness about him that caught my attention. "Why?" I asked, my voice slightly less angry than it had been before.

He moved slowly to the mantel and stood staring down into the steadily burning fire. He said, "Because we do not need to focus the attention of the country upon a criminal who is essentially insignificant."

I stiffened when he used the word *insignificant,* but I said nothing. After a minute, when he saw that I was not going to erupt, he turned to face me. "The fabric of our society is already so badly damaged, Kate, and a trial in the House of Lords will only divide the country even more. The reformers will see a chance to attack the nobility, and the government will grow even more defensive than it presently is, and it will pass laws that are even more restrictive. Nothing good can be gained from such a trial, and much that is bad is likely to result."

I stood in front of him and had no reply.

He gave me the ghost of a smile. "Mind you, I am not claiming that these were the motives which caused Barbury to allow Stade to escape."

I was quite sure they were not. Lord Barbury and his ilk simply wanted to avoid a scandal.

I hung my head. "I had not thought of . . . of all you have said."

"I realize that."

My hair came tumbling loose from its mooring behind

my right ear, and I raised my hand to push it back. I bit my lip, said, "Adrian," and looked up at him once more.

His narrowed eyes were looking at my breast. I glanced down involuntarily and saw that a single ebony strand of hair had been caught inside the low-cut bodice of my evening dress. I looked up again at his hard, intent face and felt the heat of an answering desire surge through me.

I don't know which one of us moved first, but our bodies came together and I felt the fire of his kiss on my breast. My head was tipped way back, and the full length of my body was pressed against his. I could feel every hard line of him against me, and my love for him was like a river flowing inside me, surging strongly through every part of my being.

His mouth moved from my breast to my mouth and I parted my lips to receive him. After a long, dizzy time he lifted his head and said in a hoarse, unsteady voice, "Kate, let's go to bed."

We had gotten quite adept at shedding our clothes in a hurry, and it was not long before I was lying beneath him naked on the bed. His mouth was all over me, and I buried my hands in his hair, pressing him against me, breathless with the excitement his mouth was stimulating in all the nerves of my body. I ran my hands up and down his bare back, pressing first my fingers and then my nails into his skin. I repeated his name with increasing urgency.

He knew exactly what I wanted, and I shivered with pleasure as I felt the powerful surge of him come up inside of me, penetrating deeply. Our mouths met and I shut my eyes tightly as I concentrated on the feel of him within and without. Again and again I ran my hands up and down his back, over the smooth skin, the hard muscles, the strong bones.

His mouth moved to my cheek, my ear. "Kate," he said. "Kate."

I held him tightly as he drove deeper and deeper inside of me. If he went any deeper, I thought, he would touch the baby. His hair brushed against my cheek and inside I felt my flesh softening, yielding, letting him come still more deeply inside.

He drove me up the bed until my head was pressed against the mahogany headboard. He filled me utterly, and when the consummation finally rocked through me, the pleasure of it was so fierce that I thought I could not endure it. I felt the vibration of his own release, and we hung on to each other to keep from shattering into a million pieces and floating away.

I pressed my face against his sweaty shoulder and thought that it was only in moments like these that I felt truly married. Lying here with him like this, our union was deep and complete and profoundly fulfilling. I wished the morning never had to come.

The next day dawned as it always did, however, and Adrian and I went back to acting like courteous strangers. We left for Greystone late in the morning, Harry in the coach with me and Louisa, Adrian and Paddy riding on horseback. It was a long and tiring drive, but Harry insisted that he did not want to stop over on the road. By the time we got him into bed in his own room, he was exhausted. So was I.

After we had been home for two days, I took Louisa over to Lambourn Manor and introduced her to Mrs. Noakes. The three of us partook of tea in the kitchen and had a lovely time gossiping about the neighborhood. I was greatly relieved. If Mrs. Noakes had not taken to Louisa I don't know what I would have done. But when I confided in the housekeeper that Louisa was probably going to be her new mistress, she seemed actually to be pleased.

We had been home for exactly one week when I decided to drive into Newbury to pick up a book I had ordered. Before I left I went into the library to ask Harry if there was anything I could get for him while I was in town.

He was lying on the sofa in his dressing gown reading the *Morning Post*.

"I say, Kate, look at what appeared in the engagement announcements this morning," he said.

"You poor thing, you must be really desperate for amusement if you are reduced to reading the engagement announcements," I teased. But obligingly I picked up the paper and looked. Printed there, in starkest black and white, was the notice that a marriage had been arranged between Lady Mary Weston and Mr. Richard Bellerton.

I stared at it for a long time in silence. Then I gave the paper back to Harry and asked quietly, "Has Adrian seen this?"

"I showed it to him earlier," Harry reported, "but it came as no surprise. He already knew. Evidently Lady Mary told him about the engagement while we were still at Harley Hall."

I stared at Harry blankly.

"Kate?" Harry said. "You still there?"

"She told him?"

"That is what he said to me this morning."

"At Harley Hall?"

"Yes."

"Did he say exactly *when* she told him, Harry?"

He rolled his eyes.

"It's important," I said tensely.

"Well, he did say something about her telling him in confidence at that confounded dance."

"Did he by any chance say that they were out on the terrace?" I asked breathlessly.

"He might have," Harry said.

"Good God," I said.

Harry folded the paper and put it down on the footstool that had been pulled up next to the sofa. "Would you care to tell me what this inquisition is all about?" he asked.

"I think I have been very stupid," I said.

Harry grinned. "Nothing new there."

I moved the *Morning Post* to the floor and sat on the

footstool myself. This put my face on a level with Harry's, and I gazed at him solemnly and said, "I have been very angry with Adrian because I saw him kiss Lady Mary's hand when they came in from the terrace. I thought he was still in love with her, you see. But now I think that perhaps he was only making a gallant gesture in response to her telling him that she was getting married."

Harry looked back at me and said, "You thought Adrian was in love with Lady Mary? Are you insane, Kate?"

I bristled. "It was a perfectly reasonable thing to think, Harry. After all, Adrian wanted to marry Lady Mary before he was forced to marry me. Why wouldn't I think that he was still in love with her?"

Harry said distinctly, "Adrian is in love, all right, but not with Lady Mary."

I stared at Harry like a hopeful puppy. "Do you think that he might perhaps love me?"

He gave me a look that said he must be dealing with an idiot. "Kate, the man can't keep his eyes off of you. He is clearly bewitched. I can't believe that you didn't know."

I sat in a dazed silence, wondering if Harry could possibly be right, hoping that he was, and afraid that he wasn't. "I'm afraid that he is very angry with me, Harry," I confided. "He is angry that I almost got you killed, of course, but he was irked with me even before that. We should have told him about our murder investigations. He was excessively annoyed that we kept him in the dark."

Harry said, "You are exaggerating, Kate."

"No," I said gloomily. "I am not exaggerating, Harry. When I asked him to come to the Jockey Club hearing, he wouldn't. He said that we didn't need him, that we appeared to have managed very well without him."

Harry rubbed his perfectly chiseled nose. "Well, if that don't clinch things, then I don't know what does."

"What do you mean?"

"Great heavens, Kate! Think of what you just told me.

Adrian has never sounded petulant in his entire life. That is what you have reduced him to."

As I thought back to our quarrel, another idea struck me. I said thoughtfully, "Do you know, he even sounded jealous of you?"

Harry gave me a startled look.

I bounced a little on my footstool. "He said that we were as thick as thieves," I said. "And then, when I was complaining to him about the way Lord Barbury let Stade escape, he said that I should take my childish complaints to you, that he was too grown up to take them seriously."

Harry rubbed his nose again. "Considering that I have spent almost my entire life being jealous of Adrian, that is a pleasant turnaround."

"You aren't jealous of Adrian," I protested. "You love and admire him. It isn't the same thing at all."

"Of course I love and admire him." Harry cocked an eyebrow. "But he sets a hard standard, Kate."

I said, "I once told Adrian that you wanted to be like him but you didn't know how."

Harry slanted a sideways look at me. "What did he say to that?"

"He said, 'He shouldn't want to be like me. He should want to be like himself.' "

Harry's smile was rueful. "How like him."

"He meant it, Harry. And he is right."

"I know that."

I bit my lip. "Being Adrian isn't as wonderful as you may think it is," I said.

Harry's look was skeptical.

I stared at the *Morning Post* at my feet and said a little gruffly, "He once asked me if I knew how many deaths he was responsible for."

I heard Harry grunt in surprise, but I kept my eyes fixed on the newspaper. I fervently hoped that I was not betraying

Adrian's confidence by speaking this way, but I thought that it was important for Harry to understand his brother better.

"People look at him and they see his physical beauty, his bravery, his integrity." I turned to look at him. "But there is so much death inside him, Harry." I gripped my hands tightly together in my lap. "Be glad you missed the war," I said. "It is something that Adrian will probably never get over."

There was a long moment of silence. Then Harry said, "I never thought of him that way."

"He is a man to keep his troubles to himself. I only told you this because I thought you needed to understand him better."

Harry said, "You're right when you say that he is a man to keep his troubles to himself, yet he told them to you, Kate. Do you still think that he doesn't love you?"

CHAPTER
twenty-eight

I WANTED TO TALK TO ADRIAN IMMEDIATELY, BUT MR. Crawford, Adrian's agent, had arrived the night before, and he and Adrian were closeted in the estate office going over account books, so I decided I might as well go into Newbury. Louisa and Paddy were over at Lambourn for the day, so one of the grooms came with me for propriety's sake. My errand was accomplished easily and quickly, and in less than an hour I was back in the phaeton and eagerly heading for home.

Two miles outside of town we came upon a gig that was overturned on the side of the road.

I stopped. The gig appeared to have had only one passenger, the driver, who had just finished freeing his horse from the tangled harness when we pulled up.

"All you all right?" I called to the man. "Do you need help?"

He turned to me, holding the horse's bridle close to the bit. He was a stocky, middle-aged man with dark eyes set close together in a square, powerful face. He wore plain, countryman's clothes and could have been one of Adrian's tenants. He tried to approach my phaeton, but as soon as he took a step his face contorted and I heard his breath hiss in pain. He halted.

"Are you hurt?" I asked sharply.

"Aye. It's my left ankle," the man said hoarsely. "I've done something to it for sure."

I looked at the gig, which was resting on its side. It

would take more than my groom to heave it upright, and the driver was clearly in no state to assist. I said to the injured man, "Where do you live? If I take you home, can you send some men back to retrieve your horse and carriage?"

"That I can." The man gave me a grateful look. "My farm is just outside Thatchem. I would be fair appreciative of your help, ma'am."

"Y're addressing the Countess of Greystone," my groom informed him snootily. "Mind yer manners now and call her 'my lady.' "

I said, "This is hardly the time to worry about etiquette, Charlie. Get down, if you please, and assist this gentleman to take your place. You can remain with the horse and the gig until help comes."

Charlie's wizened face looked doubtful. "P'raps it would be best for us t' send help from Newbury, my lady," he suggested. "I din't like the notion of sending ye off with a stranger."

"Don't be so stiff-necked, Charlie," I said impatiently. "The man is clearly hurt."

Charlie scowled.

We looked at each other.

"Have a little compassion," I said.

We looked at each other some more. Finally he cast his eyes upward, climbed down from the phaeton, and went to take the horse from the injured man.

"I need to ask ye for some help to get to the carriage," the man said gruffly. At this, Charlie grudgingly offered his arm. Hopping and leaning on Charlie, the farmer made his way to the phaeton. It took him several tries to heave his way up to the seat. Once he was beside me, he hung his head forward, as if he were afraid he was going to faint.

I waited until he straightened up. "All right?" I asked gently.

He nodded.

I asked the horses to move forward at a walk, afraid that a trot might jar the poor man's ankle.

We continued north for a half a mile, and then instead of taking the road that would have brought me to Greystone, I veered to the east, toward the tiny village of Thatchem. The road was empty as I drove slowly along. "Is your farm before or after the village?" I asked.

"Before," he answered gruffly. "We're almost there now."

To the left of the road was a pasture where a flock of sheep were grazing peacefully, the lambs cavorting and play-ing games in the bright afternoon sun; to the right of the road fields of wheat rippled luxuriously in the gentle breeze. We rounded a curve, and there before us, drawn up on the grass margin at the side of the road, was an elderly-looking coach with two horses still in harness. I frowned when I saw it, thinking it peculiar to find two disabled carriages on the road in one day. Once again I halted my own horses.

The injured farmer I had rescued reached over and pulled the reins from my hands. I swung around, said, "What do you think you're doing?" and tried to snatch them back.

He shoved me aside. Hard. I had to grab the seat to keep my balance, and it was then that I heard another voice say, "Get down from the phaeton, Kate. You are coming with me."

I looked back to the road, to the man who had been con-cealed by the coach and who was now approaching the phaeton. My heart began to slam, and I tried once more to grab the phaeton's reins. If I could only get control of the horses!

The erstwhile farmer brought the side of his hand down on my wrist with a numbing blow. I gasped.

"Get down, Kate," my uncle said again.

I could hear my own rapid breathing. "What do you want?" I demanded.

"I want you to get down," Charlwood said. "If you don't do so immediately, Carruthers will hurt you."

I looked at the grim face of the man sitting beside me, and slowly, favoring my aching wrist, I climbed to the ground.

"That's right," my uncle said. "Now you will get into the coach."

It seemed that Charlie had been right after all.

"I have no intention of getting into that coach," I said. My mother's brother stepped toward me, gripped my arm with one hand, and with the other he hit the side of my head so hard that the world reeled around me. Then everything went black.

When I woke up I was in the carriage. My head ached and there was a ringing sound in my ears. My wrist hurt, and when I tried to move my other hand to rub it, I couldn't. It took me a few moments to realize that the reason for this was that both my hands were tied.

I leaned my aching head back against the cushion and tried to remember what had happened to me. Eventually I did, and the recollection did not make me happy. The only encouraging thing about my present situation, I thought, was that there was no one inside the carriage with me.

I looked out the window and saw that we were driving between high hedgerows along a twisting country lane. It could have been any one of hundreds of similar country lanes anywhere in Berkshire. It was definitely not the road to Charlwood, and my heart sank at the thought. Adrian might think to look for me at Charlwood, but he would never find this anonymous lane.

A few minutes later, the carriage turned in through a broken gate and proceeded slowly up a rutted track. It stopped before a cottage with a thatched roof in obvious need of repair, a fenced pigsty in need of a pig, and a vegetable garden in need of some plants. I felt sick when I thought how far removed from the main road this place was.

Adrian would never be able to find me here.

The coach door was thrown open and a man stood in the doorway. It was not my uncle but the man he had called Carruthers.

"Get out," he said. Even his accent had changed. His dark, close-set eyes were narrowed as he looked from the sunlight into the dimness of the coach.

I pressed my back against the cushions and said, "No."

He said in a perfectly expressionless voice, "If I have to knock you out again, I will."

The thought of being unconscious and at this villain's mercy was not edifying. I slid to the edge of the seat and then to the doorway of the coach. Carruthers lifted me down, and the feel of his hands on my waist made me want to shudder.

"I will double whatever Charlwood is paying you if you let me go," I said as my feet touched the ground.

He didn't reply, merely took my upper arm in a grip that would leave ugly dark bruises and began to walk me toward the cottage. I stumbled as I was ruthlessly dragged along, and his fingers bit deeper into my flesh as he held me up.

We reached the cottage door and Carruthers pushed it open. He shoved me into the dark interior and I lost my balance, tripped on my skirt, and couldn't recover because of my tied hands. I went down to my knees. The man towered above me in the narrow passage and waited silently for me to scramble to my feet. Then he opened a door that led into a room that had probably once been someone's parlor, and nodded for me to go inside.

The room I stepped into was small and low-ceilinged, with two windows in the far wall and a heavy wooden chair set in the middle of a worn grayish-colored carpet. I drew a deep breath and once again said to my captor, "I meant what I said, Carruthers. I will double Charlwood's price."

A flicker of amusement flashed across his face and then was gone. "If I sold out my customers, I wouldn't have any more," he said.

"My husband will give you so much money that you

won't ever need another customer for as long as you live," I said.

"Oh, I doubt that, my lady," he responded calmly. "Now, sit down in that chair so I can tie you up."

I stared at him in frustration, thinking that I must be able to say *something* that would get through to him. His face was absolutely calm. It was amazing how so calm a face could look so brutal.

"Sit down," he said again, and I realized that if I did not obey he would have no hesitation about making me. I did not want to be hurt so badly that I was incapacitated. I was going to need all my strength if I hoped to get out of this trap.

I sat in the chair. He tied my feet to the chair's legs, then took a knife from his coat pocket and cut the rope that was binding my hands together in front of me. The instant my hands were free, I grabbed for the knife, hoping to catch him unaware. I could not knock his hand free from the handle, and my own hand closed around his hard fingers. I dug my nails deeply into his skin, drawing blood. The chair I was tied to rocked as I hung on, struggling to gain possession of that precious knife.

"You little bitch," he muttered, and wrenched his hand and the knife out of my frantic hold. He took my already injured wrist in a punishing grip, pulled my arm behind the chair's back, and twisted it upward.

Agony burned through me. Through the stabbing red-hot pain I heard him say, "Don't ever try that again."

I held as still as I could, sobbing with the pain in my arm and shoulder. He lowered my arm fractionally and said, "Give me your other hand."

I shut my eyes tight and reached my other arm behind the back of the chair. He lowered my arm some more, then began to bind my wrists together. When he had finished he came back around the chair to face me.

I think he would have frightened me less if he had shown some emotion. I felt sick from the pain in my wrist, but I stared at him defiantly. His face was expressionless as he slowly looked me up and down, from my eyes, to my throat, to my breasts, to my belly, and then my legs. I felt as if he had stripped me naked, and I knew my cheeks were hot with fury and fright and humiliation.

"You're a very nice package, Lady Greystone," he said. "Maybe your husband *would* pay double to get you back. But as I said before, I don't cheat on a customer."

He stepped closer until he was standing directly over me, took a fistful of the hair that was streaming down my back, and pulled until my neck arched and I was forced to look up at him. He said, "I think I deserve a payment for the scratches you just gave me," and he bent his head and covered my mouth with his so that I could not breathe.

It was awful.

Adrian, I prayed. *Please, please, come and rescue me!*

Carruthers lifted his mouth from mine and for the first time in our encounter I saw emotion on his face. I cringed away from the lust that was making his close-set eyes so hard and bright.

"A very nice package indeed," he said.

I tried to kick him, but my legs were too tightly bound.

"My husband will have your head for this," I said.

"I don't think so," he replied, and bent to kiss me again. This time I bit him.

He jerked away from me, swearing furiously. I was pleased to see that there was blood welling up in his mouth.

He said, "You slut," and hit me. My head rocked back with the blow and the world reeled around me.

I struggled to clear my vision. "Villain!" I panted. "Bully! Is this the only way you can get a woman to kiss you? By tying her up and making her helpless to refuse?"

My breathing was the only sound in the room. Then he said with great deliberation, "Now we have a score to settle, Lady Greystone. But not until the customer is finished with you first."

Things did not bode well for me, and after Carruthers left I had nothing to do but think about my dismal situation and try to work my hands free. I pulled on the rope that bound my hands until I was sobbing with the pain in my injured wrist, but the knots would not loosen.

I was going to have to deal with my uncle. I remembered the expression on his face the night he caught Adrian and me kissing in the garden, and I was very afraid.

The sun was in the western part of the sky and its rays were slanting in the parlor windows when Charlwood finally came. He stood in the doorway and regarded me in silence, and I could feel myself staring back like a terrified animal.

"Adrian will kill you for this," I croaked.

"For what?" he asked lightly, and crossed the room to my chair.

"For kidnapping me," I replied.

He smiled. "Well, if I am to die for kidnapping you, then I might as well go ahead and do a few more things as well."

I did not ask him what other things. I was afraid I knew.

He took my chin in his hand and held my face up. "A little bruised, perhaps, but you are still very beautiful, Kate." He ran his forefinger across my lips. "Such a lovely mouth. Greystone likes it, doesn't he?" I stared at him mutely, incapable of thought even. "I gave him a juicy little plum when I forced you on him, didn't I, Kate? You opened your legs for him and he liked it. He liked it very much. It's unfortunate, because that is not what I intended."

"You can't hurt Adrian through me," I said. "I won't let you."

He said, "I am going to lie with you, and I don't think your precious Adrian will like that at all."

My mouth was absolutely dry. I said hoarsely, "If you rape me, Adrian will surely kill you."

He smiled. His sea-green eyes were filled with a torturous mixture of hate and desire, and I had to stop myself from cringing away from him. "Rape?" he said. "Surely not rape,

Kate. I think you will enjoy it. You like the idea of a man under your skirt."

"You are my mother's brother!" I cried in agony. "How can you say such things to me?"

His face went pitilessly cold. "I know you are Lizzie's daughter," he said. "That will make it even better."

Fear pumped through me with every beat of my pulse. He was warped and twisted, and nothing I could say would mean a thing. He put his hands on the neck of my pelisse and ripped it open. Buttons bounced off the floor.

The blood beat in my head as I realized the strength of those slim hands. I said, "Adrian will . . ."

His laugh stopped me, it was so full of malice. "Adrian, Adrian, Adrian," he said, mimicking my voice. "Adrian won't do a damn thing to me, Kate, because he won't want a scandal."

"You're wrong," said a voice from behind my uncle. "I have every intention of killing you, Charlwood."

It was my husband.

Charlwood spun around to face the man who filled the doorway. *"Greystone!"* he said.

I couldn't believe he had come. I had prayed and prayed for him to find me, but I hadn't really thought that he would.

"Kate," Adrian said, his eyes still on Charlwood, "are you all right?"

"Yes," I croaked.

I couldn't see Adrian's face very clearly, but I knew I had never heard that tone of voice from him before. I shivered.

Adrian spoke again in that same chillingly quiet voice. "We started something ten years ago, Charlwood, and now we are going to finish it." He stepped into the room, and for the first time I saw that he was holding two swords.

I felt chilled to the bone. My lips formed his name, but no sound came out.

My uncle's laugh sounded genuinely amused. "Are you proposing to duel with me, Greystone?"

"I was a boy the last time we fought," Adrian said. "I didn't know then that I should have killed you. Now I do."

"We were both boys," my uncle returned. "You forced the swords on me then because you knew you could defeat me. But you can't defeat me now, Greystone. I have had ten years to perfect my swordplay. It's you who are going to die."

I said in a trembling voice, "Adrian, can't we just leave? I am very uncomfortable tied up like this."

He came across to me, went behind the chair, and used one of the swords to cut the ropes that tied my hands. Then he did the same for my feet.

I moved my arms painfully and rested my hands in my lap. I looked up into Adrian's face, and as soon as I saw his eyes I knew that nothing I could say would weigh with him. He was in a white-hot fury.

"Get out of the center of the floor, Kate," he said to me.

I tried. I put my hand on his arm and said again, "Please, Adrian? Can't we just go home?"

He didn't even hear me; his whole attention was concentrated on the other man. Slowly, trying desperately to think of something I could do to stop this, I retreated to the wall. Adrian picked up the chair and plunked it down next to me. Before he turned back to my uncle, however, he reached inside his coat and took out a pistol, which he handed to me. "If I lose, Charlie is outside with the horses," he said.

My heart stopped. *If I lose . . .*

"No!" I said loudly, but Adrian had already turned his back on me.

Charlwood smiled with honest pleasure, and I felt terror surge through my veins. He had been preparing for ten years for this moment, and he was elated that finally it had come.

Adrian himself had not exactly been idle during the past ten years, but neither had he been perfecting his *demi-voltes* at Angelo's in London! How could a man who has been using nothing but a heavy saber hope to compete with a man whose chosen weapon was the dueling sword?

I watched in petrified horror as both men removed their coats and their boots. When they were standing in their shirtsleeves, Adrian offered Charlwood his choice of swords. My uncle accepted one, raised it, and attacked.

His thrust was lightning fast, but just as quickly Adrian's sword lifted to parry it. I forgot to breathe as I realized how close he had come to being skewered. Then the swordplay began in earnest.

They stood barely a sword's length apart, and their blades slid and tapped against each other with almost unbelievable speed. If this had been a sporting match, it would have been beautiful to watch. The rich glow of late-afternoon sunlight illuminated the white shirts, intent faces, and bright heads of auburn and blond. Their stockinged feet were quiet and the blades gleamed like flashes of lightning as the men engaged and disengaged. Only, it was death that waited in every flicker of those elegant swords, death that waited for one of the duelists at the end of this game.

The picture changed as Charlwood began to increase the rhythm of his attack, pressuring Adrian's blade so forcefully that he was forced to retreat slowly toward the door. My hand was pressed hard against my teeth as I watched.

This can't be happening. This can't be happening.

The thought repeated itself again and again in my brain, and I stretched my eyes wide, hoping that I would wake and discover that the scene before me was only a nightmare.

I didn't wake up, and the duel went on.

The concentration on my uncle's face as he pressed the attack was fearful to see. His whole being was consumed by only one desire: to avenge the loss and the humiliation he had suffered ten years earlier. Adrian parried and took another step backward.

Both men were breathing audibly, their shirts soaked with sweat. I could see that Adrian was aware of the wall coming up behind him, and suddenly, with a movement that I could not follow it happened so fast, he leaped to the side, out of Charlwood's reach, while at the same time launching a thrust of his own.

Charlwood cursed and sprang out of the way, and I saw blood stain the sleeve of his sword arm. Adrian took advantage of the break in Charlwood's rhythm to increase his own, and he began to drive my uncle back across the floor in the other direction, his attack coming so swiftly that all Charlwood could do was retreat and parry.

The swordplay was incredibly fast. I did not know how the men could sustain such a continuous effort. Both of them were gasping for air by now, but the relentless play of the swords went on. Back and back and back my uncle went, Adrian striking, Charlwood parrying. Back toward the window Charlwood was driven, and it was only when they had reached the pool of sunlight that I saw the danger to Adrian.

I cried out a warning, but it was too late. The sun shone through the windows directly into Adrian's eyes, blinding him. A second later he had leaped like a giant cat, back to the safety of the unlit room, but not before Charlwood had successfully landed a thrust of his own. Blood stained Adrian's right shoulder. Sweat was running down his face, and I could see the muscles in his back rippling through his soaked shirt.

Charlwood was in no better a case. He was almost sobbing for air as he followed Adrian out of the sunlight and back to the center of the room, where the match had started.

I was beginning to hope that perhaps they would continue on this way until neither of them was able to stand up. They were once more standing a sword length apart, and their breath was shaking their ribs. The swords were still going, but it seemed to me they were moving more slowly than they had. Both men were exhausted.

And then it happened. A stronger pressure on my uncle's blade, pushing it downward, a second's opportunity while it was harmlessly lowered, then, instead of the lunge my uncle was prepared to dodge, a hard blow on the upper part of his blade knocked the weapon from his hand.

Charlwood was disarmed.

The only sound in the room was the men's raucous breathing. They stared at each other. Charlwood empty-handed, Adrian with his own sword raised and pointed very steadily at the other man's throat.

Adrian's eyes were narrowed, his expression utterly ruthless, and for the first time I truly understood what a terror he must have been on the battlefield. But I could not let him kill Charlwood.

"Adrian!" I said loudly. "No!"

He said to my uncle, "You are a sick and twisted excuse of a human being, Charlwood. The world will be better off without you."

He hadn't even heard me. If I didn't act quickly, he was going to run Charlwood through, and then he would have to live with it. I raised the pistol he had given me, aimed carefully, and shot my uncle in the shoulder. He fell like a stone.

Adrian looked at me. Finally I had gotten his attention.

"Jesus, Kate," he said. A little color came back to his face as he looked down at Charlwood. "Did you kill him?"

"I don't think so," I said shakily. "I was trying to aim for his shoulder."

"Jesus," he said again.

I put the pistol down on the chair and ran to him. "Oh, Adrian," I said, flung myself into his arms, and began to cry.

CHAPTER
twenty-nine

ADRIAN BANDAGED MY UNCLE'S SHOULDER WOUND using his neckcloth, and then I bandaged Adrian's using my uncle's. Charlwood's eyes had been open when Adrian first began to work on him, but he had soon passed out. This was just as well, I thought. Certainly neither Adrian nor I wished to speak to him.

Of course, it was Charlie whom I had to thank for my salvation. Adrian told me the story as he worked on bandaging Charlwood's shoulder. "Somethin' about that accident smelled bad" is how Charlie had described his feeling as he had watched me drive off with Carruthers. So he had not stayed with the overturned gig as I had ordered, but instead rigged a bridle for the unharnessed cob and followed me. He had rounded the curve in the road to Thatchem just in time to see Carruthers loading my unconscious body into the coach, and he had followed behind the coach all the way to the cottage before going for Adrian.

"Thank God for Charlie," I said. "I would have been in deep trouble if he hadn't followed me."

Adrian didn't reply, but the set of his mouth bespoke his feelings clearly enough. I said, "Sit down so I can take care of your shoulder. You're too tall for me to reach it properly."

"It's only a scratch, Kate," he said. "It can wait until we get home."

"Sit down."

He began to protest again, looked at me, and stopped.

Apparently what he saw on my face convinced him that I meant business, because he walked to the chair where I had been tied up and sat down.

His shirt all around the shoulder area was soaked with blood and the rest of it was soaked with sweat. I made him peel the whole thing off.

Charlwood's sword had not cut deeply, thank God, and I wrapped the neckcloth tightly around his shoulder and under his armpit and said, "That will do until Dr. Matthews can look at it."

"I told you it wasn't bad," he said. "What did you do with my shirt?"

"Just put your coat on, Adrian. You will be warmer without that disgusting shirt."

"All right." He stood up and took his riding coat from me. "What's wrong with your wrist?" he said as he began to button the coat over his naked chest.

I realized for the first time that I was cradling my right wrist with my left hand. "Carruthers hit it when I tried to grab the reins from him," I said. "It's just a little sore."

I saw a muscle tighten in his jaw, and for a moment that scary look was back on his face. I said quickly, "It isn't broken or anything, Adrian. Truly, it's just a little sore."

After a moment he nodded. But his voice sounded very clipped when he said, "What precisely do you want to do with Charlwood? Quite obviously you don't want him dead."

"It's not his death I object to so much," I said honestly, "it's that I don't want you to be the one responsible."

He finished buttoning his coat as he walked toward my uncle's unconscious body. He stood over Charlwood, stared down into the pale, insensible face, and said, "What worries me, Kate, is that if he lives I won't be able to prevent him from attacking you again."

I regarded my husband's profile, which at the moment looked as chiseled and as stern as a Greek statue's. That, of course, was precisely why he had been prepared to kill

Charlwood. I understood that, but still I didn't regret what I had done.

I said, "I don't want a scandal, Adrian, and there will surely be a scandal if it comes out that you killed Charlwood in a duel. I don't want the whole world to know that my own uncle kidnapped and tried to rape me."

He pushed a strand of damp hair off his forehead. "I can't argue with that," he said wearily.

The dusty gray carpet under Charlwood was soaked with blood, and blood was beginning to seep through to stain the white neckcloth that bandaged his wound. I said in dismay, "Whatever are we going to do with him?"

"The first thing to do is take him back to Greystone and get Dr. Matthews to patch him up properly," Adrian said. "Matthews is a good man; he'll keep his mouth shut."

I spoke with a feeble attempt at humor in order to disguise the fact that I felt like crying again. "Too bad we can't pack him off to the Continent with Stade."

Adrian's gray eyes turned to me. They narrowed thoughtfully. "That's an idea," he said.

"It would solve our problem, of course, but I don't see how we could possibly bring it off."

"Let me think about it for a while," he said. "In the meantime, Charlie and I will load Charlwood into the coach and then we'll get him home to Greystone."

Charlie drove the coach and Adrian and I followed in my uncle's curricle. It seemed hardly the moment for a declaration of love—we were both exhausted and emotionally wrung out—but I was determined to delay no longer. The look on Adrian's face when he had held his sword to Charlwood's throat had convinced me that his feelings for me could not be lukewarm.

I pulled my buttonless pelisse closer around my shoulders and said, "Harry showed me the notice about Lady Mary and Mr. Bellerton this morning."

"Um," he said. One of the horses was throwing his head about restlessly, and Adrian spoke to him soothingly. My husband was clearly so uninterested in Lady Mary's projected marriage that I had to smile.

"I saw you kiss her hand when you came in from the terrace with her," I said. "I thought you were still in love with her, and I have hated the both of you for weeks."

I had gained his attention. "Kissed her hand?" he said in bewilderment.

"At the Barburys' dance. I saw you do it, Adrian." I folded my arms across my chest and regarded him sternly. "In fact, that was the reason I was so upset that I did not think clearly when I received Stade's note."

He glanced at me out of the side of his eyes. "You were upset because you saw me kiss Lady Mary's hand?"

"Wouldn't you be upset if you saw me kissing the hand of the man I was supposed to have married instead of you!"

"I saw you kissing Harry on the mouth," he said quietly.

It took me a moment to remember, and when I did I frowned direfully. "Harry had just saved my life, Adrian. You certainly could not be stupid enough to think that I was in love with *Harry*."

"Lady Mary had just told me that she and Bellerton would be announcing their engagement shortly," he countered. "I kissed her hand because I was happy for her."

We looked at each other.

"It seems, Kate, that we both have been wearing blinders," he said softly.

I stared at him, my lips parted in hopeful wonder.

"I have loved you for so long, sweetheart," he said. "I thought I would go mad sometimes, thinking that you did not love me back."

By now the horses were ambling along the road at their own rate, their driver completely oblivious of their direction. I said in amazement, "Are you serious, Adrian? You really did not know that I loved you?"

He stopped the horses completely and turned to face me, sliding one arm along the back of the seat. "You married me to get away from your uncle," he reminded me. "And I was not very kind to you, Kate. There was every reason in the world for me to think you did not love me."

"Not kind to me?" I said. "You were magnificently kind to me!"

One long finger traced a gentle path along my cheekbone. He shook his head and a lock of hair slipped over his forehead. He said quietly, "You are the most generous person I have ever known, Kate. And the most gallant."

I literally stopped breathing. To hear such a thing from Adrian! I inhaled shakily and blurted, "Oh, Adrian, I love you so much!" And I flung my arms around his neck and squeezed him so tightly that the poor man was in danger of being choked.

He didn't complain, however. In fact, his own arms came around me in such a crushing grip that for a moment the air in my lungs was quite constricted.

We stayed like this for rather a long time, his mouth buried in my hair, my nose pressed against his neck, my mouth against his collarbone. Finally he said into my hair, "You would never confide in me. You always seemed to turn to Harry."

"You were always so busy," I said. "I thought it wouldn't be fair to burden you with my affairs."

"Stupid," he said.

"Well, you never confided in me," I defended myself.

"I didn't think you would be interested."

"Stupid."

He chuckled.

I felt as if I were in heaven. I kissed his jawbone and felt the faint prickle of incipient whiskers. I buried my hand in the thick silver-gilt hair just above his nape. I sniffed the scent of him. It was heaven to be with him like this.

He said reluctantly, "We are embracing in the middle of a public road."

I loosened my grip on him. "I know." I kissed his jawbone once more and moved away. His hands opened slowly to let me go. We looked into each other's eyes.

"I adore you," I said.

"Sweetheart," he said, "let's finish this discussion later. Preferably in bed."

"To do that, we have to get home first," I pointed out.

"True." He picked up the reins and started the horses moving forward again.

I went upstairs as soon as we reached Greystone, but Adrian had to cope with the doctor and my uncle as well as give explanations to Harry and Louisa. Shamelessly, I let him do it alone. I had some supper sent to my room, and then I soaked for a half an hour in a deliciously hot tub.

Jeanette was scandalized when she saw my bruises. They were not a pretty sight. The worst was the bruise on the side of my face where my uncle had hit me.

"Someone tried to kidnap me," I told Jeanette, "but Lord Greystone came to my rescue."

Her eyes grew starry. *"Mon dieu,"* she said. "Monseigneur is all right?"

"Yes."

She sighed.

"Where is my dressing gown, Jeanette? I am ready to come out of the tub."

She emerged from dreams of her hero and went to collect my robe.

It was another hour before I heard Adrian come into the room next door. I sat up against the pillows, looked at the door through which he would come, and felt such excitement inside that I could scarcely contain it. The door finally opened and his tall, familiar figure came into the bedroom. My heart did a very satisfactory flip-flop.

"Did the doctor see Uncle Martin?" I asked.

"Yes. He didn't have to dig for the bullet, Kate, it passed through his shoulder. Matthews says there is no reason why he shouldn't make a full recovery."

"Oh," I said.

He had reached the bed, and now he touched the bruised side of my face with fingers so gentle that I scarcely felt them. His face did not look gentle at all when he asked, "Did Charlwood do this?"

I nodded.

"You should have let me kill him."

"Adrian," I said, "at the moment I am not terribly interested in Uncle Martin."

He grinned.

"I love you," I said.

He got into bed and gathered me close. "I was furious with you when I left you at Lambourn," he said. "And then, when I was in France, I couldn't stop thinking of you."

It was so blissful to be lying here with him like this, to be hearing such wonderful things. "That kiss," I said wisely.

"It packed a pretty potent punch," he agreed.

"I didn't really love you until you came home," I offered. "It was seeing you with Elsa that did it. You were so gentle. And she nickered for you."

I could feel the laughter rumbling in his chest. "I should have known a horse would figure in this somehow," he said.

"Of course you should," I replied.

He turned me over onto my back and looked down into my face. "Are you feeling too bruised and battered for this right now, sweetheart?" he said softly.

"No," I said.

He gave me another flash of that irresistible grin, and my heart lit like an explosion of candles. "I love you," I said. "I love you I love you I love you . . ."

I didn't stop saying it until his mouth stopped words altogether.

*   *   *

We talked before we went to sleep, and the talking was as precious to me as the lovemaking had been. I told him how extraneous I had felt to his life in London, and he told me how he had felt left out of mine.

"You were always so busy, always being taken away from me," I said tentatively. "We could never go anywhere without someone wanting to talk to you."

"I know," he said wearily.

I lay quietly beside him, trying to find the words that would make him understand how I felt about what had happened in London. How could I explain that it wasn't just that I felt personally neglected. Yes, I had bitterly resented all those midget men who grabbed at him at every party and every dinner, but I resented them because they were trying to diminish him by making him a participant in their petty-minded policies.

I leaned up on my elbow and looked down at him. His tumbled hair framed his face and the eyes that looked back at me were dark and troubled.

I said, "Everyone seems to want a piece of you."

He looked surprised. "That is exactly how it feels sometimes, Kate. As if everyone wants a piece of me."

I lowered my head and kissed him lightly on the mouth. "Let's not go back to London, Adrian. Let's stay here at Greystone. You haven't had any respite from the war and its aftermath, and you need one."

He shook his head in disagreement. "I'm not the only one," he said. "Look at Wellington. He's still in France trying to administer the peace."

"The Duke of Wellington's wife can look after her husband," I said, "and I will look after mine. I think you need a period of peace and quiet."

He didn't reply.

"They want you as a trophy, Adrian," I said. "They want

your honor, your reputation, your stature. But they don't want your ideas."

He looked up into my eyes. "You're right," he said. He reached up to draw me back down beside him. "I think we both could use some peace and quiet, sweetheart. We'll stay here at Greystone until the baby is born."

He had listened to me. I felt boneless and warm with contentment. He settled me in the curve of his body and said softly, "Go to sleep, sweetheart."

It took me perhaps one and a half minutes to obey.

It was late in the morning when I finally awoke. My shoulder hurt, my wrist hurt, and the side of my face hurt as well. Adrian was gone.

Jeanette gave me a disapproving look when she came in response to my bell.

"Where is his lordship?" I asked her. Jeanette could usually be relied on to know Adrian's whereabouts.

"He send for his attorney," she informed me condescendingly. "He said for me to tell you when you wake up that they are in the libraire, my lady."

His attorney?

"Do you wish tea in your room, my lady?" Jeanette asked.

In fact, I was starving—my morning sickness had quite disappeared this last week—but I was too anxious to find out what Adrian was doing with an attorney to waste time with food.

"No," I said. "Help me to dress, Jeanette, and be quick."

When I entered the library twenty minutes later, I found Adrian and his attorney from Newbury, Mr. Marley, with their heads bent over a piece of paper that was reposing on Adrian's desk. They both looked up when they heard the door open.

"Kate." Adrian smiled at me and my insides melted.

"I've confided our problem to Marley here, and he has come up with a confession for Charlwood to sign."

"A confession?" I crossed the room to my husband's side. "I thought we had agreed to keep this affair quiet."

Adrian nodded at Mr. Marley, who was a man of about thirty-five with a sharp, intelligent-looking face. "It will be kept quiet, Lady Greystone, for as long as Charlwood agrees to remain out of the country," the lawyer said.

Understanding began to dawn. "Ah . . ." I said.

"Read it, Kate, and tell us what you think." Adrian put the paper into my hands.

It was as he had said, a complete confession, not only of Charlwood's designs upon me, but of his desire for revenge against Adrian. It was comprehensive, couched in all sorts of legal terminology, and it was utterly damning.

I looked up and found Adrian's eyes waiting for me. I nodded my agreement.

"Is Lord Charlwood in good enough condition to sign this document?" Mr. Marley asked.

"We can pay him a visit and see," Adrian replied. "Matthews dressed his wound last night, and when I looked in on him this morning he didn't seem to be feverish."

I frowned, remembering how ill his wound had made Harry. "You haven't left him alone, have you, Adrian?"

He shook his head. "I left one of the footmen sitting with him." He turned to the lawyer. "Come along, Marley, and we'll see what sort of state he's in," Adrian said.

"I am coming, too."

Mr. Marley looked at Adrian, obviously expecting him to forbid me to accompany them.

Adrian said, "Come if you want to."

Mr. Marley picked up the unsigned confession, held it carefully so the ink wouldn't smudge, and the three of us left the library together. We walked through the Roman splendor of the anteroom and went up the magnificent staircase to the cozier ambience of the bedroom floor.

"He's in the yellow room," Adrian murmured to me, and I nodded and accompanied the two men to the door at the very end of the passageway.

Adrian was in front of me, and I watched as he put his hand on the knob and pushed open the door. Then, before I had a chance to receive anything more than a fleeting glimpse of the bedroom, he spun around and pulled me into his arms, pressing my face hard into his shoulder. I could feel the bandage he wore under the blue superfine. Still pressing my face to him, he moved me a few feet down the passageway. I heard Mr. Marley's steps as he ran into my uncle's room.

"Don't look, Kate," Adrian said. "Go on back to your bedroom and wait for me there."

But I had received a shadowy impression of what was in that room. "Adrian?" I faltered. "Is Uncle Martin . . ."

"He's dead, Kate," Adrian said. "He's hanged himself."

EPILOGUE

I STOOD IN THE MIDDLE OF THE RIDING RING AT Greystone and watched Adrian and Euclide perform the *passage*. This is a light, elevated trot in which the horse swings himself from one diagonal pair of legs to the other, hovering in the air for a moment without touching the ground. It is a beautiful movement, proud and solemn, and Euclide was performing it with wonderful energy and softness.

"It's perfect," I said to Adrian. "Come down the center line and see how he holds it away from the fence."

They made the turn.

"Think soft," I said. "Use your back, Adrian, not your legs."

Down the center line they came, full of impulsion, Euclide's strides seeming to float in the air.

"And halt," I said.

They did. Beautifully. I was grinning like a fool, and Adrian's smile was no less wide than mine. We had been working on this *passage* for a month, and today it had been perfect.

Adrian patted Euclide and praised him, then he dismounted and gave him a piece of sugar. "He's so light!" he said to me. "I never knew a horse could be this light."

"Papa used to become enraged when he saw riders constantly pushing their horses into the bit with their legs," I said. "The contact should always be soft and generous. That is the only way to have a light horse."

We began to walk out of the ring. "The show is finished for today, lads," Adrian said to the grooms who were lined up along the fence, watching him ride and keeping the dogs from getting underfoot. "Time to get back to work."

Charlie came to take Euclide from Adrian. "That horse fair dances, my lord," he said as Adrian handed him the stallion's reins. "You put on a better show than anything we saw at Astley's in London."

"Thank you, Charlie," Adrian said with amusement.

Charlie shot him an impudent look. "If you work real hard, my lord, p'raps in a hundred years you'll ride as good as her ladyship."

Adrian turned to me. "Do I have to put up with this cheekiness just because he rescued you from a fate worse than death?" he complained.

"Yes," I said. "You do."

"Take the horse back to the stable, Charlie," Adrian said.

Charlie grinned. "Aye, my lord."

We walked together up the path to the house, Adrian shortening his steps to match mine, the dogs sniffing the ground in front of us. We were talking about our favorite project, which was to go to Portugal after the baby was born to try to persuade the Portuguese to sell us a Lusitano mare to breed to Euclide, when Adrian suddenly stopped dead and turned to me.

I gave him an inquiring look.

"I have just had the most wonderful idea," he said. And fell silent.

"I can't raise my eyebrows any higher, Adrian," I complained. "Speak!"

"I've just thought of something for you to do while you're waiting for the baby to be born," he said. "You must write a book on equitation."

I stared at him. "Write a book!"

His face was very serious. "What could be a more fitting tribute to your father? You always quote him to me, and everything you say is so wise, so revealing. What better way to keep his name alive than to pass that wisdom along to future generations of riders?"

"Oh, Adrian," I said softly. "What a wonderful idea. It will make Papa live again."

He nodded. "Make the book good enough, and he will live for as long as horses are ridden, Kate. Think of that."

"There hasn't been a decent equitation book in English since the Duke of Newcastle's," I said.

He nodded, and we talked seriously about what kind of book I could write all the way back to the house.

The nuns' parlor on the ground floor was filled with baggage waiting to be loaded into the coach. We were leaving for London the following day so that Adrian could participate in the official opening of London's new Waterloo Bridge. It was to be a state occasion, and the Duke of Wellington was to be present as well as the Regent and his brother, the Duke of York.

Adrian had tried to persuade me to remain in the country while he went in for the bridge opening, promising that he would be home within the week. But I had chosen to accompany him.

It wasn't that I didn't trust him to return quickly; it was that our happiness was so new that I didn't want to be parted from him for even so short a period as a week. And Caroline was coming to London for the opening, and I wanted to see her very much.

Harry had been visiting Caroline for the last two weeks—he would be coming to London with her and would return to Greystone with us—and Paddy and Louisa had been married just before Harry left, so Adrian and I dined alone. We spent the remainder of the evening in the library, discussing an outline for my projected book. Then we went upstairs to bed.

All day long I waited for this moment, the moment when

Adrian put his hands on me, and I felt the flood tide of desire surge through my body.

We would join together in the big bed, impelled by passion and by another need that went even deeper: the need to affirm our unity, our oneness, our marriage. When he was buried deep inside of me, powerful and potent, driving me, lifting me toward the heights of an almost unendurable ecstasy, then we were one. As we were one afterwards, when we lay quietly together, his arm cradling my body, my head tucked into the hollow of his shoulder.

It was then that I knew I had truly come home.

Caroline, Harry, and I waited in the first row of spectators on the city side of the magnificent new bridge that had been designed by John Rennie and named after the battle that had ended Napoleon's rule forever. The bridge was hung with Allied flags, and the guns had been shooting for almost a full minute, firing a 202-shot salute.

Most of the aristocratic spectators were watching the show from wherries on the river, but I had balked at the idea of getting on a boat. I was not a good sailor under the best of circumstances, and the memory of my recent morning sickness was all too vivid. Adrian had tried to convince me that the crowds that were bound to be at the bridge opening would make it no place for a pregnant lady, but I had insisted that I wanted to come. He had given in and arranged for my phaeton to be parked in a place of honor, and Caroline and Harry had come with me.

It was a glorious June day. The colors of the flags on the bridge shone brilliantly, and the barge carrying a full contingent of Waterloo heroes bobbed up and down on the sparkling water that, from where I sat, looked almost clean. A fair was being held all along the riverside, and the bright colors of the tents and the people's clothing added to the air of festivity that surrounded the day.

The last shot boomed out across the water.

Harry stood in his stirrups to get a better view. "They're starting to move," he said.

A moment later, Caroline and I saw the beginning marchers in the short but eminent parade that was taking the first walk across Waterloo Bridge.

First in the procession were the Prince Regent and his brother, the Duke of York, who had been the titular commander-in-chief of the army. After the royal contingent came the Duke of Wellington, the real commander-in-chief, and the Marquis of Anglesey, who had commanded all the cavalry at Waterloo. Anglesey had left a leg behind in Belgium, and he walked with a noticeable limp. Behind Wellington and Anglesey came Adrian.

He was not alone, of course; men—all heroes of the battle—walked on either side of him. But it was at Adrian that I looked.

He had refused to wear his uniform. He had not even wanted to come, had only agreed to it on the personal request of Lord Anglesey. In the midst of a sea of smiling faces, his was sober. His head was uncovered and his hair, bared to the sun, shone like a Viking's in the brilliant afternoon light.

It wasn't just his beauty that drew the eye like a magnet, I thought. There was something else about him, a quality of . . . I will say *nobleness* for lack of a better word. Perhaps in medieval times there had been knights like Adrian; in today's age he had no peers.

Caroline's voice said in my ear, "Isn't Adrian magnificent?"

I nodded.

The crowd behind us, Londoners who had flocked to see the show, set up a roar. No one shouted for the Regent. A few called hurrahs for the Duke of York, who was more popular than his brother. Wellington, of course, was loudly applauded, and sympathy was expressed for Anglesey. But it

was Adrian who got the longest and most enthusiastic round
of cheers.

I thought of his tears on the field of Waterloo and knew
he must be hating this. The man walking next to him said
something into his ear, and I saw him shake his head.

Harry leaned down from his horse. "What's it like to be
married to such a great hero, Kate?" he asked.

I looked at him. He was laughing.

"It's a bloody nuisance," I said distinctly. "No one ever
lets the poor man alone."

Harry drew in his breath in a loud parody of shock.
"Lady Greystone! Such language!"

"Really, Kate," Caroline said. "Suppose someone else
should hear you?"

"They will think the great hero is married to a shrew," I
said.

"He is," Harry informed me.

I stood up and lifted my reticule as if I was going to
whack him with it. He pretended to cringe away from me, lifting his arm to protect his face. He made me laugh, he looked
so funny.

By now the procession had reached our end of the
bridge, and I resumed my seat. The Regent and the Duke of
York stepped off the bridge. The band struck up. The Duke
of Wellington and Lord Anglesey disappeared behind a protective circle of Household Cavalry. Adrian veered off from
the procession and began to make his way toward us through
the crowd.

"You should have ridden Euclide," I told him when he
finally arrived. "Think of him *passaging* all the way across
the bridge. No one would have paid any attention to you; they
would all have been looking at him."

The tense look left his face and he grinned.

"What is a *passage*?" Caroline asked.

"You will be able to read all about it in Kate's book," Adrian informed her.

"Kate's *book*! What book?" Both Harry and Caroline were staring at me with looks of identical astonishment.

"The book she is going to write about equitation," Adrian replied.

"Oh I say, Kate, that is a splendid idea!" Harry said.

"Yes," I returned placidly. "It will be utterly brilliant, and then when Adrian and I go out together, people will look at me, not him."

"Well, the Regent wants to look at you," Adrian retorted.

"Now?"

"Now." He held up his arms. "Come along, Lady Greystone, royalty awaits."

I wrinkled my nose. I did not approve of the Regent.

"And I would like to introduce you to Anglesey," Adrian said. "Perhaps we can get him to order copies of your book for the entire cavalry."

"Well, they can certainly use it!" I retorted.

I placed my hands on his shoulders and felt his hands encircle my slightly swollen waist. His thumbs moved up and down in a brief, private caress, and then he was lifting me to the ground.

"You can drive Caro home," Adrian said to his brother. "Leave your horse with me, and I'll have someone bring him back to Grosvenor Square."

"All right," Harry said, beginning to dismount.

Adrian had kept one protective arm around me and I leaned against him for a minute, relishing the feel of his big, solid body against mine.

Caroline and Harry began to brangle over something trivial as he took up the reins of the phaeton. I rested against Adrian and listened to their voices, and knew that I was happy.

Harry began to back the horses.

"I hope he doesn't run someone over," Adrian muttered.

The sun shone warmly on my head. The sky was deeply blue. Adrian's arm was still around my shoulder. We stood and watched until Harry was safely clear of the crowd, and then we turned and went together to meet the Regent.

Please turn the page
for a bonus excerpt
from Joan Wolf's
May, 1997 release:

The Guardian

a new romance
coming from
Warner Books

CHAPTER ONE

My God, my God, my God, he's reading Gerald's will.

It was as if someone had just dealt me a sudden and stunning blow to the head.

I stared at the lawyer standing in front of the closely clustered family group, and my fingers closed convulsively around each other in my lap.

I thought again, with shocked comprehension, *He's reading Gerald's will.*

I think it was the first time I truly understood that my husband was dead.

A deep voice from the chair next to mine murmured, "Are you all right, my dear?"

I pressed my lips firmly together and nodded. Uncle Adam reached over to pat my clenched hands gently, and then he returned his attention to Mr. MacAllister. The dry, dispassionate legal voice droned on:

"In the event any part of my estate becomes payable to my son, Giles Marcus Edward Francis Grandville, before he attains the age of twenty-one, a separate trust shall be established for him, to be held by a Guardian, hereinafter named, upon the following terms, conditions and for the following purposes."

As Giles was only four years of age, it came as no surprise to me that the estate would be tied up for him in a trust.

Giles was the Earl of Weston now. Gerald was dead. I drew a long unsteady breath and stared fixedly at the splendidly carved mahogany chimney piece that rose behind Mr. MacAllister's long narrow head.

I had not been prepared for this kind of emotional reaction to the reading of the will. Perhaps that was why it had happened, I thought. It had caught me unaware.

The last few days I had felt as if I were living through an unreal nightmare.

After Gerald's death, the servants had shrouded the house in black, and for twenty-four hours his body had lain in state in the Great Hall. All day long neighbors and tenants had filed past his coffin. Then yesterday, hundreds of black-robed mourners had formed a great funeral cortege from the house to the church. Giles had been beside me all during the church service, and his small hand had held tightly to mine when the vicar had said the prayers over the casket before it was lowered into the vault that already held six Earls of Weston.

Giles had helped me. I had needed to be calm for him.

But Giles was not here today. Nor were there hundreds

of eyes watching me. And Mr. MacAllister was reading Gerald's will. I breathed deeply, moved my eyes to the lawyer's face, and struggled to focus my attention.

Mr. MacAllister was still on the topic of the trust: "The Guardian herein named shall have the power to manage, sell at public or private sale, lease for any terms or otherwise convey without the order of any Court, and to invest and reinvest the trust property. . . ."

It seemed unbelievable to me that my little son was now the Earl of Weston.

The atmosphere in the room changed subtly. I sensed a faint rustle, as of people coming to stricter attention. I brought my own attention back to Mr. MacAllister and realized that he was coming to the naming of Giles' guardian.

Mr. MacAllister sensed the drama of the occasion and paused. He glanced up from the long legal document he was holding and let his eyes run consideringly around the semicircle of faces assembled before him in the library of Weston Hall.

There were not many of us. I sat in the middle with Uncle Adam and his wife, Fanny, on one side of me and my mother on the other side. On the far side of Mama was Gerald's uncle Francis Putnam, and next to him was Gerald's cousin, Jack Grandville. The rest of the Grandville family had returned home directly after the funeral.

Mr. MacAllister returned his gaze to Gerald's will and began to read slowly and clearly: "I hereby name, constitute and appoint my brother, Stephen Anthony Francis Grandville, as Trustee and Guardian for my son, Giles

Marcus Edward Francis and Executor of this my Last Will and Testament. . . ."

There was more, but we didn't hear it.

"*Stephen!*" Jack's voice completely drowned out Mr. MacAllister's nasal drone. "Gerald can't have named Stephen!"

Mr. MacAllister lowered his document and looked at Jack over the rims of his spectacles. "I assure you, Mr. Grandville, the earl did most certainly name his brother Stephen. I was the one who made the will for him, so I should know."

Mama's clear cool voice made itself heard next. "Stephen is in Jamaica," she said. "He has been in Jamaica these last five years. He cannot possibly act as Giles' guardian from halfway around the world. You will have to name someone else, Mr. MacAllister. I cannot imagine what Gerald was thinking when he named Stephen."

Mr. MacAllister said calmly, as if he was totally unaware that he was dropping a keg of lighted gunpowder into our midst, "Mr. Stephen Grandville will have to be called home to assume his responsibilities. In fact, I have taken it upon myself to write and apprise him of the contents of Lord Weston's will."

"Well, that was damn cheeky of you, MacAllister," Jack said furiously. His handsome face was flushed with anger.

"One of the family should inform Stephen of his brother's death." For once my mother agreed with Jack; she had always been a stickler for form. "Such news should not come from an attorney."

"I also wrote to Stephen about Gerald's death," Uncle Francis said quietly. "Both letters will doubtless arrive in Jamaica on the same boat."

"Suppose he refuses to come back?" Jack said. "After all, he could still be arrested for that escapade of five years ago, couldn't he?"

"There was never any question of an arrest," Mr. MacAllister said coldly. "The authorities were fully satisfied by his father's promise to have him leave the country."

"No charges were preferred," Uncle Adam agreed. "Stephen is perfectly free to return to England should he choose to do so."

My mother turned to me and demanded, "Did you know Gerald had named Stephen, Annabelle?"

"No, I did not." I looked at the family attorney. "When was this will executed, Mr. MacAllister?"

"Shortly after Giles was born, Lady Weston," he replied gently.

I pressed my lips together and tried to keep my face blank.

Mr. MacAllister attempted to reassure me. "Mr. Stephen Grandville is to be Giles' guardian, Lady Weston, but I can assure you it was always Lord Weston's intention that the care of your son should remain with you."

I nodded.

"I cannot understand why Gerald did not name Adam," Mama said.

I stood up. "This discussion is pointless. Gerald named Stephen. I am quite certain, however, that when Gerald made this will he had every expectation of living well beyond Giles' majority." My voice shook treacherously. "I am going upstairs," I said.

"Mr. MacAllister has not finished with the will, Annabelle," my mother said.

I didn't answer. I simply walked out the door.

The dogs were waiting for me in the hall passageway and as usual they trailed close behind me as I went up the stairs to the nursery that was situated on the third floor of the house. I looked first into the schoolroom and found it empty. The dogs and I went along the corridor, past the governess' room and into the playroom. There I found my son and his governess, Miss Eugenia Stedham, sitting at a table putting together a puzzle of a map. I had allowed Giles to resume his regular daily schedule today hoping that the familiarity would help him cope with his grief.

Giles pushed back his chair the moment he saw me. "Mama!" he cried and came running to throw himself against me. The dogs went to curl up on the blue hearthrug in front of the unlit fire.

I caressed the back of my son's head, rejoicing in the feel of his strong sturdy body pressed against my legs, his face buried in my stomach. I looked at his governess and said, "I think that Giles and I will go for a walk this after-noon, Miss Stedham."

Giles pulled away from me and clapped his hands. "A walk! Just what I would like to do, Mama."

"Have you eaten your luncheon?" I asked him.

He nodded, his eyes bright with anticipation. "I ate it all," he said.

Miss Stedham had gotten to her feet. "It is rarely a prob-lem to get Giles to finish his meals," she said.

I smiled for the first time that day.

"Let Miss Stedham dress you warmly, Giles," I said to my son. "It may be sunny but it's still rather cold."

Miss Stedham said, "When shall I have him ready, Lady Weston?"

"Right away." I ruffled my son's sleekly brushed hair.

"Come along to my dressing room when you're ready, Giles. I have to change my clothes too."

"All right, Mama." He turned to Miss Stedham. "Come on, Genie. Let's go!"

I turned to leave, and the dogs got up and followed me.

Outside the March day was sunny but blowy and chill. Giles skipped along beside me, delighted to be outdoors after a morning spent in the schoolroom learning his letters and his numbers. We set out from the south entrance of the house, the dogs racing before us, leaping wildly, circling back to us again, then racing on ahead once more. The path we took led us through the formal gardens, where the blue and pink hyacinths were coming out and a few early trees were showing promise of the blossoms to come.

A small stream marked the end of the formal gardens and we leaned over the wooden bridge and admired the marsh marigolds and violets and lady's smock, whose brightness colored the grass along its banks. We continued on, following the path between two fenced paddocks where some of my thoroughbred hunters were turned out on grass that was beginning to green up nicely. We stopped to say hello to the horses and to pat their necks before we continued on our way to the wooded hillside that was our destination.

Spring was showing herself in the woods also. The birds were singing, and we saw daffodils and periwinkles, primroses and the blue speedwell whose color I loved. The pussy willows were out, and Giles and I picked some to bring home to Miss Stedham.

Like my son, I was very glad to be outdoors. I had spent seemingly endless days sitting beside Gerald's sickbed, holding his hand and listening helplessly as his breathing became progressively more difficult. And then there had been the funeral.

I drew the crisp, cold air deep into my healthy lungs and felt life course through me. I looked up at the intensely blue sky, with high white clouds scudding along it like sailboats, and thought, *Stephen is coming home.*

"Mama," Giles' voice said, "where is Papa now?"

I looked at my son. His cheeks were ruddy and the knees of his breeches were caked with dirt. I sat down on a fallen log, heedless of my skirt dragging in the mud. "Papa is in heaven, darling," I said gently.

"But we putted him in the floor of the church yesterday," Giles said. "How can he be in heaven if he is in the church?"

"Papa's spirit is in heaven," I said. "When we die our spirits leave our bodies and go home to God. Papa doesn't need his body any longer, Giles, so he left it behind in the church."

Giles scowled. "I didn't *want* Papa to die, Mama."

I reached out and drew him close. He had always been a cuddly child and now he pressed his face against my breast. "I don't *like* him being in the church floor," he said.

Tears flooded my eyes and I shut them tightly, forbidding them to fall. "I don't like it either, Giles," I said. "But Papa got very sick. There wasn't anything we could do to keep him with us."

He said, his voice muffled by my breast, "You're not going to die, are you, Mama?"

"No, darling. I am not going to die." I managed to say the words very clearly and firmly.

He lifted his face from my breast and looked up at me. "Never?"

His cheeks were flushed with healthy color, but his light gray-green eyes were filled with apprehension. "Everyone has to die someday, Giles, but I am not going to die for a long time." The apprehension still clouded his gaze, and I added, "Not until you are a grown man with children of your own."

The idea of himself as a grown man with children of his own was sufficiently impossible to him now; he was reassured, and his eyes cleared. He began to turn away, but I put my hands on his shoulders and made him look back at me. "Papa left a will, Giles. Mr. MacAllister read it to us this morning."

He was intrigued. "What is a will?"

"It's a . . . a list . . . of things that Papa wanted to have done in case he died. One of the things he wanted was for his brother, your uncle Stephen, to come home to look after Weston for you."

"Uncle Stephen?" Giles said. "I don't know my uncle Stephen. He lives somewhere else."

"He has lived in Jamaica for the last five years, so you have never met him, but Papa has said he must come home to look after Weston for you until you are big enough to do it yourself. You are the earl now, darling. I know it is hard to understand, but you have taken Papa's place."

Giles gazed solemnly back at me. "I know," he said. "Genie said I was Lord Weston now."

"You are Lord Weston," I agreed, "but Uncle Stephen will take care of running Weston Hall and the farms until you are twenty-one. People will call you 'my lord,' but none of the responsibilities for Weston will be yours for many years."

Giles frowned. "But Uncle Adam takes care of Weston Hall and the farms."

I nodded. "I imagine he will continue to do that."

"Then why do we need Uncle Stephen?" my son asked.

"Papa named him to be your guardian," I said.

Giles, who was as sensitive to my moods as a tuning fork to a note, shot me an alert look. "Don't you like Uncle Stephen, Mama?"

I laughed. I stood up. I gave my son a hug. "Of course I like Uncle Stephen. You will like him too. He is fun."

We began to walk back toward the house. "Does he like to play?" Giles asked eagerly.

I drew in a deep breath of air. I could feel a headache coming on. "Yes," I said. "He likes to play." Something flashed by the edge of my vision. "Oh look, Giles," I said enthusiastically. "I think I just saw a bunny."

"Where?" he demanded, his attention, as I had hoped, neatly diverted from the subject of Uncle Stephen.

When I walked into my dressing room some forty minutes later, my mother was waiting for me. The dressing room, which opened off the bedroom I had shared with Gerald, was supposed to be my private domain, but I could not seem to make my mother understand that. Of course, the room had belonged to Mama during all the years that she had been married to Gerald's father, and I suppose she still felt a proprietary right to it.

She was seated in a chinz-covered chair in front of the fire, sipping tea when I entered.

"I cannot understand why you did this room over," she

said, as she said every single time she came in here. "It was perfectly elegant when I had it. You have made it look so common, Annabelle." Her exquisitely straight nose wrinkled as if it had been assailed by an unpleasant odor. "Flowered chinz," she said in disgust.

When Mama had used the room it had been done in straw-colored silk. It had indeed been extremely elegant, but I had always been afraid I would dirty the upholstery when I sat down, and the dogs had rubbed mud on the silk draperies. For my purposes, the cheerful chinz was much better.

Mama's green eyes moved to regard my person. "Really, Annabelle," she said, her disgust deepening, "how can you allow yourself to be seen in such disgraceful garments?"

"I took Giles for a walk," I said. I sat down on the chinz sofa that faced Mama's chair, stretched out my legs and contemplated my muddy boots. "We both needed to get outside. It has been a difficult time."

In respect for my grief, my mother forebore to comment on: a) the mud, b) my posture and c) the dogs, who had curled up in the pool of sunlight in front of the window. "Poor Gerald," she said. "How could so young and healthy a man get an inflammation of the lungs severe enough to kill him?"

She made it sound as if it were Gerald's fault that he had died.

"I don't know, Mama," I said wearily. The headache was now securely lodged behind my eyes. "The doctor said that these things happen."

"Well, they shouldn't," she said.

I had no answer for that.

She took another sip of tea. The silence lengthened. I

looked at my mother and for the first time I noticed a few strands of silver in the pale gold perfection of her hair. "I cannot understand why Gerald would name Stephen to be Giles' guradian," she said.

I went back to looking at my boots and kept my voice carefully neutral. "Stephen was his only brother. I should think it was a natural choice."

"Nonsense. Gerald and Stephen were never close."

I shrugged and said something about blood relationships.

Finally Mama got to the point. "Did *you* have anything to do with this decision of Gerald's, Annabelle?"

I looked up from my boots. I met her eyes. "No, Mama, I did not."

After a moment she looked away. "Gerald must have been insane," she said. "What does Stephen know about running an estate like Weston?"

"He has been running the Jamaica sugar plantation for five years now," I pointed out. "He is not without experience, Mama."

My mother gave me a pitying look. "His father sent him to Jamaica because the plantation was in such bad financial condition that even Stephen couldn't do it any more damage."

"I understood from Gerald that Stephen has actually done a good job, Mama. At any event, the plantation has not gone bankrupt, like so many others in Jamaica."

I heard what I was saying and scowled as fiercely as Giles. Why was I defending Stephen?

"At any rate," I went on coldly, "I am quite certain that Stephen will want Uncle Adam to continue to look after Weston as he has always done."

"I certainly hope so," my mother said. "Stephen has always been sadly unsteady. He couldn't even stay in school; he was always fighting."

I opened my mouth, then shut it again. I *was not* going to fall into the trap of defending Stephen to my mother.

"If Stephen does come home, he cannot live in this house with you," my mother said.

I stared at her in bewilderment.

"Don't be so dense, Annabelle," she snapped. "You cannot live here unchaperoned with Stephen."

My bewilderment turned abruptly to disgust. I said, "Mama, Gerald is not yet cold in his grave."

My mother lifted her chin. She is an incredibly beautiful woman, but the beauty is all on the outside. I have never liked her.

"I am only thinking of your reputation," she said.

I do not think I have ever been so angry with her. I stood up. "Mama," I said, "please leave."

She looked at my face and wisely decided it was time to retreat. She swept to the door and paused for a moment, looking back at me, clearly intent on having the last word. "You should be wearing black, Annabelle," she said.

She closed the door firmly behind her, leaving me alone with my headache.

THROUGHOUT THE NEXT YEAR, LOOK FOR OTHER
FABULOUS BOOKS FROM YOUR FAVORITE WRITERS
IN THE WARNER ROMANCE GUARANTEED PROGRAM

FEBRUARY
HOT TEXAS NIGHTS   MARY LYNN BAXTER

MARCH
SWEET LAUREL   MILLIE CRISWELL

APRIL
PASSION   MARILYN PAPPANO
THE LISTENING SKY   DOROTHY GARLOCK

MAY
BEHOLDEN   PAT WARREN
LOVERS FOREVER   SHIRLEE BUSBEE

JUNE
GOLD DUST   EMILY CARMICHAEL

JULY
THIS LOVING LAND   DOROTHY GARLOCK

AUGUST
BRIDES OF PRAIRIE GOLD   MAGGIE OSBORNE

SEPTEMBER
SUNSETS   CONSTANCE O'DAY-
                                      FLANNERY

OCTOBER
SOUTHERN FIRES   MARY LYNN BAXTER
BELOVED   STELLA CAMERON

NOVEMBER
THE DECEPTION   JOAN WOLF
LEGACIES   JANET DAILEY